Published in the United States by Amazon KDP & Barnes and Noble Press

ISBN 978-1-7351059-0-1

Editing by Michele Rubin of Cornerstones US Editing

Cover Design by Anthony Sullivan

Maps by The Map Archive

For Jacquelyn. All my love.

Historical Note

What follows is a work of fiction, but is based on the events leading up to the fateful raid on the city of Dieppe in the late summer of 1942.

The political and bureaucratic circus that supervised the planning of this raid is based on historical accounts and interviews by personnel who participated in the raid.

All SOE events included are based in the realm of fiction, but it is well known that SOE agents were operating in and around Normandy in the time leading up to the raid. The Dieppe raid was one of the few times when all three RAF Eagle Squadrons participated in a joint operation, and all ground forces cited to have participated in the raid are real.

Where actual historical characters appear – Lord Mountbatten, Trafford Leigh-Mallory, Bernard Montgomery, Charles Hambro, to cite the more prominent- all actions they are said to perform and do are pure fiction but are based on known documented interactions. That said, events such as General Montgomery's interaction during a planning meeting with Admiral Hughes-Hallet, and Lord Mountbatten taking time away from planning the Dieppe raid to assist in the filming of his war exploits for the film *In Which We Serve*, are factual. All interactions by these individuals, although fictional, are grounded in historical evidence. Other characters are composites or inventions.

JUBILEE

Prologue:

"Arrêtez! Arrêtez!" The German SS soldier shouted, as the crack of a pistol ripped through the Parisian quiet. Arthur Cutter ignored him and quickly ducked down a narrow alleyway. "Come on, Victor," he called in French.

Victor scrambled after Cutter, his breath ragged and coming in short gasps. He wheezed and leaned against the wall, struggling for air. "I'm shot," he gasped, a red splotch spreading on his shirt.

"But you aren't dead, so move!" Another gunshot echoed down the alleyway as the German soldier caught up to them.

"Bollocks." Cutter pulled his Walther from his waistband and let off two shots.

The German ducked for cover as one of the rounds snapped against the brick wall inches from his head.

"Let's go, Victor! If we stop the Gestapo will torture and kill us."

"I can go no further!" Victor wheezed as he slouched against the wall. He struggled to stand, but his legs buckled underneath him.

Cutter looked at his friend with a combination of concern and urgency. "Victor, if we stop we're dead."

"I can't go on." Victor choked, his breath becoming more erratic as one of his lungs collapsed.

Cutter gritted his teeth, Victor wasn't one to quit. "Please."

Victor looked up at Cutter, his face set in a grimace. "I can't go on. You know what you have to do."

Cutter shook his head. "No. I won't do it."

The shouts of their German pursuers grew closer. By the sounds it was more than just one or two members of the SS chasing them. Victor coughed and spat out a globule of blood. "We don't have time. Stop acting like a fucking child and do your job!"

Cutter froze. He couldn't do it. All the training, all the cautionary tales, none of it prepared him for this. His pistol dangled limply at his side as he stared down at Victor.

"If you don't do this, they'll torture me and my family." Victor looked up at Cutter, his eyes pleading. "Please, just get it over with. Do your job."

Cutter's vision blurred as he adjusted his grip on the Walther. His stomach tightened as he raised the pistol. "*Je suis désolé.*" The crack of the Walther reverberated down the alleyway. He fired two more rounds, one in the chest and another in the head to insure Victor was dead. "I'm so sorry, my friend." Cutter whispered and turned and ran. The Gestapo wouldn't capture another SOE agent tonight. Cutter was hell bent on making that a reality. He sprinted down the alleyway and made a few quick turns and found himself at a Christmas market. He took a deep breath and fought back the tears.

With all the willpower he could muster, he holstered the Walther and casually walked out of the alleyway and strolled through the market. He could hear the German soldier shouting as he ran out of the alley but didn't turn to look. He had to make it to the Seine. He had to get out of Paris and back to London.

"You there, stop!"

Cutter froze. His body tensed and his hand slowly moved to the Fairbairn-Sykes knife sewn into his coat.

"Don't move!" The voice was closer than before.

Cutter counted the seconds, waiting to make his move. A hand grabbed him and spun him around, bringing him face-to-face with a young, blond-haired, blue-eyed Aryan.

The boy glared at Cutter, his ill-fitting uniform making him look like he was playing soldier in his father's clothes. His mouth was half open, prepared to demand Cutter's papers, but Cutter didn't give him the opportunity.

In a quick motion, Cutter pulled the knife from his coat and drove it up through the boy's chin. The knife slid easily through the soft tissue of his neck, surprising and unnerving Cutter. He had never killed someone before, and the realization that he had killed two people in less than five minutes almost made him lose his bearing. Cutter's jaw muscles tightened as he struggled not to vomit. His eyes drifted to the SS Death Skull perched atop the boy's cap. The skull leered at Cutter, daring him to escape. It all transpired in the blink of an eye, but for Cutter it could have been an eternity.

The German grabbed at Cutter's coat, struggling to stand, but Cutter kept his eyes transfixed on the skull. He quickly pulled the knife from the boy's chin, crimson blood oozing out of the hole he had left. A woman next to him let out a scream as the German collapsed.

Cutter averted his eyes and darted past her, quickly walking away from the body. He kept his fedora low over his eyes, avoiding eye contact with the people on the street and turned a corner. He wouldn't dare run, running was what guilty people did, what spies did.

His mind raced as he tried to map how he would get out of the city. His worst nightmare had come true. He was on the run from the Nazis, and the one person he knew in Paris, he had just killed.

Cutter traced his way down to the Seine and took a moment to collect himself. "Goddammit," he whispered softly. He looked out at the inky black water, but all he saw was Victor's deformed face after his bullet had entered the center of his forehead. He cursed the three Special Air Service commandos who had shown up at Victor's house with little warning. If it weren't for them, Victor would still be alive and he wouldn't be on the run. If by some miracle he made it back to England, he swore he would break the jaw of the SAS sod who had planned this.

Cutter took a deep breath and forced himself to calm down.

"Think, you idiot. What do I do now?"

Cutter checked his watch and looked around. He wasn't far from Gare Montparnasse. With a little luck he could catch a train to Spain. Without another thought he darted down an alleyway and started to make his way to the train station. In the next twenty minutes the entire arrondissement would be flooded with Nazis. He did his best to keep to the alleys and only used the major streets when necessary.

When he was a block from the train station he dumped his pistol and knife in a trash can and made his way to the ticket counter. One of the many German soldiers patrolling the station stood next to the counter and demanded his papers before he could purchase a ticket.

Cutter gave him an annoyed look and shoved his papers into the German's hands, playing the part of a disgruntled Parisian.

The German ignored him and examined the papers with the practiced diligence of a Prussian drillmaster. Satisfied, he handed the papers back to Cutter and motioned him to the counter.

He hurriedly bought a ticket for Bordeaux and raced to the platform; with a little luck he could be in Barcelona by morning. Cutter thrust his ticket into the conductor's hands and stonily stared at him as the old man inspected the ticket. Satisfied that all was in good order, the conductor nodded and moved his arthritic hands to return the ticket. Cutter impatiently snatched it from him and, without a word, darted up the stairs onto the train.

As soon as he sat down the train whistle bellowed and the conductor called, "All aboard."

Cutter swayed in his seat as the train gently pulled out of the station, slowly accelerating toward Bordeaux. Only when the City of Light swept away did Cutter allow himself to crack. His hands started to tremble violently and his stomach turned. He pulled his fedora low over his eyes to hide his tears and sobbed softly. He struggled to calm himself and slowed his breathing. He leaned his head against the cool glass window of the train car and watched as the twilight landscape of France swept by. His sobbing reduced to an occasional hiccup as he steadied himself. Victor was gone, the fact that he was the one who had snuffed out his life was still a surreal fact to Cutter. He watched in a daze as trees whipped by, and said a silent

13

prayer hoping he would never return to France while it was under Nazi control.

PART I:

CHAPTER 1

RHUBARB

Normandy, France

November 1941

The roar of the Supermarine Spitfire Mk. VA's Rolls-Royce Merlin Five engine vibrated through the airframe of the aircraft, drowning out all other noise inside the cockpit. Flight Lieutenant Ian Faraday of No. 71 Squadron adjusted the trim tabs as he leveled out at 15,000 feet. He checked his course and double-checked the map attached to his kneeboard, and marked his location. He was twenty miles inland off the French coast of Normandy.

He turned and looked toward the horizon; the skies were remarkably clear.

"Ulster Leader, this is Ulster 2, no luck finding a holiday house today, or anything else for that matter," one of Faraday's wing mates, Flying Sergeant Stokes, called.

Faraday looked down along the French fields. He couldn't see anything either. *"Alright, Ulster 3, we're zero for three, what do you say we call it a day?"* he asked his other wing mate, Flying Officer Tombs.

"You yanks sure do have strange idioms; we must be hunting in the wrong place," Tombs said in his clipped English accent.

"Ulster 3, you joined an American squadron, we speak the President's English here."

"Sorry, old boy, but might I point out that you are in the RAF and we speak the King's English like proper fighter pilots."

"Not in 71 Squadron," Faraday fired back. He checked his fuel gauge and checked his wing mates. They were both brand new with less than 100 hours of flight time between them, and were still prone to rookie mistakes in Faraday's opinion.

"Ulster Leader, might I point out that 71 Squadron is no longer exclusively American."

"Alright, cut the chatter, otherwise you may both suffer the same fate as your American predecessors. The only reason you're with 71 is because we don't have enough American pilots."

"Roger," they both chorused.

"Damn kids," Faraday muttered. They were still green. Their tendency to joke on the radio displayed that easily enough, but Faraday trusted them. He checked his map and clicked his mic, *"Ulster Flight, turn to heading 3-2-5. How copy?"*

"Ulster 3, roger."

"Ulster 2, copy."

The flight turned northwest and started a track back to England, the French coast coming into view. Faraday could see Cherbourg over his left wing; in a matter of minutes the English coast would be visible.

"Bandits! Five o'clock low!" Tombs called over the radio.

Faraday searched the sky frantically and spotted them. A flight of five yellow-nosed Messerschmitt 109's were roughly two miles away flying toward them.

Damn. Faraday had hoped to make it back to England without issue. He could tell the German fighters were on an intercept course with his flight. He adjusted his goggles and mask and pushed down on his mic. *"Tallyho! Six*

Messerschmitts, break left." He pulled back hard on the stick and pushed left. The Spitfire banked and turned over, rolling into a descent. Tombs and Stokes followed suit, hot on Faraday's tail.

"*We can't outrun them, but we're more maneuverable. Use it to your advantage!*" Faraday reminded.

"*They've spotted us.*"

"*Watch the split!*"

The five ME109s broke off into two groups. One hung back while the other took off toward Faraday's flight.

"*They're coming at us head-on.*"

Faraday jotted down their location on his kneeboard and looked up. One of the flights of ME109s was hurtling toward them as though they were playing an angry game of chicken.

"*Control, this is Ulster Leader, we are engaged with five, I say again, five ME109s. We are at Angels 1-5 near Cherbourg.*"

"*Roger, Ulster Leader,*" a woman's voice responded in a curt tone. "*At this time we are unable to assist; all aircraft in the area are engaging with German bombers.*"

Faraday gripped the circular joystick tightly, "*Ulster 2, Ulster 3, we're outnumbered. Hit them head-on, take your shots and when we pass you two will break off and head home. I'll try and draw them off for a few seconds.*"

"*Ulster Leader, we're staying with you.*"

"*Do it, that's a bloody order!*"

Faraday gingerly nudged the joystick, pushing the gunsights onto the middle ME109. He took a deep breath and relaxed his grip. Waiting until the last possible second, he squeezed the trigger as the ME109s raced by. His rounds raked the left wing of one of the planes as it hurtled past. Faraday whipped around, not losing sight of them. He smirked in satisfaction as he spotted smoke trailing from two of them.

"I got one," Tombs shouted jubilantly.

"Great, now bugger off," Faraday snapped. He pulled up hard on the stick and put the plane into a sharp turn. *"Go, I'll be right behind you."* Out of the corner of his eye he spotted the two Spitfires split off in the direction of England. Faraday leveled off and checked his fuel gauge; he had maybe another minute. Most of the ME109s appeared to be uninterested in going after Stokes and Tombs, but Faraday spotted two giving chase.

In a calm as if he were discussing the weather, Faraday warned them, *"Ulster 2, Ulster 3, you have two bandits giving chase. Stay your course, I'll break them off."*

"Roger, Ulster Leader. Godspeed."

Faraday pushed the throttle forward. The Rolls-Royce Merlin engine revved and the odometer began to rocket up into the red. Faraday's body sunk back in his seat as the Spitfire careened toward the two German fighters. He started to line up a shot with his gunsights. As he inched closer and closer, he peeked at his fuel gauge and saw it start to sag closer to empty. He performed some quick math in his head and doubted he would be able to make the English coast.

His thumb hovered over the trigger of his eight .303 Browning machine guns. He was almost in range.

"Come on, ya bastards, just a little to the left." He was close to a shot. One more kill and he'd be a double ace,

Faraday realized and chuckled softly. Just as he was about to depress the trigger, both ME109s broke right and away.

"Goddammit!" Faraday swore, before he even turned to look behind him he instinctively knew what had happened. He had been outmaneuvered and was a dead man.

He looked over his shoulder and spotted two more ME109s bearing down on him. Faraday rolled the aircraft and put his plane in a corkscrew dive, attempting to shake his pursuers.

Tracers shot past his cockpit as one of the ME109s opened fire. Faraday struggled to shake them, but as he tried to lose them in a turn, another spurt of tracers danced around the cockpit. *Where the hell did they come from?* He felt the plane shudder and checked both wings. Several large holes peppered the right wing two feet from the cockpit. *Sloppy, I should have seen them.*

Red hydraulic fluid and fuel oozed from the holes and Faraday didn't need to check his gauges to know he was about to begin losing control of his aircraft. He checked his altitude: 10,000 feet. He pushed the stick forward and went into another dive and banked hard to the right. *"Control, this is Ulster Leader. I've been hit and will need to ditch in the Channel."* He looked at the map on his kneeboard. *"I am approximately fifteen miles due south of Dover."*

"Roger, Ulster Leader, search and recovery boats are being alerted, Godspeed." The sorrow in the controller's voice was barely masked. She knew better than Faraday what his chances of survival were.

Faraday scanned the skies again and spotted the flight of ME109s, they had regrouped, accepting Faraday's fate as a cold death in the Channel. He checked his gauges again; the fuel needle was bouncing between full and empty, as though it were teasing him with the possibility of staying airborne. For a moment Faraday dared to hope the engine had a chance, but was quickly dismayed as the grinding screech of the engine pierced the air and it sputtered and died.

"Bugger."

He set the Spitfire on a glide path and looked down at the Channel, he could glide for roughly four miles, but would have to ditch soon after to deploy the parachute. He scanned the horizon, searching in vain for any sign of a boat.

Faraday queued his mic and desperately tried to hail any search and recovery boats in the area, but was only met with silence. After what felt like an all too quick four miles of gliding, there was still no sign of a rescuer.

"Christ, this is it," Faraday groaned. He leveled out the aircraft, opened the canopy, and clambered out on the wing. The wind buffeted him, nearly knocking him off his feet, but he kept his balance.

Faraday looked out over the wing and eyed the white crests of the waves. The sea was rough, and, without question, cold. He stared out at the frigid water, the knowledge that he most likely would freeze to death terrifying him.

He looked back at the cockpit and wondered if he could land the Spitfire in the ocean, and decided to give it a try. As he turned around to move back to the cockpit, a jolt of turbulence jarred the aircraft, breaking Faraday's grip on the airframe and pushing him off the wing. Faraday hung in the air for a moment, completely confused, but he quickly recovered and pulled the rip cord to his parachute.

The chute caught the wind and he started to slowly glide down into the chilling blue Channel. He looked around and watched as his plane crashed into the water, breaking apart on impact.

His descent was slow, making his splash in the water all the more nerve-racking. He prayed a fishing trawler or even a German U-boat would appear. As Faraday hung in the air another thought entered his mind that made him nearly soil himself: sharks. What if instead of freezing to death he was eaten alive by some invisible monster? His mind was transfixed on the thought of some unseen mouth coming up from the black depths of the Channel and tearing through his legs with no warning. The thought terrified him so much that he didn't realize he was about to enter the water until his head submerged.

The water was as cold as Faraday expected. He shuddered as his body hit the water and couldn't breathe from the shock of the frosty sea. As fast as he could, he moved to get out from under his chute, its shroud threatening to drown him.

He quickly inflated his Mae West and looked around. Waves bounced him up and down, bobbing him around as he curled his legs up tight to his chest to conserve body heat. His teeth chattered and his body shook uncontrollably. As the cold seeped into his bones, Faraday replayed over and over in his head the dogfight. *Why did I have us hit them head-on?* he wondered. *Had we just waited and let the ME109s catch up we could have gone into a high roll. We could have gotten behind them without giving them a shot!* Faraday shook his head and grunted. He couldn't help but question his decision. After all, it was the reason he was floating in the Channel freezing to death.

Two hours ticked by before Faraday was finally picked up. When he was pulled out of the water his face was a deep tinge of blue. Wrapped in blankets and guzzling hot tea, it took Faraday nearly four hours to stop shaking.

"You're one of the lucky ones," an old toothless sailor said, as he handed Faraday a fresh cup of tea.

"How's that?"

"Normally we just recover bodies. We don't always conduct rescues."

"Thanks for that cheery bit of information."

The sailor scurried away under Faraday's glare, and resumed his duties on the deck. Faraday rode the rest of the way home in silence, save for the occasional groan of pain as feeling returned to his arms and legs.

"Your arms hurt?" the sailor asked.

"Like they're on fire."

"That's good, means warm blood is circulating through your limbs and thawing them out. It'll hurt like hell for a couple hours, but it's supposed to."

"Fantastic," Faraday mumbled, and resumed his silence. When he arrived at his airfield at RAF Martlesham Heath, Stokes and Tombs were eagerly waiting for him.

"Catch anything while you were in the Channel?" Tombs asked cheekily.

"Just pneumonia."

"The old man wants to see you."

Faraday looked over at the ready room and back at his two protégés. "Any trouble on your way across the Channel?"

"None, thanks to you."

Faraday nodded silently while Tombs and Stokes exchanged an uneasy look. "Boss we . . ." Tombs hesitated, his voice thick with emotion.

"We thought we lost you," Stokes finished.

Faraday nodded to them, not trusting his voice. What he had done was incredibly thickheaded. *Who the bloody hell sacrifices themselves for others in real life?* That stuff was for the silver screen. Unsure of what to say, he gave a thin smile and shrugged. "You nearly did."

Stokes bit down on his lip and stayed silent while Tombs grunted and averted his eyes.

"Thanks for getting us home."

Faraday gave an understanding nod. "Best not dwell on it." He was as eager as they were to let it go, more even. He could venture a guess that until five minutes ago, they had thought they had lost their flight leader in an act of selfless heroism. He could tell by Tombs's bleary eyes and Stokes's hoarse voice that his presumed death had extracted a heavy toll. He patted them on the shoulder and started toward the ready room. "Oh, and lads, if either of you are stupid enough to question my order to scatter again, I'll ground you in a heartbeat. Daft heroic acts are reserved for your flight leader and flight leader only, understood?"

Stokes and Tombs chuckled and bobbed their heads. "Understood, sir."

Faraday nodded and kept walking. As he strode across the grass a handful of pilots gave him soft praise.

"You got bigger balls than Leigh-Mallory."

"Well done, old boy."

"You're a mad geezer."

Faraday gave a polite smile and tried not to make a big deal out of it. As he got closer to the ready room, stuffed couches and flimsy chairs littered the grass around the shack where pilots lounged in a standby status. The chairs were beginning to show mold as rain started to pick up with the end of autumn.

"Hello, Ian, nice to have you back with us!" Clyde Baker, Victor Flight's Australian Flight leader, called to him from the comfort of one of the armchairs.

Victor Flight lounged in the grass and chairs around their leader and jeered Faraday with mock congratulations for his amphibious landing.

"How's the water this time of year?"

"Bloody cold."

"That was daring, to say the least."

"Didn't have any better ideas," Faraday called over his shoulder.

"Yeah, well next time, try and make landfall," Clyde shouted as Faraday walked into the shack.

"Is he in?" Faraday asked the clerk in the outer room.

The outer office of the shack was no bigger than a shed someone kept gardening tools in. It consisted of a window to the outside, and sitting next to it a flying officer whose head was permanently attached to a telephone listening for the order to scramble the pilots for takeoff, as well as a clerk who assisted the squadron leader with the mundane paperwork necessary to run the squadron.

"Go on in, sir, he's waiting for you," the clerk said.

Faraday nodded and knocked on the door.

"Enter," a muffled voice behind the door called.

Faraday opened the door and started to march toward the desk.

"Oh, please, just sit down in the damn chair." Squadron Leader Michael King impatiently motioned toward a chair that looked like it wouldn't support Faraday's 180-pound frame. "You look like shit."

Faraday sat down hard in the chair and chuckled, "You ever go in the drink?"

"Twice, at Dunkirk and during the Battle of Britain."

"Well, maybe if I do it one more time they'll promote me."

King's face tightened. "I do hope that's not a dig at me being the youngest squadron leader in the wing."

Faraday grinned. "Never, it was more a dig at you being a prize pupil of Air Vice-Marshal Park."

"You tosspot," King said icily.

"Oh, relax, Mike. You know I'm kidding, and no one thinks that, especially here in 71," Faraday said with a wave of his hand. He reached into his pocket and fished out a carton of cigarettes and plucked one out. He placed it between his lips, but hesitated.

King looked at him in bemusement.

Faraday pulled the cigarette from his lips and threw it and the carton in the waste bin next to King's desk. "Still waterlogged," Faraday explained.

King chuckled softly. He opened a desk drawer and pulled out another carton and tossed it to him.

"Thanks." Faraday caught it, pulled a fag out, quickly lit it and inhaled deeply.

"Good to see you in one piece."

"Nice to be seen at all after that, sir."

"The operations officer will debrief you, but I wanted to see how you were first."

Faraday took a heavy draw on his cigarette before responding, "I'm fine, sir."

King leaned back in his chair and eyed Faraday coolly. "Jolly good, stiff upper lip and all that, but I'd honestly be worried if you were okay." King knew the look on Faraday's face all too well. Faraday was mentally exhausted but refused to tell anyone.

"When was the last time you had a day off?"

"About a month ago when I went to a meeting in London with you."

King nodded; he figured as much. He had watched Faraday cross the flight line and had observed his interactions with the other pilots. He was levelheaded and in control but King could see he was close to cracking.

"How many missions have you been flying a day?"

Faraday squirmed in his seat at the line of questioning. "Oh, not nearly as much as the rest of the lads, I'd reckon."

King wordlessly pulled a file from one of his desk drawers and thumbed through it to Faraday's flight file. He silently scrolled through the flight logs and found what he was looking for. "Ian, you've been flying at least a mission a day for the past three months and have lost three of your flight in the last two weeks. You have over three hundred hours more flight time than the next flight leader and over six hundred hours more than the next one."

"What are you saying? You think I've lost my nerve?" Faraday couldn't believe what he was hearing, it was one thing for him to question himself, but another to be questioned by King. "I just sacrificed my aircraft to save my flight, and ditched into the Channel and froze my ass off for two hours; I don't think I've lost my edge."

King held his hands up in surrender and changed tactics. "Calm down, that's not what I'm saying. I'm saying you've been going out daily running rhubarb and rodeo sweeps of France, and you're one of the few that has beaten the life expectancy curve for pilots running missions in France. That makes you valuable. I've submitted your name and it has been approved for you to become an instructor up with 13 Group at RAF Turnhouse near Edinburgh."

"What?"

"Stokes and Tombs are as ready as they are going to get. We're getting a new crop of pilots and I'm sick of watching half of them die before the other half becomes competent enough to make a difference." King leaned forward in his chair and locked eyes with Faraday, the timbre in his voice changing, "I'm sending you north so the new pilots we get won't be as inexperienced as we both were when we went into our first dogfight all those months ago."

Faraday absently toyed with a worn button on his navy blue tunic and eyed King for a long moment. "The Squadron is losing all her Americans."

King placed his fingertips together and nodded slowly. "Command is reshuffling the Squadrons. We don't have as many Americans as we once did, and I doubt we will be getting more. You all will stay in the Eagle Squadrons, but more and more of British pilots will be entering the ranks. Especially Aussies and Kiwis."

"Great. More characters like Clyde."

"Yeah, I tried to send him away but he's like that damn boomerang he plays with. Always comes back."

Faraday finished his cigarette and tossed it in the waist bin. "When do I leave?"

"Tomorrow afternoon."

"Anything else?"

"You may want to get your uniform serviced; that button you play with isn't the only one that looks like it's about to fall off. Come by in the morning and we'll have a copy of orders for you."

"Will do, sir." Faraday stood up and brought himself to the position of attention, stamped his foot and saluted and departed the office. He walked out of the ready shack and found Stokes and Tombs loitering outside.

"Well?" Tombs asked.

"I've got orders for RAF Turnhouse to begin instructing students. I depart tomorrow."

"What? What about Ulster Flight?" Stokes asked.

"We didn't discuss it, but Tombs will be taking over. You'll be getting a new batch of pilots soon so you'll have to teach them everything I taught you."

Tombs and Stokes exchanged an uneasy look.

"Hey," Faraday said sharply, "you both are ready. I've taught you everything I know and you don't need me to babysit you. It's time for you to do the same for the new pilots."

Both Tombs and Stokes shook their heads slowly. "Damn," Tombs said softly. He ran a hand through his sandy blond hair. "What now?"

"I've got to go debrief, but I'll meet you at the pub." Faraday nodded to the pair of them and started to make his way toward the operations building.

Tombs and Stokes watched him walk away in disbelief, the news hitting them like a ton of bricks.

"Christ, we're in trouble now," Stokes said, punching Tombs's arm.

Tombs nodded uncertainly, the thought of taking over the flight making him queasy.

"Come on, we better go pass the word," Stokes said, gesturing to the crowd of pilots watching intently from their lawn chairs.

Faraday turned and watched them from the doorway of the debrief room as Clyde Baker started to interrogate them. Although Tombs thought he wasn't ready, Faraday was confident he would make a good flight leader. Both he and Stokes were some of the better rookies in the squadron. *Rookies*. Faraday snorted. *I guess they aren't that anymore.* Today's engagement had been their fourth dogfight, and fifth rodeo sweep of Normandy. Between that, and the six rhubarb missions they had done to interdict German targets of opportunity, they were more than ready.

Faraday smirked as Clyde started to argue with Tombs. The Aussie's arms flailed angrily about as he shouted at Tombs. But Tombs stood his ground. Faraday guessed that Tombs had just told him that he was going to be taking over Ulster Flight. Clyde continued to shout and work his arms vigorously, but Tombs seemed unperturbed.

Faraday watched a few seconds longer and smiled. Tombs's first challenge as a flight leader would be earning the other flight leaders' respect, and by his body language and how angry Clyde was getting, Faraday could tell he had made the right decision in picking Tombs.

He turned from the doorway and continued into the debrief room. He still couldn't believe his luck. The thought of being sent north and leaving the squadron was a bitter one, but it was quickly overwhelmed by the relief that he wasn't going to be in aerial combat for a while. He was secretly happy he was being sent north. He would never admit it publicly, but he *was* burned out. He couldn't remember the last time he had taken a respite from the war.

"Faraday, take a seat." The Operations Officer pointed to the lone chair in front of his shoddy, weathered desk and started to scribble down a quick set of notes. "Alright, let's get this over with, quick and as painless as you like."

The debrief went smoothly and lasted only an hour. The Operations Officer asked the usual questions: "How high were you flying? At what speed? At what time did you engage the enemy? What did you see on your patrol?" It was tedious, but it helped the Operations Officer construct an image from all the pilots' debriefs. Each debrief was like a puzzle piece the Operations Officer could use to build a picture.

Fortunately for Faraday, Tombs and Stokes had provided a very clear sight picture of their mission earlier so there were only a few questions Faraday had to answer. When the debrief finished, Faraday made his way back to his room at the local inn. He changed into a set of warm clothes and turned the sink on. He dunked his head under the hot water and groaned in pleasure. He stood there for a few minutes musing about his future as the water's warmth seeped into his skull.

He could hardly believe that he was transferring. The shock of it still hadn't worn off. He pulled his head from the sink and studied himself in the mirror. The youthful Princeton student who had traveled to England in search of adventure was gone. He was only 23, but he looked closer to 30. His face hadn't particularly aged, but it was thinner and sharper from the lack of sleep and a proper diet. He had been fighting for nearly a year and already he felt like a changed man. He had killed and seen friends killed. He had watched helplessly as friends burned alive, listening to the radio like a helpless bystander as they screamed and moaned as fire burned through their cockpits and they spiraled down to the earth in a fiery pillar of smoke and metal. Faraday had seen all of this, and the thought of taking a respite from the war was such an enticingly sweet dream that Faraday rarely permitted himself to think of it. Now hearing that this dream may become a temporary reality brought a thin smile to his face. He finished with the sink, toweled off and reached for his bomber jacket and made his way to the pub.

As he walked through the door he was greeted with the raucous sound of what could only be the entire squadron packed into the tiny, dark establishment. A beer was thrust into his hands before he was fully through the door.

"Hey, cobber! Couldn't let you go quietly into the night!" Clyde Baker roared.

"Cheers." Faraday raised his glass in thanks and took a sip. He navigated his way over to the bar, his back being patted the entire way and congratulatory remarks being spouted with every step.

"Although you're an ugly bastard, I hate to see you go," Craig Bolden, the flight leader of Swift flight, called from a corner where he was playing a game of darts with Squadron Leader King. Faraday meandered through the crowd and joined them.

"Is there going to be another late-night bare-knuckles brawl?"

King chewed the tip of his cigar in thought. "You know, that's not a half-bad idea. Maybe I'll step in the ring."

"Sir, you keep trying, but no one is going to fight the pride of Sandhurst, especially when you're the commanding officer," Bolden mused with a chuckle. "Besides, it's only Aussies and Kiwis that ever want to bash each other's brains in."

"Right, well, we'll see where the night takes us," King said jovially. "Craig, be a good lad and go grab us another round."

Craig nodded, but before he left he raised a dart to eye level and took aim at the board, his tongue stuck out in devout concentration. When the dart left his hand and hit the bull's-eye, King let out a groan.

"I win. You're buying, sir."

"Bloody conman," King grumbled as he dug some money from his coat. He thrust a few quid into Bolden's hand and waved him away. Once he was out of earshot, King looked at Faraday, his face serious. "You tell Stokes and Tombs?"

Faraday nodded. "They're a little unsure of themselves, but give them some pilots to train and they'll quickly stop worrying about their own feelings."

"I can only make one of them flight lead. Who will it be?"

"Tombs," Faraday said simply. "The kid has a good understanding of aerial tactics. To him it's not just a science but an art."

"That was my thoughts exactly. Are you all packed to leave tomorrow?"

Faraday snorted. "What is there to pack? All I have are the clothes on my back and the small trunk and toiletry kit I brought with me from the States."

"I figured you may have bought some new things since you've been here."

"Clearly you've never seen my lodgings. It resembles a dingy closet."

"Well, maybe when you make squadron leader you can get a bigger dingy closet."

"Maybe." Faraday looked over at the far end of the bar. Clyde Baker had snatched a bottle of whiskey from behind the bar and was lining up a row of shot glasses. He caught Faraday's eye and aggressively motioned for King and him to come over.

"Oh Christ." King grimaced. "Baker is going to get us pissed out of our minds."

"I have a feeling I'm still going to be drunk tomorrow morning when I leave."

When Faraday awoke the next morning back at camp, a wicked headache and a mouth as dry as dust greeted him. He rolled out of his cot with a groan. He hadn't been this drunk since his going away party at Princeton when he left for England. He stumbled over to the wash basin and dunked his head under the cold water. The water had its necessary effect and helped clear his head.

He surveyed his room and made sure he had packed all of his worldly possessions into the small trunk, and slowly, carefully, hobbled down the stairs. As he walked outside he found King leaning against his car waiting for him. His face was pale and the pool of vomit on the ground next to the tire indicated that he was suffering just as much as Faraday.

"All packed up?" King belched.

Faraday nodded, "Just need to fill up the bike and I'll be ready to go."

"You're taking that grimy motorcycle?"

"I like to think of it as a sentimental possession."

King snorted and handed him a sheaf of papers. "Your orders and a couple rations cards for petrol. They should get you to Turnhouse."

"Thanks." Faraday took the documents, and the pair of them walked over to his motorcycle. It was a 1938 Norton 16 home model. Faraday had bought it almost immediately after flight school from another pilot who was selling it on the cheap prior to deploying to Burma.

"If you need anything, don't be afraid to give me a call," King said, extending his hand.

"Will do, sir. Keep an eye on Tombs and Stokes for me."

"They'll do fine."

Faraday nodded but didn't say anything. A silence fell over them. For some reason, Faraday couldn't say goodbye; it felt strange and the words caught in his throat.

King gave a knowing smirk. "Good luck." He patted Faraday's shoulder and started to walk away.

"Thanks." Faraday smiled and straddled his bike and started the engine. As he did so the claxon started to sound for an incoming German raid. He watched as pilots scrambled to their planes, Stokes and Tombs among them. The determined looks on their faces gave Faraday a vote of confidence in their chances of success. He had taught them everything they knew, now it was time for Faraday to do the same to another batch of students. He revved his engine, not wanting to be around when the first German strafing run hit the base. He pulled back on the throttle and accelerated away.

***

"Durand, what's the hold up?" Francois Crevier demanded.

"It must be the weather; the signal is strong," Durand said, double-checking the radio battery and instruments.

Francois grunted in annoyance. He shouldered his Sten submachine gun and pulled out a carton of cigarettes in one deft movement. "Damned weather, we rarely get in touch with England and the one time we can the weather is against us." He fought the urge to pace about the barn and stood silently behind Durand as he tinkered with the radio controls.

"If we don't hear from them soon, we'll need to break down the radio. The Germans will be triangulating us as we speak."

"Yes, yes, I know." Francois scanned the barn and spotted his niece near the barn door. "Talia!" Francois beckoned her over to him.

Talia looked up from her place by the door. She could tell by the look on her uncle's face that something was wrong. It was the same look he had had when the news came that the Nazis had taken Paris. "Climb up into the loft and keep watch."

"Is something wrong?"

"There will be if you don't do as I say, girl."

Talia frowned but did as her uncle commanded.

"Wait, take this." He rummaged through the pocket of his coat and pulled out a pair of binoculars and tossed them to her. "Shout if you see something." Without another word he resumed his position hunched over Durand as he struggled to get a signal.

Talia clambered up the ladder into the loft and rearranged a hay bale near the loft door and sat down. She took a moment to let her eyes adjust. The sun was dipping below the horizon and the twilight dusk had already set in. The long shadows cast by the hills and the forest gave the landscape a hollow feel, as though the French countryside knew the plight of her people. With the German occupation, nothing felt the same. The woods and hills, once sites where Talia would go to play as a girl, were now ominous and threatening places. Danger lurked everywhere, as German soldiers scoured the countryside in the search of Maquis fighters: people like Talia and her uncle.

Talia squinted and struggled to keep watch. With the sun fading, she had a hard time seeing in the shadows. She scanned the rolling hills and watched the three roads that intersected a half mile from the barn. If a vehicle came she was sure they could get away quickly.

As she watched the landscape, the angry shouting of her uncle floated up into the loft.

"Dammit, Durand, why won't it work!"

36

Talia shook her head, if they would let her she was sure she could get the radio to work. It was infuriating, ever since she had moved from Paris to live with Francois it had been a struggle to prove her worth. Getting Francois to simply agree to let her help the French Resistance had been a Herculean task. But she had quickly proved to him, if not everyone else, that she was up to the challenge. Francois had not been keen to the idea of letting his niece run around sabotaging Nazi supply lines, but she had given a persuasive argument: No one would suspect an eighteen-year-old girl to be a member of the Resistance. This made her valuable because the Nazis would pay her no mind.

Francois had relented and had in turn convinced Claude to let her help, but her argument to help also proved fatal to her chances of advancement. Claude had agreed with Francois to let Talia help, but all he saw in her was a messenger and a lookout. The idea of using her for sabotage or anything more was out of the question.

Talia silently grumbled and picked up the binoculars and resumed her watch. There were other assignments she could perform well. Smuggling munitions and weapons was a constant requirement, and one they were shorthanded for. She knew she could do more if she was given the chance. She looked through the binoculars and scanned the roads. She would speak to Francois about it later. As difficult as he was, he was family and was always looking out for her, unlike the others. Talia swept the three roads and scanned the woods. The sun was halfway below the horizon, making it difficult for her eyes to adjust to the semi-darkness. She blinked and struggled to focus on the trunks of the trees. As she did so, a dozen figures appeared from the darkness of the forest. Their gray tunics and matte black guns made Talia's heart skip a beat. They stopped at the edge of the woods as their commander surveyed the barn, his blond hair jutting out beneath his gray cap.

"*Merde.*" Talia leapt up from the hay bale and scrambled to the edge of the loft. "Francois! Amsel is coming with his men!"

Francois stopped what he was doing and looked up at his niece. "Are you sure?"

"Yes!"

"Durand, break the radio down and make for the fields."

Durand frowned but started to turn the radio off and pack it. "What about you?"

Francois grabbed two magazines for his Sten and pocketed them and started up the ladder to the loft. "I'll buy you some time."

Talia watched as her uncle moved to the loft's window. She had no weapon, but she knew she could help. "I'm staying with you."

"Don't be foolish, go with Durand."

"No."

"Dammit, girl, you're as stubborn as your father. Go!" Francois shoved her toward the ladder and turned back to the window and started to fire the Sten.

Talia clambered down the ladder as the staccato of the Sten pierced the evening quiet.

"I'm nearly done. Go to the field, Talia," Durand ordered as he finished packing the radio.

Talia wordlessly ducked out the back of the barn and scampered through the wheat field. The wheat was taller than her, and with a few steps she was hidden by its golden stalks. Since the Nazi occupation, many farmers had abandoned their harvests rather than give it to the Germans. Talia was thankful that the farmer that had fled these fields hadn't burned his crops. She ran through the field and came out near a large clump of trees where another member of the Resistance was waiting with a car.

"What's happening? Where are the others?"

"Behind me," Talia gasped as she caught her breath.

The man stared at Talia uncertainly and brandished a shotgun as a heavy rustling emanated from the field. "Who goes there?"

"Don't shoot, it's Durand! With Francois and Fabrice. Francois is shot, we must go!" Durand staggered out of the field with the radio over one shoulder and Francois struggling between him and Fabrice.

"No!" Talia screamed and darted toward them.

"Get him in the car!"

Francois grimaced in pain but struggled to move under his own power. "I'm fine, Talia, just get in the car."

"You've lost a lot of blood."

"Are you a doctor? Get in the car." Francois climbed into the back seat with some difficulty while Durand loaded the radio into the trunk.

Talia sat down next to him and inspected his wound. A dark hole gushed blood next to his navel. "We'll get you help."

Francois inspected the wound and shook his head. His face was pale and his voice shaky, as he said, "Don't bother. You may not have been a doctor but I was. The bullet hit my liver . . . with the amount of blood I've lost, I don't have much time."

"Don't say that," Talia whispered.

"Let's go!" Durand called as he clambered into the car and sat down next to Talia. He looked over at Francois. "You okay?"

"No one can know that I was part of the Resistance. If the Nazis find me like this they'll ask questions."

The tires screeched as the driver pressed down on the pedal. The car shot through the woods and came out on a dirt road a mile from the barn. Durand looked around, searching for any Nazis, but the road was empty. He looked over at Francois. "What should we do?"

"Crash the car and burn it. If anyone asks, tell them I was drunk driving."

"We can take you to a doctor," Talia argued. She gave Francois a pleading look. "Please, don't die."

Francois smiled weakly and put a hand on Talia's face. "You're strong, but I need you to be stronger. Survive this war for me . . . for your parents and brother."

Talia stifled a cry as Francois's head drooped to the side and his hand slid into his lap.

Durand reached across her and checked for a pulse, "He's gone. I'm sorry."

Talia wordlessly nodded. The pain of knowing that Francois was no longer there for her felt like a noose around her neck. Her last living family member had died and she was alone. She struggled to breathe and fought the urge to wretch. She refused to let Durand see her in such a vulnerable state.

Durand put a comforting arm around her. "I'm sorry, Talia." He grabbed a blanket off the floor of the car and gently draped it over Francois's body. "Fabrice and I will do what needs to be done. We'll take you home."

Talia stifled a sob and dried her eyes. "No, I will do it."

"This isn't something a girl your age should do," Fabrice argued softly.

Talia stole a glance at her uncle. The warmth was slowly fading from his face, his skin was starting to take on the pale tone of the dead. *I'm alone.* The realization hitting her again. She swallowed bitterly and bit her lip. She needed to be strong for her parents, for her brother, for Francois. She turned and gave Durand a hard look, her eyes like granite. "I'm a member of the Resistance, not some innocent girl. Now let's get this done."

***

CHAPTER 2
RUTTER

London, England

Hambro hated Boodles. He hated gentlemen's clubs in general, but he hated Boodles the most. It wasn't because it was a poor establishment; quite the opposite. It was well regarded and magnificently furnished, and as such, it attracted a number of snobbish aristocratic patrons. And for that reason, he disliked it.

The thought of coming here would never have entered his mind had the Earl Mountbatten and Air Vice-Marshal Leigh-Mallory not recommended it as a place to meet.

So here he was, a disgruntled, unwilling participant at a venue he disliked with two men he despised. If Hambro had it his way, they would have met at the War Office. It was a perfect place to discuss classified information. "Boodles," he grumbled.

His driver looked at him through the rearview mirror in confusion. "Sir?"

"Clark, if you wanted to discuss classified information pertaining to the war, where would you do so?" Hambro already knew the answer.

"Either at HQ or the War Office, I'd say, sir."

"My thoughts exactly," Hambro grunted. To be fair, his disdain for the venue was only amplified by the people he was meeting. Hambro recalled with a grimace what his predecessor, Sir Frank Nelson, had said about Mountbatten and Leigh-Mallory. On Hambro's first day as the head of the Special Operations Executive, Nelson had told him that they were the two best political minds to ever wear a uniform and waste the time and manpower of the British military. Upon working with the pair of them, Hambro quickly realized that Nelson had made an understatement.

Clark pulled the car up to the curb in Pall-Mall and brought it to a stop.

"Thank you, Clark." Hambro struggled out of the back seat. He stepped onto the curb and attempted to straighten his rumpled tweed suit. His clothes were a day old and he hadn't had a chance to go home and change. A late-night communiqué from one of his spies had kept him at the office until the wee hours of morning. He pulled on the hem of his jacket but quickly gave up, as the stubborn creases refused to smooth out. He let go of the fabric and looked around, surprised by the amount of sandbags barricading the front of the club. They served as a constant reminder that Britain was under threat by the German Luftwaffe.

As he walked up to the front gate, he stopped as an olive green military vehicle approached. The lorry came to a halt in front of the gate and an aide-de-camp got out and opened the rear door.

Hambro looked in bemusement as he waited to see who was in the back. To his surprise, it was Field Marshal Bernard Montgomery.

The Field Marshal stepped onto the curb, straightened his military tunic and casually looked around. He spotted Hambro and a slight smile spread underneath his neatly manicured mustache. "Oh dear, what has Leigh-Mallory gotten me into now?" He walked over to Hambro and extended his hand.

"General." Hambro took his hand.

"My dear fellow, it is good to see you. How are things?" He motioned Hambro through the gate.

"Fair, thank you. I can only assume you too were roped into this meeting."

"Indeed, I nearly canceled attending, but maybe something of worth will come out of it since you are here."

Hambro couldn't help but chuckle; it was a left-handed compliment if ever he had heard one. It was always flattering to know that you ranked higher than an air vice-marshal and English lord. "I understand you have Southeastern Command?"

"Indeed, ever since Dunkirk, I have voiced my discontent as to the handling of the Army thus far both in training and tactics." Montgomery removed his garrison cap and tucked it under his arm. "The squeaky wheel gets the grease, as they say."

"Well, I must offer my congratulations, as delayed as they may be."

"Thank you. Any idea what the usurper wants?" Montgomery's distaste was dripping from his voice.

"With Leigh-Mallory you never know."

"His betrayal of Air Chief Marshals Dowding and Park is something I still have trouble with. He's a bloody politician in uniform."

Hambro remained silent, struggling to hide the approving smirk curling up at the corners of his mouth. "What is Mountbatten up to these days?"

"The Good Idea Fairy? I can only assume he is trying to ingratiate himself with the King and PM. His failure at Crete and the sinking of his ship really besmirched his naval career. Hence, the reason he's in Combined Operations. No one really knows what they do, including his boss."

"Isn't his boss the PM?"

Montgomery smiled coyly. "Yes. He's a clever one."

Hambro grunted as they walked into Boodles. A valet, elegantly dressed in tails, opened the door for them. "Good afternoon, gentlemen."

"Good afternoon, is Lord Mountbatten here? We have a meeting."

The valet looked distastefully at Hambro's wardrobe but slowly bobbed his head. "Yes, sir, right this way." He motioned for them to follow, and led them down the hallway to a thick oak door. He knocked and slowly opened it. "My Lord, General Montgomery and another gentleman to see you, sir."

Hambro snorted in delight. *Some other gentleman.* Anonymity had its uses, especially as a spy. Any other day the state of his dress would have been a concern. Prior to the war, Hambro prided himself on his appearance as a banker. First appearances were an essential part of the occupation. But now, with the strange hours he was pulling and the rationing of everything from fuel to cloth, he was lucky if his shirts didn't have sweat stains.

"Oh! Well, let them in!" Hambro heard Mountbatten exclaim from behind the door. He couldn't help but admire the discretion of the valet, keeping the Boodles patron's privacy even while attempting to bring the member's guests to him. The valet swung the door open wide enough for them to enter and quickly secured it after Hambro walked in.

Hambro looked around. The room was an ornate study with rich mahogany bookcases and paneling that left the room in a dark red hue accented by a marble fireplace along the far wall. In the center of the room a decanter sat half full.

Mountbatten stood in the center of the room, arms outstretched in greeting. A toothy grin filled his narrow face. Hambro suspected his good humor was a result of the half-full glass of whiskey he held in his hand. Over Mountbatten's shoulder, Hambro spotted Leigh-Mallory inspecting what he had thought was a napkin, but now realized was a map next to the decanter.

"Monty! Mr. Hambro, how nice to see you."

"Hello, Dickie," Montgomery said in amusement. "Drinking the firewater early, are we?" His words were friendly but his tone had an undercurrent of chastisement. They shook hands and Montgomery turned and took Leigh-Mallory's.

"Can we indulge you with a glass?" Leigh-Mallory asked, motioning to the decanter.

"Thank you, no," Montgomery said curtly. Hambro walked over and extended his hand. "Mallory."

"Hambro." Leigh-Mallory took his hand and quickly let go, not offering him a glass. *A git just like he always is*, Hambro thought as he turned to Lord Mountbatten.

"I don't think we've ever officially met," Lord Mountbatten said, extending his hand.

"Charles Hambro, SOE."

"Louis Mountbatten. Your predecessor, Mr. Nelson, spoke very highly of you. How is he, by the way?"

Hambro's eyes flickered slightly, softening, but returning to his usual steely gray. "Frank is getting better. The job weighed on him heavily."

"Gentlemen, I beg your pardon, but if we could dispense with the pleasantries, I do need to return to Kent this evening. So if we could get started," Montgomery said as he took a seat, setting the tempo for the afternoon.

Hambro gave an amused smirk, which he could have sworn was returned for a split second by Montgomery.

"Of course, of course," Mountbatten said as he recharged his glass and sat down. He crossed his legs and gently tapped his signet ring against his whiskey glass while Leigh-Mallory took a seat across from him. The smug looks on their faces reminded Hambro of the cavalier, self-entitled nobles he attended Eton with all those years ago and whom he had dealt with for years while working in his family's bank.

Montgomery gave Mountbatten an annoyed look, and the tapping on the glass ceased.

"Well?"

Mountbatten grinned mischievously, leaned forward in his chair and in a conspiratorial tone began, "Our American cousins want a timeline for when we will invade the continent."

"We aren't ready," General Montgomery said simply, providing no further explanation.

"Indeed, that is what *Winston* told *Franklin*," Mountbatten said matter-of-factly. "I assume you all are familiar with Operation Sledgehammer?"

"The draft plan to invade the continent?" Hambro asked. "It's a template. It'll take months of planning to finish, and we don't have the manpower to execute it."

Mountbatten gave an icy glare, not used to being interrupted or dismissed. "Gentlemen, like you, I am aware of the plan's shortfalls, and you'll be happy to hear that the other day I was at a meeting where that plan was scrapped in favor of an American-led invasion plan for next year."

"I suspect even by 1943 we won't be able to invade either."

"Well, we can cross that bridge when we get to it," Mountbatten said with an arrogant smile as he sat back in his chair, crossed his legs again, and smiled in delighted anticipation of what he was about to say. "In the meantime, my chaps in Combined Operations headquarters may have a solution to scoring a few points on the Continent."

"Well, don't keep us waiting, Dickie, I haven't got all day," Montgomery growled in impatience.

"Of course," Mountbatten said, annoyance at being interrupted breaking through his amicable facade. "The Russians risk brokering a peace treaty with the Nazis if we don't start attacking the mainland. We need to begin opening this war on a second front and Combined Operations is going to do it."

"How?"

"We are going to raid Normandy."

"What?"

"Dieppe to be precise."

"Not with my men."

Mountbatten looked at the general in surprise. "What do you mean, Monty? Southern Command's support is vital to pulling this off."

"They aren't ready," Montgomery said simply. "The Canadians aren't fighting fit, and I have concerns about our own troops."

"This is our first chance of bloodying Jerry's nose on the Continent and you immediately say no?" Leigh-Mallory fumed. He had been silent the entire time, listening to his co-conspirator lay out the plot. Montgomery's refusal clearly was not part of the plan.

"Trafford, your *Big Wings* may not take as long as I do to form my forces, but when I strike, I ensure it is swift and vicious. With my forces in their present state, I cannot do so."

"Monty, *Winston* wants this."

"Well, if *Prime Minister Churchill* wants Southern Command to support a raid he need only tell the Joint Chief of the Army and I will do so." Montgomery looked at Hambro as he said, "If that will be all, I really must get going. Mr. Hambro, may I offer you a lift?"

Hambro, realizing this was his chance to escape, stood up. "Thank you, General, that would be much appreciated."

"Trafford, Dickie, if there is anything Southern Command can do to help, please let me know. We will support training any way we can."

"Yes," Mountbatten said softly, his voice betraying nothing. "A pleasure, Monty. Be seeing you." His icy blue eyes penetrated Hambro and Montgomery as they quickly departed the study.

"Bloody fools," Montgomery muttered when they were outside Boodles. "Who drinks in a meeting? No discipline." He shook his head in disgust and spun around and shoved a finger in Hambro's chest. "He has no business running Combined Operations. None." He turned and continued walking. "The man has held command on three separate occasions while in the Navy. On three separate occasions his ships were sunk. He has no clue how to win a battle."

"What will you do if he goes to Churchill to order your assistance?"

"I suppose I'll have to make my own plan." Montgomery mused, as his lorry pulled up to the curb and they clambered in.

"I thought you wanted nothing to do with this?"

Montgomery sighed, his fingers plucked at his mustache as he weighed his answer. "I won't deny the idea of raiding Normandy has merit, but the idea of Mountbatten planning and orchestrating it leaves me anxious about risking my men's lives for some half-cocked plan. The only person I trust to do this right is myself."

"Perhaps SOE could be of some assistance?" Hambro offered, as the lorry shot off down the street.

Montgomery shot Hambro a suspicious look. "Why would SOE offer to help?"

Hambro took his horn-rimmed glasses off, ran a cloth over them and readjusted them on his nose. "I don't trust Mountbatten. I've lost enough spies to the Gestapo. I'd like to avoid losing more. One way or another, SOE will have to assist with this raid. If I can pick who plans it I'd pick you."

Montgomery smirked. "Your faith in me is flattering. What can you get me?"

"No promises, but I'll see what I can build. When would you try to conduct the raid?"

"Spring would be best."

"Christ, that's ambitious. I'll see what I can do. Where are you looking?"

Montgomery shrugged. "Dieppe, I suppose. Dickie may not be a tactical genius, but I'm sure his staff is. They picked Dieppe for a reason. Let's see what reconnaissance we can gather."

Hambro stayed silent, his mind whirring as he started to think through how he would get a man to Dieppe. "I'll start looking at viable landing sites. If your man can drop me off here." He pointed up at the corner of the upcoming intersection. The lorry slowed and pulled up next to the curb.

"I'll see what I can find for you and will let you know in two weeks."

"Thank you, Charles. Have a good evening."

"You as well, General." Hambro closed the door to the car and took off down the street. He strolled past the Thames as the sun started to set, casting a shimmer along the water. Hambro absently watched as a riverboat slowly glided up the gray river. He decided to duck into a nearby pub. *Dieppe*, he thought. After Dunkirk and the Blitz he wanted just as much as anyone else to hit the Nazis on their own turf, but was it worth the risk? Mountbatten was a paper tiger as was Leigh-Mallory. For all their bluster, Hambro doubted they had the objectivity needed for such a high-risk operation. *But what about Montgomery?* Hambro thought, as he sat down at the bar. He was aggressive, orderly, and disciplined, but did Hambro just align himself with a similar cat with just a different coat? *Time will tell*.

"Bartender! A brown ale please."

In the meantime it made sense for him to send someone into Normandy to nose around. Worst case, he could recall the agent if things didn't pan out. But whomever he sent into Normandy needed to be smart, experienced, and reliable most of all. Hambro sipped his ale and smirked. He had someone in mind.

***

CHAPTER 3
JEKYLL & HYDE
London, England

Arthur Cutter grimaced; the beer was flat. He beckoned to the bartender to come over and placed the beer in front of him.

"There a problem?"

"My beer is flat. I'd like a new one."

The bartender gave him a hard look. "Are you even old enough to drink?"

"My good man, I'll have you know that beneath this Celtic collegiate exterior is the heart and soul of a connoisseur of fine spirits."

"What's a connoisseur?"

"It's French for professional drinker. I learned it at Oxford," Cutter said solemnly.

The bartender scratched his beefy neck and shrugged. "Ehh, sounds like a tosspot of an education." He poured Cutter another glass and handed it to him.

"You most likely are correct." Cutter took a sip of the beer and nodded his head in satisfaction.

"Oi, why aren't you in uniform?" asked a patron at the other end of the bar.

"Too small, War Office was afraid that if the Germans took one look at my small freckled face we'd lose the war."

The bartender snorted in amusement. "They aren't wrong. If Jerry thought we all looked like you, we'd have already lost the war."

"Steady on, my good man, no need to kick me when I'm down!"

"You oughta be in uniform!" The bar patron declared, not satisfied with Cutter's excuse.

"My dear fellow, I wish I could be, but the War Office said no."

The patron's eyes narrowed and he pointed a bony finger at Cutter. "I want to see your papers. You could be a deserter."

Cutter set his beer down and looked at the patron. As if on command, his eyes changed from a pale friendly blue to a glazed icy gray. When he spoke, his voice was hard. "Sir, I really think you should let this line of questions lie."

The bartender shifted uneasily behind the bar and looked at the patron. The patron held his gaze for a moment longer but blinked under Cutter's unyielding glare. The patron mumbled an apology and sheepishly moved further down the bar.

Cutter nodded and turned back to the bartender, his eyes friendly and jocular again. "Happens all the time," he explained and took another sip of his beer.

The bartender grunted, "I think Jerry would have second thoughts facing you." A phone rang from behind the bar and the bartender went to answer it.

Cutter took a heavy draft from his glass, the memory of Victor saying something similar washing over him like an unwelcome rain.

"Damn." After three weeks he still hadn't told anyone about Victor. The guilt was nearly unbearable. He had conducted numerous missions behind enemy lines over the past two years, and this was the first time he had ever killed someone with his own hands. The fact that he had been forced to kill a contact and friend had only made the pain of his actions worse.

It was him or me. Cutter took another sip from his beer and tried to control the swirling emotions that were ricocheting around in his head. As he did so, he watched as the bartender set the phone down and looked at him. Cutter had a hunch that SOE was on the phone.

"You Arch?"

"Depends who's asking?"

"Your uncle, he wants to talk to you."

Cutter bobbed his head and walked over to the other side of the bar and reached for the phone. "Uncle?"

"Christ, where the hell have you been? I've called every single bar within four blocks of your flat." Cutter recognized the voice on the other end as his control officer, Frederick Atkinson.

"Calm down, no need to be such a mother hen."

"Control wants to see you in the morning."

"What about?"

"Can't say, this channel isn't secure. Be at HQ by 8:00 a.m."

Cutter nodded absently. "I shall be there. Care to join me for a pint?"

"Afraid I can't; I have an early dinner with Lucy this evening."

"Your loss, old boy. I'll see you in the morrow." Cutter hung up and walked back over to the bar and sat back down.

The bartender eyed him in mild curiosity. "Everything alright?"

"Who knows? There is a war on after all." Cutter picked up his pint and finished it.

"Care for another? The environment just got a bit prettier." The bartender inclined his head towards a gaggle of girls who had sat down in the corner while Cutter was on the phone.

Cutter looked over at them. They were his age he thought, and by the looks of them had gone to university, maybe even classmates of his at Oxford. He debated introducing himself but thought better of it. "You can just close me out. Women prefer a bloke in uniform, not some git in tweed."

Cutter walked out of the bar and meandered back to his flat. The next morning he woke up early and left for Baker Street before sunrise. Cutter liked walking the streets at this hour. The pale glow of the sun as it burned through the early morning fog gave London an ethereal feel, and for a moment it made Cutter forget that there was a war on. He ambled down the street in no rush, taking his time and grabbing a copy of the *Daily Mirror* along the way to see the latest news. As he perused the paper a cartoon stood out to him: a man clinging to a piece of debris in the ocean, holding on for dear life. The caption below read: THE PRICE OF PETROL HAS BEEN INCREASED BY ONE PENNY— OFFICIAL.

Cutter chuckled at the cartoon and stuck the paper under his arm, saving it for later. The thought of antagonizing Freddy with unpatriotic propaganda delighted him. He turned down Baker Street and surveyed the road. The street was empty save for three men dressed in street clothes and overcoats and a fourth on the roof of 64 Baker

Street, the SOE headquarters. Cutter strolled down the street, paying the four heavily armed guards no mind.

"Morning, Jimmy," Cutter said as he passed one of the guards.

"Arch. Haven't seen you in a minute."

"You kill anybody this week?"

Jimmy shot Cutter a look of distaste. "Not yet, but it's early."

Cutter opened the gate to 64 Baker Street and walked in. Another guard stopped him and asked for identification before he could make his way up to Atkinson's office.

Cutter hated headquarters. The constant echo of women's shoes clicking against the wooden floors and the cacophony of typewriters almost made Cutter long for fieldwork. He ambled up the stairs and strode into Atkinson's office. "Morning, Freddy, how goes the war?"

"Arch, how nice to see you," Frederick Atkinson said with a smile, closing a dossier he was reading and setting it down. "We were beginning to wonder if you had been killed in a bombing."

Cutter grinned wryly. "I was given three weeks of holiday, I wasn't about to give you a way to find me and interrupt it."

"Yes, I can hardly blame you." He sat back in his chair and gave Cutter an inquisitive look. "Rested?"

"Would it matter?"

The corners of Freddy's mustache drooped down into a frown. "Personally, yes; professionally, no."

"Control has work for me?"

Freddy nodded silently.

"I was promised a desk after Paris. What is this? Hambro punishing me for how things shook out?"

"Paris wasn't your fault, everyone knows that. Sometimes things just go wrong."

"I'm known to the Gestapo. Sending me back gets us nowhere."

"Control disagrees. Our contacts in the Resistance tell us that they are still hunting you in Paris, but don't have a solid description of you. They think you're from Toulouse and have no photo. Your cover survived your exodus from the Continent."

"I daresay I barely did," Cutter said sitting down across from Freddy. "It could be a ruse by the Gestapo to get me back to the Continent so they can capture me."

"We don't think so."

"So what does Control want?"

"I can't say for certain. He's keeping this close to his chest. I suspect it has to do with the invasion."

Cutter clucked his tongue in amusement. "Mysterious, aren't we?"

"Well, you know the Abwehr has spies just like us, no doubt one or two floors below us."

"Surely you can't be serious."

"Nothing is confirmed, but we suspect we have a leaky ship." Atkinson checked his watch and stood up. "We'd better get going. The boss wants to see us."

"Any more word on me taking on more administrative duties?" Cutter asked as they walked down the hall.

"Ask Hambro. That decision is out of my hands."

"Freddy, you have the worst bedside manner. How the hell are you my handler? At least string me along a little."

Atkinson chuckled. "Sorry, Arch, what I meant to say was the paperwork is pending approval by Hambro. Upon his review you'll be behind a desk in no time, provided you pass one final evaluation. Better?"

"Moderately."

They walked into the waiting room for the head of the SOE; Hambro's secretary gave them a questioning look.

"We're here to see the boss. He's expecting us," Freddy provided.

"You can go in, Mr. Atkinson, he's expecting you."

Freddy nodded and knocked on the door.

"Enter," Hambro called from inside.

Atkinson opened the door and let Cutter in first.

"Gentlemen, good to see you. Take a seat," Hambro said from behind his desk, motioning to a pair of shabby chairs in front of him. "Give me one minute to finish this brief."

Cutter sat down in the chair and looked around the office. It was shabby and cramped; it reminded Cutter of his father's office at Oxford. A smile crept over his face at the thought of the university. He still had a semester to complete before he could get his degree. The war had put that on hold, but Cutter had every intention of finishing his studies and eventually receiving his doctorate in archaeology.

Hambro finally finished reading and looked up at them. "Arthur, how are you?"

"I'm well, sir. Curious as to what's going on."

"You just cut right to the chase."

"Best not to delay bad news, sir."

"Curiosity killed the cat, as they say."

"I'm pretty sure that's your job, sir," Cutter shot back.

Atkinson bristled and shot him a glance, a combination of annoyance and embarrassment.

"Arch, as always your petulant attitude is very refreshing." Hambro gave Cutter a patient look and pulled a dossier from a stack.

"It's part of my charm, sir."

Atkinson coughed and attempted to steer the conversation into friendlier waters. "Sir, I think what Cutter means is, we've heard talk about the invasion. Is that why we're here?"

Hambro's forehead creased in frustration. "Damn rumor mill. I haven't even told anyone about this and speculations begin to fly."

Cutter and Atkinson exchanged glances and eyed Hambro suspiciously.

"No, it's not the invasion. We need to send Cutter back to France," Hambro rumbled as Atkinson and Cutter reviewed the file.

Cutter looked up at Hambro with an annoyed expression.

Hambro put his hands up in mock defense. "I know you just returned, and we usually give you a couple weeks to reset after a mission, but this is important, old boy."

"Ideal locations for a raid?" Atkinson read; he gave Hambro a questioning look. "A bit ambitious, wouldn't you say?"

"Yes, it is, but it's going to happen with or without our help. General Montgomery has begun planning to conduct a raid and has requested intelligence on suitable targets and beachheads to land at." Hambro deliberately failed to mention anything about Mountbatten and Leigh-Mallory. The last thing he wanted was to bog SOE down in the political quagmire of senior military leadership, aristocracy, and political buffoonery.

"I'm assuming that's why you want me to go back to France?"

"Indeed." Hambro rummaged through his desk and found a cigarette and lit it. "I need you to get in contact with your sources in Normandy and begin setting the stage for a raid."

Atkinson handed the file to Cutter and he thumbed through it. "Am I to assume that I am picking where the raid will be occurring?"

Hambro inhaled deeply on his cigarette and exhaled. "You'll be providing recommendations and cursory reports on troop locations. You'll be in France no longer than a month and we will pull you back. Once the location for the raid has been determined, reconnaissance flights will scout the area monthly providing updates on the region."

Cutter stared intently at Hambro, his sharp gray eyes never leaving his face. "That's what you told me before I went to Paris. Three months later, three Special Air Service commandos showed up unexpectedly on my doorstep, and within twenty-four hours they, along with my Resistance contact, were dead and I was almost captured."

"Yes, I know, what of it?"

"If I'm going to be sent to France for a month to reestablish contacts and to scout raid locations, I better not be fucking told while in the field that I will be supporting additional missions that can compromise my own."

Hambro ignored Cutter's temper and kept his cool when he responded, "What happened last time was not something SOE endorsed and fought aggressively against."

"That won't help my credibility the next time I meet with the French Resistance. They'll think I'm an Abwehr plant."

"That's why we're sending you and your winning personality rather than some stony git," Hambro groused as he checked his watch. "Fred, as usual you will be Arch's control officer. I expect a brief from you in two weeks."

"Will do, sir." Atkinson and Cutter stood up. "Come on, Arch, we've got a lot of work to do."

"Always a pleasure, sir," Cutter said with a hint of impudence. "Come on, Freddy, try and *control* me."

"Go ahead, Arch, I need to talk to the boss about something real quick."

Cutter eyed them both suspiciously but said nothing. He shrugged and walked out of the office.

When Freddy was sure Cutter was out of earshot he glared at Hambro. "Sir, you promised him an office job after Paris."

"I know, and I had every intention of delivering on that promise until this raid business came up. Cutter is just too damn valuable in the field. Do you know how many agents we have that speak French, Greek, and German well and can read Latin?" Hambro grunted. "It's not as many as we lead people to believe."

"I can think of at least three other agents we could send in Cutter's place. Two are already in France and negate the requirement for infiltration."

Hambro shifted his weight in his chair and leaned forward, his tone fatherly, "Freddy you're a great handler because you give a damn, but you don't let it get in the way of what needs to be done. Cutter needs to do this. He's been inserted into France seven times, and except for Paris, he's exfilled smoothly. His success in the field isn't because of luck."

"Then why not send him north to be an instructor?"

The corners of Hambro's mouth twitched into a smirk. "Cutter has something that can't be taught, you have to learn it on your own. He's very cunning and he plays off people's needs like a conductor directs an orchestra. He's a devious, Machiavellian bastard. That's why he's such a great agent. He can be your friend in a moment's notice and kill you the very next if you risk the mission."

"The typing pool calls him Dr. Jekyll and Mr. Hyde."

"Well, they aren't wrong." Hambro leaned forward in his chair further. "You read his after-action report, about how his Resistance contact was killed?"

"Yeah, he said a stray bullet penetrated his skull."

"I don't think that's what happened. Cutter has never been so dour when a contact was killed by the Germans. I think he killed the contact himself."

"Jesus."

"How many agents have the bollocks to do that?" Hambro asked. He leaned back in his chair and took a pull on his cigarette. "We need Cutter on this mission because I firmly believe no one else can complete it. Once it's done, I promise Cutter will be done with fieldwork."

"I intend to hold you to that promise, sir," Freddy said, the veiled threat clearly understood by Hambro.

***

CHAPTER 4
FNG

RAF Turnhouse

"*Tighten up, Red 3, there's a hole the size of my mother's house between your wingtip and mine!*" Faraday shouted.

"*Copy, Red Leader,*" the student chirped obediently, tentatively inching his Spitfire closer to Faraday's.

Faraday turned and checked on the student on his other wing. "*Red 2, climb, you're too low. You're no good to me in a dogfight below me!*"

"*Copy, Red Leader.*"

Faraday shook his head and checked his fuel. He had a quarter of a tank left. "*Alright, Red Flight, that's enough for one day, we'll work on it again tomorrow. Red 2, go ahead and land; Red 3, follow in after him. We'll debrief on the ground.*"

"*Roger, Red Leader.*"

Faraday broke away from the pair of them as they began the landing cycle and climbed to survey their landings. After a month at RAF Turnhouse he could see he was already effecting a change in the skill level of his students. He watched as Red 2 went in for landing.

"Sloppy," he muttered as red flares exploded from the control tower signaling that Red 2 had forgotten to lower his landing gear.

"I couldn't have been this green?" Faraday asked himself as he started his descent. His students had much to learn, but they were quick studies, Faraday reasoned. With the exception of formation flight and dogfighting, which came with experience and practice, they showed promise. Faraday pushed them hard, but he was ensuring that before the students went into the war, they received as much flight time as possible to sharpen those things that couldn't be taught but had to be experienced.

As both of his students' wheels touched the ground, Faraday lined up an approach and started his descent. When he landed, both his students were waiting for him.

Faraday shut down his aircraft and climbed out. "You two need to learn to follow my lead in the air. If you don't, you won't last longer than twenty minutes against the Nazis."

Both students nodded their heads vigorously and followed after Faraday as he hopped off his aircraft and started to walk toward the ready shed. Faraday looked over his shoulder back at his two students and locked eyes with Flying Officer Faust. "Danny, you need to keep your little eye on my wing and big eye on the air. If we were in a dogfight you would be too busy watching my ass to see a German closing on your tail." He turned and looked over his other shoulder at his other student, Flying Officer Chambers. "Alex, ease up on the control. You're too jerky in your movements." He deliberately didn't mention Chambers's mistake of forgetting to lower the landing gear. He was a good lad and wouldn't make the same mistake twice. Faraday was sure.

"Will do, sir," the pair of them echoed.

"Good, now bugger off. I'll see you in the morning. We'll keep working on it."

They both saluted and turned toward the barracks.

"How're they looking?" Squadron Leader Peter Bailey called from the doorway of the ready shack.

"A few more weeks and they'll be fine. Were we the last flight?"

Bailey nodded. "I'm heading to the pub, care to join?"

"Sure." Faraday pulled his Mae West off his shoulder and tossed it and his flight harness in his locker in the shack.

"I meant to ask, how's the transition from flight leader to instructor?"

Faraday shrugged and closed the locker. "It's harder than I thought it would be." He walked out of the shack and joined Bailey on the stoop. A light, misty rain began to fall, coating their flight suits in a damp. Faraday turned his collar up against the wet and they set out across the grassy field. "I thought I would be more relaxed teaching, but I think I'm more scared for my students than I was during the Battle of Britain."

"I know the feeling. You're scared shitless for your own life in a dogfight, but when you have to teach others to fight for their lives you're bloody petrified that you'll fail them."

"I'm just scared that I'll forget to teach them that one thing and they'll die for it."

"Just wait till you have children," Bailey chuckled. The sun started to set as they walked into the quaint pub down the road from the airfield.

Bailey ordered a round from the bartender and handed a beer to Faraday. "Other than that, how do you like instructing?"

"Well, the hours are great, my schedule is predictable and I'm not on ready status every day, so it's bloody marvelous."

"Not to mention the pub isn't too crowded."

"That is a perk. I must admit I do love watching the students stride in here after they earn their wings. The look on their faces as they've earned the right to drink with real pilots is stimulating."

Bailey nodded and looked at the far end of the bar. The wall was littered with pilot wings and patches that students had left as part of a tradition. He chuckled as he pointed toward a corner of the wall.

Faraday looked where he was pointing and let out a laugh. On the wall sat a pair of wings with BAILEY and FARADAY emblazoned underneath them. "It feels like a lifetime ago."

Bailey chuckled, "I remember your first solo. You forgot to lower your landing gear when you were coming in to land. The control tower personnel all but ran out into the middle of the runway to stop you from landing. They must have fired twelve flares."

Faraday laughed at the memory. "If memory serves me, I recall you nearly falling out of the sky because you forgot to check your fuel gauge and never noticed a steady fuel leak."

"It's a miracle I still have an ass after the chewing I got from the instructor."

"I bet you don't let your students make the same mistake."

"Never." Bailey toyed with his mug, spinning it with his hands just fast enough for the beer to touch the lip of the glass. "I'm debating whether or not to go back south."

Faraday looked over at him but didn't say anything.

"Sharon thinks I'm crazy, but I can't in good conscience stay here. I'm rested and my mind is fit. I'm ready to get back into the fray." He looked over at Faraday. "Seeing men like you, seasoned pilots, come up here for a respite makes me feel awful that I've been up here nice and safe for the past eight months."

"Shut up, Pete, you have no reason to feel ashamed," Faraday said taking a sip from his beer. "You're an ace who was shot down and wounded over France. You've earned your time here to heal and help teach the next crop of pilots."

"Well, I'm healed, and it's time for me to get back in the fight."

Faraday didn't say anything; he knew the feeling. He already felt like he was cheating his friends by coming up to Turnhouse to teach students in the safety of Scotland while they were fighting and dying back south. What made him feel worse was the relief he felt every morning when he woke up, knowing with some certainty that he would be alive in the evening.

"Where would you go?"

"Twelve Group most likely, they need an experienced commander since Eleven is getting the most experienced pilots."

"Less chance of being shot down in France, too."

"That, too." Bailey drained his mug. "I expect orders will come through in the next few weeks."

"Who will take over the squadron?"

"Banner, I believe. He's a good man. He'll do fine."

"Well, we'll have to have a banger before you depart."

"That would be grand," Bailey agreed. He motioned to the bartender for another beer.

They sat quietly for a few moments, lost in their own thoughts. Faraday eyed the wings on the far wall, recognizing a handful of names underneath the wings, and knowing that a few of them hadn't survived the Battle of Britain.

They both finished their beers and Bailey finally broke the silence, "Bloody Nazis. Wankers really know how to botch up the world."

Faraday shook his head absently. "They really know how to cock it up." He ordered another round from the bartender and nudged Bailey and raised his glass. "For our friends long gone."

"Cheers."

Faraday finished the glass and ordered another.

The two of them talked for another hour about their students, past missions, family life and everything else before they both decided it was time to return to their homes. The next day both met with their students and discussed the day's lessons and went up, ready to continue teaching the latest batch of fighter pilots.

***

The British War Office

Hambro gazed impassively at the map of Europe. German swastikas littered it, dotting the landscape of the continent and surrounding England on all sides. England's situation was dire, and as cynical as Hambro was he believed they would survive the German onslaught. He ignored the handful of staff officers in the room. He had no interest in making small talk, nor was he inclined to interact with anyone from Combined Operations. Mountbatten's style of leadership had attracted similar personalities to his unit, many of whom were eager to make a big splash into politics after the war *if* they could curry favor with Mountbatten. Hambro was leery of trusting them with a budget, let alone organizing a raid.

"I hate that map more often than not," Montgomery said from behind him.

Hambro turned and gave a thin smile. "Feels more like a Gordian knot than a statement of fact."

"That says a lot about the type of person you are. Some people look at the map and take it as a resolute fact of our circumstances."

"I don't believe in circumstances. The people who get on in this world are the ones who look for ideal circumstances, and if they don't exist they make them."

"You do know George Bernard Shaw is a socialist."

"The Germans must've taken him to heart. They were on their knees after the Great War; look at them know."

Montgomery grunted in annoyance, "Is this what we're here for?" He turned toward another map in the room.

"It is," Hambro said simply. "It's not much, but it's a start."

Montgomery nodded as he inspected the map absently. "I have some bad news, old boy. The Joint Chief has tied my hands on this raid."

"What do you mean?"

Montgomery shrugged uncomfortably, a trait unusual for a general. "It seems Dickie went to Churchill and complained about my involvement and now I've been forced to go along with Combined Operations taking the lead. This is now a Combined Operations meeting."

"So you're telling me that we've been politically outmaneuvered and Combined Operations is running the show now?" It was a rare occasion for Hambro's emotions to betray him, but he couldn't believe what he was hearing. He could feel his cheeks burn as rage gripped him. He struggled to steady himself.

"I'm afraid so," Montgomery grunted, his face made up into a scowl as though he had smelled something repulsive.

"So who is leading this meeting?"

Montgomery turned and beckoned a vice admiral over to him, "John, are you the senior Combined Operations representative?"

Vice Admiral John Hughes-Hallett bobbed his head. "Yes, General, I am."

"Well, let's get this meeting started, shall we?"

"Whenever you are ready to be briefed."

Montgomery gave Hughes-Hallett a confused look. "What do you mean? You're leading this meeting."

"Sir, you're the senior ranking officer, this is your meeting."

"I was told Combined Operations was taking over planning for this raid?"

"Yes, General, but as senior ranking officer, it is the custom that you lead the meeting."

Montgomery turned and stared at Hambro in disbelief. The look in his eye was a combination of annoyance and contempt. With a grunt he turned back to the vice admiral and shot him a disgruntled look. "Very well, if Combined Operations doesn't wish to plan their own operation I will do it for them." Without another word he strode over to the head of the table and sat down. He shot

Hughes-Hallett a venomous look but said nothing. Taking the general's cue, the rest of the personnel in the room quickly found their seats. "Mr. Hambro, please orient us to the map."

Hambro nodded, he was still a little bewildered as to what was going on. Did Hughes-Hallett shift control of the meeting to Montgomery to shirk responsibility? If Mountbatten pushed so hard to have this raid, why did he just have one of his chief planners give it back to Montgomery? Hambro struggled to find a logical answer, but could only settle on one. Mountbatten wanted all the credit but didn't want to do all the work. He had never before seen such a spectacle in his life. He walked over to the map and pointed to Normandy. "Gentlemen, for those of you who are not aware, over the past few days there has been talk of exploring the viability of conducting a large-scale raid on the French coast. Our target is Dieppe." Hambro locked eyes with Montgomery as he said the town. "For my part, SOE is currently gathering intelligence to assist in the development of a raid in the coming months, and identify targets of opportunity."

Montgomery nodded and looked around the room. "Admiral, I assume Combined Operations has a working template for how this raid will occur. How long will this raid last?"

Admiral Hughes-Hallett shifted uncomfortably in his seat. "I'm afraid the Navy can only provide fifteen hours of support, so we are tethered to that time schedule."

"Fifteen hours? How the bloody hell do you expect the raiding party to unload and seize their objectives in that amount of time?"

Hughes-Hallett started to answer but was cut off by Montgomery, "Dammit, man, have you never planned a raid? This isn't some outpost in Norway we're looking at. It's a large, heavily occupied city. The raiding party won't be a fifty-man team; expect a thousand men to land in Normandy!"

"Combined Operations is confident we can accomplish our objective within fifteen hours."

"Admiral, I can tell you with certainty that the raiding force will need closer to forty-eight hours to land, attack and retreat successfully. If the Navy cannot provide this, then this raid needs to be reevaluated."

"General, Combined Operations will have to evaluate this and reconvene."

"Admiral, you do as you please. As far as I'm concerned, this is a Combined Operations mission. The only reason I am leading this meeting is because you refused to do so." Montgomery didn't wait for him to respond and turned to Hambro. "Mr. Hambro, as soon as intelligence begins to come in, please contact Major General Roberts. He will serve as my liaison for South Eastern Command."

Hambro bobbed his head silently, surprised by this unexpected turn of events. At the moment he had no clue who was in charge of the raid and whom exactly he needed to provide intelligence to.

Montgomery turned and glared back at Hughes-Hallett, his lips pursed beneath his mustache. "Admiral, who is the planning officer for this raid at Combined Operations?"

"I am, General."

"Then I leave it in your hands." Montgomery briskly stood up from the table. "Gentlemen, if there is nothing further, I recommend you convene next week to further develop your plan." Without another word, he strode out of the room.

Hambro watched in confusion as Montgomery walked out of the room and he quickly went after him. "General."

Montgomery stopped and turned. "Yes, Mr. Hambro?"

"What is going on?"

"I honestly am as confused as you, but I will not let Combined Operations demand my cooperation and then expect me to plan their entire raid. When they have a plan, they can let me know."

"I am literally about to send a man into the field for this in a matter of hours," Hambro growled. "It's highly dangerous and better be worth it."

"Charles, forgive me, I don't mean to disregard the risk your agent is taking, but I am in a political quagmire. I can't fight Mountbatten as long as he has Churchill's ear, and I can't waste time arguing over the details of this raid with him. I have other responsibilities with Southern Command. I'll do my best to help where I can, though."

Hambro nodded but said nothing.

"Keep calm and carry on, old boy, that's all we can do here." He squeezed Hambro's arm in encouragement, turned and left.

"Goddammit," Hambro swore furiously, receiving a handful of dirty looks from a group of generals walking through the hallway. He was furious about Mountbatten's political subterfuge, and was even more angry at Montgomery for allowing himself to be so easily outmaneuvered. But most of all, he was furious with himself for letting himself and Cutter be put in this difficult situation.

***

RAF Biggin Hill

Freddy Atkinson stood outside the hangar and waited for Cutter. He took a heavy draw on his cigarette to steady his nerves. He didn't like last minute missions, and in his opinion this was as last minute as it could be. There were too many unknowns. His mind wandered; he was concerned Cutter wasn't ready for this mission. Since Hambro's revelation that Cutter may have killed Victor, Freddy had reservations about sending him back into the field. He needed to be sharp for this mission, and if he had a guilty conscience about Victor's death he could easily cock up the whole operation.

Freddy watched as the C-47 pilot and copilot walked around their blacked-out aircraft and inspected the wings, tires, and stabilizers. He hated C-47s and had requested a Lysander for this mission. It was smaller, faster, and more nimble. The C-47 needed a large, flat field to land, and due to the aircraft's size it was less forgiving if the pilots made a mistake on approach.

Atkinson spotted Cutter, blew out a puff of smoke and flicked his cigarette into a puddle of water on the flight line and waved to him. Cutter saw him and nodded. He walked toward him, keeping an eye out for any incoming aircraft as Spitfires and Hawker Hurricanes taxied to and from the runway. He didn't look the part of a spy. He was dressed in a brown serge suit and carried a small trunk. If Atkinson didn't know better, he would have thought Cutter was going out to the country. The tailors at SOE had done a thorough job of making sure Arthur looked like he was from Normandy.

"All set?" Atkinson asked, shaking Cutter's hand.

"Well, if I'm not it's too bloody late now."

"Do you have your cipher?"

Cutter nodded and patted his breast pocket. Inside was a code book that held all of Cutter's code words to communicate with SOE. At first Hambro hadn't liked the idea of Cutter keeping a lexicon of code words on him. If he was captured, the Germans could exploit it. Cutter had argued against it; with the amount of data he was trying to relay, it would require extensive use of code words and a dictionary was a necessity if he was to provide accurate detailed information. Being fluent in Greek he had devised a basic cipher for the code book using the Greek alphabet. In order to even read the code book you needed to know the cipher. It had stumped the SOE codebreakers for a time, and Hambro had relented.

They spotted Hambro near the rear hatch of the aircraft conferring with the pilot. He looked up and spotted Cutter and Atkinson and beckoned them over.

"Arch, Freddy, how are we?"

"Ready for the return flight."

"I just wanted to see you off and remind you that the more sites you can inspect the less likely you'll have to go back."

"Thank you for the pep talk, sir," Cutter said blandly, only to be shoved cautiously by Atkinson.

"What legend are you using?"

"Olivier Deschamps, French archaeologist and student of naval history, home as a result of the war,"

Cutter furnished. "It's an old legend I've used and I have a contact in the area who can verify me."

Hambro nodded and exchanged a knowing look with Atkinson. "Best of luck, Arch. Freddy, I'll wait for you in the car." Atkinson watched Hambro amble back toward the car and when he was out of earshot shot Cutter a cautionary look, saying, "You may be a good spy but you need to learn to check your mouth and keep your temper."

"Oh, come off it, Fred! We both know this mission is a kick in the bollocks," Cutter flared, pent up anger boiling over. He was more than angry; he was tired of the risk. People always talked about the glory of war, the glory and heroism of making sacrifices for King and country, but they never mentioned the other things. Like being interrogated and tortured for the locations of French Resistance fighters. Like having your fingernails pulled out after being captured and questioned by the Waffen-SS, or dying in a ditch and no one knowing about your death. In real life, war didn't have music playing in the background like it did in the movies, and Cutter had seen enough friends die horrible deaths that he didn't want to join them.

"When the hell is my request to become a control officer going to come through?"

Atkinson sighed heavily and put a comforting hand on Cutter's shoulder. "Arch, I know this is tough, believe me I do. I have spoken with Hambro about your request, and he assures me it will come through as soon as this raid is completed."

"Not after this mission."

"No, we need your contacts for this. Once this raid is done we can replace you with someone else to work with the Resistance and you can manage them."

Cutter didn't say anything, anger visible on his face.

"Arch, keep it together for a little while longer and I'll get you out of the field, I promise."

Cutter swallowed and licked his lips, not trusting his voice. SOE agents didn't have the best life expectancy. He had beaten the odds, but he didn't expect that to keep happening. He wanted to survive this war, and his best chance of doing so was behind a desk. He had done his part and felt he didn't owe Hambro, the British people, or the King for that matter, anymore. He had already done seven insertions, and the average for an SOE agent was five. It was time for him to come in from the field and train the next crop of agents.

"Ready when you are, gentlemen," the pilot interrupted, as ground crews started to pull back the tarp covering the hangar.

Freddy inclined his head and extended his hand to Cutter. "Stay safe, I'll see you soon."

Cutter nodded and forced a mischievous smile. "Stay out of trouble." He walked over to the C-47's hatch and clambered in. He gave Atkinson a wave and shut the door.

Atkinson waved and started to walk away. As soon as Atkinson was far enough away, the pilot started the engine and conducted his preflight check. When he was done he unlocked the brakes and started to taxi away from the hangar.

Atkinson watched the plane taxi to the runway before hopping in Hambro's car.

"Will he be alright?"

"It's just nerves. Arthur will be fine once he gets there. It's the anticipation prior to jumping into an icy pool: standing over it is always worse than getting in."

"Let's hope so. We've lost enough agents this past month; we can't afford to lose him."

"He had a right to know that Billy Ealey and Eamon Royce were killed in the last two weeks."

"You know why I didn't tell him, the same reason you didn't as his control officer. Your job is to make sure he has everything he needs to get the mission done and hedge off as much risk as possible so if his mission is compromised he can't damage other missions."

"It's a dirty business we do."

"It is, but it's necessary," Hambro agreed. He waved to his driver, signaling it was time to go. "I have a meeting with the PM tomorrow morning. I'll be sure to let him know our agent, code name Cartographer, has been inserted."

"Why did we change his code name from Merlin?"

"It helps keep the Germans on their toes. With all the radio traffic being intercepted by them, they'll think Cutter's code name is one for a new spy. We'll keep sending chatter using Cutter's old code name, letting the Germans think we have more spies than we actually do."

"Won't that endanger Cutter?"

"No, the Germans don't know that we know they've cracked a few of our codes. The codes we will send referring to Cutter will be saying he is in the South of France, and we can send the Abwehr and the Gestapo on a merry chase."

"That's bloody clever of you."

"That's why the PM doesn't meddle in my affairs," Hambro murmured as he lit a cigarette. He didn't mention anything about Montgomery and the Combined Operations meeting. It was the last thing Freddy needed to know about.

***

Five Miles West of Quiberville, France

Cutter silently thanked God one more time for not having to jump out of the plane as he cleared the field his C-47 landed in. The aircraft was on the ground no longer than half a minute. Just enough time to land, spin around, and take off. By the time Cutter had scrambled over the hedgerow onto the road, the sound of the C-47 was an inaudible rumble. Cutter dusted a few leaves off his pants and checked his watch. The luminescent hands showed that it was two in the morning, which meant he had three hours to make it to the safe house before anyone was awake. He put his trunk on the ground and opened it. Inside was the typical set of clothes, but underneath were a few components to a radio Cutter expected the French Resistance needed and a Colt M1911 pistol. Cutter fumbled around in the dark and checked to make sure they were secure in the trunk and then double-checked the F-S fighting knife in a sheath in the flat of his back. Satisfied, he shut the case, picked it up, and started walking.

***

Hambro chewed his lip in silence. He was annoyed that twice in twenty-four hours he was forced to deal with Combined Operations. He glowered at Mountbatten who sat across from him. The casual look on Mountbatten's face as he reviewed the brief Hambro had brought for the meeting infuriated him to no end. "So you have a man on the ground in Normandy?" Mountbatten asked in surprise as he closed the brief.

Hambro glared at General Montgomery, who was sitting between them, but nodded. "Should have landed a few hours ago."

Montgomery remained silent throughout the discourse, avoiding Hambro's gaze, still feeling guilty for the situation Hambro was now in.

"Incredible," Mountbatten said in awe. "I don't think I've ever told you how damn impressed I am with SOE."

"We aim to please."

"How soon will we begin receiving intelligence?"

A vein started to bulge on Hambro's forehead but he kept his calm. "Difficult to say. Could be a week, maybe a month. My agent is one of our best. He's thorough, and if the report takes some time it will be all the more worthwhile."

"Leigh-Mallory tells me his aircraft will be able to gather sufficient information about the town alone. We may not even need your man there."

Before Hambro could fire off a violent retort, Montgomery cut him off. "Dickie. Only amateurs dismiss the opportunity to gather more intelligence. You'd do well to use Hambro's intelligence in your decision-making process."

Mountbatten shrugged, closing the brief with finality. "Of course, my dear fellow. I am merely saying Hambro's man may not need to skulk around Dieppe as much as we thought."

"If you wish to plan this raid without SOE, you need only say so." Hambro had never been a man for physical violence, but he leaned forward in his chair hoping for Mountbatten to offer a glib response.

"It seems I'm out of the frying pan and into the fire," a familiar voice grumbled behind them.

Hambro, Mountbatten, and Montgomery stood up as the Prime Minister walked in.

"Just a discussion of strategy, sir."

Winston Churchill grunted and shook each of their hands. He walked over to his desk and sat down heavily, giving them a wave of his hand signaling for them to sit.

"Where are we with the Africa Campaign?"

Hambro cleared his throat and replied, "Not good, sir. We got a good thrashing at Gazala, the commander was a man named Erwin Rommel."

"Who?" Montgomery asked.

"Erwin Rommel. He's a tank commander and a clever tactician. Heavily decorated in the Great War and wrote a book on military strategy called *Infantry Attacks.* He's a huge proponent of blitzkrieg tactics, and I think he'll give Field Marshal Wavell a hard time."

"What makes you say that?" Churchill asked as he lit a thick cigar and began puffing on it.

"He's an unorthodox fighter, and when he invaded France he was in the lead of the entire German army the whole time and took 10,000 prisoners in seven days." Hambro handed Churchill a sheaf of documents. "The chaps call him the Desert Fox."

"Sounds like your kind of man, Monty."

"Just say the word, sir."

The Prime Minister chuckled deep in his throat and started to investigate the sheaf of papers. "What is this?"

"Latest intelligence on the Empire of Japan's conquest of China. Mao Zedong has started a vigorous defense and has halted the Japanese advance. At the moment Japan has a firm control of Manchuria and the north, but I don't think they'll be able to push any further south."

Churchill scanned the documents and placed them on his table. "What about India?"

"It's difficult to say. Before they can even contemplate India they'll have to take Burma."

"Why Burma?"

"They need to secure their supply lines, sir," Montgomery furnished. He placed his fingertips together and looked intently at the ceiling. "The Japanese have grossly expanded their empire. Before they can go any further they need to solidify their supply lines."

Churchill nodded slowly. "I'll want to hear more about this, but let's get to the matter at hand." He turned and looked at Mountbatten. "Dickie, what is the latest on this Dieppe business?"

Hambro watched as Mountbatten flashed his Cheshire cat grin. "Good, sir. Monty has promised us some of his Canadian troops and we're looking at June for execution."

"What is the purpose of this raid? I've heard we're committing thousands of troops to land and take the city. Why do this if we aren't staying?"

A thin smile formed at the corners of Montgomery's mouth, but he said nothing.

"The Army Chief of Staff has voiced some worries," Churchill continued. "What makes Dieppe so worthwhile to invade?"

"Sir, a good question. But it's not an invasion, it's a raid. It will only take fifteen hours."

"Nevertheless, I have some initial concerns. Can the raid be done in fifteen hours?"

"I believe so, sir."

Churchill's gaze slid from Mountbatten to Montgomery. "What do you think, Monty?"

"I think Combined Operations will need to figure out how to land the whole raiding force within an hour, and retreat just as quickly if they only have fifteen hours."

Churchill nodded as he read through Hambro's brief. "Charles, you have a man in the area?"

"Yes, sir. He was inserted last night. He should be en route to the safe house right now."

Churchill nodded slowly and looked up at Mountbatten. "If experience has taught me anything, you don't just jump into the fray when it comes to an amphibious landing. Too many things can go wrong if not properly prepared. I think we need to build up to this."

"An excellent idea, sir. It's interesting you say that. I was thinking the same thing!" Mountbatten exclaimed.

Hambro rolled his eyes and looked over at Montgomery who had a similar disgusted look on his face.

"We were looking at the town of Saint-Nazaire as a possible raid location. It would be ideal to conduct a medium-size raid as a proof of concept prior to Dieppe."

Hambro couldn't believe his ears. He truly wondered if Combined Operations had done any investigation into Saint-Nazaire or if Mountbatten was just making this up as he went.

"What's at Saint-Nazaire?"

"A dry dock, sir. We could go in and disable the dry dock and attack any other targets of opportunity."

The Prime Minister stayed silent for a time. Hambro wondered what was going through his head. Surely, after his experiences with Gallipoli and the fiasco at Dunkirk, he was wary of committing troops to an amphibious landing on the shores of Normandy or Brittany without a well-thought-out and objective plan. Hambro suspected that Churchill did not see Mountbatten as the most objective individual when it came to planning and risk assessment.

The Prime Minister cleared his throat, plucked the cigar from his mouth, and leaned forward in his chair. "Dickie, as always, you have something up your sleeve. We've known about Saint-Nazaire for some time, but before I authorize a large-scale raid, I want to know more as to why it needs to occur."

"Of course, Prime Minister, but might I point out that every day we wait is an opportunity for the Russians to broker a peace with the Nazis."

"Dickie, I'm grateful that you concern yourself with the political ramifications of our military actions, but leave those concerns to me. Give me a plan and a reason why we must go after Saint-Nazaire now rather than later." The Prime Minister looked over at Montgomery and Hambro. "Any questions or concerns, gentlemen?"

"No, sir," Montgomery and Hambro chorused.

Churchill nodded and turned to Mountbatten, who had a disappointed look on his face. "It's a clever idea, Dickie, but I need the details for something this . . . grandiose."

Mountbatten bobbed his head eagerly, stealing a quick glance at Montgomery and Hambro. "I will have the particulars within a fortnight, sir."

Churchill smiled and gave a nod. "Good man." He rose from his chair and the three of them followed suit. "Well, gentlemen, thank you for your time, but if you'll excuse me I have a meeting with the Home Secretary right after this followed by my weekly meeting with His Majesty."

The three of them nodded and quickly departed the Prime Minister's office.

"Well, that should slow Dickie down," Montgomery murmured when they were outside the Prime Minister's office.

"It's just another raid we may have to assist," Hambro groaned.

"Yes, but he has to do his homework before he can bring it to the PM. It'll take months for a Saint-Nazaire raid to occur. There's still a chance that the Dieppe raid will die in the planning stages."

"I hope so," Hambro said soberly. He had significant concerns about Mountbatten's cavalier way of running Combined Operations.

***

Cutter arrived in Quiberville just as the sun was beginning to peek over the horizon. He said a silent prayer in thanks for the thick fog that had rolled in almost out of nowhere. It had made it all the easier to avoid being spotted as he walked to the village.

He ambled up the dirt road toward the edge of town and spotted his safe house. "Perfect," Cutter muttered in satisfaction, surprised that he wasn't lost or in the wrong place. It was easy enough to spot, it was the last in a row of houses that lined an alley that led to the main street of Quiberville. He walked up to the front door of the cottage and knocked. As he waited, he looked around and surveyed the area. The town was charming, like something out of a postcard from a relative on holiday. Cutter breathed in deeply. The smell of the sea coupled with the smell of the fields was something he had sorely missed. Of all the regions of France, Normandy was his favorite.

He stopped looking around as he heard footsteps moving toward the door from inside the house. Cutter half expected a German soldier to open the door and was surprised by the woman who stood in the doorway. She couldn't have been older than eighteen, Cutter guessed. She was tall, lithe, and very pretty with dark brown hair and gray, almond-shaped eyes. She took Cutter off guard, and alarm bells went off in the back of his head. His contact at the safe house was Francois Crevier, not some girl.

"*Bonjour?*" The girl looked at Cutter questioningly.

Cutter quickly recovered from the shock. "*Bonjour,* how are you?" he said in French.

"*Bien,* can I help you?"

"Yes, I hope so, I was told—" he said, then paused and looked around in confusion. "Forgive me, maybe I am in the wrong place. I'm looking for Monsieur Crevier."

The girl nodded. "This is his house. Who are you?"

"Olivier Deschamps. Who are you?" Cutter said, a hint of annoyance in his voice. He wasn't in the mood to sit around outside talking this early in Nazi-occupied France.

"Talia Crevier."

Cutter didn't hesitate. He had no idea who she was, but his occupational specialty was improvisation. "Pleasure to meet you." He tipped his hat to her. "I'm a good friend of your father's. If I may say so it is quite rude to not invite me in. It's rather cold out here."

Talia made a face, a cross between annoyance and anger, but let him in. Cutter walked into the kitchen and put his case on the kitchen table. "I need to see your father. I—" He stopped talking as he turned around. Talia stood by the doorway, her eyes fixed on him, a Walther P38 trained on his chest.

"Who are you?"

"Olivier Deschamps. Where is your father?" Cutter slowly put his hands up. *Goddammit.* A sinking feeling crept into the back of his head. Just once he wished things would go smoothly. Cutter kept his cool and eyed Talia for a long moment, studying her body language, trying to estimate what she would do next. He had drastically misjudged her, and he wondered if that was common for her. Cutter could tell by the way she held the pistol and asked him questions that she wasn't afraid or uncertain; two things he had hoped to use to his advantage.

"Francois is dead. He was my uncle."

Cutter looked at Talia but said nothing. His face remained emotionless as his mind raced. Francois Crevier was the only person in Northern France who knew him by sight. No one else had ever met him, and the Resistance had already had numerous cells destroyed from the inside by Abwehr agents posing as SOE agents. There was a good chance the Resistance would kill him if he couldn't prove who he was quickly. "How did he die?"

"Gestapo raided one of our meetings. Francois was shot. I helped him escape, but he bled out in the woods. We knew you were coming, but I need some proof that you are who you say you are."

"'Our,' 'we'?" Cutter asked suspiciously. Francois must have told his compatriots that an SOE agent named

Olivier Deschamps was coming. At least he was expected by them, he thought. Cutter's eyes narrowed as another thought entered his mind. For all he knew Talia could be a German plant and the entire cell was dead.

"Yes, I am part of the Resistance."

Cutter eyed her coolly, but didn't say anything. She wasn't what came to mind when he thought of a Maquis fighter. She was young, maybe a year younger than he was.

"Is it that difficult to believe? Because I am a woman?"

Cutter remained silent, but he found his opening. *A chink in the armor!* If he could get her to lose her temper, maybe he could get her close enough to disarm her. He sat down slowly, keeping his hands visible to Talia. "No, it's just you aren't even old enough to drink."

"I could say the same about you."

Cutter looked about the room. If she was a plant, the Germans would be in the area, and he would be better off trying to shoot his way out than being captured. She still hadn't searched him and he still had his knife and pistol. On the other hand, if she was in fact part of the Resistance, then she was the only friend Cutter had at the moment. "Where are your parents?"

"Killed by the Gestapo in Paris. I was brought here by my uncle when they died."

Cutter nodded and slowly stood up. "Right. Well, take me to the Resistance." He kept his hands visible but started to walk slowly toward the door.

Talia shook the gun, reaffirming her willingness to shoot him. "Stop moving."

Cutter stopped. He was arm's length from her. "Come on, let's go." He motioned to the door.

Talia's eyes followed the motion and looked at the door for a split second. Cutter took full advantage of the misdirection and grabbed Talia's forearm and the top of the pistol with both hands; he swiftly pushed her forearm away and ripped the gun in the opposite direction simultaneously. It was over in an instant; Cutter grabbed her by the forearm and propelled her into the wall. He covered her mouth suppressing a scream. "Stay quiet and I'll take my hand off your mouth."

She squirmed for a moment, then stopped. She glared at Cutter in cold fury. Her gray eyes betrayed the frustration and anger she felt, but it wasn't directed at Cutter so much as at her own carelessness.

Cutter slowly removed his hand and nodded to her. "Look, I honestly don't have time for this rubbish. Take me to the Resistance. Someone there can verify who I am." He sat back down at the kitchen table and field-stripped the P38.

Talia looked at Cutter in contempt, but sat down across from him.

"Nice to know we can be civil."

Talia murmured something under her breath that Cutter didn't quite hear, but assumed it wasn't a compliment.

Cutter looked around the kitchen. It was small but it had the essentials, and he was ravenous. While in the C-47, he had emptied his stomach twice over the Channel when they had hit turbulence. His stomach growled and he walked over to the stove and lit it. "Tea?" he asked Talia as he filled the kettle with water and tore a piece of bread from the loaf that sat on the kitchen counter.

She shook her head. Cutter shrugged and put the kettle on the stove and sat back down. She was being difficult. Whether it was the stubbornness that came with adolescence, or the genuine distrust of Cutter, she wasn't being cooperative. It was time to play rough. Cutter didn't want to stay in Normandy any longer than he had to, and he had a schedule to keep. "Alright, Ms. Crevier, the way I see it we have two options. I can kill you and go out on my own and find the Resistance or you can help me." He leaned forward in his chair, his hand moving slowly toward the F-S knife in his waistband. "So what's it going to be?" It was an empty threat, but she didn't know that.

Talia eyed Cutter, surprised by the ease with which he threatened her with death. "We'll meet with the Resistance this afternoon."

"Splendid." Cutter flashed a warm smile and got up as the water began to boil in the kettle, mixed in tea leaves, and let it steep. "Do you have milk?"

***

The morning went by in a relatively civil fashion. Cutter spent the better part of their time asking about the surrounding area, getting an understanding for the village and their relationship with the Germans. Talia had stonily answered his questions, but had refused to give much in regard to her own personal history. By the time they left the safe house to meet with members of the Resistance, Cutter had a fair understanding of the town and felt like he could pass as a local.

Before leaving, Cutter had worked out a solid cover story with Talia. If anyone asked who Cutter was she was to tell them that he was a family friend from Cherbourg. Cutter had given Talia details to his own legend, and had made sure not to give any information about who he really was. As far as she was concerned he was a history student without a school because of the war. He suspected that Talia knew he was lying when he told her he was a French native, but she said nothing. As they left the safe house, Cutter inquired about the neighbors, "Anyone I need to worry about?"

"No. Madame Delacroix lives in the white cottage down that alleyway." Talia pointed out the kitchen window toward it. "She's nosy and loves to watch people from her window, but is for the most part harmless. She hates the Germans."

"We'll have to remain cognizant of her. Is there an alternate way into the house?"

"There's an entrance in the living room that leads to a small backyard with a low wall separating it from a street that leads up to the main road," Talia said as she tied a purple scarf over her hair.

"We'll alternate entrances so as to keep Madame Delacroix on her toes; see if we have any observers or tails."

"You should see the town center. There's a bakery we can stop at that will give you a chance to inspect the area."

Cutter agreed and they made their way into town. As they walked, Cutter made mental notes about the town layout, the width of the streets, and how easily the town could be fortified. The village was tiny, quiet, and had potential as a possible assembly area for a raid. It wasn't too far from the beach and, by the looks of it, was a crossroads with roads leading inland and east and west. "What is the enemy disposition around here?"

"A platoon of Germans patrols the surrounding villages. They come through every other day."

Cutter eyed the roads and noticed the dirt was churned up running through the town. Probably a half-track, if Cutter had to guess. The tracks weren't deep enough to be a tank. He would have to request anti-armor equipment as soon as he started setting up supply drops.

Talia led Cutter to the town center; it was nothing expansive. The center consisted of one long road that, for the most part, was empty on both sides save for a bakery, a butcher's shop, and the local constable's office. They walked into the bakery and were greeted by the warm, sensuous aromas of baked bread and pastries.

"*Bonjour*, Claude."

"*Bonjour*, Talia, how are you?" Claude, the baker, smiled as he walked up to his cash register. His thick eyebrows furrowed as he gave Cutter a questioning and suspicious look. "And who is this?"

"This is my friend from Cherbourg, Olivier Deschamps. He's visiting some family in the region and decided to come visit."

"Nice to meet you, Olivier. What do you do in Cherbourg?"

"The pleasure is mine," Cutter responded in French. "I was a student at the university but with the German occupation it closed down, so now I'm a scholar without an occupation trying to survive the war."

Claude grunted but didn't respond. He turned to Talia. "What can I get you?"

"Two baguettes, please."

Cutter didn't like Claude's dismissive behavior. Something about it seemed off. *I'm one of the few strangers they encounter from a big city and he's not asking me questions. Why?* Claude's lack of curiosity put Cutter on edge. *Maybe he's just a prick?* It was an easy reason for his behavior, but it didn't satisfy Cutter.

Claude turned around and grabbed two baguettes from the oven, wrapped them, and gave them to Talia. "Any plans today?"

"I think we're going to see Madame Renault and then maybe have a picnic."

"Wonderful. Be sure to announce yourself before barging in on Madame Renault. Her condition has worsened these past few weeks. Nice to meet you, Olivier." Claude nodded to them and, without another word, returned to his work.

"You as well." Cutter forced smile and a wave. As they walked away from the bakery, Cutter looked at Talia. "What the hell was that?"

"What was what?"

"You told him where we were going."

"He asked."

Cutter opened his mouth to say something but thought better of it. Maybe he was being too paranoid. They walked on in silence for a few moments before Cutter spoke, "Who is Madame Renault?"

"A widower. Her husband was killed in the Great War and her two sons died when Germany invaded. The community takes care of her as much as we can. It's a good excuse to take you around the village."

Cutter grunted but didn't say anything. He didn't like that his contact had been killed a week before his arrival and he was being ferried around by his contact's never-before-mentioned niece. It was all all a bit too

94

coincidental for his taste. They walked down the road toward the coast and finally arrived at Madame Renault's cottage. It was an isolated house at the edge of the town. As they approached, Cutter eyed the empty windows of the house and the unkempt grass covering the path to the front door. He had a feeling something was off.

Talia stopped and looked at him. "What is it?"

Cutter wasn't sure. Something *was* off, but he couldn't place it. "I don't know."

"Well, come on." She gave him an annoyed look and turned around and started for the cottage. She knocked on the door, but there was no answer. "Madame Renault?" she called, but there was no response. She hesitated, then opened the door.

Cutter followed her, but stopped at the doorway. His sense of unease amplifying as he eyed the unkempt nature of the living room. A musty smell of decay filled his nostrils, and he wondered how an old woman could live this way.

"Madame Renault? It's me, Talia!" Talia made her way into the kitchen, searching for the old lady. As she did so Cutter took a step into the living room. Before both feet were planted, the sound of a floorboard creaked behind him to his left. He tried to spin around to face the noise, but before he could, he felt a sharp pain in his head as something cracked against his skull.

He groaned and staggered to the ground and looked up. He locked eyes with Talia as she walked out of the kitchen and looked down at him. Before he blacked out, Cutter met her eyes and saw the calm and collected look she shot him, and realized he was a dead man.

***

CHAPTER 5
SHOOT AND SCOOT

Faraday checked his tail and pulled back on the stick, making sure to not fly the same line for more than 15 seconds. He scanned the skies and rolled over to check below him. As he did so, he pulled back on the stick again, going into a steep dive. The cloud cover was scattered but gave him good concealment for an ambush. As Faraday leveled out he spotted his two students above him. He darted into a cloud and started to climb, anticipating where they were heading. As he pulled out of the cloud he spotted his students. He was directly below and behind them, right in their blind spot. Faraday grinned and lined up a shot.

"Red 2 and 3, you make beautiful corpses. I'll enjoy watching this highlight reel during the debrief. That's three for three that you've lost! Set up again, and remember, watch each other's back!" Faraday pushed down on the stick and darted back into the clouds, when the control tower came on the radio: *"Red Flight, this is Control, we are tracking a formation of German fighters and bombers heading in your direction."*

Faraday checked the map on his kneeboard; they were twenty miles south of Edinburgh. *"Control, this is Red Flight, copy, where are they heading?"*

"It looks like Edinburgh, maybe Glasgow."

"Do we have fighters on an intercept vector?"

"We have fighters scrambling, estimated time of intercept is ten minutes."

"Ten minutes? They may as well not bother. We're closer," Faust called over the radio, pointing out the same thing Faraday was already thinking.

"Red Leader, we can assist. We should go," Chambers agreed.

It took Faraday a minute to respond. His students were his responsibility, but his flight's guns were armed for aerial gunnery practice in the afternoon; they were in a spot to assist when no one else could. *"Control, Red Flight is moving to intercept. Estimated time of intercept is five minutes."*

"Negative, Red Flight, your orders are to return to base." Control's voice was frantic. Faraday could hear in the background someone shouting a delayed intercept.

"Didn't quite catch that, Control, you're coming in broken and unreadable. If you are receiving, we are moving to intercept. Red Flight, this is Red Leader. Form up on me."

"Copy, Red Leader." They both fell in behind Faraday's Spitfire.

What was he doing? Faraday prayed he hadn't made a rash decision. He knowingly had just put his flight at risk. It wasn't their responsibility; no one had told them to do it. They could turn back to base and let the seasoned fighter pilots engage the bombers over the city. Faraday swore softly. He *knew* they needed to intercept. If they could shoot down just one bomber, it may save hundreds.

"Alright, you two, listen up. We're the nearest flight to intercept. We're going to make two gun runs. Our targets are the bombers. Ignore the fighters and stay on my ass." His flight turned east, and the coast quickly came

into view. *"Remember what I taught you: lead your target, two seconds bursts on the gun."*

Both students responded, but otherwise stayed silent, no doubt a little jittery about their first dogfight.

Faraday checked his fuel and tried to steady his breathing. His grip on the stick was like a vice. This would be his first engagement since getting shot down, and that knowledge left room for doubt in his mind. Was he making the right decision? Was his plan the right thing to do? Self-doubt nagged at him as his flight cruised closer and closer to the German formation. He tried to relax and looked over at his wing mates. Whatever he was feeling he was sure it was worse for them. *"If we get separated, don't engage, just dive toward the deck. Their fighter escort won't* follow."

"Copy."

"Roger."

As they closed on the enemy formation, the controller came on the radio, her tone resigned to help them, *"Red Flight, this is Control. Turn northeast to 0-1-5 degrees, climb to Angels 1-5, you are five miles to intercept."*

"Copy, Control. Estimated time of reinforcement?"

"Three minutes."

"Great, we'll be dead in two," Faraday muttered under his breath. They turned to 0-1-5 degrees and climbed to 16,000 feet. *"Eyes up, boys, watch for enemy fighters."*

"I see them, a flight of enemy bombers below us, one mile away!"

"Calm down, Red 2, don't get excited. I see them." Four wings of bombers were flying northwest toward

Edinburgh. Faraday could see ME109s buzzing around them like angry bees. *"Alright, listen up, we're attacking from above and behind. We'll hit them from above, and when we dive below we'll strafe the front and then run like hell back to base."*

"Roger."

"Copy."

"Do NOT engage the ME109s. Neither of you are ready to tangle with them. If you try to be a hero I will ground your ass permanently, understand?"

"Understood."

Faraday pushed the throttle forward and sunk back into his seat from the acceleration. The ME109s caught sight of Faraday's flight and started to move toward them.

"Don't worry about the fighters; they have strict orders to stay with the bombers," Faraday said, hoping the Luftwaffe's tactics hadn't changed since the Blitz. They climbed high above the German formation, quickly catching up with the bombers.

As predicted, the ME109s stayed with the bombers until they were very close. They were half a mile away before ME109s started to peel away from the bombers to engage them. Unfortunately for the ME109s, Red Flight was too close and too fast for them to attack. Faraday's flight crashed past the cordon of fighters and went straight for the bombers at the rear of the formation.

Faraday lined up a shot on the lead bomber of the rear flight. *"Engage targets at will!"* He pulled the trigger back for two seconds and watched as an angry streak of tracers shot through the right wing of a bomber. They dove through the formation and in seconds were already under them. Out of the corner of his eye, Faraday saw smoke billow from at least two bombers as they flew under them.

Turret gunners quickly recovered from the shock of the lone Spitfire flight's daring attack and started to fire at Faraday and his students. Tracers streaked down between the three Spitfires as they hurtled toward the front of the formation for one last gun run.

"*Shoot and scoot!*" Faraday called as he opened up on another bomber. He could see the tail gunner moving his gun frantically, trying to hit his aircraft. As he did so, Faraday's rounds found the left engine of another bomber which started to flame out.

"*Bandits on our tail!*"

"*Dive toward the deck!*"

Red Flight dove toward the ground and away from the formation. Faraday looked over his shoulder, expecting to see ME109s giving chase, but saw nothing of the sort.

"*Red Flight, this is Baker Leader. Nice work. We have Able, Charlie, and Easter Flight one mile from intercept. We'll take it from here.*"

"*Roger, Baker Leader. Red Flight is returning to base.*"

"*Holy shit, that was incred—*"

"*Cut the chatter, Red 3,*" Faraday barked. They continued the rest of the flight in muted silence except for a comm check and an inspection of everyone's aircraft. Each aircraft had bullet holes covering the frame, but they were surprisingly intact. Faraday exhaled a heavy breath and loosened his grip on the joystick. His heart was still beating a mile a minute. He struggled to control his breathing and steady his heart rate. After a minute he gave up and pulled his oxygen mask off. "Christ!" He grinned and laughed hysterically. It felt good getting back into the fight. After all these months up in Scotland after bailing in the Channel, Faraday had started to wonder privately if he had lost his nerve. Tangling with those bombers had assuaged his fears. He smiled as he put his mask back on, the confidence he felt making him feel invincible.

When they landed the aircrews greeted them raucously. A crowd gathered around Faust and Chambers's aircraft as they clambered out. Fellow students greeted them with jubilant cries, both jealous and amazed that they survived their first intercept mission.

Faraday clambered out of his aircraft and found Squadron Leader Bailey and fellow instructor, Flight Lieutenant Ben Royce, waiting for him.

"Sir." Faraday saluted once he was on the ground.

Bailey returned it. "On the one hand I'm very happy to see you in one piece; on the other I'm a bit peeved that you disobeyed a direct order from Control to return to base."

"Nice to see you too, sir."

Bailey smiled weakly and extended his hand. "Nice work." He nodded up to Faraday's aircraft. "She'll need some repairs." Faraday turned and looked at his aircraft. She was streaked with bullet holes all down the fuselage, including one directly behind the cockpit.

"If you were a little slower, that one would have gotten you," Royce pointed out.

Faraday shot him a look.

Royce chuckled and clapped him on the back. "Nice job, Ian."

"Thanks, Ben."

"We're giving the lads an evening liberty pass. We'll hit them in the morning with a lecture on not trying to go off and be a hero."

"I assume everyone and their brother now wants to be called on to conduct an intercept mission."

Royce snorted. "My students are already begging me to do one."

"Won't happen again," Bailey said simply. The three of them started to make their way toward the crowd of students.

"I'll get them debriefed, sir, and deflate their bubble a little before they go out on the town."

"Good man. The chaps are talking about going to Edinburgh this evening and I don't think it's a half-bad idea."

"I'll brief and change over and meet you in town." Faraday walked toward his students. "Faust, Chambers! If you want to survive your next dogfight without me being there I suggest you get your asses to the debrief room."

The pair of them exchanged sheepish grins with their classmates and trudged after Faraday. Debrief took longer than expected simply because it was Faust's and Chambers's first dogfight. As they reviewed the shot film, both of them learned more than Faraday could have taught them in a school environment. By the end of the debrief both of them walked away with a greater understanding of dogfighting as well as intercept tactics. When they finished, Faraday sent them off to enjoy the night and went home to change. As soon as he was ready, he hopped on his motorcycle and headed toward Edinburgh. As he drove into town he surveyed the damage from the day's bombing raid, and was impressed by the limited destruction. Thirteen Group had done a good job repelling the raid. They had done a nice job mopping up the remaining bombers.

Faraday parked his motorcycle and walked down the street. It was a cold evening, and a frost hung in the air. Even with his wool-lined bomber jacket and wool turtleneck the wintry air made him shiver. He turned his collar up and made his way down the cobblestone streets of Edinburgh. After walking a block, Faraday found the pub he was looking for: The Plump Goose.

When he walked in he found the pub crowded with people, including Bailey and half the instructors, most of whom were half in the bag.

"The hero of Edinburgh!" someone called as he walked in the pub.

"Hey, can I get your autograph?" another instructor called.

"All of you can piss up a rope."

"Oi, were you Red Leader today during that intercept?" a man Faraday didn't recognize asked up at the bar.

"Yes."

"You got balls, mate. I was Baker Leader and we came in right after your run and cleaned up. You set us up nicely to clobber them. Half of them gave chase down toward the deck after you, but had to stop midway to climb back upstairs to defend the bombers from us." Baker Leader laughed and clapped Faraday on the back, ordering two rounds from the bartender.

"Well, your lot came just in the nick of time. We surely were at the end of our rope."

"Well, hopefully you can return the favor one day. By the way, we confirmed that your flight shot down three Heinkels. No doubt they would have killed a lot of people had they made it to the city." The bartender showed up and handed over the beers, which Baker Leader then offered to Faraday.

"Cheers." Faraday nodded his thanks and walked over to Bailey and handed him one of the beers. "Made some new friends."

"I know. They've been regaling the women in here with how they stopped the bombing raid for the past hour. A couple of them are now eyeballing you with the entrance you just made. You just became the man of the hour."

Faraday looked around the pub and caught the eyes of a few women. He took a sip from his beer and prepared to walk over to a blonde with inviting eyes, when the air raid siren started to go off.

Faraday swore under his breath.

"Alright, everyone to the shelters, everyone out!" the bartender called calmly. Patrons started to make their way out of the bar. It wasn't a frantic stampede but a hurried walk as though they were late to work.

"Rotten luck old chap." Bailey snorted as he watched the blonde steal away out of the bar.

Faraday shrugged and walked over to the bar and pulled out a wad of bills.

"Hey, what do you think you're doing?" the bartender called in annoyance as Faraday reached over the bar for a bottle of whiskey. He showed the bartender the bills and laid them on the table.

The bartender nodded his consent, realizing Faraday was paying nearly double for the bottle. Faraday grabbed the bottle and rejoined Bailey near the door. "Sod it, I'm getting drunk tonight." He took a hearty swig from the neck of the bottle and passed it to Bailey. "Call it an early going away party, Pete."

Bailey hesitated but took the bottle and drank deeply. He coughed and checked the label. "Damn. I haven't had Irish whiskey in a while."

"Good, right?" They looked on as they walked outside. Spotlights lit up the sky as they swept the night in search of German bombers. Tracer fire began to stitch upward as bombers were spotted.

"They're going for the factories."

Faraday nodded and took the bottle. "I'm not going down into that bloody shelter."

"Neither am I."

Faraday took a heavy sip from the bottle and belched. He could hear the whistle of the bombs as they screeched through the air. The ground rumbled and the air cracked thunder as the bombs impacted. Vibrant orange plumes of fire billowed up as West Edinburgh burned. He couldn't help but feel anger well up in the pit of his stomach.

"Pete, I think I wanna go back south."

Bailey looked over at him. "You're drunk."

"Doesn't change what I want."

"You've only been an instructor for three months. You can't just say I want to go back to an intercept squadron. Who would replace you?"

"I'm sure someone would be willing. They'd be getting the long end of the stick."

"We'll talk about it when you're sober," Bailey said dismissively. He had known Faraday long enough to know that he wasn't someone you could keep on the sidelines for long. Mike King had warned him that Faraday wouldn't stay in a training squadron; and Bailey knew from flying with Faraday in the Battle of Britain that he wasn't one to step aside when he could help. Twice he had nearly run out of fuel while flying because he had refused to leave a wing mate in a fight. Bailey knew his time at Turnhouse was short. He took another sip of whiskey and looked around. The street was deserted. "Christ, fucking Jerry knows how to ruin a good night. I'm going back to the airfield. I'll see you in the morning."

Faraday nodded silently and continued to watch the raid, imagining what he would do if he was in an aircraft right now.

***

Cutter shook his head; it hurt as he moved it. He opened his bleary eyes and looked around. His vision was still blurry and took a moment to refocus. He tried to stand up, but realized he was tied to a chair. He looked around and saw that he was surrounded by a large group of people.

"Monsieur Deschamps, apologies for the rugged treatment, but I'm sure you can understand our precautions," Claude, the baker, said. He walked over to Cutter and crouched down to eye level.

Cutter regarded him and then looked over at Talia and chuckled, "That's why we went to the bakery."

"*Oui.*" Claude nodded and looked over at Talia. "Talia is a clever girl; knew how to cordon you off so we could isolate you and take you somewhere secure."

Cutter looked around. They appeared to be in a barn. Hay bales cluttered the floor and farm tools hung from the walls. Cutter counted six people, but assumed there were more. "So what now?"

"Well, you certainly walk, talk, and are equipped like an SOE agent," Claude said in English as he unsheathed Cutter's F-S knife and inspected the blade. "Question is, are you?"

"Have you spoken with SOE?" Cutter asked, also in English.

"We have. They confirmed that Olivier Deschamps was inserted, but Francois Crevier was the only one who could confirm your identity. You can understand why we are hesitant."

"A bit of a conundrum."

"So what do we do?"

"How about untie me, give me a stiff drink, and behave like gentlemen?"

Claude chuckled and shook his head. "I think not, *monsieur.*"

Cutter smirked, trying to appear in control even while tied up. "Well, you can put me in contact with SOE, and they can prove who I am."

Claude stood up and thought it over. "I was thinking something similar, but I have concerns."

"Like what?"

"The Germans are able to not only intercept our radio communications, but are able to triangulate where we are. If we get on the radio, we have maybe thirty minutes before the Nazis get here."

"So?"

"We've already used it twice in the past three hours."

"Well, I'm not staying tied up the whole bloody night, so let's do this."

Claude toyed with the tip of the F-S knife absently and turned to two of his men. "Get the radio ready." Both of them nodded and departed. Claude walked over and started to uncut Cutter's bonds using the F-S knife.

"Claude what are you doing?" Talia asked in surprise.

"We need to verify him, and we don't have time to wait," Claude said in annoyance. He finished cutting the bonds, but did not hand Cutter his knife.

Cutter stood up shakily and rubbed his arms where the rope cut off circulation.

"Follow me," Claude said, and started to walk off. Cutter jogged after him, noticing two Resistance members staying close to him, weapons at the ready. They walked into an adjacent room of the barn and found the two men next to a portable radio.

Cutter didn't immediately go to the radio. He watched as the two men fumbled with the device. He still wasn't entirely convinced this wasn't a German ploy, and didn't move to the radio until one of the radio operators started using the proper codes to get SOE on the net.

Without asking for permission, he walked over and grabbed the mouthpiece. *"Tackley Station, this is Cartographer. Come in, Tackley Station."* It took Cutter three tries before finally getting a response.

"Cartographer, this is Tackley Station. Send your traffic."

"Roger, I have made contact with Tempest, but need assistance with proving my identity. Can you assist."

SOE took a moment to respond, *"Roger, Cartographer, stand by."*

Cutter put the mouthpiece down and waited. Claude and Talia stood near him, listening in to the whole conversation.

"Cartographer, this is Tackley Station, come in."

"Go for Cartographer."

"Aardvark would like to know how many dates his wife has set you up on."

Cutter snorted and clicked the mic. *"Zero."* Freddy's wife didn't like him one bit.

There was a pause on the other end. *"Affirmative. Name the counter code to Emerald."*

"Tranquility." They went through three more challenge and return code words before Tackley Station was satisfied. *"Identity confirmed for Cartographer. Tackley Station out."*

The line went dead. Cutter put the mic down and looked at Claude and Talia. "You heard that, right?"

Claude nodded and handed over the F-S knife. "Never can be too sure."

"I understand. Wasn't personal."

Cutter noticed the look of disappointment on Talia's face but ignored it. "So what now?"

"Run like hell," Claude said simply, he pointed to the two radio operators. "Break it down and get out of here." He turned to the two guards. "Make sure they get out of here safely." He motioned for Cutter and Talia to follow him.

"Where are we going?"

"The safe house; we can talk there," Claude said and motioned toward a car. "Get in."

***

Faraday's head was throbbing and his clothes were wet. He woke up shivering and looked around and realized he was in the middle of a field. He searched the area and spotted his motorcycle leaning against a stone wall near the road. It took him a minute, but he slowly remembered stopping to relieve himself by the wall in the night. He must've sat down and dozed off at some point. He stood up unsteadily and looked down. The bottle of whiskey sat at his feet, empty, save for a few stray drops. He checked his watch: seven o'clock. He had half a mind to lie back down in the field and sleep for another hour if he wasn't so damn cold.

Faraday shook his arms and stamped his feet to try and warm up. How the hell didn't he die in his sleep from hypothermia? He trudged toward his bike, the hangover hitting him like a hammer with every step. His head buzzed making it all the more difficult to concentrate. As he sat down on the bike, he realized the buzzing in his head was actually above him. He looked up and saw contrails streaking across the sky.

A dogfight waged overhead as bombers vectored toward Edinburgh. "Christ, you bastards are persistent," Faraday muttered. He watched as Spitfires and Hurricanes tangled with ME109s. Black smoke coughed out of one of the fighters. Faraday couldn't tell whose aircraft it was, but watched as it went into a nosedive.

The aircraft was losing altitude quickly; as it got closer to the ground Faraday could see that it was a Hawker Hurricane. Flames licked the cockpit as fuel leaked from the engine and ignited. It was only a matter of moments before it would explode.

"Get out, dammit! Bail!" Faraday shouted as he watched helplessly from the ground. When the plane looked to be no higher than three thousand feet, the pilot bailed out. Faraday watched as a chute deployed, and the pilot started to drift back down to earth. Faraday revved the engine and took off toward where he expected the pilot to land.

The pilot touched down a mile away from where Faraday had woken up. He arrived just as the Hurricane pilot was detaching himself from his chute.

"You alright?" Faraday asked as he killed the engine to his motorcycle.

The pilot looked at Faraday and shrugged. "I could be a hell of a lot worse, I suspect." His thick Scottish brogue was barely understandable.

"Need a lift?"

"Sure. Do you mind giving me a ride to my aircraft? It looked to have crashed a few fields over."

"Sure, hop on. What's your name?"

"Flight Lieutenant Seamus Kilgore. You?" Kilgore asked as he hopped on the back of the motorcycle.

"Flight Lieutenant Ian Faraday. Nice to meet you." Faraday revved up the engine and started off in the direction of the billowing smoke.

"What squadron are you with?"

"One-eleven. You?"

"I'm an instructor at Turnhouse." Faraday pulled the motorcycle to the side of the road next to the field the plane had crashed in, and killed the engine.

Kilgore hopped off the bike and surveyed the wreckage. Flames licked the airframe as petrol and canvas burned. They both kept their distance in case the fuel tank exploded.

Kilgore ran a hand vigorously through his hair in frustration. "Dammit, I really liked that bird." He looked over at Faraday. "You've any idea how hard it is to find an aircraft that doesn't have any sort of equipment malfunction?"

"It's a rare occurrence."

"Aye, and she was one of them. Now they're gonna give me some hangar queen who no doubt will have a gun jam in the middle of a scrap," Kilgore moaned. He kicked a tuft of grass and meandered back up to Faraday's bike. "What's your deal anyway?"

"Got drunk and passed out in a field."

Kilgore laughed. "If it weren't for your accent I'd swear you were from the Highlands with that tale."

"I can take you to Turnhouse and you can get a ride back to your airfield from there." Faraday watched as the aircraft started to blaze.

"I appreciate that." Kilgore didn't move for a moment but looked at Faraday thoughtfully. "So you're an instructor?" a hint of envy filling his voice. "You lucky sod."

Faraday nodded but didn't say anything.

"How do you like it?"

Faraday shrugged. He loved not being on standby to intercept at every hour of the day, but he meant what he said last night to Bailey. He was ready to get back into the fight. "It's the first time my schedule was my own in a long time."

Kilgore nodded in understanding. "Aye, not having to worry about the enemy for a day is a grand thing." He took one final look at the burning wreckage that was his aircraft moments before and without another word hopped on the motorcycle.

The ride was short, and as they entered the front gate a few dogfights could still be seen waging over the outskirts of Edinburgh.

Kilgore eyed an instructor briefing his students, a look Faraday recognized as he'd had it in his own eyes a few months ago. He looked over at the flight line and saw Ben Royce prepping his boys to go up. "You know, I'm actually going over to request a transfer, if you want to get a foot in the door."

Kilgore looked at Faraday in surprise. "You better not be having a laugh."

"Dead serious. Come on." Faraday brought the motorcycle to a stop and hopped off. He motioned for Kilgore to follow him to the ready shack.

"Why give this up? Away from the war? You'll survive," Kilgore asked suspiciously.

"I've spent three months here and have trained nine students. Yesterday my two students and I were in the scrap over the city and I realized how much I missed it."

"Shitting yourself when Jerry gets behind you in a scuffle?"

"No. I missed being relied on."

Kilgore nodded in understanding. "It's one thing to know that you can rely on your mates, but it's a whole other when they can rely on you."

113

"That's why I want to go back."

They walked into the ready shack and found Squadron Leader Bailey packing up his office.

Faraday knocked on the open door. "Morning, sir."

"Where the hell have you been?" Bailey groaned. He looked to be suffering from a hangover similar to Faraday's.

"I'd rather not say."

Bailey grunted, and looked over at Kilgore. "Who's this?"

"He's a stray. Found him in a field on my way home."

"Shot down?"

"Yes, sir."

"What's your squadron?" Bailey asked in a perfunctory manner, as if this was a regular occurrence.

Kilgore leaned against the door frame. "One-eleven Squadron out of RAF Acklington."

"Sir, I was wondering if before you leave you could do both me and Kilgore a favor."

Bailey stopped packing and looked up. "I have a horrible feeling I'm not going to like this."

"Kilgore is looking to transfer here, and I'm looking to transfer back south."

"I thought that was just drunken rage last night when you were blathering about going south." Bailey sighed and walked around his desk and leaned against it. "Why?"

"I'm rested. It's time I got back into the mix. I ask that you give Kilgore my slot and send me south."

"How nice of Mr. Kilgore to take your position. What about your students?"

"If we learned anything yesterday, it's that Faust and Chambers are ready. I'll take them with me. Surely there is a squadron in need of a new flight."

Bailey grunted, crossed his arms, and chewed his lip as he thought it over; his desk creaked under his weight. "I'll make a few calls. Flight Lieutenant Kilgore, head back to your squadron. You can await word there. Wait outside and I'll arrange transportation for you."

"Yes, sir." Kilgore stamped his foot, saluted, and departed. Bailey eyed Faraday for a long moment. "Ian, don't make me regret this." He reached for the phone on his desk and started to dial a number.

"One more thing, sir."

Bailey looked up and glared at him. "What?"

"Faust and Chambers go back to 77 with me."

"Sure, why not? Let's just send you to the busiest group in all of England." Bailey grumbled, talking to no one in particular, "Oh, top of the morning to you, Air Vice-Marshal Leigh-Mallory. Mind if I spot you three new pilots?"

"Thanks, sir, I'll go get my kit ready."

"Sod off, Ian. If you get shot down it's on your head."

***

The car came to a halt on the gravel drive of the safe house back in town. Claude, Talia, and Cutter clambered out and crunched across to the house, making their way back into the kitchen where Talia and Cutter had first been introduced to each other. Claude sat down heavily in one of the chairs and stretched his legs. "So what do you need from us?"

Cutter leaned against the countertop and crossed his arms. His initial concerns about Talia and Claude being part of an elaborate ruse by the Gestapo were allayed, but he still didn't trust them. He weighed his response carefully. He needed to ensure that he didn't give up too much information, so that if Claude or anyone were captured and interrogated they wouldn't compromise the raid or him. "I need information: troop strengths, locations, and capabilities in the surrounding area."

"Shouldn't be difficult. What for?"

"We're looking for targets of opportunity for the RAF to interdict," Cutter lied. It was a weak lie, and Claude knew it, but didn't respond. Cutter could tell he understood why he wasn't being told the truth. The man was professional enough to not get upset. "Shouldn't be too difficult. How soon do you need it?"

"You have a week."

"It'll be done. What will you be doing?"

"I have my own mission. I'll need a vehicle."

"You intend to go around the region alone?" Claude asked in surprise.

"Yes, why?"

Claude shook his head. "No. You'll be picked up by the Germans before you even leave the village. Nothing screams Resistance like a young solitary man in a car driving around Normandy. Talia will go with you."

Talia had been silent the entire conversation, but was taken aback by the proposal. "Excuse me?" she exclaimed, clearly not approving of the idea. Her almond-shaped eyes darted between Claude and Cutter. A look of distaste crept over her face. "Send Durand or Fabrice."

Claude looked at Talia and pointed at Cutter. "Deschamps will need a guide. It's less conspicuous if he isn't alone, and even less conspicuous if he is with a woman.

116

The cover you used at the bakery was that he was your friend from Cherbourg. We can stretch that and say he is your lover."

"We will do no such thing!" Talia hissed. She walked over to Claude and dug one of her fingernails into his chest as she pointed at him. "I will not go around pretending to be this English cad's lover."

"Please contain your excitement for the notion."

"Shut up!" Talia growled.

Claude grabbed her by the arm none too gently. "Talia, I don't care what your preferences are. You will pose as his lover. This is how you can best serve the Resistance. You've been pestering me for new responsibilities for months. Here's your chance."

"I can fight!"

"Be quiet. Combat is no place for a girl," Claude hissed. "You *will* escort Olivier around. That is my order as your commander and that is final." He turned and shot Cutter a wary look. "As for you. If you take advantage of her, you won't be going home with everything intact."

Cutter nodded in understanding. "Don't worry, I happen to like my crown jewels very much."

"Come by the bakery on Wednesday and we'll discuss whatever information we have gathered." Claude looked at the pair of them and stood up. "Good luck." He shot Talia a dark look, and without another word walked out the door.

As the door shut, Talia stormed out of the kitchen and out of sight. Cutter heard the sound of footsteps climbing up a flight of stairs and a door shut violently.

"Alone at last." He stood up from the table and walked over to the stove and lit it and set a kettle of water on it to make some tea. He set his pistol on the table and walked over to his trunk. The radio components were missing; the French Resistance had searched his bag and had seen fit to liberate him of it, along with a pair of his socks.

Cutter took the kettle off the stove and poured the water in with the tea leaves. He returned to the table and absently stirred his tea. Talia would be a challenge, he thought. He couldn't help but feel sorry for her after the way Claude had treated her. Unlike Hambro, he was very heavy-handed in dispensing his authority. But still, the girl had fire. Cutter had seen the defiance in her eyes. She wasn't one to take anything lying down. She was very different from the girls Cutter had met while at the university. He deliberated over how he would win her over to aiding him willingly. In the past, learning about and befriending his contacts had been the simplest way to conscript aid, but he wasn't sure he had the stomach to do that. Since Victor, he was unsure how willing he was to continue with his usual methods of achieving results.

"Do your job." Victor's last words echoed in Cutter's head. He doubted he would be able to kill Talia in order to preserve himself or the Resistance if he formed an attachment to her. He needed to find another way. What did he know about her?

Talia was ambitious, that much was clear in her willingness to fight. But she despised being treated like a child. No, a girl, Cutter corrected himself. She hated being looked upon as lesser than the men of the Resistance because of her sex. Cutter stopped stirring and took a sip of his tea, a plan beginning to form in the back of his head.

An hour passed before Talia came back downstairs. She gave Cutter a contemptuous look and made a point of never being in the same room as him for more than a few moments. Cutter let her prance about in a rage for another hour before addressing her. "Are we going to continue this way the entire time I'm here?"

Talia looked up from a book Cutter suspected she was pretending to read. "Like what?"

Cutter rolled his eyes in exasperation. "Come on, where's the car?"

"Where are we going?"

"Saint-Aubin and Sotteville," Cutter said as he put his F-S knife in his waistband and checked his pistol. He inspected the magazine, inserted it in the pistol, and chambered a round.

"Why?"

"I figured a drive through the French countryside may do our relationship some good."

Talia shot Cutter a stony look, but did not respond.

He walked over to the kitchen and placed his pistol in one of the cabinets. "Where's the car?"

Talia put on her coat. "It's on the street."

Cutter nodded and opened the door. "Alright, let's go." They walked out toward the car and saw Madame Delacroix tending to her garden, her long bony fingers working deftly to manicure her flowers. She was an elderly woman with gray hair and a weathered face. Cutter could tell she was of a prying nature and made a mental note to keep an eye on her.

She spotted them and waved. "*Bonjour*, Talia, how are you? And *who* is this?" She gave Cutter a leering smile as she batted her eyes and smiled mischievously at him.

Talia smiled warmly. "Madame Delacroix, how nice to see you! Have you met Olivier? He's a friend of mine." She motioned to Cutter, who walked over and introduced himself.

"*Bonjour, madame*, it is a pleasure to meet you."

"Talia you never told me you had such good looking friends." Madame Delacroix winked.

Talia gave a strained laugh. "Well, he's been in Cherbourg this whole time and I hadn't had a chance to see him until now."

"Oh, you're from Cherbourg. What a wonderful city."

Cutter put an arm around Talia's shoulder and smiled. "It is indeed." He felt Talia's shoulder stiffen under his touch. "Darling, I don't mean to be rude, but we are in a bit of a rush."

"*C'est vrai*, we are meeting with some old friends of Olivier's and we can't keep them waiting."

"Well, I don't want to keep you," Madame Delacroix said, meaning quite the opposite.

Cutter nodded and said goodbye, steering Talia toward the car. "She's a man-eater, by the looks of her," Cutter murmured when they were out of earshot.

"She'd eat you alive," Talia murmured as she clambered into the car. It was a faded 1937 Citroen, but by the way the engine started it ran as good as new.

"Which way?" Cutter asked as he put the engine in gear.

"Turn left up here." Talia pointed at the T-intersection straight ahead. Cutter turned onto the road and drove out of the village.

They drove in silence for a few kilometers before Cutter spoke, "If we're supposed to be lovers, it would be a good idea to get to know each other a little better." He wasn't keen on the idea, but he needed to know who Talia was.

"Why?"

"So we don't get killed. Look, I've been at this for a while. The better we know each other the better our chances of survival."

Talia looked out her window and leaned her arm against the sill. "Whatever you tell me won't be true, so why should I tell you personal things about me."

Cutter hesitated for a moment, unsure how to respond. "I know you don't like this situation, but—"

"You have no idea what I like and don't like!"

Cutter paused, unsure how to proceed. "You clearly dislike me, but I don't understand why." He could understand the hostility for Claude pairing her with him, but from the start she had disliked him. Since he had knocked on the door of her house to proving that he was here to help, Talia had hardly warmed up to him. He couldn't understand where the contempt was coming from.

Talia looked out the window and didn't respond for a long time. Then she looked at Cutter and said, her voice soft, "I'm supposed to pretend to be the lover of a man who yesterday threatened to kill me if I didn't help him and is the reason my uncle was killed."

Cutter took his eyes off the road for a second and looked at her. "What do you mean I'm the reason your uncle was killed?"

Talia turned back toward the window and remained silent.

Cutter looked at her in confusion. He had only met Francois once and it had been over six months ago. *How is his death my fault?* "How did your uncle die?"

"He was covering the escape of a radio operator after they received your communiqué that you were coming. Your message took too long to receive and the Germans found them. My uncle fought the Germans, giving the operator time to escape with the radio." Talia turned back and looked at Cutter, struggling to blink back the tears.

"I'm sorry," Cutter murmured, not entirely sure what to say. They continued the rest of the drive in silence and arrived at Saint-Aubin. For all his efforts trying to remain detached from Talia, it was already proving to be difficult. How was he going to get to know her and pose as her lover without forming some kind of attachment? It was a paradox he realized. Cutter drove through the small town and turned toward the beach and parked. "Let's go for a stroll." He hopped out of the vehicle, walked around, and opened the door for Talia, then reached for her hand. Talia hesitated but gave it. "Remember, we're lovers," he reminded gently as they walked.

"I know," she said, through gritted teeth.

They meandered out onto the beach. The sky was overcast and a cold breeze blew along the water, putting a chill in the air. The pair of them walked up to the water's edge and stood in silence watching the tide. Cutter looked around as they walked and made sure they were alone. "You're not mad at me about your uncle's death."

"Are you a mind reader or something?"

Cutter shook his head. "No, but I see how Claude treats you. You're mad at anyone who expects less of you."

"You don't know the first thing about me."

"No, you're right. But that pugnacious overly hostile persona you put on isn't you."

"You've known me less than twelve hours and you think you have me figured out?"

"I can take a guess. You lived with your uncle; your parents are either missing or dead, most likely because of the war. You're one of the first women I've ever met in the Resistance that is younger than me, and I suspect you're one of the only women in this circuit. You're mad because of all these things, and with your uncle's death you lost the one person you could talk to openly." Cutter picked up a pebble off the beach and rolled it between his thumb and finger. "Am I close?"

Talia, opened her mouth and prepared to give a sharp retort but was cut off by Cutter. "Look, I don't really care if I'm close. I don't care if you need to hate me to get through this, that's fine, but don't think for a second that you're the only person that has suffered because of this war." Cutter tossed the pebble into the surf and took a step closer to Talia. His voice softening, he said, "This war has cost us all something, but I'm here to see that I don't pay any more for it. What about you?"

"Of course!" she snapped. "I'm willing to do anything and everything I can to get rid of the Nazis, but I'm not some whore Claude can use to satisfy you and keep you safe."

"Then help me. You have an opportunity to do a lot of good for your country and take something back. Don't throw this chance away just to spite Claude."

He could tell by the look on Talia's face he had touched a nerve. "I'm here to help, but I need yours to do it." He searched Talia's eyes, his voice calm and measured, "Will you help me?"

Talia hesitated, surprised by Cutter's candid words. His declaration angered her but at the same time something inside her felt liberated by his harsh observation. None of the Resistance members had ever asked her how she was after her uncle's death. As the only woman in the cell it was always difficult to be taken seriously. In Claude's eyes she was just a remnant of her uncle and had little to no value to the Resistance. As harsh as Cutter was, he wasn't treating her as a frail girl but as someone he needed to rely on, as an equal. As much as she disliked Cutter's acerbic nature, the idea of having a purpose and a chance to do something to fight the Nazis, other than being a decoy or messenger for Claude, excited her.

"The Nazis took my family from me. They took my life. I don't want anything else taken."

A faint smile curled at the corners of Cutter's mouth and he extended his hand. "Then let's crack on."

They spent the rest of the day scouting Sotteville and Saint-Aubin. Cutter made mental notes as they went, planning to write everything down back at the safe house. Both towns provided little in regard to possible raid locations, but it helped Cutter develop situational awareness of the surrounding area. As they drove back to the safe house he looked over at Talia. She had thawed over the day and had become much less frosty toward him. "What will you do after the war?" he asked. As much as he wanted to avoid forming an attachment, it wouldn't do to know nothing about her.

"That's a long way away."

"You think so?"

Talia looked at him skeptically. "Do you honestly see an invasion occurring anytime soon?"

"It's possible."

"Not that possible."

"What did you do before the war?" Cutter asked. He had interacted with contacts numerous times and had been able to extract information easily for the most part. Usually his contacts had been men, which had made it easier to find common ground, usually over a glass of liquor. With Talia, it was a whole different game. His rousing speech on the beach had been a huge gamble. Cutter had no clue how to handle a woman, and hadn't been sure if his caustic and candid talk with Talia would be successful. Her willingness to work with him after what he said had left him more confused than confident about what motivated her.

"I was a student in Paris."

"Really?"

"Yes at the Sorbonne."

"Not many women get into the Sorbonne. That's impressive. What did you study?"

"Music." Talia shifted in her seat and looked outside as they continued through the French countryside. "I played the violin."

"Do you still play?" Cutter asked as they approached Quiberville.

"I haven't really had time," Talia said, a hint of sadness in her voice.

Cutter noticed and quickly changed topics. "What do you know about Eglise Saint Valéry?" He had studied a map of the area extensively, and he was eager to inspect the church. It was backed up along a cliff on the beach, but a couple topographical charts indicated that it could be scaled easily from the coast.

"It's one of the oldest churches in the region. The priest is sympathetic to the Resistance. It's also along the coast." Talia paused and eyed Cutter suspiciously. "Why are we visiting these places?"

Cutter remained silent.

"Are you going to go silent every time I ask a question about your mission, or will you trust me?"

Cutter weighed his answer carefully. If he didn't tell the truth, he ran the risk of sabotaging a fragile working relationship with Talia. On the other hand, if he told the truth, he ran the risk of compromising the mission if she turned out to be an informant. Cutter never had a contact betray him, but he had heard stories of other agents being double-crossed; as a result he was incredibly cautious. "We're screening for ideal beachheads for a potential raid in the coming months." He decided telling her the truth was worth the risk.

Talia looked at him in surprise, and then smirked. "Was that so difficult to say?"

"You have no idea."

Cutter rounded a blind bend in the road and hit the brakes. Up ahead a German half-track sat parked with a squad of Nazi soldiers standing in the road with a checkpoint set up.

"*Merde.*"

"Relax," Cutter said in French, "just act normal." He eased on the gas pedal and they crept forward.

A German corporal motioned for them to stop.

"Dammit, Oberleutnant Amsel is with them."

"Who?"

"He's in charge of the detachment that patrols this region. He's a pig."

Cutter looked around the squad of Germans and spotted Amsel. He stood out easily, not only with his Oberleutnant boards on his collar, but also because he was tall, blond, and blue-eyed; the perfect Aryan. Cutter could tell he had seen Talia as he strode over to the passenger window and motioned for Talia to role the window down.

"Mademoiselle Crevier, how nice to see you." Amsel leaned into the window aperture. He smelled nauseatingly of cologne, and wasn't afraid to invade Talia's personal space.

"Oberleutnant, it's been too long. How are you?" Talia broke into a friendly smile. Her eyes shined amicably and her voice rose an octave, Cutter noticed.

"I am well, thank you, and who is this?" Amsel leered at Cutter. His lupine smile reminding Cutter of a Gestapo agent he once encountered.

Talia reached for Cutter's hand and gripped it warmly and leaned closer to him. "This is my dear friend Olivier Deschamps. He's come from Cherbourg to pay his respects to my uncle."

Amsel frowned at Talia's affectionate display. "Yes, I heard about his untimely death. I am so sorry for your loss."

Cutter frowned. Talia had told him he had been shot by the Germans. This conversation was not how he expected a German officer to interact with the niece of a saboteur.

"Yes, a horrible way to die, burning in an automobile accident. But Francois loved to drive as much as he loved to drink. I warned him countless times of the dangers," Talia said, for Cutter's benefit.

"Indeed," Amsel agreed. "Mr. Deschamps, how do you know the Creviers?" His eyes looked sharply at Cutter. The question was innocent enough, but Cutter saw it for what it was, an interrogation.

"My parents were close with Talia's back in Paris. Unfortunately they were taken from me at an early age."

"I'm sorry to hear that," the Oberleutnant said sympathetically. "Where are you staying?"

"With me. It has been too long since I have seen him; it didn't seem right having him stay at an inn," Talia answered, the tone of her voice further cementing the romantic nature of her relationship with Cutter. This received the desired effect from Amsel, who was visibly annoyed, much to Talia's pleasure.

"Well, that is gracious of you. If you will please show me your papers, we can let you go."

Cutter rummaged through his pockets as Talia searched her purse for her documentation. They both handed their papers over to Amsel. He inspected the documents and handed back Talia's to her but lingered on Cutter's. "Monsieur Deschamps, I do not see your pass to travel here from Cherbourg." He motioned to one of his soldiers who marched over to open Cutter's door.

"Oh! I have it right here. Sorry, I forgot I had it." Cutter rummaged back through his pocket and quickly produced it.

Amsel took it with a disappointed look. The soldier stopped in his tracks and waited for an order from his commander. Amsel inspected Cutter's documents closely, but couldn't find an issue with it and returned it to him. Cutter took it and said a silent prayer promising to buy the forgers back at SOE a case of whiskey when he returned.

"Everything is in order." Amsel motioned to his troops to move out of the way and waved them through. Cutter pushed lightly on the gas and the car rolled forward. When they were clear of the checkpoint, he pushed down on the gas and accelerated to a moderate speed.

"Well, he's delightful," Cutter said dryly as they drove, "and infatuated with you."

"He's incorrigible," Talia said as she removed her hand from Cutter's, her warmth and effervescence evaporating.

"He could be a problem."

"I can handle him."

"Tell me about him."

"He's from Bremmen. A bit of a narcissist."

"I haven't met a German who wasn't."

"He tries to come across as a gentleman whenever he wants to impress a woman, and has never forced himself on a girl, from all the reports we've received. He enjoys the hunt, as he puts it."

Cutter tapped the wheel with his fingertips. Amsel sounded like an amateur. A man more interested in wearing a uniform than actually doing his duty. "Corrupt?" Cutter asked as he downshifted on the clutch.

"Not that we've heard."

"Have you two ever . . . you know."

"What?"

Cutter's cheeks reddened. "Made the beast with two backs?"

Talia gave a disgusted look. "No, I would never let him. He is fun to toy with, though."

Cutter nodded, the look of annoyance on Amsel's face when Talia grabbed his hand stood out in his mind. "Maybe you should ease up on him. I'd rather not have him make life difficult for me because of jealousy."

"Jealousy, why would he be jealous?" Talia asked innocently.

"Calm down, I'm not trying to get in your knickers. Amsel is self-infatuated. The idea of you choosing me over him must drive him crazy. The only way I see throwing him off is by playing off his jealousy for you." Cutter blushed further as he said it. He was a good agent but lacked any grace when it came to talking to women. He always managed to say the wrong thing. They continued on in silence for a while until Talia turned and started to stare at Cutter.

"What is it?"

"You're not very good at talking to women." Talia smirked.

"What makes you think that?"

"You're young, your face turns crimson whenever we talk about romance. Have you ever been with a woman?" She smiled coyly.

"Of course I have!" Cutter lied. In truth, he had never been with a woman, let alone on a date. When he had been at university he barely looked eighteen and was always mistaken for one of his friend's younger brothers. Since the start of the war, little had changed and Cutter had never mastered the art of seduction.

Talia watched his face turn flush with rage from the inquisition. "It's okay if you haven't; it's actually quite cute."

Cutter shot her a glance but said nothing. She was toying with him. They arrived back at the safe house as the sun started to set. Cutter parked the car in front of the safe house and got out and opened the door for Talia. "We can worry about Amsel tomorrow," he said, quickly changing the topic of discussion.

They walked into the house and Cutter made for the kitchen while Talia sat down in the living room; he started to inspect the cupboard. He hadn't eaten since breakfast and was starving. He grabbed a slice of bread from Claude's bakery and tore into it. He walked into the living room still nibbling on the bread. "Is there a spare bedroom?" he asked, feeling fatigue begin to creep into his body. He hadn't slept in 36 hours.

Talia's lips pursed into a thin, unsympathetic smile. "No, just my room. You can sleep on that couch." She nodded to an old dilapidated couch that sat along the wall.

Cutter grunted and walked back into the kitchen, took off his jacket, shirt, and pants and hung them carefully on a chair. Dressed in only a pair of briefs and an undershirt, he defiantly strode back into the living room past Talia and collapsed on the couch. Talia gave him an annoyed look but said nothing. Cutter grabbed and wrapped himself in a blanket that was draped over the backrest of the couch. "We'll go back out tomorrow." Without another word he drifted off to sleep.

***

The streets of London were slick with rain. The dreary skies were a welcome sight, as they offered the country a respite from the incessant bombing of the Luftwaffe. The citizens of London had survived much over the past year. The Blitz had tested the English resolve, but the people had proved to be unyielding. Hambro watched as a group of Londoners salvaged what they could from their bombed-out apartments. Not a tear was shed for their loss, Hambro noticed as he looked over their faces. They all had similar expressions on their faces, a look of stubborn defiance and a refusal to let the Luftwaffe affect their way of life. Hambro continued down the street and turned left onto Baker Street. He spotted the four guards watching the entrance to SOE and nodded to the nearest one.

"Morning, James," Hambro said as he walked past the guard dressed in plain clothes.

"Morning, sir."

"Anything suspicious?"

"Henry had an old whore proposition him earlier, but other than that, nothing."

"Didn't he tell her he was spoken for?" Hambro joked as he walked into SOE. He took his bowler hat off, made his way upstairs, and was greeted at the top of the stairs by his secretary. "Good morning, Charlotte."

"Good morning, sir. We received word from Bishop and Tiger last night."

"We'll talk about it in my office after I check the operations room," Hambro said as he led her down the hall.

"Sir, Lord Mountbatten is in your office."

Hambro stopped and turned around. "What the hell does he want?"

"He wouldn't say."

Hambro tapped his bowler against his leg in thought and made up his mind. "Don't brief me on Tiger and Bishop yet. We'll talk after I get rid of him." He turned back around and strode toward his office. He could check on the operations room later.

"Admiral, what an unexpected surprise. Belated congratulations on the promotion by the way," Hambro said as he walked into his office.

Lord Mountbatten was already seated in one of the chairs in front of Hambro's desk and looked over his shoulder and smiled at Hambro. "Charles, apologies for the unannounced visit." He extended his hand to Hambro, not bothering to stand up from his seat.

Hambro deliberately took his time setting his briefcase down, taking off his coat and hat, and hanging them on the coat hanger. He turned back and finally took Mountbatten's outstretched hand, much to the admiral's chagrin. "So what can the SOE do for you?" Hambro sat down and adjusted his glasses.

"Well, after our little discussion with the Prime Minister, I've yet to hear anything from SOE in regard to Dieppe."

"Why would you? My man has been there less than 48 hours."

Mountbatten's lips cracked into a Cheshire cat smile. "Yes, but due to the short timeline we have for planning not just this raid but the Saint-Nazaire one we really need more from you."

"Dickie, I'm doing all I can, but what the bloody hell do you want from me for Saint-Nazaire? Generating intelligence for these locations takes time, and at the moment I don't have any personnel in the area around Saint-Nazaire."

Mountbatten nodded, a hint of annoyance etched on his face. "What about your man in Normandy? Can't you send him?"

"No. Too risky, and it would raise too many questions with the Germans."

Mountbatten nodded in feigned understanding and leaned forward in his chair threateningly. "Charles, SOE really needs to be more of a team player with Combined Operations."

Hambro remained silent, not trusting his temper.

"SOE has been sandbagging or disregarding Combined Operations' requests for intelligence repeatedly. Naturally, I assume that is due to the SOE providing support to British forces around the globe. But Charles, you heard Winston." Mountbatten leered at Hambro as he used the Prime Minister's Christian name. "Combined Operations is the priority."

"Dickie, Combined Operations isn't the priority," Hambro replied coolly, "winning the war is."

"Which is what we are doing," Mountbatten snapped. "If SOE can't support us then perhaps we need to narrow your scope of tasks to ensure you can accomplish your missions."

Hambro smirked and took his horn-rimmed glasses off and started to clean them. "Dickie," he started, then paused and put his glasses back on. "If Combined Operations is a priority for the PM, then I will need a memorandum stating that. At this time I am accomplishing all tasks and mission requirements that the PM and the

Chief of Staff task me with. If you have any issues or qualms, please see them."

Mountbatten's smile faded as he realized he had been outmaneuvered, but he quickly recovered. "Well, thank you for your time, Charles, and the clarification. I hope to be seeing more of your reports." He stood and acknowledged Hambro, not willing to loiter in his defeat. "If you'll excuse me, I really must be going."

Hambro nodded but didn't bother to stand up and walk him out. "Always a pleasure, Dickie. If you need anything at all, don't be afraid to let us know."

Mountbatten nodded and strode out of his office, ignoring Hambro's secretary as she gave him his hat.

"Shit," Hambro mumbled once his office was empty.

"What was that about, sir?" Charlotte asked from the open doorway.

"I swear to God, politicians will end this country," Hambro groaned and started in on a stack of papers on his desk. "Charlotte, I need a meeting with the PM as soon as possible." He looked down at the papers and back at Charlotte. "Damn. Brief me on Tiger and Bishop in an hour. I need to whittle this paperwork down first."

***

The smell of eggs wafted through the house. When Cutter woke, he spotted Talia in the kitchen. Her long brown hair was down her back and covered half of her robe. She hadn't dressed yet; her feet and legs were bare. She had a nice body, Cutter thought, eyeing her shapely alabaster legs as she made breakfast. He silently stood up from the couch, stalked into the kitchen, and grabbed his trousers and put them on. "Smells good," he said as he strapped on his belt.

Talia turned her head and smiled thinly. "Sit down, I'll make you a plate."

"I'm getting breakfast?"

"Why wouldn't you?" Talia asked as she put a plate in front of him.

Cutter eyed the eggs suspiciously, but grabbed a fork. He dug into the eggs and wolfed them down quickly.

"Would you like some more?"

"What about you?"

"I'll eat in a moment." Talia smiled. She leaned forward with the pan and shoveled some more eggs onto his plate. As she did, her robe dropped slightly, exposing the top of her breasts to him.

Cutter couldn't help but stare. His eyes transfixed on the low cut of her robe. His eyes slowly drifted up and saw her smirking. She was toying with him. Cutter glared at her but she pretended not to notice. She continued to move about the kitchen, the thin fabric of her robe stretching and pressing to her body as she leaned over the sink or reached for something in the cupboard.

Cutter watched her movements and realized she was trying to bait him. It was all an act after seeing him fumble around the other day trying to interact with her. In the night she must have realized that his floundering behavior was something she could exploit. Cutter watched a moment longer as she bent over to pick something up from the floor. Her robe rising up along her pale hips. He frowned and set his utensils down on the plate.

"We need to get ready," he grunted as he stood up. "Get dressed."

Talia turned and smiled, relishing Cutter's annoyance. "I'll go change and we can leave."

Cutter nodded and started to get ready. As soon as she went upstairs he walked into the kitchen and checked the cabinets for his pistol and found it where he had left it. He checked the magazine; the rounds were still there. Was he being paranoid? No, paranoid was what had kept him alive so far. She was trying to get in his head. Unfortunately for him, it was working. He walked over to the sink and stuck his head under the facet and turned it on, letting the icy water clear his mind. Watching her turn on the charm with Amsel, and how she handled a pistol, left little doubt in Cutter's mind that she was more dangerous than she let on. He grabbed a towel and dried his head vigorously. The thought of Victor bubbled to the forefront of his brain and Cutter wondered if he'd be able to kill Talia if necessary. *We'll cross that bridge when we get to it*. He was so close to the end, to being done with fieldwork. Now wasn't the time to lose it over some girl. All he had to do was keep his nose clean and he'd be back in England in no time. He started to button his shirt, the memory of Victor's head caved in by the bullet in his skull lingering on his mind. Cutter fumbled with the buttons as his hands started to shake.

He looked down at his trembling hands in revulsion. "I'm a bloody coward." He struggled to finish buttoning his shirt but as he fumbled with the buttons the memory of Freddy congratulating him on his escape made him queasy. He stopped what he was doing and took a deep breath. How did anyone before him survive as a spy? The high risk, low life expectancy, and diminishing reward made him wonder why anyone would volunteer in the first place.

The memory of how one of his college professors approached him about joining the SOE flickered through his mind. The promise of adventure and a solid recommendation for graduate school after the war being the bait Cutter took. "You silly bastard." He had certainly gotten his fill of adventure, and at this point, graduate school was the last thing he cared for. Had he known joining the SOE would be a Faustian bargain, perhaps he would have done things differently. *Maybe.* He slowly resumed buttoning his shirt, his mind shifting back to the here and now. It didn't pay to dwell on past choices. *Do your job.* Victor's last words came back to him. He was right, Cutter thought. No point reminiscing about past mistakes. But what about Talia? He thought they had come to a shaky truce the other day. But with the way she was behaving, Cutter couldn't help but wonder if her intentions were more than just to help him. What was she playing at?

Talia came down a few moments later. She was dressed in a blue sheer dress and a white cardigan. Cutter deliberately ignored her appearance and led her out of the safe house, managing to dodge Madame Delacroix. Talia reached for Cutter's hand, catching him off guard. "Lovers, remember," she muttered as they walked toward the town center.

Cutter nodded and grudgingly accepted her hand. Her quick acceptance of playing the role was off-putting. Was she doing this because Cutter had convinced her to help, or was she trying to keep him off balance? He doubted he would ever get an honest answer to that question. They ambled down the lane out onto the main street of the town without a word. Silence being the mutually approved preference when it was just the two of them.

The town center was a bustle of movement as local farmers delivered goods to the bakery and the butcher's shop. A lone farmer unloaded bags of grain at Claude's bakery, tossing the heavy bags into the storage room like they were nothing. Talia and Cutter strode inside and found Claude double-checking his records. He stopped what he was doing when he saw them. "Good morning! Don't you two make a pretty couple?" He grinned and shot a sly wink at Cutter.

"Claude, nice to see you." Cutter ignored the bait. He looked around making sure the three of them were alone. The farmer remained outside emptying his truck. "Can we talk?"

Claude nodded and pointed at the farmer. "You don't have to worry; Durand is with us."

Cutter shot a glance at Durand as he continued to throw sacks of grain from the wagon bed into Claude's storage room. He appeared to be focused solely on his work, but Cutter had his doubts. The Resistance had as many moles as a farmer's field. Claude and the rest of his circuit had a long way to go to earn Cutter's trust. "Do you have any information yet?"

"It's been less than a day. I'm not a miracle worker!"

"The sooner you get it done, the faster I can start coordinating supply drops."

Claude grunted and threw his hands up in frustration, stray flour flying off his apron and forming a small cloud above his head. "*D'accord*, I need another day. I promise I'll have it by tomorrow."

Cutter gave a satisfactory nod. If he could fast-track the timeline there was no reason he couldn't be home in two weeks instead of four. The sooner he did his job, the faster he would be away from Talia and the rest, and tucked away in a small office at HQ.

Claude jotted down a note on a stray piece of paper and snapped his fingers, beckoning Durand to come inside.

Durand hefted a sack of grain onto his shoulder with a grunt and walked in. "Durand, you know Olivier, right? Olivier, Durand was with us the other night operating the radio."

"A pleasure." Cutter extended his hand, and shot him a distant look. He wasn't interested in making friends this time.

Durand gave a lopsided smirk and took Cutter's hand in a bone-crushing handshake, his eyes darting coyly at Talia as he did. "Nice to meet you, Olivier."

Cutter winced but did his best to keep his face expressionless. A hint of jealousy flickering inside him as Durand continued to shoot Talia demure looks.

Claude ripped the note from his ledger. "Durand, I need you to go out and get a head count of the German armor in the area. Memorize these locations and burn it."

Durand bobbed his head and took the note. "*D'accord*, me and few of the others will take care of it." His eyes darted back to Talia. "Would you like to come, Talia?"

Talia's eyebrows shot up in surprise at the invitation. After months of being told she couldn't, it was a shock that Durand was now willing to let her help with anything more than ferrying messages.

Claude shook his head and responded before Talia could, "She has her own mission. You can manage without her."

Durand shot Cutter a dark look, reminding Cutter of the look Amsel gave him when Talia had said that they were romantically involved.

Christ, does everyone want to get in Talia's knickers? Cutter wondered. He looked over at her and saw the wheels turning behind her eyes. *She must know the only reason Durand wants her to come is because he's jealous we're working together.*

"Durand, I need it done quickly. Get going." Claude put a hand on Durand's shoulder and pushed him out of the bakery. "Don't come back till it's done." Claude turned around and looked at Cutter. A look of visible annoyance etched on his face. "He's a good lad, but he thinks it's all a bloody game."

"So did I at first."

Claude snorted as he looked Cutter up and down. "What do you mean at first? You can't be more than a year older than Durand. What are you, twenty?"

Cutter shot Claude an icy look, his eyes turning a cold gray. "I'd say experience outranks age."

Claude locked eyes with him but after a few seconds blinked and looked away. The way Olivier glared at him reminded Claude of Talia's uncle. It was like looking at Francois's ghost. The boy was as bellicose as that old goat. He clearly wasn't afraid to stand up for himself when he needed to. Claude had clearly mislabeled Olivier as a weak and yielding boy. He clearly had some iron to him.

Claude coughed and tried to recover some semblance of his pride after yielding to Cutter's gaze. "Perhaps you're right." He ran a hand uneasily through his balding black hair and quickly changed subjects. "Where are you going today?"

"The chapel of Saint Valéry."

Claude looked at Cutter in confusion, but said nothing. The chapel was a curious place to go, but he didn't desire to prod for an answer.

"We better get going. I expect those numbers tomorrow." Cutter's words were friendly but the coldness remained in his eyes.

"*Oui, oui*. We will have them."

Cutter nodded and motioned to Talia that it was time to leave. They strode out of the bakery and started to make their way back to the car.

"Well, Durand is a strapping young lad."

"He's a good friend, one of the few members of the Resistance that's my age."

"Are you two close?"

Talia arched an eyebrow and looked at Olivier. "Is that jealousy in your voice?" She liked how the tables had turned. Olivier had arrived yesterday as the big man in charge, but Talia suspected he was no older than she was. His ineptitude at speaking with her had at first been a source of amusement, but as she went to bed the other night she had realized that it was a weapon she could use to keep Olivier off balance.

"Of course not, just curiosity."

Talia smirked. Seeing Durand had been a lucky coincidence. It annoyed her to no end that Durand was willing to invite her to help him after Claude had asked her to work with Olivier, but it was also nice to see her position rising, even if it was fueled by primal jealousy. They walked the rest of the way to the car in silence and made their way to the church.

"So how long have you known Durand?"

"Years. When we were children we used to play together in the summers when my parents brought me here to see my uncle."

"What was that like?"

"Paradise." Talia smiled as she looked out the window, remembering a time before the war. "Durand and I would do everything together. We would fish on the Saâne river or go to the beach. I remember we used to wrestle in my uncle's barn, but as we got older wrestling started to turn into—"

"So you two were close."

Talia turned away from the window and smiled, enjoying Olivier's discomfort. "I'd say we were *very* close." She bit down on her lip and struggled not to giggle as she lied. The first time Durand had tried to kiss her, she had slapped him so hard her hand hurt for two days.

"But not anymore?"

"What makes you say that?"

Olivier shrugged. "Your body language when you saw him. You kept your distance from him when we walked into the bakery."

"No, not anymore." Talia couldn't stand Durand. But she didn't want Olivier to know that. They continued to drive in silence for a time. Talia drummed her nails on the dashboard as she watched the countryside roll by. "Can you ever talk about sex without turning crimson?"

"What?" Olivier turned and stared at Talia, nearly swerving off the road in the process.

"You were talking about my body language. I thought we could talk about yours."

Olivier scowled but didn't answer.

"Do you not like women?" Talia teased.

"Look, I like you. But we have a job to do so can we stop the fucking mind games?"

Talia frowned, taken aback by Olivier's temper. "What do you mean?"

"Since breakfast you have been playing heavily on your sexuality to get a rise out of me. I'm here to do a job and to help you and Claude; you aren't making it easier."

"You were the one asking about my relationship with Durand!"

"Yes! I was just trying to learn about who Durand was, I wasn't asking about your sexual exploits!"

It was Talia's turn to be embarrassed. Her cheeks reddened and she struggled to give a retort. After two failed attempts to continue her argument, she silently turned her eyes back to the road. She struggled to find a defense, but couldn't. At first her plan had revolved around peaking Olivier's desire, but between breakfast and now it had turned into childish delight at torturing him. Embarrassment and a hint of shame burned through her.

They drove the rest of the way to the church in silence.

"Turn here. You can park by the church."

Olivier turned down a narrow lane and drove the car up to the church and parked. He clambered out and absently motioned to Talia to follow him. The action infuriated Talia to no end. She didn't take orders from him.

She followed Olivier into the church and obstinately made her way to a pew and pretended to pray. She had been to this church hundreds of times. As a girl her parents used to bring her and her brother for the Sunday service. She eyed the stained-glass windows and she pursed her lips in a little smile at the memory of her and her brother playing outside after the service. Talia watched as Olivier surveyed the architecture and looked with mild interest at the old inscriptions about the church's construction four hundred years ago. After spending what felt like a sufficient amount of time in the church, Olivier beckoned Talia to follow him back outside.

Talia gritted her teeth but kept her frustration bottled. Olivier wasn't deliberately trying to annoy her. He had a job to do and was trying to do it quickly. Talia could appreciate that. His outburst in the car wasn't without merit, but his obstinance when it came to women was frustrating. He was brusque and controlling and it made her mad. Her mind drifted to the altercation between him and Claude. A shiver went down her back as she recalled how Olivier almost transformed right before her eyes. In the blink of an eye the small, bookish collegiate was replaced by an intense, detached saboteur.

They walked behind the church where an open field spanned out 200 feet and suddenly dropped with a view overlooking an intercoastal waterway and beach. Talia wondered what his interest was in the cliff. She followed him as he meandered toward the edge of the cliff and looked out at the Channel. "Looking for anything in particular?"

Olivier grinned and gave a shrug. "Figured we could save some time if we could see the entire coast from one vantage point."

Talia nodded, keeping her thoughts to herself. She walked up next to him and he pointed toward the east. From their vantage point they were able to see all the way down the coast for roughly six miles.

"What town is that?"

Talia looked where he was pointing and frowned. The town he pointed at had colorful houses along the waterfront and a harbor cutting through the middle of the town, splitting it in half. "That's Dieppe."

"Anything of interest there?"

Talia shook her head. "No. Dieppe is the nerve center for German forces in the area. Since the invasion they have had the city under lock and key. We've heard that the Abwehr and the Gestapo have agents there roping up Resistance cells."

"How many cells have been captured?"

"Two."

Olivier nodded slowly. "SOE isn't privy to that information, or to the fact that the Gestapo and Abwehr are in Dieppe."

"Saint-Valéry-en-Caux would be a better town to raid. It's to the west and has a smaller detachment and is already in ruins from when the 51st Division fought Rommel."

"Are there any targets of opportunity in that area?"

Talia bit her lip, her arms akimbo as she racked her brain. There wasn't much worth raiding other than Dieppe or Le Havre. As she mentally ticked through the possibilities a sea breeze swept up the cliff from the Channel and pushed the skirt of her dress up. Talia quickly pushed her hands down and stopped the skirt from rising any higher than her knees. She looked up in annoyance and spotted Olivier staring.

"Do you mind?"

Olivier averted his gaze and blushed slightly. "Sorry," he mumbled.

Talia continued to stare at him as he looked away. He looked genuinely embarrassed and Talia couldn't help but feel bad for him. She had tortured him all day with her promiscuity. For all the things he did that annoyed her, he seemed willing to help as best he could and was willing to include Talia in his efforts. He treated her fairly in comparison to Claude or Durand, but still, why didn't she like him? *He's too arrogant*, she realized. *He reminds me of Francois*. His demeanor was identical to how her uncle had been. Francois had always tackled a problem in the same sanitized way he tackled a problem of a patient when he was a doctor: without emotion and in the most effective, unbiased way. Like Francois, Olivier always had a solution ready. Was that why he annoyed her?

"We should go back up toward the church," Olivier said, interrupting her thoughts.

"Of course." Talia brushed past him toward the church. "To answer your original question, I'm not sure. We would have to check, but that could take some time."

Olivier nodded but stayed silent, not trusting his voice.

They walked back toward the church and perfunctorily inspected the inside again. After what seemed like a decent amount of time in the church, they walked back outside and saw a German half-track driving up the gravel lane.

Talia watched as the half-track came to a crunching halt and Oberleutnant Amsel hopped out of the back. "Oh no."

"Bollocks." Olivier reached for her hand and gave her a reassuring squeeze.

"What the hell is he doing here?"

"I don't know. Keep walking to the car," Talia whispered, pulling him toward their vehicle.

"Monsieur Deschamps! Talia! What a pleasure to see you again in such a short time."

Talia stopped in her tracks and looked up at Olivier. He grimaced, but forced a smile and turned around. "Oberleutnant, how are you? We came to see the church. Talia told me about the Gothic architecture and the beautiful view, and I had to see it."

"Indeed, it's wonderful," Amsel agreed as a squad of his men barreled into the church. Talia watched as two more soldiers blitzed into the rectory and brought the priest out. She wondered why they were here.

"What's happening?"

Amsel absently inspected the medals on his tunic and absently pulled at a loose thread on his cuff. "We received intelligence that fugitives of the Reich are being held here." Satisfied with his appearance, Amsel placed his arms behind his back and strode over to the priest. "Good afternoon, Father."

"What is the meaning of this?" the priest demanded in a fury. Blood trickled from the side of his head where one of the soldiers had hit him with a rifle buttstock.

"Father, you have been charged with the crime of harboring criminals of the Reich." As Amsel said this, the sound of screams emanated from the church. Two men and four women were shoved out of the church. They were herded up by the half-track and ordered to kneel.

Amsel looked over at the six fugitives and bounced on the balls of his feet as though he were preparing for an athletic competition. His hobnail boots crunched against the gravel as he shifted his weight. "Do you have anything to

148

say for yourself?" His tone was dripping with disdain as he nonchalantly watched his men toss the family next to the priest.

Talia watched in horror as she recognized them. It was the Veil family. She had thought they had fled to Portugal months ago. She watched as the youngest daughter, Sybil, was shoved to the ground by one of Amsel's men. Mr. Veil struggled in protest but was cracked in the mouth by the buttstock of another soldier's rifle. He clutched at his broken jaw, tears streaming down his face, a handful of teeth littering the ground in front of him.

Olivier put his hand on Talia's lower back and motioned her toward the car. "Let's go."

"I know them."

Olivier ignored her and forcibly propelled her toward the car.

Oberleutnant Amsel turned and locked eyes with Talia and gave her a cruel smile. She could tell he was enjoying himself. Amsel turned back to the priest. "Well?"

"You call yourselves Christians? God will judge you, all of you!" the priest roared, pointing at all of them. Olivier helped Talia into the car and quickly got behind the wheel and started the engine. Talia didn't understand why Amsel was searching for the Veil family. She watched as Amsel asked them a handful of questions while Olivier drove the car down the lane. He gently reached over and grabbed Talia's shoulder and forced her to look at him. Just as she turned, the crack of a pistol went off.

"What was that?" Talia whirled around to look through the rear window, but Olivier grabbed her and pulled her tight to him, not letting her look. As the crack of the pistol dissipated, a quick staccato of rifle fire went off and then it was eerily quiet.

Talia squirmed in Olivier's arms and struggled to break free. "What just happened? We need to go back!"

"No, we don't." Olivier held her tight, and accelerated down the lane.

Talia stopped squirming and looked up at him, her eyes pleading. Olivier slowly released his grip on her and she turned to look out the rear window. She let out an anguished gasp as she saw the priest and family lying in the gravel. A pool of blood starting to spread, turning maroon as it mixed with the dirt.

"Why?" she moaned. "Why did this happen?"

She looked up at Olivier, searching for answers. "I don't understand. They had nothing to do with the Resistance."

"That's not why."

She sat upright and looked at him, tears streaming down her face. "Why, then?"

Olivier gave a heavy sigh, and looked her in the eye. "We've received reports that the Nazis have begun to cleanse Europe of certain ethnic groups they see as polluted or not befitting their view of the perfect race. From what we know, they've been killing Jews in large numbers."

"Oh my God. That's horrible." Talia shuddered at the thought of Mr. Veil being brought to his knees while his children cried in terror. The image evoked the memory of her uncle's own death and she let out a silent sob. "How did this world turn so ugly?"

Cutter hesitated, the thought of Victor's corpse flashing through his mind. "I don't think it changed, I think it just bubbled to the surface. It's always been there. War brings out the worst in people." He parked the car in front of the house and helped Talia to the door. Still visibly shaken from the executions, her footing was wobbly and the color had drained from her face. He helped her upstairs to her bedroom. It was a small room, and the bed took up most of the space. Talia sat down on the bed and rubbed her eyes. They were red and puffy from the tears. Olivier went back downstairs and brought her a cup of tea.

"Thank you."

"My pleasure." Olivier looked around the room for a moment but quickly turned to head back downstairs.

"Stop, where are you going?"

Olivier turned around and smiled comfortingly. "I have to see Claude, and you look like you could use something to eat."

Seeing the Veil family and the priest killed had been an all-too-fresh reminder of her own loss. The memory of her parents, brother, and uncle burned through her head on a never-ending loop. A feeling of isolation started to creep into her thoughts and a panic at being alone seized Talia. She grabbed Olivier's hand and held on for dear life, as though if he were to leave he would never return. "Please, don't go."

Olivier squeezed her hand and instinctively kissed her on her head. "I'll be back soon."

His hand slipped out of hers and without another word she was alone.

Talia finished the tea and lay back in the bed. She felt numb. She had witnessed cold-blooded murder, and aside from the loneliness she was feeling there was another emotion, relief. Relief that she was still alive. The feeling sickened her but she couldn't help it. She had once told

151

Francois that she was willing to die for the Resistance, but after today she wasn't so sure. She had no desire to end up like the Veils, that priest, or even Francois. Francois had died for something but the Veils hadn't. They were just a casualty of the Nazis, but that didn't matter. They were all still dead, no matter the reason, and she was alive. Fresh tears started to well up and Talia struggled to blink them away. Everyone from her childhood was dead, and part of her was just happy she wasn't among them. She sobbed softly and wrapped her arms around her knees, desperately wanting Olivier to return to the house.

***

Cutter walked back downstairs and out the front door toward the bakery. *What the hell did I just do?* He didn't even think when he bent down and kissed Talia on the head, but now a shudder of panic crept through him. He knew better than to let his guard down in such a way.

"Pull yourself together, man," Cutter whispered. He checked his watch as he walked. It was seven o'clock; the sun would be going down soon, and he didn't want to be caught out after dark. The last thing he needed was to be spotted by Amsel during dusk. He had a feeling Amsel would see it as an opportunity to get rid of him.

Was he playing the role of a rival lover or was it something real? The image of Talia struggling to keep her dress from billowing up past her knees on the cliff by the church lingered fresh in his mind, but was slowly replaced by thoughts of the priest and Jewish family. Cutter shuddered at the thought and banished Talia's image from his mind as he arrived at the bakery. Claude spotted him as he was locking up and gave him a confused look. "Olivier, is everything alright?"

"We need to talk."

Claude frowned but beckoned him inside.

"Can I have a baguette?"

Claude walked behind the counter and grabbed a loaf of bread and gave it to him. "What is it?"

"We just returned from the church. Oberleutnant Amsel just executed the priest and a family of Jews."

"What?" The look of surprise on Claude's face was genuine, but Cutter doubted this was the first he had heard of such a thing happening.

"How long has that been happening?"

"This is the first I've heard of it."

Cutter shot him a skeptical look, his frosty gray eyes digging for the truth behind Claude's soft brown ones.

Claude averted his gaze and shrugged in surrender. "This is the first I've heard of it happening *here*."

"Where else?"

"Dieppe, Le Havre, Cherbourg. Rumors are circulating among the senior Resistance commanders that camps are being set up to do similar things."

"Where? In France?"

Claude's arms flapped helplessly at his sides as he shrugged. "I don't know. You asked me to search for Nazis, not Jews."

Cutter rubbed the bridge of his nose in frustration and shot Claude a withering look. "Do you have any word on the enemy situation?"

"I'll have it for you tomorrow."

Cutter snorted and shook his head in disgust and impatience. "Christ, Claude, the way you sandbag me one would think you were helping the Germans."

"Go to hell, Olivier." Claude shoved two baguettes into Cutter's arms and motioned him toward the door. "If you don't like the aid I'm giving, go somewhere else. It's not easy getting troop counts, especially when the Gestapo is looking for us. Anyone who even looks at a military convoy the wrong way gets detained."

"You're right, I'm sorry." Claude was doing the best with what he had. Cutter realized he was being unreasonable. "What you and your men are doing is incredibly dangerous, and they're doing a good job. Please accept my apology."

The sincerity in Cutter's voice caught Claude off guard, but had the desired effect. Claude scowled suspiciously at him but nodded his head. "*C'est bon.*"

A faint smirk tugged at the corners of Cutter's mouth. "Thank you. Also, I'd really appreciate it if you could get me in contact with SOE."

"What for?"

"I figured it's about time we started to coordinate a few supply drops."

A thin smile spread across Claude's face and he pumped his arms in jubilation. "About time. Be here tomorrow morning and we'll take care of it."

Cutter nodded, and without another word departed the bakery and walked back to Talia's house and opened the door. The sun had set while he was at the bakery, leaving the house pitch black.

An eerie quiet filled the home, putting Cutter on edge. He looked around and strained his ears, the frantic heartbeat pounding in his chest the only sound he could hear. He reached for the F-S knife and started up the stairs.

154

"Talia?" He walked upstairs and found her curled up on the bed. She had changed into a nightgown and had fallen asleep on top of the sheets. He sheathed the knife and started to back away quietly.

"Wait. Please don't go."

Cutter stopped moving but didn't say anything. He could see the curves of her body underneath the thin gown as she sat upright. The fabric strained against her breasts and a lock her auburn hair obscured one of her pleading eyes making her request all the more enticing.

Cutter's breath caught in his chest and he felt a rush of blood burn his cheeks. His throat felt dry and he didn't trust his voice to speak.

"I don't want to be alone tonight."

Cutter's primal urges bucked against his logic. His mind screamed for him to walk away but his body refused to budge. He looked at her for a long moment, unsure what to do. "Okay," he said finally. While she slid under the sheets, he changed out of his clothes and joined her. His movements were wooden and uncertain. Talia wordlessly watched him and didn't remark on his insecurity. Gone was the prickly exterior, Cutter had dealt with the past few days. It had been stripped away.

Talia slowly moved closer to him, the scent of honeysuckle and lavender filling his nostrils. Her fingertips traced across Cutter's chest as she wrapped an arm around him and pulled her body close to his. Cutter hesitated but gently put his arms around her and held her tight. She trembled in his arms and nestled her head underneath his chin. Her body heat radiated through him, making him cognizant of his own excitement of being this close to her.

He could feel her breasts pressed against his chest and felt excitement fill his body.

In the back of Cutter's head a voice was screaming at him, but he didn't care.

***

CHAPTER 6
STRANDED

    The next morning Cutter woke before Talia. They had made love during the night, and Cutter spent the next ten minutes after waking up cursing himself silently for his lack of control. He argued with himself that he had done it to comfort Talia and continue to develop her as an asset, but that was a lie. That was what the spy in him said. He had wanted to sleep with her. Before last night he had been a virgin, a boy. Over the last two years he had done all that was expected of a man. He had killed, drunk to friends' deaths, and served his country; but he had never slept with a woman. Part of him was excited about the connection he had formed with Talia, but it was slowly overpowered by the resumption of his duties and reminder that there was a war on. He crept out of the bed silently and padded across the room to where he had left his clothes. As he put his pants on, Talia stirred and looked over at him.

    "Morning."

    Talia smiled and sat up, the sheets falling to her waist. "Good morning."

    Cutter checked his watch. "We have a meeting with Claude at nine."

    Talia frowned, her eyes narrowing.

    "Come on, we're in a rush." Cutter put his shirt on and did his best to avoid making eye contact with her. Talia glared at him and covered herself. "Give me some privacy."

    Cutter wordlessly walked out of the room and went downstairs.

    Talia quickly shut the door behind him and put on a pair of black trousers. She didn't like the brusque manner

Olivier had used. The tender compassion he had shown in the night had evaporated. It was like he had turned into another person. She put on a white blouse and buttoned it. In a moment of vulnerability she had let Olivier in, and he had taken full advantage of it. For the smallest of moments, Talia had thought that their faux relationship could have been real. *You silly girl,* she chastised herself. Olivier was here for one reason, and as soon as his mission was done he would pack up and leave. She checked her appearance in the mirror. *A pig, like any other man*, Talia thought in disgust. She refused to wallow long on the matter, but wouldn't give Olivier the opportunity to get close again. Without another thought she opened the door and went downstairs. She found Olivier in the kitchen and shot him a dark look. "Let's go," she ordered, and walked to the door, not waiting for him. They got into the car and drove over to the bakery, where Claude was waiting for them.

The baker took one look at them and chuckled to himself. Between Talia's unkempt auburn hair, which she struggled to hide underneath a scarf, and the love bite that cheekily poked above Olivier's collar, he didn't need to be a detective to figure out what had happened in the night. He walked over to the car and handed them a picnic basket and leaned through the open passenger window. "If anyone asks, you're going for a picnic. We'll meet at the windmill in an hour."

"Where is that?"

"I know where it is," Talia interrupted, casting a stony look at Olivier.

Claude eyed Talia and wondered what Olivier had done to trigger such a cold front, but thought better of asking. "I'll see you there." He nodded to the pair of them and walked back into the bakery.

Cutter and Talia drove through the French countryside further inland. Cutter drove in silence unsure of what to say, or how to explain his feelings. In an attempt to correct and return their relationship to something resembling professional, Cutter had overcorrected. He knew his treatment of Talia that morning had been cold and selfish, but he had no idea how he should have behaved or how to fix it now. For Talia's part, she seemed disinterested in anything Cutter would say and kept her eyes transfixed on the rolling scenery as it sped by. She gave a few curt directions when necessary, and after thirty minutes they arrived at the derelict windmill. A maze of hedgerows and ruins ran along the road leading them up to the mill. Less than a half mile away a large intersection split off into four different directions and then split off again a few miles further down the road. It was an ideal location to transmit because of its elevation and multiple escape routes.

They parked a hundred yards from the windmill under an oak tree, the tree's shade making it difficult to spot the car from a distance. They got out of the car and walked over to the mill. Moss climbed the sides and the tower and the sails had long ago crumbled away, Cutter suspected as the result of a storm. They spotted Durand sitting on a large piece of debris in front of the mill, tinkering with the radio. A lookout sat at the highest point of what was left of the mill, a rifle in his lap and a pair of binoculars clamped to his eyes as he scanned the roads and fields for any signs of trouble.

"*Bonjour*, Durand."

"*Bonjour*, Olivier." Durand nodded to him coolly, a cigarette dangling from his lips as he played with the radio. "We should be online soon."

"Okay."

Cutter looked around and spotted Claude walking toward him, a piece of paper in his hand. "Here's the list of the enemy situations in all nearby coastal cities."

"There isn't much here," Cutter replied.

Claude opened his hands in apology. "Like I said, our resources are limited."

Cutter grumbled and quickly memorized what was on the paper. There wasn't much to memorize and after a few seconds he was confident he could recite it by heart. He balled up the paper, pulled out his lighter, and touched the flame to it.

"Marvelous. Talk about a waste of a week." Cutter looked over at Talia, instantly regretting his choice of words. For a split second a look of hurt covered her face but was quickly replaced by one of disinterest.

"How long till we're online?"

"Five minutes."

Cutter nodded. He looked over at Talia and, making up his mind, walked over to her. "Can we talk?"

"Now is the worst time."

"Maybe, but I'd like to talk about last night."

"What does it matter?"

Cutter paused, unsure how to go forward from here. He reached for her hand. Talia tried to move it out of his reach but he was quicker. "Do you know how many people I've seen killed because they became emotionally attached while in the field?" He didn't wait for an answer.

"Six. All better spies than me. I need you to understand that."

"Why?"

"Because I don't want to die."

"So was I just a casual roll in the hay for you?"

Cutter's face turned crimson. "No, not at all. It was a mistake."

Talia's nostrils flared and her cheeks reddened. "Oh, I was a mistake?"

"No! That's not what I'm saying!" Cutter paused, unsure how to answer, something that had become a norm. "I don't want you to think I don't like you." He debated telling her about Victor but decided against it. "I'm just trying to keep us alive."

"Well, thank you so much."

Cutter opened his mouth but closed it. This wasn't how he had seen this conversation going. Why couldn't she see that he was trying to keep her safe? Before he could answer, Durand waved, beckoning for them to come over.

He handed the mic to Cutter. "We have Tackley Station."

Cutter pulled a notepad from his pocket and checked his notes. He slowly gripped the mic and pressed down on the key. *"Tackley Station, this is Cartographer, over."*

After a moment's pause SOE responded, the woman's voice from the previous communiqué coming over the radio, *"Roger, Cartographer, this is Tackley Station. Send traffic."*

"Roger. Initial mission incomplete, unable to conduct BOOKER over." Since the radio wasn't encrypted,

Cutter had to resort to code words he had stored in the code book. He had dozens of code words for various towns in the area as well as words for various other things such as objectives, personnel, and German equipment and personnel. Booker meant assessment.

"*Roger. Stand by,*" Tackley Station replied. There was an additional pause as Hambro and Freddy no doubt deliberated over what to do.

"*Cartographer, be advised you are to swisher billy goat and cobble herring when able.*" Cutter matched the code words in his notebook. Hambro wanted him to develop the French Resistance and assess the Germans in the area.

"*Roger, Tackley Station. What about blitz?*" he asked, referring to his extraction.

"*At this time that has been put on hold.*"

"*Roger, Tackley Station. No further traffic on this end.*"

"*Roger, Cartographer. Tackley Station out.*" The line went dead. Cutter handed the mic to Durand.

"Goddammit."

"What is it?"

Cutter grunted and started to walk back to the car. "My orders changed."

***

CHAPTER 7
REESE FLIGHT

Faraday, Faust, and Chambers sat in 71 Squadron's ready room at RAF Martlesham Heath in Suffolk. The ready room sat on the bottom floor of the control tower. It was a stark contrast to past ready rooms; it was dry, warm, and comfortable. Faraday leaned back in the wooden chair and listened as it creaked under his weight.

Faust cast a sidelong glance at Faraday as the wood groaned. "Not quite as comfortable as the armchairs we had outside the ready room back in Scotland."

Chambers shrugged. "At least we're inside. I hated sitting out on the field in the rain. Bloody awful."

The squadron had come a long way since Fenton Hill, Faraday observed. They had been at Martlesham Heath for a month and had conducted seventeen Rodeo and Rhubarb missions since their arrival. The flight tempo was not as crazy as what Faraday had experienced prior to going to RAF Turnhouse. As soon as they had arrived it had been two weeks before Faraday's flight had gone on a mission. The hours weren't as hectic as what Faraday was used to, but he wouldn't call it a relaxed assignment.

Faust looked around the empty ready room and shot Faraday a questioning look. "Any idea why we're here?"

"No clue; maybe something to do with that locomotive you hit yesterday."

"Or maybe we're here because Danny and I just got our fifth kill!" Chambers grinned. "We're aces now!"

"Join the club." Faraday shot his two protégés a flat look, deliberately deflating Chambers's ego.

"Maybe we're getting new aircraft?"

"I highly doubt it. The squadrons intercepting the bombers get priority over us."

"Boss, you really can be a dour sport."

Squadron Leader King strode into the ready room with two unknown Flying Officers following behind him in full flight kit. Faraday, Faust, and Chambers all stood up as he walked in.

"Keep your seats." King walked up to the podium at the front of the room and shifted his gaze between the three members of Reese Flight. The flying officers who had entered with him took a seat near the door.

"Gentlemen, I know you are going out on a Rhubarb mission; and based on our analysis you should have limited opposition in the air. As a result, I'm integrating two more pilots into your flight." King motioned to the two flying officers. "Flying Officers O'Brien and Argyle are being attached to Reese Flight. They both were part of Victor Flight until I disbanded it yesterday."

Everyone knew why Victor Flight had been disbanded. Seventy percent of the flight had been shot down the week before during a Rodeo mission over Brittany. Faraday had taken the news hard, since Clyde Baker had been the flight leader.

King looked around the room. "Unless there are any questions, you are dismissed." He pointed at Faraday. "Except for you, Flight Lieutenant." The rest of Reese Flight trickled out of the room.

"Argyle, right?" Faraday heard Faust ask. "I'm Danny Faust, and this is Alex Chambers."

"Damn shame about Clyde," King said once Faraday's flight was out of earshot.

"His wife is in London. She's four months pregnant."

"I know, I've sent a letter. I plan to check in on her at the end of the month."

Faraday ran a hand furiously through his hair. "What about Victor Flight?"

"We won't be standing that flight up for a while. Fighter Command has diverted all new pilots to 12 Group; they're getting hit pretty hard."

"That leaves Reese and Swift Flights; we've already stood down Ulster Flight. We're now at fifty percent," Faraday said in disbelief. "How the hell are we supposed to conduct sweeps like this?"

"Other squadrons will be picking up our slack, but we will be at seventy-five percent readiness at all times."

Faraday played with the straps of the Mae West life preserver hanging from his shoulder. He thought back to the constant state of alert last summer and grimaced. "If we go up any higher in our readiness posture we'll begin to see losses due to fatigue. And unlike during the Battle of Britain, if our pilots bail out they won't be landing in a friendly farmer's field in Suffolk."

"I know, I know," King agreed. "I am pushing Leigh-Mallory for more men."

"Push harder, Mike," Faraday pressed as he started to secure his Mae West and move toward the door.

"I am." King followed him out the door. "You've lost your accent."

"Scotland killed the Boston in me. I have that Cary Grant mid-Atlantic accent now."

"Don't tell Leigh-Mallory. He'll pull you from the Eagle Squadrons and send you to a proper English one."

Faraday chuckled and looked back over his shoulder at King. "My squadron leader wouldn't dare sell me out like that!" Faraday walked over to his aircraft where Reese Flight was huddled around his wing.

"Alright, lads, quick meet and greet. I assume you've become familiar with Faust and Chambers. Who are you and where are you from?"

"Cameron Argyle. I'm from Hartford, Connecticut."

"Harry O'Brien. I'm from San Francisco, California."

"A long way from home," Faraday said and grinned, trying to lighten the mood. "Alright, lads, I'm Flight Lieutenant Ian Faraday of Boston, Massachusetts. Before you ask, no, I didn't always talk like this; I had a very annoying Boston accent that I lost when I was in Scotland."

The pair of them chuckled dutifully, and Faraday continued, "Clyde Baker was a hell of a pilot and will be missed, but you are no longer flying with Victor Flight. You're with Reese now, which means I'm flight leader, and we're flying my way."

Both O'Brien and Argyle made a face but kept their mouths shut and nodded slowly. They understood the situation; they just needed a sharp jolt to realize things had changed.

Faraday studied the pair of them for a moment. "Not to dig through old injuries, but did Clyde bail out?"

"We aren't sure, sir. I could've sworn I saw him jump, but I never saw a chute."

"Stevens said he saw a chute, but seconds later he was blown out of the sky, too."

Faraday nodded soberly. "Best leave it then. Losing your flight is hard but you're with Reese now; we're your family."

O'Brien and Argyle shook their heads solemnly but said nothing.

"We've got a Rhubarb mission into Brittany, in addition to engaging targets of opportunity; Command wants us to keep our eyes open for any sub pens or airfields along our route. Since nothing has been spotted so far in the area, if you see something say something." Faraday looked around at the group, pausing for any questions. "Alright, get to your aircraft and stand by for takeoff."

Reese Flight dispersed to their Spitfires and started to conduct their preflight checks. Faraday clambered up on the wing of his aircraft after conducting a walk-around check to ensure nothing was out of the ordinary. He checked the feed belt for his guns on both wings and made sure they were clear of any debris that would trigger a jam. He walked across the wing back to the cockpit and inspected all his controls, making sure everything was as it should be. He sniffed the air, checking that there wasn't a petrol or hydraulic leak. Satisfied, he climbed into the cockpit and put on his parachute and then strapped on his safety harness. He took his flight cap off the joystick and put it on and adjusted the chinstrap. The head of his flight crew, Sergeant Taylor Roland, hopped on the wing and crouched next to him.

"Everything alright, sir?"

Faraday nodded as he put his gloves on. "Everything looks in order. Were you able to fix the sluggishness in the rudder?"

"I hit it a few times with a wrench, sir, so you should be fine."

"Oh, marvelous. I don't know what I would do without you." Faraday wiggled the stick and checked the ailerons. He turned around and looked at the vertical stabilizer as he pushed on the rudders. "Looks good."

"I aim to please. If you aren't satisfied, maybe you can find a mechanic in France who can fix it for you."

"Roland, I honestly would if only I spoke German. Now bugger off and let me do my job."

Roland smiled. "Best of luck, sir." He walked off the wing and stood a good distance away and motioned for Faraday to start the engine. Faraday primed the engine and pressed the ignition plunger. The engine coughed and the propeller slowly started to turn. The engine continued to sputter until just when Faraday thought there was an issue, it caught. The engine growled to life and the propeller accelerated into a spinning disc as the engine settled to a steady purr. Faraday keyed his mic and said, *"Reese Flight, this is Reese Leader. Radio check, over."*

"Reese 2, loud and clear."

"Reese 3, loud and clear."

"Reese 4, loud and clear."

"Reese 5, loud and clear."

Faraday switched channels. *"Ops, this is Reese Flight, requesting permission for takeoff."*

"Reese Flight, stand by. We are awaiting word from Control."

"Roger, Ops. What is the delay?" Faraday's radio chirped but no one responded. "Guess we're playing the waiting game."

After twenty minutes, Faraday looked around the airfield in annoyance. *"Ops, this is Reese Leader. How much longer are we to sit here, my engine is overheating as is my temper."*

"Roger, Reese Flight, you are cleared for takeoff when ready. The field is yours."

Faraday switched channels back to Reese's interior channel, keeping the channel with Control open but not speaking with them.

"Reese Flight, cleared for takeoff. Assemble at Angels 7, heading 2-0-5. Over." Faraday turned to Roland and gave him the signal to remove the safety chocks in front of the wheels. Roland repeated the motion and two flight crew moved under the wings and removed the chocks. Faraday pushed down on the brakes, keeping the plane in place as he increased power. Roland waved his hands and motioned for him to conduct a brake check. Faraday released the brakes just enough for the plane to inch forward and reapplied pressure and stopped. He decreased power and looked down at Roland.

Roland nodded and motioned that Faraday was cleared to depart. Faraday pushed down on the left rudder and continued to apply pressure on the left brake, making the aircraft turn left toward the runway. He let go of both brakes and increased power so that he was moving toward the runway at a steady pace. He looked around, keeping an eye out for any aircraft or animals that may move into his path. He had seen a flight of geese fly across the path of a Spitfire before. The result had been three geese turning into tiny pieces across the windshield and the aircraft being dead lined until all the bones and feathers had been removed from the engine.

Seeing that he was clear, Faraday pushed down on the throttle giving the engine full power. The Spitfire accelerated quickly down the runway. As he started to climb he banked sharply and found his heading. He reached

7,000 feet quickly and started to search for the rest of Reese Flight.

"*Reese 4 on your six,*" Faraday heard Argyle call over the radio.

"*Reese 5 on your left wing.*"

"*Reese 3 on your right.*"

"*Reese 2, I'm on five's left wing.*"

"*Reese 4, move to three's right wing. Wing formation,*" Faraday called as he inspected their formation. It wasn't bad. A few things that could be fine-tuned, but for the first time working together they looked good.

"*Alright, gentlemen, looking good. Loosen up and keep your distance. We aren't up here to impress anyone. One-hundred meter distance between each wingtip.*"

"*Copy,*" everyone called over the radio.

Faraday looked out the front of his cockpit. Cloud cover was low and scattered. He could see the Channel shining through the clouds.

"*Control, this is Reese Flight. We are Angels 7 at 2-0-5, over the channel.*"

"*Roger. Be advised we are tracking bogeys twenty miles west of you.*"

"*Roger, Control.*"

"*Reese Leader, are we intercepting?*"

"*Negative. Swift Flight is on standby to intercept.*" Faraday checked his map and marked the bogeys with his grease pen. "*Increase speed to 3-2-5.*" He increased power to the engine and inspected the odometer and did some rough math. They would be over France in five minutes. He pulled back slightly on the stick and started to climb. The rest of Reese followed suit. He leveled off at 18,000 feet and adjusted his oxygen mask, double-checking to make sure it was working. Normandy started to come into view to the south as they continued to cruise at a fast speed.

"Alright, Reese Flight, head on a swivel, we're in Indian territory now."

The rest of the flight rogered up. Faraday looked out his window to the south; he could see the Cotentin peninsula and could barely make out Cherbourg at the tip of it. They flew past and continued on, straddling the isles of Jersey and Guernsey. Faraday checked his watch; twenty minutes had passed since they had taken off. He checked his fuel and made sure there wasn't a leak. As they passed the isles, Faraday called over the radio and started to turn. *"Reese Flight, turn to 1-7-0."* The rest of Reese Flight acknowledged him and the flight started to turn south. Faraday spotted the town of Saint-Malo, a catching feature he had marked to help identify that they were on course.

Seeing the town of Saint-Malo, Faraday keyed his mic and said, "Alright, Reese, proceed to drop external tanks and switch to your internal fuel lines. Keep an eye on your petrol." He pulled the lever and felt the tank drop with a thud. "Descend to Angels 2." Faraday didn't wait for a response but went ahead and started to drop to 2,000 feet.

As they crossed the coastline and started to penetrate into the French countryside, Faraday kept an eye peeled for antiair emplacements. The last thing he wanted to do was repeat what happened to Victor Flight, which was the reason they were flying so low. The lower they were, the harder it was for antiair guns to hit them. The ground flew past as they crossed forests and farms into Brittany. Minutes ticked by without an issue, and Reese Flight came upon their second terrain marker a few miles to the south where the town of Rennes stood.

"*Reese Lead, this is Reese 5. We've got flak firing above the town to the east,*" Faust called. "*No idea what they're shooting at; we're well out of range.*"

"*Roger, I see them. Continue on present course and watch for enemy fighters.*"

They continued south. As they went, the intensity of flak continued to increase. Shells started to explode around the flight, but with limited effect. Reese was moving too fast and too low for the antiair to be effective. Nonetheless, the German forces tried all the same. *What the hell is around here?* Faraday never encountered such heavy flak this far west. They started to approach the city of Nantes, split in two by the Loire river and along the Bay of Biscay it was easy to identify. As they got closer, tracer fire erupted on the edge of the city and raked Reese Flight. Tracers whizzed past Faraday's cockpit.

"*Watch the fires!*"

"*I'm hit,*" Argyle called.

"*How bad?*"

Argyle paused before responding, "*I'm clipped pretty good, but I'm still flying.*"

"*Bandits! Coming in fast. Check six! Check six!*"

Faraday turned around and searched the skies. A flight of three ME109s was bearing down on them.

"*Reese 5 and 2, break off, Reese 4 and 3 stay with me.*"

"*Roger,*" Faust called, taking the lead of his element with Chambers. Argyle and O'Brien stuck with Faraday.

Faraday turned west, breaking away from the tracer fire, his eyes scanning for any other fighters.

The three German fighters were alone and ignored Faust and Chambers and took off after Faraday.

"*Break formation!*"

Both Argyle and O'Brien peeled out of the formation in different directions, but the Germans stayed with Faraday, no doubt looking for a quick kill. They didn't see Faust and Chambers come in behind them until it was too late.

Faust and Chambers opened fire on the last ME109, scaring the flight and making them break ranks.

The flight scattered and Faust and Chambers took off after one lone ME109 that had broken a little too far from his compatriots.

Faraday whipped back around, clear of the city, and angled for the two ME109s still together. They were chasing after Faust and Chambers, trying to save their wing mate.

"*Reese 5, watch your tail. You have the other two coming after you.*"

"*Roger, Reese Leader. We almost have this one.*"

Faraday angled for a better vector and started to sight in using the pipper in the windshield. He was close to having a shot. His thumb hovered above the trigger, ready to shoot.

"*Bandit down. Breaking right.*" Faust and Chambers banked and yanked, turning hard right and away from the two ME109s on their tail. As they banked, the two ME109s tried to follow suit, flying straight into Faraday's pipper. Faraday depressed the trigger, leading both planes and raking them with rounds from his eight Browning machine guns. The lead ME109's left wing tore off as it went into a spin. Faraday smiled in grim satisfaction as he watched the ME109 slam into a grassy hill on the edge of the Loire.

"*The other bandit is fleeing!*"

"*Leave him, reform up on heading 2-7-0.*" Faraday leveled his wings and a hail of tracer fire started to erupt all around him. "Jesus Christ." He pulled on the stick and climbed, evading the fire.

"*Scatter! Scatter! This fire is too intense. Push west out to sea and reform.*" Faraday looked around for the source of the fire. Their dogfight had dragged them closer to the coast and the mouth of the Loire. Faraday looked out the side of his cockpit and saw angry flashes emanating from the town on the north bank. He continued to search the city as he flew away. He spotted something as he flew out of range of the guns. Along the north bank, right on the river, dredging of the harbor was underway. Faraday consulted the map on his kneeboard and made a note of the dredging next to the town of Saint-Nazaire. As far as he was concerned it wasn't anything special, but the head shed would want to know about it.

Reese flight linked up two miles out over the ocean and turned north back home. Once England was in sight they called into Control and vectored for RAF Martlesham Heath. When they landed at the airfield Faraday was greeted by Sergeant Roland.

"How nice to see you, sir, and without a single hole, I daresay."

"That's a miracle, considering the amount of flak we received. Argyle's aircraft got dinged up."

"I already saw. I'll have to check her out, but she may be our new hangar queen. She looks like a dingy bird; most of her parts may be cannibalized."

Faraday grunted and hopped out of the cockpit.

"Just see what you can do."

He hopped off the wing of his Spitfire and took a moment to get his footing. His knees were shaky and his mouth was dry. It took a minute for his heartbeat to settle. He looked over and spotted Faust and O'Brien and nodded to them.

"Get over to the ready room for debrief."
Operations would definitely want to know about dredging
at Saint-Nazaire.

***

"Dickie, I have some good news!" Air Vice-Marshal
Leigh-Mallory shouted excitedly as he walked into Lord
Mountbatten's office.

Mountbatten looked up from the brief he was
reading, annoyed at the unscheduled interruption. "What is
it Trafford?"

Leigh-Mallory said nothing but grinned broadly and
laid a pair of photos on Mountbatten's desk.

Mountbatten stopped what he was doing and
inspected the pictures. "My God. Where did you get these?"

"One of my Eagle Squadrons flew over Saint-Nazaire
the other day during a scrap and spotted this. This is the
validation we need to move forward with the Saint-Nazaire
raid." Leigh-Mallory tapped the photos eagerly. "As soon as
we do this, we can raid Dieppe."

Mountbatten inspected the pictures diligently. He
had been struggling to find concrete proof that could justify
the raid; with this he could finally silence Hambro and
Montgomery. A smile started to spread across his face.
"Trafford, this is exactly what we needed. With this,
Churchill will approve the raid."

"What're you going to do now?"

Mountbatten paused, deep in the thought. "If I
show that fool Hambro or Monty, they'll try to stop the raid
or try and take the mission away from Combined
Operations." He drummed his fingers on the desk as he
weighed his options. "I need to go see Churchill this
morning and get his approval. I'm in no mood for a fight
with that slippery bastard Hambro."

Leigh-Mallory nodded. "I'll have a few sorties flown
to gather more photo reconnaissance for the raid."

"Damn, this is spectacular! We finally have a chance to show how effective a large scale raid can be."

***

Freddy Atkinson looked up from the newspaper he was reading and shot his boss a look of concern. "What's going on? Is it Cutter?" Hambro walked past him, continued down the SOE hallway, and motioned for him to follow.

Freddy jumped from behind his desk and fell in step with Hambro. "We just got word that the RAF spotted dredging operations at Saint-Nazaire."

Atkinson gave him a confused look. "What does that mean, sir?"

Hambro shot him a look of mild annoyance. "Since the sinking of that behemoth battleship, *Bismarck*, the Kriegsmarine has been building its replacement, *Tirpitz*. It was a damned herculean effort to sink the *Bismarck* it will be just as difficult to defeat the *Tirpitz*. If Saint-Nazaire is able to harbor the *Tirpitz* that blasted ship can cut off our lifeline to America." Hambro frowned, his pace quickening as they raced down the hallway. "Dammit, this is not good. I thought we had more time."

"What are we going to do?"

"Mountbatten outmaneuvered us. Leigh-Mallory brought the reconnaissance photos solely to him and he went straight to the PM with them. If this goes well, Mountbatten will get his Dieppe raid."

"Sir, is that such a bad thing? If he succeeds we—"

Hambro impatiently raised his hand, cutting Atkinson off before he could finish. "Freddy, normally I would say yes." He stopped walking and turned to face him. "Victory, no matter what, is ideal, but the way Mountbatten plans these missions is atrocious. Even with multiple defeats and failures he has managed to advance his military and political career dramatically. If these raids are successful it will be because of blind luck and someone else's doing."

"So what do we do?"

Hambro sighed and continued walking. "There really is nothing we can do, but help as best we can. If the mission fails no one wins, men die, and the Germans cut off our supply lines. I will not let Mountbatten fail due to grudges or lack of trust in him. As much as I hate to say it, we must ensure his mission is a success."

"So where are we going?"

"Mountbatten's people are developing a plan, but will want everyone to assist," Hambro groused as they walked out of the building to the car. They both clambered in and sped off.

"Who are we meeting?"

"Leigh-Mallory; a Combined Operations gentleman; Lieutenant Colonel Newman, commander of No. 2 Commandos; and a Commander Ryder."

"Anyone else?"

"I bloody well hope not. Changing topics, what's the latest *with* Cutter?"

Atkinson exhaled between his teeth and shrugged. "Well, as you can imagine, he is royally offed about having to stay in Normandy for another month. His reports are showing that he is making progress, particularly to the south, but the east around Dieppe is proving difficult."

Hambro looked up from cleaning his glasses. "Oh, why?"

Atkinson rubbed the edges of his mustache. "Apparently Dieppe has become a hotbed for the Gestapo and Abwehr."

"That's news to us. I want an exit ready for him if things get too heated."

"I have that covered, sir."

The car came to a halt in front of the War Office. They both climbed out and walked past the checkpoint and made their way inside. They found everyone in a conference room waiting for them. Leigh-Mallory was the first to greet them and introduced them to Commander Ryder, Lieutenant Colonel Newman, and Commander Jacobs of Combined Operations. Each man had brought a handful of additional staff, filling the room to maximum occupancy. Once introductions were made, they all sat down.

Commander Jacobs spoke first, beating Air Vice-Marshal Leigh-Mallory to the punch. "Gentlemen, it has come to our attention that the port of Saint-Nazaire has begun preparations for the *Tirpitz*. If we do not shut down the port, our supply lines with America will be severely debilitated."

"Well, he just gets right to the thick of it," Atkinson muttered.

Commander Jacobs pointed to a board that stood along the wall opposite from the table they all sat at. A table of equipment and personnel was listed outlining what the Navy, the RAF, and the commandos were providing for the raid. "At this time, the Navy has provided us with two destroyers and a handful of gunboats in order to move a raiding party." He looked at Lieutenant Colonel Newman and said, "It is my understanding that Commander Ryder has provided you with enough boats?"

Lieutenant Colonel Newman exchanged a smirk with Commander Ryder and nodded his head. "Yes, we're retrofitting the *Campbeltown* to ram the dry dock. One way or the other we'll at the very least delay the operational capabilities of the port. Once in the port, my commandos will break off into teams and attack multiple objectives to neutralize critical targets to the port's operation."

Commander Jacobs frowned and looked up from his notepad. "I'm sorry, can you say that again? What are you doing with the *Campbeltown*?"

A mischievous smile curled at the corners of Newman's mouth. "We're gonna ram her into the dry dock." The statement got the desired effect. A flurry of side conversations erupted. Hambro watched a few people shake their heads while a few others shot Newman skeptical looks.

"Everyone quiet!" Commander Jacobs bellowed, restoring order to the room. "Commander Ryder, I assume you are aware of this plan?"

"I am."

Leigh-Mallory cast a doubtful look at the young naval officer. "And you're okay with this plan?"

Commander Jacobs shot Leigh-Mallory an annoyed look but kept his mouth shut.

Commander Ryder exchanged looks with Newman and shrugged gamely. "We're attempting to sabotage a dry dock while conducting an amphibious raid in the early hours of morning. We have no beachhead to land on that gives us direct access to the dock and we aren't confident that the explosives we bring will actually destroy the dry dock. I'd say this is the best way to ensure that it's destroyed."

Leigh-Mallory leaned back in his chair and looked at Jacobs. "I have concerns about this plan. We should land our forces on the Old Mol."

Commander Jacobs tapped his pencil in agitation but kept his temper. "Sir, I appreciate your input, but Old Mol is nothing more than a narrow dock that leads to the outskirts of the port. In order for this to work we need to come up with a creative way to deliver our commandos inside the dock."

Hambro nodded in agreement. He was surprised at Jacobs candidness and willingness to stand up to Leigh-Mallory. He suspected that Jacobs was cut from a different cloth than his boss.

Leigh-Mallory shot Jacobs a withering look, which Jacobs ignored. "That's easy for you to say, Commander. Both you and Ryder won't be aboard the *Campbeltown*. In my opinion it's too risky. Too . . . unorthodox." Leigh-Mallory looked around the room, daring anyone to challenge him. No one spoke up. Leigh-Mallory's gaze fell upon Lieutenant Colonel Newman, believing he had an ally in the man who would be riding the *Campbeltown.* "I'd like to hear your thoughts, Newman. Surely, as the man who would be riding that amphibious battering ram, you have some concerns?"

Lieutenant Colonel Newman paused as he measured his words. His lips pursed under a neatly manicured mustache in the style of Montgomery. "If I daresay, sir, as the man riding the battering ram, I'd rather much prefer the *Campbeltown* to a rubber dinghy landing anywhere other than my objective." He paused and for a brief second exchanged a knowing glance with Commander Jacobs. "No. 2 Commandos thrive on the unorthodox."

Jacobs looked down at his journal and quickly jotted down a few notes, not bothering to look up as he spoke. "I think that settles it, sir."

Leigh-Mallory shot him a murderous look, but Jacobs ignored him and finished making his annotations.

Oh, he's nothing like Mountbatten. Hambro thought with a smile.

"What about air support, sir?"

Leigh-Mallory cleared his throat. He eyed Jacobs coolly but didn't attempt to challenge him. "We have squadrons prepared for bombing runs as well as diversionary raids; we just need a date."

Jacobs nodded his head again and made a note. "Ryder what is your recommendation?"

"With the small boats, I'd recommend early May at the earliest."

"That's four months away! If *Tirpitz* pushes out to sea even a month prior we'll be in hot water."

"Fine, no earlier than March," Ryder grumbled, not pleased with the idea.

Jacobs nodded and turned to Hambro. "Mr. Hambro, do you have anything to add?"

"Whatever intelligence you are receiving from the RAF recces I believe they will be far more reliable than whatever I can gather in the next month."

"You have no further input?"

"I will attempt to develop intelligence for the raid, but at this time I have nothing in place for anything this imminent."

Jacobs jotted down some final notes and looked up. "Anything else?" The room was quiet.

"Alright. Lieutenant Colonel Newman and Commander Ryder are the action officers for planning and coordination. We will reconvene a month from now for final planning prior to the raid." Everyone stood up and started to depart the conference room, each person having either another meeting or another pressing issue to attend to. Hambro and Atkinson made their way back to where their car was waiting for them.

"Do you want me to retask someone to the Loire valley?" Atkinson asked. "Maybe Chessman or Artemis?"

Hambro paused and thought about it before answering, "I appreciate the initiative, Freddy, but I don't think the juice is worth the squeeze. You saw how perfunctory that meeting was. The War Office is planning a major raid as though it were a weekly business meeting they hold in poor taste. I don't want to create a precedent of retasking agents at the last minute."

"What do you think about Jacobs?"

"I think he's a step or two ahead of his colleagues in Combined Operations."

"He ruffled Leigh-Mallory's feathers quite a bit."

"He better watch himself. Trafford isn't one to let that lie."

"I'm getting a report from Cutter tonight. Is there anything you want me to pass?"

Hambro shook his head. "No. Just keep me in the loop."

***

PART II

CHAPTER 8

THE CARTOGRAPHER

Cutter grimaced as he surveyed the map of enemy locations. "I've been here two months and we barely know anything outside the immediate area of Quiberville." He looked around the room at Claude, Durand, and a handful of other Resistance members. "This isn't enough. What else have we found?"

Claude studied the map for a long moment and shrugged, his bushy eyebrows merging into one as he frowned. "We've received reports from Fécamp and Le Havre; they are establishing concrete defenses near the beaches." He looked up at the other Resistance fighters in the room hoping for further confirmation, but received none.

"Forces are being diverted from Rouen to bolster defenses," Claude continued. "In addition to this, the cell we established in Dieppe has been unresponsive for the past week."

"Who was the cell controller? Is he still in contact?"

"He is. We heard from him yesterday." Unlike the cell, the cell controller didn't operate in Dieppe. He worked on the outskirts of the town and served as the buffer between Claude and the cell operating there.

Cutter nodded. *It could always be worse.* If the controller had been captured they all would already be dead. "He's our cutout. Have him moved to another city and start again. We can't risk him interacting with other cells. He could be compromised."

Claude took a sip from a glass of wine and nodded. "I'll take care of it tomorrow."

"What else?"

"We've received a supply drop the other night from SOE. I'm attempting to set up additional radio personnel to the south to coordinate additional drops." Durand pointed out where on the map.

"What are we getting?"

"Sten submachine guns and some explosives. I have a man going around and teaching a class on how to use the explosives as well as the Stens."

Cutter nodded but said nothing, they weren't ready to start attacking the Germans but it was a decent start. "Let's pull our forces away from Dieppe. This is the third cell to be destroyed in the city. The town is too hot right now."

"What about attacking Germans in other areas? I think we are ready to start conducting attacks."

Claude nodded his head in agreement. "Durand is right, we need to start fighting back."

"We aren't ready yet." Cutter looked up from the table and spotted Talia in the back of the room staring at him. Since the night he had slept with her, their relationship had become tepid. Some days she would be friendly and helpful, other days something Cutter would say would aggravate her. Today was one of those days. He could tell she was brooding on the idea of being active, and by the look on her face was preparing to give a heated argument. Cutter knew that if he didn't ask her opinion there would be hell to pay. "What is it?"

"We need to start killing German patrols."

The room went dead quiet and all eyes turned to Talia. Cutter rubbed his forehead in frustration. "We can't just go and start offing German soldiers. We need to kill their informants and limit what the Gestapo and Abwehr can do before we start attacking actual troops."

Talia didn't respond, but stared frostily at Cutter. Cutter stared right back at her, not blinking. "Why do you want us to start targeting troops?"

"Oberleutnant Amsel has been asking about you with renewed interest."

Claude swore under his breath and the room erupted into a buzz of hushed whispers.

Cutter kept his eyes on Talia and she stared right back. He couldn't help but wonder if she was telling him this because she worried about him or because it affected the Resistance. Either way it was unwelcome news. Amsel had proved to be a nuisance. Cutter's initial impression of the man had turned out to be accurate. He wasn't a professional soldier. Like a rat casting a long shadow, the man enjoyed the fear and respect that came with his title; and, like any good Nazi, enjoyed instilling fear through murder, brutality, and bullying.

"Everyone, calm down," Claude barked, restoring order.

"Why is he asking about me?"

"I don't know."

"Did anyone in Dieppe know about me?"

Durand shook his head. "No, they never met you and we never mentioned you."

"Then why is Amsel asking about me?"

Talia shrugged uncertainly. "I'm not sure, but the other day I saw him and he asked when you were returning to Cherbourg."

Claude leaned over the table close to Cutter's ear. "Do you think the Abwehr knows about you?" he asked softly in English.

Cutter shrugged. Amsel's reasons for asking about him weren't limited to professional queries. He still strongly disliked Cutter because of his "relationship" with Talia. "It's possible. It could be that he just doesn't like me."

Durand frowned. "Do you think he would hurt you because he's jealous?"

"I doubt it, but you never know."

Claude vigorously rubbed the scruff on his neck and shook his head. "He shot the LeBlanc boy last week because he accidentally spilled a bucket of milk on his boots." He reached for his wine glass and took a heavy sip. "Two weeks before that he beat a farmhand within an inch of his life for not moving his cows out of the road quick enough for him to pass."

"We should kill him before he can kill you." Talia looked over at Cutter, waiting to see his reaction.

Cutter eyed her for a long moment, unsure of what to say. She was clearly trying to protect him. "If it's simply a matter of a love triangle and not a professional interest, let's leave it be. Nothing attracts the Abwehr or the Gestapo like a curious death of a Nazi officer."

"We could do it," Claude said.

Cutter shot him a dirty look for even contemplating it.

"What? We could! We would need something to shift the blame from here, though."

"Such as?"

"Amsel likes his alcohol, and he is known for driving after a hefty night at the bar," Durand provided.

"We should do it the next night he is at the bar," added Claude.

Cutter shook his head slowly. "If we kill Amsel, no matter how it looks, we are inviting trouble."

"How so?" Durand crossed his arms and leaned back against the kitchen counter. "If it's an accident, no one will suspect us."

"Amsel is an oaf. His primal urges are something we need to be concerned about, but we can mitigate the risk. If we kill him he will be replaced."

"What's the problem with that?" Talia asked.

"Amsel's interest in me is purely as a competitor for *you*. His own men know this. As long as we keep our distance from him we are fine." Cutter paused to collect his thoughts and looked around the room. "However, if we kill him, we know nothing about his replacement. He will be an unknown quantity. I can only suspect anyone who replaces Amsel will begin his duties by becoming overly familiar with his surroundings. That means we'd be put under a microscope, and as a result it will delay our operations."

"The devil we know is better than the devil we don't." Claude grumbled.

"Precisely."

"I think it's worth the risk," Talia stubbornly persisted.

Cutter looked over at Claude for help. Cutter was solely an adviser; he made recommendations but couldn't issue orders to Claude's men. Claude would make the decision.

Claude was silent for a long moment, drumming his fingers on the table. "Alright," he said with finality, "we leave Amsel alone. For now."

No one said anything, but there were silent nods. "Alright, gentlemen, that should be it. Continue with training, we will not be conducting attacks until Claude says otherwise."

Claude's declaration was met with a handful of nods. Without another word, the meeting was finished. Resistance members slowly trickled out of the house, moving in small groups of two or three, scurrying out into the fields and avoiding the roads. Durand and Claude shook Cutter's hand and walked toward the door. As the pair of them left the safe house, Cutter looked at Talia. "What is it?"

Talia didn't say anything but picked up the wine glasses and brought them into the kitchen. Their relationship was anything but simple. Cutter walked up behind her and placed his hands on her arms.

Her arms flexed taut and she stiffened. Cutter gently let go. "We need to talk."

She snorted. "Now? About what?"

"That night we slept together. We've been tiptoeing around each other for the past two months. We can't keep doing this."

"Don't be silly, it was a moment of weakness for me. It won't happen again." Talia waved her hand dismissively and started to clean the glasses. Cutter could tell by her tone that that was not the end of the matter. Since the night they had made love she had changed. Although Cutter had barely known her, he could see the change. She was more serious and smiled even less now. He knew that he had hurt her when he had called what they did a mistake. He could tell that the emotional pain he had inflicted had hardened into resentment, and he despised himself for it, but didn't know what else he could have done.

"Talia, I told you why this wouldn't work. It's too risky."

"Yes, you've said that before." She stiffly turned to look at him. Her eyes were set in her default frosty look. She eyed Olivier coolly but said nothing more. She wasn't looking for a fight, nor was she interested in reconciling with him.

"So why does it feel like you want to kill me as well as Amsel?"

Talia's lips puckered into a frown as she set the glass she was cleaning down. "Do you remember what you said to me on the beach? You said you were here because you didn't want this war to take anything else from you."

"I know, and I meant that."

"Well, what's the point if it's already taken your ability to feel?"

Cutter paused, unsure of what she was getting at.

"Every time you begin to open up to me you immediately shut down. That night when we made love, that was the real you. Not some *nom de guerre* the SOE gave you. My uncle used to say that you spies had a split personality. Normally we only see your alias; Olivier, in your case. But you can normally start to see through the disguise and start to piece together the type of person a spy was before the war. With you that's not the case, and I wonder if one of the things this war has taken from you is your identity."

Cutter struggled to respond, uncertain of what to say. "Talia, I know you think I'm a bastard, but I mean well."

Talia's eyes glistened as she struggled to control herself. "Even a bastard feels."

"I'm trying to keep you safe, dammit!" Cutter shouted in English.

After spending two months speaking French, his switch to English shocked both of them. They both remained quiet for a few moments before Cutter spoke, "Being romantically involved with a British spy is a sure way for you to be killed if I were captured. Do you have any idea what the Gestapo would do to me, to both of us, if I was caught? Death would be a mercy."

"That's why we need to kill Amsel," Talia argued. Her tone was gentle, but her voice was firm.

"No, now is not the time. If the Abwehr or the Gestapo suspects me, Amsel's death, no matter how well staged, will cause such a stir we'll be scrambling to survive."

"So what now?"

Cutter switched to French and said, "We'll continue with establishing networks, and I plan to have a handful of raids occur to the south soon." He locked eyes with Talia. "I promise, we will begin to kill Nazis."

***

Atkinson didn't bother to knock, but brushed past his secretary and opened the door to Hambro's office. "I've received word from Cutter."

Hambro looked up from a document he was reviewing and set it down. "What is it?"

Atkinson sat down across from him. "They're preparing to start conducting guerrilla operations. We should be seeing a relocation of German soldiers to Normandy in response in the next few days."

Hambro placed his fingertips together and leaned back in his chair. "This will benefit the Saint-Nazaire raid." His lips curled into a smirk. "I don't think we could have planned this any better."

"When does that occur?"

Hambro reached for a cigarette and put it between his lips. "Combined Operations decided that the raid will go 28 March." He pulled out his lighter and lit the cigarette and inhaled. "Lieutenant Colonel Newman's commandos are conducting rehearsals and Commander Ryder is finishing his retrofits of the *Campbeltown*." Hambro raised his eyebrows as he looked at Atkinson. "Did you know she's originally an American ship, given to us courtesy of Roosevelt's lend-lease program?"

"I was not aware, sir."

Hambro grunted and took another drag on the cigarette. "I also found out that it has been requested by our American cousins that an observer accompany the raid."

"Looks like the Yanks are finally getting in the war."

"Took them bloody long enough."

Freddy nodded and examined his boss. Hambro's suit was disheveled and covered in creases. Freddy suspected he never made it home the night before. "With this raid going on, I suppose it means we can pull Cutter out?"

"Once the raid ends, the Germans will relocate their forces back south to Brittany. We'll let things settle, then extract him."

"What about the Dieppe raid?"

"The Resistance circuit should be able to provide us with the necessary intelligence without Cutter being there."

"Arch will be happy to hear that."

Hambro snubbed out his cigarette and nodded. "The raid goes in a few weeks. Go ahead and start planning to pull him out."

***

First Lieutenant Malcolm Parker of the 1st Ranger Battalion looked around the port of Falmouth, Cornwall, in confusion. British soldiers and sailors passed him by giving him no notice as they went about their days. He turned his collar up against the rain and looked around. He assumed he was in the correct place since he had spotted multiple gunboats and destroyers in the harbor being loaded up. His orders had lacked information and his commanding officer had basically told him to make it up as he went. The only solid piece of information he had been told was that he was to take part in a raid by British commandos in order to provide an assessment and further develop ranger doctrine.

The American Rangers were still a novel concept modeled after the British commandos, and as a result Parker was excited to be working with the people who created the groundwork for the unconventional warfare philosophy.

"Lieutenant Parker?" a voice called, pronouncing it "left-tenant." Parker turned around and spotted a British soldier on the pier waving at him. Parker walked toward him and recognized the pips on his collar signifying the rank of captain. Parker fired off a salute which the captain returned lazily. He looked Parker over and nodded. "Welcome to Two Commandos."

"Excited to be here, sir."

"I'm Captain Corran Carver. You'll be with Baker Troop."

Parker took his hand and shook it.

"I hope you have your battle dress readily available?"

Parker looked at Carver in confusion. "Battle dress?"

"I believe you call them fatigues?"

"Oh, right," Parker chuckled and gestured to what he was wearing. "I'm already wearing them."

Carver cocked an eyebrow and nodded slowly. "Very clean. You haven't been in the mud much?"

Parker frowned and noticed the weathered nature of Carver's uniform. His trousers were sun-bleached a faded green and the multi-pattern raincoat he wore was just as ragged. The only things that looked clean and well maintained were the boots on his feet and the maroon beret perched jauntily on his head. It was a stark contrast to Parker's freshly pressed new fatigues that he had purchased after Ranger training. He looked back up at Carver and shrugged sheepishly. "Well, I'm not afraid to get a little dirty."

"I was hoping you'd say that. Now you'll forgive me, but we're going to have to forego the usual administrative formalities of your arrival."

"I understand."

"Good, now follow me. We'll toss your gear and get you settled later. We have an imminent training exercise that you need to be a part of."

Parker nodded and wordlessly fell in step next to Carver.

"Where are you from?"

"South Carolina."

"Is that near New York?"

"No."

"Then I haven't the foggiest where it is," Carver chuckled.

Parker kept his mouth shut, unsure of how to respond. This was his first interaction with a British officer, and it was hardly what he expected. Carver's cavalier attitude and grimy uniform seemed out of place with his clipped accent. In his mind he had expected a British officer to be fussing over tea and biscuits not someone eager to get in the muck and dirt with his troops.

"What do you think?" he asked, nodding to the ships. "Ever see something like this?"

"No, never." Parker looked around. Nearly a dozen ships of different sizes sat moored in the harbor. He couldn't believe it was all for a raid. If he didn't know better, he would have thought they were invading Normandy.

"Jerry won't know what hit him." Carver motioned for Parker to continue following him. "Roughly two hundred fifty commandos and three hundred fifty sailors will be participating in this raid. We're looking to do a lot of damage in a short amount of time and be out of there before anyone is the wiser." Carver led Parker toward an inn. "This is billeting for Baker. Drop your gear and we'll head over for training. You can get situated this evening after the briefing at eighteen hundred."

Carver led Parker into the inn and found him a room. Once his gear was dropped, he followed Carver back out to the pier where the rest of Baker was waiting.

"Just try not to fall in the water and you'll do fine. Do what the man next to you does."

"Will do, sir." Parker watched as the rest of the troop adjusted their gear. He had no idea what he was doing.

A yeoman navigated a gunboat up next to the dock and the commandos hopped in.

"You gonna stand on the pier and wait for us to come back or you gonna get in the damn boat?" Carver called.

Parker grinned sheepishly and jumped into the boat after them. *What the hell am I doing?*

"Right. So we're still figuring out if we're gonna be on the HMS *Campbeltown* or come in behind her. I expect we'll know soon, but for now we're training for the worst case."

Parker nodded, still not entirely sure what Carver was talking about. "So what do I need to do?"

"Just work on getting your sea legs and we'll go from there."

They spent the afternoon training in the gunboats, sailing out of the harbor and back in and disembarking. They did this for roughly four hours until Carver was satisfied with the efficiency of their movements. The whole time, Parker struggled to stay out of the way of the commandos as they performed their designated tasks. By the end of the day Parker had found a sufficient corner of the boat where he wasn't an obstruction.

"Don't worry, sir. As long as you're handy with a gun, you'll do fine," one of the team leaders, Sergeant Callum, encouraged as they exited the boats after the last exercise.

Carver grinned as Parker clambered off the boat and back onto the dock. "I daresay, they have the hang of it."

Parker gave a low whistle and nodded his agreement. "They look good, sir." He was dead tired and his knees ached from cracking them against the deck when he lost his footing.

Carver nodded and motioned for Parker to follow him down the dock. They made their way down the pier toward the *Campbeltown*.

"See anything unusual about her?"

Parker looked around the destroyer, not entirely sure what he was searching for. His eyes locked on the forward deck and he saw what Carver was talking about. Multiple steel plates had been welded to the railings and the twelve-pound gun attached to the deck was new.

"She's been retrofitted with that gun, and two Oerlikon cannons on the upper deck," Carver said, seeing the recognition on his face. "Armor plating to reinforce the front decks and a few extra funnels have been added." Carver jerked his thumb to the aft of the ship. "To make her look more like a Nazi ship."

"A lot of trouble for a simple raid."

"Well, there's nothing simple about this raid. This beauty is going to be laden down with commandos and a shit ton of explosives and will be ramming the Saint-Nazaire dry docks."

Parker eyed Carver in annoyance. He wasn't in the mood for jokes. When the knowing smile never came he realized Carver was being serious. "That's insane."

Carver's eyes twinkled and he smiled wryly. "Suicidal is a more apt descriptor in my opinion."

"What about the gunboats?"

"Teams will be aboard the boats, but the main assault force will be aboard the destroyer. With the *Campbeltown* ramming the dock, the gunboats will be the only way the raid can escape."

Parker scratched his neck as the scope of the mission started to come into view. "So the *Campbeltown* rams the dry docks, the teams disembark and destroy various objectives, and . . ."

"Fuses are lit on the *Campbeltown* and we move like hell to the gunboats to retreat," Carver finished and expanded his arms out wide in a motion similar to an explosion. They walked away from the ship and back toward the inn.

Carver walked through the entrance to the inn and looked over his shoulder. "The brief is in an hour. We have one more rehearsal tomorrow before the raid."

Parker grunted, unsure how to respond. A hundred different things were going through his head, but the biggest one was how he would repay his company commander for throwing him under the bus by sending him on this raid.

***

CHAPTER 9
CHARIOT

Faraday checked his fuel gauge. *"Reese Flight, how are we looking on fuel?"* They had taken off an hour ago and had spent the last thirty minutes flying over Cherbourg low and slow. Operation Chariot was happening at midnight and Faraday's flight along with seven others had been tasked with buzzing Normandy in multiple Rhubarb missions in an effort to pull German forces from the area around Saint-Nazaire to better protect northern Brittany and Normandy.

Since their return from their initial flight over Saint-Nazaire, the only topic of discussion coming down from Air Vice-Marshal Leigh-Mallory's headquarters concerned that town. Reconnaissance flights were sent out weekly all over Brittany as pilots scoured the region looking to get a firm understanding of the Nazi disposition there.

Faraday pulled back power and checked his map one more time. It felt good to hit the enemy on their own turf. Since his commissioning into the Royal Air Force, Faraday had spent the majority of his time defending the island. Aside from Rodeo and Rhubarb missions, they had never attacked the Nazis on their side of the Channel. He checked his trim tabs and listened as the rest of his flight checked in.

"Reese 4 here. I'm a little over half a tank."

"Reese 5. Same."

"Reese 3. Similar."

"Reese 2. Same."

"Roger. Swift Flight identified enemy targets in vicinity of Saint-Malo. Break off into sections and prepare to engage," Faraday called. He pulled back gently on the stick.

Argyle and Chambers followed him as Faust and O'Brien broke off into their section with Faust acting as section leader.

"This is Reese 5 beginning initial run," Faust called as he began to descend on Saint-Malo, O'Brien hot on his tail. Faraday watched as the pair of them descended over the city, and scanned the skies for any aggressors.

"Reese Leader, this is Reese 5. Enemy ships have been spotted inside the harbor. Beginning gun run."

"Roger. Where in the harbor?"

"The harbor looks like a giant C. They're at the bottom of the C."

"Roger. Following after you," Faraday called and pushed forward on the stick. He watched as Faust and O'Brien bore down on the harbor, tracer fire coughing from their guns.

An explosion erupted from one of the ships. Faraday blinked, letting his eyes adjust to the bright light. *That was unexpected.* They hadn't expected their guns to do anything more than make the sailors duck and hide.

"You must've hit a fuel line or powder magazine!"

"Reese Flight, orient on that explosion, engage targets around it." The explosion illuminated the harbor, casting an orange glow on the remaining ships. Six of them were stacked neatly in a row, moored near the mouth of the Rance river. Faraday lined up on the ships so that he would fly over all of them and maximize the effectiveness of his guns. He lined up the pipper with the first ship in the row and depressed the trigger for three seconds. Tracer fire stitched up the side of the first ship. Faraday pulled back gently on the stick and the pipper jumped up to the next ship in the line. He depressed the trigger again and watched

a spurt of rounds impact. He repeated the motion twice more and gained altitude. He checked both wings and made sure that Argyle and Chambers were still with him, and then surveyed the damage they caused. Two of the ships were smoking heavily. Faraday suspected that they would need to be put into dry dock for repairs.

"*Reese Flight, form up and return to base. Nice job.*" Faraday started to gain altitude, quietly hoping they had caused enough damage to help the raid.

***

Cutter grunted. He hated ambushes. Especially when he was the diversion. He looked up and down the road one last time to make sure Durand, Talia, and the seven other Resistance members were hidden.

Cutter checked his watch. The weekly supply convoy was late and he was growing impatient. Nothing ever truly went according to plan, he knew this all too well, but that understanding didn't help his nerves. To make matters worse, he hated waiting in the dark. It was pitch black out save for the limited illumination from the moon. As difficult as it would be for the convoy to see them, it was just as difficult for Cutter to see if someone was ambushing the ambushers. When he heard the crunch of footsteps behind him it nearly scared him out of his skin.

"Sorry," Durand whispered as he dropped into a crouch next to Cutter.

"Jesus Christ, Durand, I almost killed you."

"Everyone is in place," Durand said. "You think the other raids will be successful?"

"I hope so. I'm more concerned about ours at the moment."

"The convoy is late."

200

"It'll be here." Cutter did his best to sound confident. He shifted his weight and looked up from the ditch. It ran parallel to the dirt road and gave him a good field of vision both ways. He looked over to where Talia lay hidden. Her female figure silhouetted against the moonlight made her easy to identify.

Durand followed his gaze and chuckled, "How are things with you and Talia?"

"What do you mean?"

"Olivier, the tension between you and her is so apparent even a blind man can see it."

"It's difficult to explain."

"You slept with her and didn't mean to."

Cutter turned and snapped his eyes on Durand's shadowy figure. "Who told you?"

"It's obvious. Like I said, the tension is obvious." Durand flashed a grin, but his tone was serious. "You're trying to take back what you did by keeping her at arm's length."

Cutter said nothing but toyed absently with the pin of his grenade.

"May I offer some advice?" Durand didn't waiting for Cutter to respond. "Don't push her away, we all don't know how much time we have. Her life is hard enough with her family killed and her country invaded. Is it so hard to love her?"

Cutter said nothing, surprised by Durand's candid observations. Maybe he wasn't the big thick brute Cutter had characterized him as. He wondered if Durand was speaking from experience. But he missed Cutter's motivations. It wasn't about love, it was about survival. That was the problem with members of the Resistance, they were all willing to die for France. Cutter had passed that stage in his career and wanted to survive the war desperately. The last thing he wanted was for his emotions to get him or someone else killed. Victor's death had been enough.

"Like I said, it was just some advice."

Cutter shivered slightly as the damp ground soaked his wool sweater. "You sure you'll be able to shoot the driver?"

"Yes, just make sure you throw your grenade accurately."

Cutter looked around the road. The faint sound of car engines could be heard in the distance. Cutter checked his Sten submachine gun one last time. "It's time."

He inched down a little in the ditch and pulled a grenade from the bandolier slung over his shoulder. He guessed the rest of the team was doing the same. He hoped none of them had nodded off while waiting.

He looked up over the ditch and spotted the hazy glow of vehicle lights as they drove through the light fog that had crept in. They were half a kilometer away, Cutter guessed. As they moved closer, Cutter pulled the pin from the grenade, keeping the spoon in place, waiting for them to get in range.

As they got closer, Cutter tensed, waiting for Durand to fire the first shot. He steadied his breathing and kept a firm grip on the grenade. He clenched his teeth. The convoy was close. Durand needed to take his shot now.

Crack!

The sound of Durand's rifle split the air and tires screeched as the lead truck in the convoy swerved. Cutter flicked the spoon of the grenade and lobbed it over the ditch, bouncing it in front of the second truck.

He ducked back down, and listened as his team's grenades all detonated. He wasted no time and pulled another one from his bandolier.

He quickly pulled the pin and stuck his head up above the ditch and spotted a truck stopped in front of him. German soldiers were scrambling to open the tent flap in the back.

Cutter watched, waiting until the flap was open and threw the grenade. The grenade arced through the tent flap and bounced off the opposite tent wall into the bed of the truck.

Cutter heard a few Germans scream to get out of the truck, but it was too late. A small flash and a loud explosion detonated inside the truck and a German soldier went careening out of the back onto the road.

He struggled to get up, but Cutter didn't give him the opportunity. Cutter grabbed his Sten and brought it to his shoulder and fired a quick burst. The rounds stitched down the German's back and he collapsed.

Not stopping to admire his work, he scanned the truck, waiting to see if anyone else would get out. He motioned to two members of his team to sweep the convoy.

They clambered out of the ditch and systematically checked each vehicle as they had practiced early in the day.

A few Germans struggled out of their vehicles, but were quickly killed by either Cutter or Durand's team. As Cutter's two teammates swept the trucks, they deftly set explosives on each vehicle and activated the acid fuses.

Cutter looked around and spotted Talia striding toward a wounded German. Without a word she fluidly raised her Sten to the German's head and depressed the trigger. Cutter winced at the gunshot, and watched as Talia silently continued on past the now-dead German to take up a position guarding the demolition team. *Christ, she has more bollocks than half the men in her circuit.*

Once the charges were set, they checked one more time that there weren't any German survivors and quickly departed.

"This will get their attention," Cutter muttered to Durand as they ran to a car that was waiting for them.

***

Parker checked his watch; it was a little past one o'clock. The *Campbeltown* had crept into the Loire estuary roughly an hour ago, and was now making its way closer to the coast.

Parker struggled in vain to make out the shoreline. It was pitch black, a result of the Nazis implementing blackout procedures. He walked across the deck, his Thompson submachine gun hanging from his shoulder and banging lightly against his hip. He spotted Carver and walked over to him.

Carver looked up and nodded in greeting. "Nervous?"

"Little bit. Your men look pretty calm." Parker nodded to the entire forward deck, which was covered with commandos.

"Oh, they're scared shitless. They just hide it well."

Parker gave Carver a dark look, a combination of annoyance and wishing he hadn't heard that.

Carver smiled, his white teeth reflecting in the moonlight. "Sorry mate, how's your team?"

"I'm just along for the ride, as Sergeant Callum explained to me."

"Callum is a good soldier, one of my best. If he says to do something, do it."

Parker nodded but said nothing.

"I know it's awkward for an officer to be led by a Sergeant but—"

"Sir, I get it," Parker interrupted. "Your guys are seasoned veterans who have been working together for a long time. I showed up literally yesterday and I'm not a commando, I'm tracking."

"You have no idea how few people understand that." He extended his hand. "Good luck with Team Five. Hit your targets, then get the hell out of the town."

"I wi—"

Parker was cut off by the muted thud of an explosion and the whistling sound as artillery rounds started to land around the ship. "Get down!" Carver shouted, shoving him behind one of the steel plates. One of the commandos ran to the ten-pound gun and started to prep it to return fire. "Stay that gun!" Carver shouted, pointing at the commando. "No one fire."

After a few seconds the bombardment ceased. Parker stood up from behind the steel plating and looked around in confusion. "What the hell just happened?"

"We obtained a German code a few months ago, the Captain must have radioed in saying they were firing on friendly forces." Carver walked up to the prow of the boat and found a spot next to the other commandos. "Won't take long before they realize we're not German."

As the salvo ended, the *Campbeltown* shuddered and the sound of her engines started to emanate from belowdecks as she started to pick up speed.

"All hands be to quarters, brace for collision!" a sailor called from the bridge.

"This is insane!" a commando shouted as the *Campbeltown* churned through the waves.

A pair of searchlights on the coast started to sweep the bay and locked onto the ship. The lights flashed a series of signals to the *Campbeltown,* trying to get her to slow down.

After two failed attempts, the German defenses resumed firing on the ship. Machine gun rounds pinged off the steel plating and the ship's hull, as the German shore defenses started to concentrate fire on the British ship. Sergeant Callum moved past Carver and Parker and started to shout at his fellow commandos, "Take cover! Save your ammunition! Let the Navy return fire!"

Bullets whizzed past Parker's head and cracked against the hull of the ship leaving him half deaf from the noise. He looked around and spotted a commando clambering up the ladder into the ten-pound gun's firing control. In seconds the gun started to return fire at a steady rate. Between that and the British destroyers in the convoy opening fire, Parker was hard pressed to hear anyone next to him unless they were shouting in his ear.

Parker kept his head down and did his best to keep his whole body behind the steel planking. A round ricocheted off the deck and hit a commando next to Parker in the chest, leaving a hole the size of a plump cherry where it exited his back. He crumpled backward from the force of the round and landed on Parker. He was a heavy bastard,

Parker noticed, and moved quickly to get out from under him, abandoning all observance of handling a dead man's body respectfully. It was the first time Parker had ever seen a man killed; the shock of his death was subdued by Parker's frantic drive to avoid getting shot himself. As they got closer to shore the intensity of fire started to increase. Small caliber rounds from rifles started to crack over Parker's head and crash against the bulkhead.

"Brace for impact!" commandos shouted up and down the deck. Parker grabbed a hold of a rope line that had been strung around the entire deck, and held on for dear life. He waited for what seemed like an eternity and then . . . *BANG*. Parker was airborne as the *Campbeltown* bounced into the air and landed with a crash at a lopsided angle. Parker tried to land on his feet, but his knees buckled and he cracked them on the deck. He swore loudly and struggled to his feet and looked around.

"Stay down!"

The prow of the ship was raised up out of the water at a twenty-degree angle and was canted slightly to the left making it difficult to maintain balance on the slick deck.

Two commandos shimmied up to the prow of the ship and set up two Bren machine guns and started to lay down interlocking fires.

Parker looked around the deck in a daze. His heart pumped a mile a minute and he was unsure what to do. He struggled to think. The fear flowing from the back of his neck down to his fingertips and toes was paralyzing. Gunfire drowned out all other noises, and the flash of flares and spotlights filling the interior of the dry dock was blinding. It all acted like a mental barrier, an overload of the senses. He struggled to move, and took up a position near the two commandos manning the Brens. He checked his Thompson and made sure a round was chambered and started to fire blindly. He finished a magazine and started to reload, when a rough hand grabbed him from behind and shoved him toward the shorter end of the lopsided boat. It was Sergeant Callum. "Everyone over the sides!" He didn't wait for an answer but kept moving around the deck, grabbing commandos and shoving and kicking them toward where a handful of commandos were scrambling through the debris trying to get out of the dry dock.

Parker looked around, as though being shaken out of a trance. He looked up at the *Campbeltown*'s bridge as he made his way toward the edge of the ship. The Oerlikon guns below the bridge were spewing fire as they raked the interior of the dry dock. The bridge itself was a wreckage of shattered glass.

Parker wondered if the captain or anyone else on the bridge was still alive but didn't have time to think about it. He planted his hand firmly on the edge of the ship's bulkhead and threw a leg over. The drop was a little more than he anticipated but he had little choice but to fall. He landed on his feet, then quickly rolled like he learned in jump school to spread load the impact and lower the risk of spraining his ankles. He stood up and looked around.

The outer wall of the dry dock had collapsed in and had provided the commandos with sufficient cover to rally and push out to their objectives. But water was slowly filling the dock from where the outer wall had been destroyed.

Parker spotted Carver tucked behind a piece of rubble, waving commandos forward and checking their gear. He sloshed through the calf-high water and ducked behind the nearest piece of rubble.

As he strained to hear what Carver was saying, he noticed the ten-pound gun had stopped firing, but the Oerlikons were still coughing.

"Teams Four and Five, push forward and start clearing a path for the demo teams!"

Parker moved up next to Sergeant Callum, who nodded to him and motioned for them to move out.

The seven-man team moved away from the rubble and bounded toward the nearest building and took cover. They waited for the demolition team to catch up.

"Alright, you lot, quick and clean. No mistakes." Sergeant Callum cast a fierce glare at the team and, without another word, ducked around the street corner and took off down the road.

Here we go. Parker took off after him along with the rest of the team. None of them bothered to slow down to orient on their target. Callum had instructed each man to memorize the street maps of Saint-Nazaire the day prior. As they moved, they quickly figured out where they were and, save for a few small deliberations on the quickest route, were moving quickly up the streets.

Sporadic gunfire filled the air, but as they ran it grew more distant. Their target was the outer winding house for the outer dock gate. Compared to the other targets, it was insignificant and closer to the *Campbeltown.*

The commando team moved quickly, turning corners and maintaining a weathered eye for any German soldiers. Parker gulped air and ran as quick as he could to keep up with Sergeant Callum. The middle-aged sergeant was unusually spry for his age, staying steps ahead of the decades younger commandos and ranger under his command. As he rounded a corner he came to a halt and raised a fist. "The target is up ahead," he rasped, trying not to shout. "Demo team, set your charges quickly and smoothly, take your time, but don't dawdle." He looked over at one of the commandos, a burly Scotsman wielding a Bren machine gun. "Tarbor, cover our six."

Tarbor nodded and moved to the rear. "Lieutenant, stay in the middle." Callum pointed at two commandos. "Bagger, Teach, take point and move through the winding house."

The team moved to the entrance of the building and moved in. The winding house was a large structure that housed the controls for closing and opening the dry dock as well as flooding it. Parker scanned the scaffolding that bisected the second floor of the building, expecting a few snipers to be watching them, but the building was deserted.

Both Bagger and Teach swept through the building and started to move down the walls. The demolition team broke off from the assault team and got to work. They started to lay charges while the assault team secured the entrances. Parker walked over to Callum, who was standing next to the radio operator.

"Everything alright?"

Callum shook his head, his face grave. "The Germans are counterattacking, and by the sound of it a lot of our gunboats have been sunk. I'm worried we won't be able to get out of here."

"Do we still have the *Campbeltown*?"

"For now, yes. I don't know how much longer."

Parker nodded in understanding. It didn't take a tactician to realize that if they didn't move fast they would be left behind. "We need to get back to her, it's our best chance of pulling back."

Callum agreed. He walked over to one of the commandos working with the charges and asked, "How much longer?"

"Almost done."

"Work faster unless you wanna get left behind."

"You said move quick but take your time."

"That was before I found out we may not have a way home."

The commando's eyes darted up from the charges and stared at Callum. "It's one of those raids, eh?"

"Afraid so."

The commando wordlessly nodded and returned to his work. His fingers moving quicker and less cautiously.

Callum stood up and looked around. The staccato of the Bren machine gun erupted from the doorway Tarbor was covering. "Panzerschreck! Get down!"

Parker watched almost in slow motion as the far wall of the winding house disintegrated inward. Two commandos went flying from the opening and landed with a resounding thud on the floor. Callum and Parker sprinted to them and checked for signs of life but found none.

"Leave them," Callum said grimly, and took up a position in the entrance they had been covering. Gunfire started to erupt all around them as German soldiers started to realize what the target was. They started to converge on the building by the dozens, moving between adjacent structures and inching toward the entrances.

"They're trying to cut us off!" Parker realized. He poked out from behind the doorway and fired, cutting down two Germans as they tried to move between cover.

"To hell with this," Callum groused and looked around for the radio operator. "Shepherd!"

Shepherd sprinted over to Callum and ducked down below a half-destroyed wall as German fire snapped around them. He handed Callum the radio headpiece.

"What are you doing?"

"Seeing if our mortars can help us." Callum snatched the headpiece and put it up to his ear. "*Sir, its Callum, we need the mortars to fire on the winding house.*"

Parker barely heard the conversation, but a few seconds later mortar rounds started to fall outside.

"Demo team, where are we at with those charges?"

"Done, Sergeant!" the team leader shouted. "Five minutes till detonation."

"Everyone rally up on Tarbor, we're moving back to the ship!" Callum shouted as he, Parker, and Shepherd sprinted over to where Tarbor was keeping their escape secured. Callum looked around. "Where's Bagger?"

"Dead," Teach said, gasping for air. "So are Leeds and Travis."

"Shit."

Parker looked around. Of the fourteen-man team, only nine remained. "We need to go, Sergeant."

"Tarbor, Teach, you two are on point."

Tarbor grunted, shouldered the heavy Bren, and started to move out of the building with Teach moving right behind him. They ducked behind a wall and started to fire blindly overhead.

The rest of the team quickly moved out of the wheelhouse, German gunfire snapping all around them. Callum ducked down an alleyway and motioned for the rest of the team to follow, firing his Sten intermittently as Germans started to close in on the squad.

"Move it! She's gonna blow any second," the demolition team leader screamed as they darted down the alley.

Parker scampered after him, running as fast as his legs would let him. As his feet pounded against the pavement, an explosion erupted behind him and nearly knocked him off balance. The force of the blast shook the ground, knocking a few of the commandos off their feet. Parker struggled to help Tarbor back to his feet and looked back the way they came. A column of dust rumbled down the alley after them, filling the air with a blinding film of smoke and dust.

"Stay quiet, lads!" Callum motioned for them to keep moving, and they carefully moved between the buildings. The German gunfire had ceased with the dustup, the smoke and debris hiding the commandos from the enemy. Parker looked around and gingerly moved after the rest of the team, doing his best to see where he was planting his feet in the darkness and smoke. As they moved, he double-checked their rear, making sure no Germans were following. The dust was so thick he couldn't see, but he could hear voices and the sound of mechanized vehicles.

When they finally made it back to the *Campbeltown*, the ten-pound gun was firing again, but one of the Oerlikons was down. Its barrel was twisted at a gruesome angle and jagged holes peppered the length of it.

The team traversed the rubble and made their way back up onto the *Campbeltown*, occasionally returning fire as they went. As Parker clambered onto the deck he took an outstretched hand and was helped to his feet. It took him a moment to realize that it was the captain of the ship helping him.

"Alright, Lieutenant?" Lieutenant Commander Beattie asked. He had a gash across his head and dried blood covered the side of his face.

"Objective destroyed, sir." Parker crouched down behind the steel plate next to Beattie and looked around. Sailors had taken up various positions around the ship and were doing their best to repel German soldiers trying to take her. He couldn't help but notice that a pathway wet with blood had appeared leading to the aft of the ship.

"All wounded have been moved to the back of the ship for evacuation," Beattie answered, following his gaze. "I have two gunboats ready to depart, but I'm waiting for as many commandos as I can get."

"How many are missing?"

"Too many to count. Captain Carver has yet to return, and no one has heard from Lieutenant Colonel Newman." Beattie grabbed a Lee-Enfield rifle and loaded it. Another explosion emanated in the direction of the docks. They both looked in the direction of the blast.

"That must have been Carver detonating one of the entrances into the basin."

Callum looked on in horror and shook his head. "Oh Christ, Jerry is all over that side of the dock."

Beattie looked around and coolly assessed the situation. "My ship is low on ammunition and personnel. If we don't see anyone in five minutes we are departing."

Callum turned and glared at the Lieutenant Commander. "What about the rest of our commandos?"

"I'm receiving reports that Old Mol is still under our control. We'll make a run past it on our way out and if anyone is there we will pick them up."

Callum hesitated and looked at Parker. Parker nodded. He barely knew Callum, but by the looks of it he was searching Parker's eyes for a decision. "We'll hold the ship, sir. Get your crews to the gunboats."

"Good man. My lads need to set the charges below to scuttle the ship. I need five minutes, then run like hell to the boats."

"Will do, sir." Parker looked at Callum, expecting a reaction for taking over command.

Callum gave a slight nod and started to bark orders. "Teach! Get up on the Oerlikon, Tarbor cover the left flank with your Bren!"

The remainder of team's Five and Four scrambled and took up positions where Lieutenant Commander Beattie's sailors had been seconds before, and continued to suppress the enemy. Parker ran over to the ten-pound gun and started to spin both the directional and elevation wheels on the back of it and lined up a shot on a caved-in building. He pulled on the firing chord and fired. The shell ripped through one of the walls of the building and exploded, collapsing whatever was left into a heap of rubble.

"Smith is hit!" Parker heard someone shout, but focused on lining up his next shot. He rotated the directional wheel clockwise and it spun slowly to the right. Three German soldiers were manhandling an anti-armor gun over the rubble, trying to get a clear shot on the *Campbeltown*. Parker adjusted the elevation and pulled on the firing chord again. Another shell rocketed away and impacted right in front of the gun, spraying the three Germans with shrapnel and disabling the anti-armor gun.

"Fuses are set, sir! Get back to the gunboats!" Sergeant Callum shouted as he helped Tarbor, who was limping with a piece of shrapnel in his shin.

Parker ducked away from the gun and checked the deck to make sure no one alive was being left behind. Satisfied, he ran after Callum and helped him. "Jesus Tarbor, you're a heavy bastard."

"Well, I'm real sorry about that, sir," Tarbor said through his gritted teeth, barely understandable with his thick Scottish accent.

Parker and Callum carried him to the boat. The sloping deck making it difficult for them to keep their footing. As soon as they were in the gunboats, they were away. Parker set Tarbor down and walked to the wheelhouse with Callum. The boats were less than two hundred meters away from the ship as a muted explosion reverberated from the inner workings of the *Campbeltown* as her scuttling charges were detonated. All that was left were the big charges that would detonate later in the day.

Parker walked over to the helmsman and pointed toward Old Mol, the derelict lighthouse acting as beacon in the chaos. "We need to get to Old Mol and see if we can rescue anyone."

The helmsman nodded in agreement, started to turn his boat, and motioned for the other boat to follow suit.

The two gunboats turned toward the Loire estuary and the old lighthouse that jutted out from the harbor. As they started to get close, the water around the boats started to erupt into giant geysers as German mortar teams tried to score a hit on the boats.

The helmsman pulled hard on the wheel and turned the boat.

"What the hell are you doing?" Callum shouted and whipped around. "Turn us back toward Old Mol."

"Stand down, Sergeant," a Navy Lieutenant said sternly. "We'll be blown out of the water if we bring these boats to a stop." He looked at the helmsman who was awaiting orders. "Continue your course out to sea."

Callum opened his mouth to say something but Parker grabbed him by the shoulder. "He's right."

Callum shot Parker a pained look. He slumped against the railing and slowly nodded in agreement. "I hate these bloody raids."

Parker nodded silently and looked out at Saint-Nazaire as they sailed by. As he looked around, he noticed that Lieutenant Commander Beattie wasn't aboard either of the gunboats. "Where's the captain?"

"He stayed with the ship." The lieutenant's bloodshot eyes found Parker's. "He was moving up to man the Oerlikon as we were getting in the boats."

Parker's stomach tightened and he whirled around and reached for the helmsman. "We need to go back."

Sergeant Callum grabbed Parker by the shoulder, it was his turn to be the voice of reason. "It's done, sir, there's nothing we can do."

Parker turned and looked at Callum; the bitterness in his voice and the pain in his eyes said it all. Parker nodded slowly and leaned against the rails of the gunboat. He watched as thick black smoke burned into the sky all around the docks. From what Parker could see of the dry dock, it would be years before it would be fully functional. He spotted a number of gunboats burning up in the shallows, guaranteeing no chance of escape for any other commandos left ashore. He cursed softly.

"Oh Christ, some of our lads are stranded on the beach!"

Parker turned and watched in horror as two commandos sprinted down the empty beach toward the surf. A handful of Germans chased after them, taking poorly aimed shots every few steps as they attempted to capture them. The lead commando stripped off his bandoliers as he ran, and threw his rifle aside as he crashed through the waves. Parker watched as rounds clipped the slower of the pair in the shoulder and he staggered and fell from the impact. Feet from the surf, he turned and defiantly fired a handful of rounds, slowing the Germans just a bit before their own shots found their mark. The commando collapsed backward as three well-placed rounds drilled his chest. The other commando didn't look back but continued to swim, struggling to get out to sea.

"We can rescue him!" Teach cried, "Come on, man, you can do it!"

Splashes of water started to emanate around the commando as the Germans started to fire at him. Parker watched with bated breath as the commando continued to swim. A little further and he would be out of range of the German rifles. Parker watched, confident the commando was going to make it but let out a groan as a round found its mark and the water around the commando started to turn red.

"Bastards!"

"Fucking Nazis!"

Parker said nothing but turned around and leaned against the railing of the boat. He prayed silently that Carver and the other commandos were able to escape, but he wouldn't know for sure until they returned to England.

***

Smoke hung thickly in the air above the conference room of the War Office. The stale stench of coffee, cigar smoke, and cigarettes lingered in the air, creating a stuffy environment that Hambro couldn't help but feel mirrored the occupants of the room. Mountbatten, Leigh-Mallory, and a handful of other staff members mingled about the room and Hambro couldn't help but smirk at their overestimation of their own self-worth. The only people Hambro thought actually were required for this meeting were Commanders Ryder and Jacobs, and Lieutenant Colonel Churchill, the new commander of No. 2 Commando.

Lieutenant Colonel Churchill's face was contorted into a visage of violent rage. No relation to the Prime Minister, he had taken command following the raid since Lieutenant Colonel Newman had been captured.

Hambro suspected that a number of Churchill's friends were among the dead or captured at Saint-Nazaire. His gaze floated away from Churchill and he looked around and noticed General Montgomery as he walked in.

Montgomery quietly skirted to the side, attempting in vain to be inconspicuous, and made straight for Hambro and sat down next to him.

"Fancy seeing you here."

Hambro shot him a weak smile. "General, how goes the war?"

"I'd hardly know. They still have me running that damned southern defense."

"I thought you were taking over in Africa?"

"That's been delayed a few months."

Hambro nodded sympathetically. "I'm sorry to hear that. What are you doing here?"

"I have an idea for incorporating commandos into my forces when I go to Africa; I was hoping to speak with Lieutenant Colonel Churchill about it." He gave Hambro a conspiratorial grin. "And perhaps SOE as well."

"I'll have to see what resources we have in North Africa first." As he spoke people started to take their seats around the large table in the middle of the room.

"Looks like this show is about to go on."

Lord Mountbatten walked to the front of the table, backdropped by a large map of the world that took up the entire wall. "Loves a damn spectacle," Montgomery muttered under his breath.

"Gentlemen, as you no doubt know, the raid on Saint-Nazaire was an outstanding success and the dry docks have been disabled. We've—"

"Admiral, what do you mean an outstanding success?" Lieutenant Colonel Churchill seethed. He was struggling to hold his temper, but it was evident by the look on everyone's faces that they were just as surprised at the raid being called a success.

"No. 2 Commandos was nearly destroyed," Churchill continued. "Over two hundred British servicemen captured and over a hundred fifty dead. That's half the raiding force."

Mountbatten eyed Churchill coolly. "Lieutenant Colonel Churchill, I can understand your anger, but those men sold their lives and their freedom dearly. It was necessary to deliver a crushing blow to the German Navy."

Churchill opened his mouth to fire a retort but was cut off by Montgomery. "I think what Lieutenant Colonel Churchill is trying to say is that if we continue to conduct raids with high casualty rates, then no one is going to want to participate in these suicide missions."

Mountbatten eyed Montgomery with a look of veiled annoyance. "My dear fellow, the cost was necessary. I assure you, the next raid won't be as risky." With a languid wave of his hand he turned and opened his mouth, prepared to press on.

Lieutenant Colonel Churchill looked around at the rest of the audience in confusion, wondering if he was the only one surprised by the announcement. "Next raid?"

Mountbatten stopped what he was doing and turned and directed his attention at Churchill, the way a headmaster would respond to an unruly child. His smile was strained but his tone was level. "Yes. As I was saying, we intercepted radio traffic saying that the Führer is most displeased with our success. After talking with the Prime Minister, he is very keen to continue with an even larger raid."

The news had the desired effect, if not for the reason Mountbatten had hoped. Hambro looked over at Commander Ryder who was sitting next to Churchill; Jacobs; and Lord Lovat, No. 4 Commandos' commanding officer and a good friend of Lieutenant Colonel Newman. They were all dead quiet.

Hambro knew very little about Commander Jacobs, but based on the look on his face, he was less than thrilled about the idea of another raid.

"I believe with the success of the Saint-Nazaire raid we shouldn't rest on our laurels, if you will." Mountbatten continued, "With the success of the Saint-Nazaire raid we have paved the way for the execution of Operation Rutter."

Lord Lovat raised a hand but didn't wait to be called on. "What is Operation Rutter?"

"A large scale raid on the town of Dieppe." Leigh-Mallory stood up and walked up next to Mountbatten. "The RAF has been looking for a way to get into a large-scale engagement with the Luftwaffe in an attempt to cripple their forces. Based on Saint-Nazaire, if we conduct a large-scale raid on the town of Dieppe, the Luftwaffe will scramble to interdict and provide air support to the beleaguered town."

Lord Lovat nodded his head slowly but said nothing. The look on his face was a combination of bemusement and skepticism.

Leigh-Mallory turned and pointed to the large map that ran along the wall behind Mountbatten. "By conducting a large-scale amphibious raid along the Dieppe coastline, the Luftwaffe will be forced to commit to providing air support for the defending force and our fighters will be well within range to engage."

"So we're conducting a raid so the RAF can score a few more points than Jerry?" Churchill asked hotly.

Leigh-Mallory shot Churchill a testy look, not keen on having his brainchild attacked for its merit. "No, the raid alone has significant strategic value. By doing this we are showing our Russian allies that we intend to take the pressure off them soon and make Germany fight on two fronts."

"Why not just invade rather than conduct a measly raid?"

"We aren't ready."

Hambro gritted his teeth and struggled to keep his temper. Leigh-Mallory's flippant answers and quickness to bat away any criticism or concerns weren't inspiring confidence. With every question he circumvented or downplayed, Hambro could visibly see the confidence in this operation begin to erode on the faces of the commanders who would participate. He leaned forward in his chair and raised his hand. "Didn't the Saint-Nazaire raid show the Russians our intentions?"

The question had its desired effect. Both Mountbatten and Leigh-Mallory paused and exchanged looks, unsure how to answer. If they said yes, then their audience would wonder why another raid needed to happen. If they said no, the most obvious question that would follow would be if the Saint-Nazaire raid didn't soothe Russian concerns how would a raid on Dieppe?

"Well . . ." Mountbatten hesitated.

Hambro continued, "It seems like this raid is a frivolous expenditure of manpower and offensive capability."

Leigh-Mallory took a step forward from the podium and pointed an accusatory finger down the table. "Now see here Mr. Hambro." His face grew red with frustration. "This raid has significant political and military value." No one was listening as he attempted to rebut Hambro's claims. Churchill, Lovat, and Jacobs had broken into their own discussion, as had Montgomery and Commander Ryder.

Hambro hadn't meant to derail the discussion, nor had he wanted to. He looked around the room and could hear Churchill and Lovat discussing troop deployment concerns, while Montgomery and Commander Ryder were arguing ship-to-shore movement of armor and vehicles.

Mountbatten shot Hambro a contemptuous glare and slapped the table. "Gentlemen, silence please!" He looked around the room. Satisfied that he was back in control, he turned and looked at Hambro. "Mr. Hambro, I understand your concerns, but I assure you that the benefits far outweigh the risks of this raid. Further, this raid has been approved by the Prime Minister and has been given the nod by the Canadian and American governments for Allied participation." He let that final bit of information sink in.

Hambro looked over at Montgomery in confusion. The look of perplexed annoyance on Montgomery's face told Hambro that this was news to him as well.

"What of the Joint Chiefs?" Montgomery asked, his beady eyes transfixed on Mountbatten. "Are they in agreement with this plan?"

Mountbatten smiled slyly and nodded, as though he had just moved a pawn across a chess board and captured his opponent's queen. "They were informed this morning."

Montgomery wordlessly nodded and leaned back in his chair. Hambro could tell by the fire in his eyes that he was struggling to keep his emotions under control.

Mountbatten looked around the room in Machiavellian glee. "We are not alone in this fight, gentlemen, and we cannot fall to rancor if we are expected to lead our allies."

"You mean if Combined Operations is expected to lead," Churchill murmured, and was elbowed by Lovat.

Hambro kept his expression blank, but his brain was already racing through all the possible ripples a raid on Dieppe would generate. First and foremost, he realized he needed to get Cutter out of Normandy before this raid went any further. He looked over at Montgomery one last time, hoping he was poised for a counter argument, but the resigned look on his face devastated him.

***

Cutter read the transmission a second time in surprise, and did his best to hide his joy. He was going home tomorrow; he couldn't believe it.

Claude anxiously looked over his shoulder. "What does it say?"

"Saint-Nazaire was raided." Cutter touched a lighter to the paper and let it burn. "More raids to come." He knew Claude would not react well to his departure; he needed to make sure he left on good terms and peaceably.

"That's good news!" Durand clapped his hands excitedly. "We can start attacking more Germans and blame your commandos for it."

Cutter nodded silently looking at Talia, a pang of guilt overcoming him. As rocky as their relationship was he didn't want to abandon her.

Talia read his face and frowned. "What else did it say?"

"I'm to be extracted tomorrow."

Talia stared at him but said nothing. The room erupted into murmurs as the Resistance members started talking among themselves.

Claude motioned for them to be silent and looked at Cutter. "Are you being replaced?"

"It didn't specify."

Claude leaned against the wall of the barn, deep in thought.

Durand looked around anxiously as the radio operators broke down the radio. "We should go."

Claude nodded absently but didn't move from his spot. "I don't understand." His features were a combination of confusion and agitation. "Is England abandoning us?"

Cutter shook his head. "I'm sure they have their reasons." He looked around the room and saw the look of alarm on everyone's faces. "I'll make sure supplies and munitions continue to get to you."

Claude nodded slowly, not convinced. He looked over at Durand who was anxiously waiting for him to give the word to depart.

"We should go." He turned to Talia. "Get Olivier back to the house. I'll come and get him tomorrow evening for the pickup."

Cutter was surprised there wasn't more of a fight from Claude. He had expected at least a heated argument.

Talia nodded and wordlessly walked out of the barn, not bothering to see if Cutter was following her.

Cutter jogged after her and caught up.

"Looks like you'll be escaping back to your home."

"I didn't ask for this."

"No, but you'll be leaving us all behind without a second thought."

"That's not true. You know that." They got in the car and took off away from the barn. Although Cutter was ecstatic about leaving, a part of him didn't want to abandon Talia. Her words the other week still stung, and he wondered if there was a grain of truth in them.

"You've kept your emotions in check this entire time. I doubt you'll slip up now and tell me what you're really feeling."

Cutter looked at Talia with sadness in his eyes. Was he really as apathetic as she thought? He downshifted and turned the wheel, putting the car on the main road. "I've already learned the cost of becoming close with previous contacts with the Resistance."

Talia looked at him, the ice in her eyes thawing somewhat. "A woman?"

Cutter shook his head. "Victor Boucher," his voice trembled slightly as he spoke. "He was my friend and I killed him."

Talia stared at him in surprise, unsure what to say. They drove in silence for what felt like minutes before Talia finally spoke.

"Who was he?"

"He was my contact in Paris. We had been working together for months gathering intelligence on German plans to invade England. I lived in his house with his wife and daughter for three months. And to prevent him from being captured and interrogated by the Gestapo, I killed him in an alleyway and ran for my life."

Talia looked at Olivier in surprise. This was the first time he had ever told a story that Talia actually believed was true. She had suspected that he had lost people. Who hadn't in this war? But by his own hand. She wondered if she could have done the same in his position. Could she kill her friends for the Resistance? *Am I willing to kill Claude? Durand?* She gave Olivier a pitied look as she wondered if she could have killed Francois. *Yes.* She shivered at the self-revelation. It wasn't something she wished to acknowledge, but she was willing to put the Resistance before her friends; it was what Francois had taught her to do. She looked over at Olivier and could see the discomfort on his face. Did his actions justify his distance from her? *No.* Olivier had shut himself out to others to save himself, not to do his job.

Cutter drummed his fingers on the dashboard. He had told no one about Victor. It was something SOE advocated their spies to be willing to do. But as far as Cutter knew, he was the only one who had been willing to do it. He had always thought that only a ruthless bastard would be willing to kill not just a contact but an ally and accomplice in fighting the Nazis. He had never thought that he had the stomach or the will to do such a thing and it terrified him.

"This is why you've acted so distant with me? To be able to kill me if captured?"

Cutter shuddered and avoided her gaze. "I did it because the less you knew about me the less likely you'd be of use to the Germans." He paused, the truth catching in the back of his throat. "Also, if you were killed, I didn't want to be responsible for your death," his voice cracked and he forced himself to turn and face her. The look on her face shattered any remaining barriers he was trying to keep up.

Talia looked at him in shock. Her mouth hung half open and her eyes shined as tears formed. She had never been willing to admit it to herself, but she had suspected his motives for being distant. Nonetheless, hearing them being confessed was like a vicious punch to the stomach. She struggled to control her breathing and fight back her tears. As terrible and painful as it was for her to hear Olivier say that, anger wasn't her first reaction. It was pity. She caught her breath and struggled to control her voice. When she spoke her voice was firm and matronly, "Olivier, that is part of your job. That is the risk you inherit by being a provocateur and a spy!"

"This isn't a responsibility I want. I didn't ask to come here!"

"Do you think I asked for the Nazis to invade my country? We don't always have a say in the circumstances that impact our lives. You may not want the emotional responsibility that comes with espionage, but it's your burden."

Cutter nodded but remained silent, unsure of how to respond. He parked the car in the alley behind the house and looked over at Talia. "I'm sorry."

"I don't want your apology." Talia looked over at him, her eyes hard but gentle simultaneously. "You've let fear rule your life and I pity you for that."

"I did this to protect you!" Cutter sputtered in protest.

Talia shook her head. "No, you did this to protect yourself." She opened the car door and started to get out. "I wish you the best of luck in England."

***

CHAPTER 10
SQUADRON LEADERS

Faraday landed his Spitfire and taxied to the flight line where he shut down the engine and started to clamber out of his aircraft.

Sergeant Roland, as usual, was the first to greet him as he hopped off the wing. "Good flight, sir?"

"All quiet on the Western Front. You'll be happy to know I brought your aircraft back in one piece."

"Marvelous, sir. It's the one thing that gets me through the day, knowing I have less work to do on that plane."

Cutter grinned and looked around. He spotted Squadron Leader King and a number of pilots, including a few of his own standing off away from the flight line staring at him. "What's the squadron leader doing?"

"I believe he was giving a class on aerial tactics before you landed."

Faraday shot Roland a look, suspecting some skulduggery.

Roland betrayed nothing and gave Faraday a look of innocence. Faraday shook his head and jumped off the wing of the aircraft and walked over to where King and everyone else stood.

"Had I known there was an audience, I would have charged for the spectacle of my landing!"

Squadron Leader King didn't say anything but pulled a sheaf of papers from his pocket and squinted at them, preparing to read. "Attention to orders!"

The gaggle of pilots behind him straightened up and stood at the position of attention for the orders. The smile on Faraday's lips faded and was replaced by a look of confusion.

"His Highness George VI by the Grace of God, of Great Britain, Ireland, and the British dominions beyond the seas, King, Defender of the faith, Emperor of India, etc. To our trusty and well-beloved Ian Nathan Faraday, greetings: We reposing especial trust and confidence in your loyalty, courage, and good conduct, do by these presents constitute and appoint you to the rank of Squadron Leader on this twentieth day of April 1942."

King continued reading the promotion citation as Faraday's head spun. He realized he was still gawking halfway through the presentation and quickly straightened up and looked straight ahead. The promotion took him totally by surprise. He wondered darkly if there was a shortage of squadron leaders and that was why he was being promoted.

Faust and Chambers walked up to him and replaced the flight lieutenant boards on his shoulders with those of a squadron leader. They saluted, shook his hand, and walked back to where they were standing behind King.

King finished by having Faraday recite the oath of office and extended his hand. "Congratulations, Ian."

"Thank you. This is all a little overwhelming."

King grinned wickedly and looked behind Faraday at something. Faraday turned to look and as he did so he saw King take a giant step away as Argyle and O'Brien ran up with a giant bucket between them and poured it over Faraday.

Faraday had no chance to dodge the bucket and felt the ice-cold water hit his neck. He cringed as they emptied the bucket over his head, and let out a yelp as the cold water hit him. As he breathed in, he caught a whiff of his drenched clothes and realized they hadn't poured water on him, but beer.

He looked around at the gaggle of officers as they howled with laughter. "There better be an actual mug of beer on standby for me after that!"

Roland walked up to him and handed him a canned beer. "It's not draft, but it'll do the job, sir."

Faraday took the beer and shook Roland's hand. "Goddamn, you're a good chief." He cracked the beer and took a giant sip and poured the rest over his head much to the roaring applause of the squadron. "Everyone to the pub," Faraday shouted, "first round is on me."

"Now you're talking, sir!" Argyle shouted.

"Everyone except you!" Faraday called, he crushed the beer can and chucked it at Argyle.

Everyone made their way across the flight line to the tavern that had become the de facto squadron-only social club. Faraday bellied up to the bar and threw a few quid down. "Richard, a round for the lads!"

Faraday grabbed two beers and handed one to King.

"Cheers." Faraday took a heavy drought from the mug and looked over at Faust, who was explaining to Tombs and Stokes the details of his latest mission.

"So there I was at fifty feet above sea level," Faust shouted over the din, making hand motions with both hands showing how close he was to the deck, "out of options . . . out of ideas . . ." He looked around the group and gave a cheeky grin before saying, "In a flat in London."

"What was *his* name?"

"Come to think of it Billy, I think it was your mother's house!"

Faraday and King both laughed hard and walked to the corner of the bar rather than witness Billy Hastings trying to kill Faust.

"I just got word from Group; they want me sent over to 121 Squadron. Their squadron leader got shot down a month ago."

"Pete Bailey got shot down?"

King nodded. "Yes, but we confirmed that he bailed out and was captured. He is currently in a POW camp," King assured him. "I forgot you knew Peter."

"He ran the school I was an instructor at up at Turnhouse. We also were students together."

"Don't worry about him. Peter is a resourceful chap, I'm sure he'll lead a blitz from whatever POW camp he is at."

"Anyone talk to Sharon?"

"We take care of our own, you know that."

"Who's taking care of her?"

"Her father is a professor down at Oxford; she took their son and is staying with him. She has a brother, too, does some silly work with the War Office. She should be fine."

"So who is taking over 71?"

"You."

Faraday snorted mid sip, beer shooting out of his nose. "What?"

"You're a squadron leader now, Ian, it's time for you to start behaving like one."

"I don't know the first thing about being a squadron leader."

"Yes, you do. You've commanded a flight, now you just command two. I'll see about diverting pilots here to stand Victor Flight back up before I leave."

"Mike, I—"

But King wouldn't have it. "Ian, you'll do fine. Stop doubting yourself." He looked up at the clock above the bar. "Now, if you'll excuse me, it's late, I'm tired, and there can only be one squadron leader at this bar." He grabbed his jacket from one of the bar stools and made his way over to the door without another word, leaving Faraday and the squadron to continue on without him.

***

"Hello, Arch." Atkinson shot him a toothy grin. "Welcome back."

Cutter made his way off the C-47 parked on the runway, and gave a weak smile. "Freddy, why the hell am I back in England?"

"I thought you'd be happy to be home."

Cutter walked toward him and shook his hand. "I am. Just surprised."

"Well, you set them up for success, we'll send someone else in to finish your work." Atkinson motioned Cutter to the car.

"Where are we going?" Cutter asked as he clambered in.

"Back to headquarters; the old man wants to see you." Atkinson shut the car door and started the engine.

"What's the rush? Last time I got back you drove me straight to my flat and told me to bugger off for the day and come in in the morning."

"Well last time, you were a nervous wreck and skittish as a horse."

Cutter gave a glib shrug. "Fleeing Nazi-occupied Paris tends to do that to you."

So does killing a contact, Atkinson thought darkly as he started to drive back toward downtown London.

"I heard about the raid. What's the damage?"

Atkinson grunted unhappily, "Politically or militarily?"

"Politically."

"Apparently the raid's success far outweighed the cost of human life and material. The Prime Minister was so thrilled with the raid that Mountbatten promised him another one."

"Wait, why? Mountbatten already gave him a successful raid."

Atkinson shook his head and turned the car onto Piccadilly. "Technically, he didn't. Churchill knew Commander Jacobs was the brains behind the operation, and Mountbatten was unable to steal the credit. We had hoped that Saint-Nazaire would put a pin in this talk about raiding Dieppe."

"So Mountbatten wants a raid he can take credit for?"

"Precisely." Atkinson made another turn and brought the car onto Baker Street. "His argument for another raid is to show the Russians we intend to open a second front so they won't sue for peace with Germany."

"I swear to Christ politicians will lose this war for us," Cutter swore, his mind drifting back to Normandy. Claude, Talia, and Durand were capable and cautious they would do well, provided SOE continued to support them. He thought about Talia, his mind returning to the other night, and her harsh words. The memory was interrupted when Freddy brought the car to a halt next to the curb. Cutter got out of the car and looked around.

Cutter spotted one of the soldiers dressed in plain clothes guarding SOE and grinned. "Hello, Charlie."

Charlie nodded to him and continued to lean against the fence outside SOE, a shoulder holster for a pistol barely visible underneath his coat. "Arch, long time no see."

"How goes the war?"

"I'm not stuck in Dunkirk, so it's tops."

"Glad to hear one of us is happy."

Cutter and Atkinson entered the front door of SOE and made their way through the typing pool to a conference room at the back of the building, where they found Hambro alone reading a report with a pot of tea steaming on the table.

"Good morning, sir," Atkinson greeted as he sat down opposite Hambro.

"Morning, Freddy." Hambro looked up at Cutter. "Hello, Arch, how are you?"

"Good morning, sir. I'm well."

"Did Freddy bring you up to snuff in the car?"

"I did, sir," Atkinson answered before Cutter had a chance. Being home less than an hour, Freddy hoped to keep Cutter from causing a scene.

Cutter nodded agreement and walked over to a side table along the wall, grabbed an empty teacup from an assortment that sat on the table, and walked back over to them.

He sat down and poured from the kettle. He stirred, added milk, and tested it. Satisfied, he set the cup down and looked at Hambro. "Freddy mentioned the political consequences from the Saint-Nazaire raid."

Hambro scowled darkly. "Indeed, that damn fool Mountbatten is trying to move heaven and earth to ingratiate himself with the PM. He's promised another raid."

"Anything confirmed?"

"Dieppe is still the target. As requested, you will be taking over for Freddy as the control officer for operations in Brittany and Normandy."

Cutter frowned. The thought of Claude, Durand, and Talia developing intelligence on Dieppe without him left him with a hint of guilt. "What about Freddy?"

Hambro poured some more tea into his cup. "Freddy will be taking over as my number two. Honestly, Arch, I expected you to be thrilled at the idea of taking over as control."

"Jubilant, sir," Cutter said half-heartedly. "How many agents do we have in the field at the moment?"

"Two, code-named Talent and Fowler. Freddy will brief you over the next few days on what is required of you as you two conduct a turnover."

Cutter nodded and finished his cup of tea.

"Since most of your operations are still underway, I must remind you not to speak with anyone about them," Hambro said as he stood up.

"Understood." Cutter and Atkinson mimicked Hambro and stood up as well. Hambro nodded to them and walked out of the room.

Cutter put his hands in his pockets and looked at Atkinson. "So what now, Freddy?"

Atkinson shrugged and sat back down. "We can wait a day or two to start turnover. Why don't you go see your sister?"

Cutter gave a hollow chuckle. "Both she and my father can't stand me."

"Arch, you ought to see them. It's been, what? Eight months?"

"Lord almighty, you are such a mother hen. Why don't you go and see them if you're so concerned?"

"Your brother-in-law was shot down."

"Peter? When?"

"About a week ago."

Cutter drummed his fingers on the table absently. "Where?"

"A few miles south of Caen."

"Caen is an hour's drive from Quiberville. Why the fuck wasn't I told sooner! I might've been able to get him!"

Freddy's mustache drooped down in a frown, but he kept his tone level. "We didn't find out until a few days after. By the time we found out it was too late. Besides, you jolly well know that even if we did know we wouldn't have told you."

"Oh, and why's that?"

"Because you're too emotional. Arch, if you're going to work as a control officer you need to remain dispassionate when it comes to decision-making. Had I told

238

you about your brother-in-law, you would have gone galavanting off to save him, mission be damned."

Cutter chuckled darkly. "That's funny, Freddy, because I swear I was told the exact opposite the other day."

"Rough go with your contacts?"

"Just one of them."

"Woman?"

"How'd you know?"

Freddy chuckled. "You've never hit a rough patch in dealing with the Resistance, and we both know you couldn't entice a tart even if you were wearing a coat made out of fivers."

"Thanks for the vote of confidence."

"Arch, go see your sister and father. It'll do you some good. We can talk later."

Cutter grunted absently and gave Freddy an annoyed look. "Fine, I'll go see them, but I can already tell you it's going to be a bloody mess."

"Come back Thursday and we'll start discussing your new job."

***

Hambro left the SOE headquarters grumbling. As soon as he had finished talking with Cutter, his secretary had chased him down telling him Lord Mountbatten wanted to speak with him immediately. Hambro threw on his raincoat and strode out to his car in a slowly building rage.

"Where to, sir?" his driver, Sergeant Monmoth, asked.

"The War Office, please," Hambro groused, doing his best to not direct his anger at his driver, but failing.

Monmoth nodded and put the car in gear and took off.

Hambro leaned back in his seat and started to review a dossier he had with him. It wasn't a long drive from SOE to the War Office and Hambro barely finished reading a page before they arrived.

He closed the dossier and clambered out of the car. "Stay close," Hambro instructed before he strode into the War Office. He made his way to the Combined Operations offices wing and found Mountbatten's secretary waiting for him.

"Right this way, sir."

"Charles!" Mountbatten smiled from behind his desk. "Please, grab a seat. I'm finishing a reconnaissance report from Leigh-Mallory.

"Perhaps you can tell him to start sending me those reports," Hambro rumbled as he sat down.

"You don't get these?" Mountbatten's eyebrow's shot up in feigned surprise.

"No, after repeatedly requesting them." Hambro surveyed the office as he waited for Mountbatten to finish reading. After a few moments, Mountbatten set the report down and looked at Hambro. "So what do you know about Dieppe?"

"It's a hotbed for the Abwehr and Gestapo, and the headquarters to a German infantry division."

"And you have an agent in the region?"

Hambro shook his head. "Not at this time. He was pulled out the other day. We now have strong enough contacts with the Resistance cell there that they are capable of providing us with reports."

Mountbatten nodded and pulled a cigarette out of a gold case on his desk and lit it. "I'll be candid with you. With Dieppe being the target for this raid, we need everyone to put their best foot forward." He took a puff from his cigarette and blew out. "I need reliable information before we can do anything, and if at all possible have partisan assistance."

"The Resistance is already providing us with reliable intelligence and will be able to provide support as required." He looked Mountbatten in the eye. "Dickie, must we target Dieppe? This all feels rushed and disjointed. We have less than two months to plan and train for this raid and we still haven't identified all the players to participate."

"Nonsense," Mountbatten said dismissively with a wave of his hand, cigarette smoke whisking around his head with the motion. "The success of the Saint-Nazaire raid proved we are ready to attempt an amphibious raid on a grander scale."

Hambro took his glasses off, pulled a handkerchief from his pocket, and started to clean them, an action he often did when he was annoyed. "Most people, especially the commandos and sailors who participated in that raid, wouldn't consider the Saint-Nazaire raid a glowing success. Of the six hundred eleven servicemen who took part in the raid one hundred sixty-nine were killed and two hundred fifteen are now POWs," Hambro recited the numbers from memory and continued to clean his glasses, deliberately not making eye contact with Mountbatten as he did so. "If we continue to conduct raids like this, commanders will begin refusing any order to conduct a raid due to the suicidal tendency of them. I fear that as we continue to conduct raids with such high body counts the reputation and credibility of Combined Operations as well as SOE will be strained." Hambro inspected his glasses a final time and rested them back on his nose. His pale eyes locked with Mountbatten's. "Perhaps we should wait, or find a better target to raid."

Mountbatten's face stiffened and curled into a scowl. Not accustomed to opposition, the usual charm and grace seen by many evaporated as his facade cracked. "Hambro, I don't need a damn lecture on the basics of military tactics. This raid *is* happening. If you have a bloody problem with it I suggest you bring it up with the PM, who has already voiced his approval." Mountbatten's face had turned pink and a vein was throbbing near his temple. He took a moment to regain his composure and sat back in his chair. "Both you and Monty have been attempting to derail this raid from the start and I am damn well sick of it. I will not be questioned by some banker turned amateur spy. Have I made myself clear?"

Hambro smirked but kept his temper in check, not taking the bait.

Mountbatten shook his head slowly. When he spoke, his voice was low and deadly, "We will attack Dieppe head-on and we will hold it for Leigh-Mallory to engage the Luftwaffe when they come to interdict our forces. You will begin to gather intelligence and will provide a report in one month's time. Am I clear?"

Hambro slowly stood up from his chair, buttoned his suit coat, and nodded slowly. "I'll see what I can do." Then he turned and starting heading toward the door.

"Charles."

Hambro stopped at the door and slowly turned.

"I want a man on the ground gathering this intelligence, not some drunk Resistance fighter."

Hambro gritted his teeth but nodded. Without another word he turned and walked casually out of the office, making sure to look unfazed to Mountbatten. He silently trudged through the War Office as he weighed his options. He knew he would have to send Cutter back to Normandy and cursed himself for having to do it. He found his way to the car pool outside and strode to his car.

"Headquarters," he said curtly to Monmoth, and without another word clambered into the car and rode in silence.

***

Sharon Bailey sat, legs crossed, in a lounge chair and watched as her son, Liam, played with his Uncle Arthur. Cutter gently kicked him a soccer ball and moved closer so Liam could kick it back.

"What has Father been working on lately?" Cutter asked as he swung his leg out to stop the ball before it could roll down into the creek.

"No idea, to tell you the truth. The military sent a few naval officers down a few months ago and asked him and a few other professors to help on a special project."

Cutter nodded silently. He suspected his father was helping to break Nazi codes. He took a step back and kicked the ball high into the air. Liam giggled in delight and took off after it.

"Arch, do be careful with him. I don't want him falling down."

"Relax, Sharon he's still a wee lad. If he falls he doesn't have far to go to hit the ground." Cutter walked over to the lawn chair next to her and sat down. "I heard about what happened to Peter. I'm sorry."

"We heard he bailed out in time and received word that he's in a POW camp somewhere in Germany. I just hope he's alright," Sharon said bitterly. Her eyes started to water and she quickly turned away.

Cutter leaned over and put a comforting hand on his sister's shoulder. "Peter will be fine. I know he will be."

"I just hope he comes home soon."

Liam waved at the two of them and backed up to kick the ball with all his might. With a running start he punted the ball into the air.

"Nice kick, Liam!" Cutter exulted. He quickly jumped up and picked the boy up around the waist and put him over his shoulder and spun him around.

"Easy there, Arthur," Simon Cutter called as he walked over to the other lounge chair and sat down opposite his daughter.

"Daddy, everything alright? That was a long phone call."

"Nothing to worry about darling," the elder Cutter soothed. "Peter Hilton, you remember him from when you two were children? He called asking me to help him with something."

"What?"

"He didn't say," Simon said guardedly. Cutter suspected he was lying but didn't say anything. Quickly changing the subject, Simon looked up at his son in curiosity. "Arthur, I must say that I was surprised when you called to say you were coming up for a few days. It's been months since we heard from you. What is it that you said you are doing?"

Cutter set Liam down and wiped the grass off his trousers. "I'm working in the War Office."

"Doing what?"

"Antiquity protection."

"The bloody hell is that?"

"I'm working with the War Office to help identify targets the RAF can bomb that are not of historical significance."

"You're telling them what they can and can't bomb?" A hint of annoyance pervaded his sister's voice.

"Indeed."

"Nice and safe, away from any danger."

"Sharon, be civil," their father said, though not entirely earnestly.

"I've had to go on a few bombing missions. Nearly been shot down once or twice," Cutter lied.

"Really? Good God, man."

"I took part in one of the Berlin bombings. Actually ended up manning one of the guns on my Lancaster when the gunner got hit."

Both Simon and Sharon looked at Cutter but said nothing. Liam motioned to Cutter, asking to be picked up again. Cutter forced a smile and picked him up. "Ooof, he's getting big."

Sharon's demeanor changed when she watched her son giggle and laugh as Cutter spun him around again. "He'll be as big as his father, no doubt. Have you met anyone in London?"

Cutter hesitated, the memory of Talia's last words clouding his mind. "Uh, yeah, I did actually."

"Oh? Tell us about her!"

Cutter shrugged thinking about their night together and how he had left things. "Not much to tell."

"What does she do?" Sharon probed.

"She's a musician. Plays the violin."

"How did you meet?"

"Met during a bombing raid, bumped into each other down in one of the shelters."

"Is it serious?" Cutter's father asked.

Cutter's mind immediately snapped to the memory of her pointing a pistol at his chest. He suspected if he ever saw her again it would be in a similar situation.

"It's complicated."

Sharon could tell he didn't want to talk about it and stopped asking questions. Cutter was relieved when their father changed the subject to the Prime Minister's recent speech.

Bored with the conversation, Liam scampered off chasing after the ball after kicking it too far down the hill toward the creek.

"Arch, please make sure he doesn't fall in!"

Cutter nodded, anxious to get away. He ran after his nephew, feeling somewhat guilty about how limited his relationship was with his family, unable to hold a normal conversation with them without feeling like he was on the defensive. Why hadn't he come back to see them sooner? Almost every time he had come back to England after a mission he had refused to. It wasn't their distaste in the fact that he hadn't picked up a rifle to defend the island that bothered him. In truth, he loved playing this little ruse with them. The fact that they never bothered to ask more in-depth questions other than the shallow "What have you been up to?" or "Where are you living?" annoyed him.

Sharon asking him about his love life was actually the first time she had ever taken a genuine interest in Cutter's life, and maybe that was why he didn't want to talk about it. He wasn't used to sharing his life with his family.

Father had always been obsessed with his work, and when Cutter's mother died, so too did the only parental figure Cutter had acknowledged in the household. With her death, Sharon had turned to Peter; and Cutter, like his father, had turned to his studies. Maybe that was why he was so absent on the emotional plane.

Cutter watched absently as Liam struggled to pull the ball out of the creek. The water was only a few inches deep but enough to soak his trousers.

"Let me help you, Liam."

"Thanks, Uncle Arthur!"

Cutter smiled and balanced on a pair of semi-submerged stones and scooped the ball up and handed it to Liam. "Run back up to your mum. I'll be right behind you." He jumped back onto the grass just as Liam took off back up the hill. Cutter watched with a smile as the boy's short legs propelled him as fast as he could up the hill. *Would my family like Talia?* Cutter couldn't help but wonder.

Getting on the C-47 and flying out of Normandy had been difficult. Cutter had wanted nothing more than to prove Talia wrong and show that he wasn't a feckless English spy. The more he ambled around Oxford the more he realized he should have opened up to her. He had tried to talk to a few girls at the pubs around the university but each one had gone sour. There weren't many women Cutter could meet that had similar life experiences. As Olivier, Cutter felt more like himself with Talia than he did back here in Oxford with his family.

***

Talia stared out into the darkness and silently
wondered what Claude would say if he knew what she was
doing. *To hell with him.* She fumed. It was because of his
indecision that she was forced to this course. If no one else
was going to save them, then she would.

Since Olivier's departure, her status in the
Resistance had reverted back to messenger girl, a task
beneath her. After working with Olivier she had shown a
capacity for sabotage, assassination, and ambushes. She
handled a Sten well, and she understood the tactics of
conducting an ambush better than most other Resistance
members. But still she was a messenger. She drummed her
fingers on the steering wheel of the truck and weighed her
options. It wasn't too late to turn back. She could return
Durand's truck and be home before anyone was the wiser.
No. She needed to do this, if not for the Resistance, then for
herself.

Claude and Durand couldn't see past the fact that
she was a woman, and she hated them for it. But most of all
she hated Olivier. He had given her hope. Before he had
arrived she had been resigned to her place in the
Resistance, but with him he had shown her how to do more
for her country. She loathed him for sleeping with her that
night and despised him for the cold treatment he gave her
after, but she couldn't deny he was a skilled provocateur.
She clambered out of the truck and looked around. It was
midnight, and other than the sounds of frogs and crickets in
the night it was quiet.

Talia wondered if Olivier would approve of her
decision. The surprise arrival of the SS had forced her into
action. They had come without warning, replacing the

complacent troops in Amsel's patrols and had taken over the search and hunt for the Resistance. In the last week, the SS had seized four weapons caches around Dieppe. Durand and Claude called the seizures lucky, but Talia disagreed. In less than a week, more than half of the Resistance's supplies had been seized and destroyed. Talia suspected the Gestapo's capture and interrogation of members of the Dieppe cells had borne fruit. She begged Claude to move the remaining equipment, but he refused saying it was too risky. So now here she was, in the dead of night doing what Claude should have.

She eyed the decrepit farmhouse warily. *It could be a trap.* Talia reached for her pistol and reassured herself. *It doesn't matter, I have to try.* She cautiously approached the house, straining her eyes and ears for any sign of danger. As she approached the front door, an owl hooted in warning from the caved-in roof and went flying as she opened the door. *He wouldn't be here if this was an ambush.* She walked into the house and it took a moment for her eyes to adjust to the darkness. The room was bare, save for a few rafters that had collapsed and now stood leaning against the ragged hole in the ceiling. The moon glistened through the hole, providing just enough light for Talia to see. She quickly walked to the far side of the room and found what she was looking for. A small finger hole was barely visible in one of the floorboards. She quickly pulled it up and started to pull out the contents of the secret compartment. The ammo cans were heavy, as were the burlap sacks that contained a number of rifles and machine guns. She struggled under the weight but managed to move the entire cache to the truck in three trips. As soon as the last sack was loaded, Talia hopped behind the wheel of the truck and started the engine. She had two more caches she needed to get to before the end of the night and needed to move quickly.

***

CHAPTER 11

STRANGE BEDFELLOWS

Captain Malcolm Parker shifted his weight awkwardly, feeling somewhat similar to how he felt when he had first arrived in Falmouth for the Saint-Nazaire raid.

"Feeling alright, sir?" Parker's company first sergeant, Craig Adams, asked.

"Just uncomfortable with the lack of direction we were given before coming here."

Adams grunted, "I'm of the same mind, command gave us dog shit for information for what we're doing here."

"Agreed."

Adams looked around in distaste. "So this is Newhaven?" He eyed the muddy campgrounds that were now their home. "Was it like this the last time you were with the commandos?"

"Last time we stayed in an inn."

"Well, I think I'll poke around and see if there's some similar accommodations we can get. One thing I learned during the Great War was never use what the Army gives you if you can get something better."

"You're going to get along great with the commandos, I suspect."

Adams clapped his hands together in finality. "Right, well I'll have the boys start nosing around and see what they can find for the company."

"Make sure we aren't near any of the Canadians. I don't want our boys being mistaken for the hired help and put on a working party like that major tried to do this morning."

Adams smiled mischievously, his Southern drawl more pronounced than usual as he spoke, "Oh don't worry, sir. I'll make sure we aren't with the general population."

Parker smiled and scanned the campgrounds a final time. "We need to find the No. 4 commando CO, Lieutenant Colonel Fraser. I suspect he's around here somewhere." As he scanned the camp his eyes widened in surprise at the person he saw striding toward them.

"I don't believe it; you're supposed to be dead!"

"News of my death has been greatly exaggerated," Captain Carver said with a chuckle. He extended his hand to Parker but quickly was enveloped in a huge bear hug by Parker's much larger frame.

"Get back you bloody giant! I can't breathe!"

"They told me you were killed." Parker let him go and looked him over, noticing a large scar running up the side of his neck to his chin.

"Makes sense," Carver reasoned. "We got cut off from Newman when he was making his last stand. We tried to help them make a break for the coast, but I ended up losing more than half my troop in the process. Me and three others were able to escape north, and with a little luck linked up with some Maquis fighters who were wondering what we were doing. They moved me around for a few weeks before being able to get me back here."

"How'd you get this?" Parker pointed at the scar.

"Took a chunk of shrapnel to the neck. Damn miracle it didn't kill me. Lost a lot of blood, but no arteries or veins were severed, miraculously. I lost consciousness after meeting up with the Resistance and was out for a few days. I woke up in a Resistance safe house."

"Well, I'm glad we have you back. Do you know why we're here?"

A wicked smile spread across Carver's face. "Command wants us to do another raid."

"Surely you can't be serious."

"Afraid so, old boy. The last raid was so successful they wanted another."

"So that's why my company is here?"

Carver nodded, noticing his captain's bars for the first time. "Congratulations on the promotion."

"Thanks. Happened when I returned from that goat rope of a raid. Where are we raiding this time?"

"Not sure. I've spent the last month training a new troop. They sent me to No. 4 Commando when I got back, but I managed to bring Tarbor and Callum with me."

"They're here?"

"I pulled a few strings."

"Just like old times," Parker chuckled. He looked over at Adams and noticed the confusion on his face. "First Sergeant, this is Captain Carver of the British Commandos. He was part of the raiding force that hit Saint-Nazaire."

"Pleasure to meet you, sir."

"Likewise." Carver shook his hand and looked Adams up and down. His eyes locked on his utility belt. "That's a handy relic from the last war."

Adams looked down and gripped the handle of the trench knife on his belt. It was a wicked-looking knife, with a spiked guard that covered the handle that could serve as a set of brass knuckles. A spike jutted out menacingly from the bottom of the hilt, giving the knife all the more capabilities in a close-quarters fight.

"Came in handy in the Argonne Forest."

Carver nodded. "My father served in the Great War as well. He was at Somme."

"Jesus, I'm twice the age of both of you. I'm getting too old for this shit."

Carver laughed and motioned toward a nearby inn. "We better get this geezer indoors before the weather affects his arthritis." In typical English fashion, the weather had taken a turn for the worse in a matter of minutes. Storm clouds were rolling in and the faint smell of rain was in the air.

"Call me a geezer again, I dare you."

"So what *do* you know?" Parker asked as they walked into the tavern and sat down in a booth.

Carver shrugged as Adams walked up to the bar to get a round. "I know the boss was in a meeting a few weeks ago where Lieutenant Colonel Churchill, the head of the SOE, and Montgomery himself all argued for this raid to be canceled."

Adams returned to the booth and handed each of them a pint.

"What can you tell us about Lieutenant Colonel Fraser?"

"Well, he's formally known as Lord Lovat, and he's bloody brilliant. He has extensive experience leading raids; commanded a few in Norway. He hates the military politics and has done a good job of shielding No. 4 Commandos from it. We'll do well with him. He's doing his best to make sure we succeed even if this raid fails."

Adams nodded. "So why are we going through with this raid if General Montgomery doesn't even want to do it?"

"Apparently Lord Mountbatten, the head of Combined Operations and the commandos' boss, planned this raid without telling anyone until after he gave it to the Prime Minister. The Prime Minister loved the idea so much that he told your President and the Canadian Prime Minister about it and they immediately agreed to participate before anyone in the military was told about it."

"Jesus," Adams whistled. "So we're doing this raid just because the politicians like the idea."

"More or less."

"So it's a big raid?" Parker toyed with his pint glass as he spoke.

"What makes you think that?"

Parker looked up and extended his arms out. "Look around. The amount of tents, trucks, and people in Newhaven indicate this is going to be bigger than Saint-Nazaire."

"It's going to be huge. I've seen tanks rolling into Newhaven and the RAF is constantly sending people down here for planning meetings."

Adams exchanged a look with Parker. "Are we sure it isn't the invasion?"

Parker shook his head. "The U.S. Army wouldn't send just fifty rangers if we were invading the continent. They'd have sent everyone."

Carver shrugged and took a sip from his pint. "I suppose it doesn't matter. We're in the thick of it now."

***

"Have a good holiday, sir?" Cutter's newly appointed secretary asked.

"It was marvelous, Holly." Cutter walked over to the coat rack and hung his jacket, insincerity dripping from his voice.

Holly nodded in understanding, missing his sarcasm. "It's important to see family during these hard times."

Cutter didn't say anything to correct his meaning. "Any messages?" He wasn't entirely sure what else to do with his secretary, since it was his first day on the job and Freddy had only given him an office prior to his departure to see his sister and father.

"Mr. Atkinson called; asked if you could come speak with him once you got in."

Cutter nodded, and without a word slipped back out into the hallway and headed toward Freddy's office.

"What is it, Freddy?"

Freddy looked up from a pile of documents in annoyance. "Can you for once just let my secretary do her job and let you in?"

"Sorry, old boy."

"I doubt you are, but I'm glad you came. How was your holiday? Did you see your sister and father?"

"Yes, it was as expected."

Freddy nodded sympathetically, understanding his meaning. Cutter was similar to a number of agents SOE recruited. An unstable childhood and certain personality traits often laid the foundation for a successful spy. Freddy wasn't sure why, but suspected it was easier for those types of people to form attachments in the field and sever them quickly and immediately when it was time to depart or put the mission before a contact. He had seen many reports about spies being killed because they refused to leave or finish the mission at the risk of their contacts. It was loyalty and it was indeed admirable, but SOE wasn't in it for the moral high ground, Atkinson thought darkly. They were here to defeat the Nazis, winning the war was the War Office's problem.

"Hambro went and saw Mountbatten while you were gone." With a wave of his hand he motioned Cutter to a chair and handed him a folder.

"Oh? What did that fool want with Charlie?" Cutter sat down and opened the folder. As he started to peruse it his eyes widened after reading the first sentence. "Initial reports based on aerial reconnaissance show that a raid on Dieppe, France, is *highly* feasible and capable of providing the RAF with a concentrated focal point to engage the German Luftwaffe within range of No. 11 Group's Airfields . . ." He stopped reading aloud and looked at Atkinson. "What is this horseshit?"

"Latest brilliant idea from the head shed up the road."

"Good, let's send them instead of the commandos." Cutter looked up in thought for a moment. "I suppose I better radio Claude and start having them put a concentrated effort on Dieppe."

Atkinson nodded absently but held his tongue.

Cutter shook his head in disbelief. "God, I still can't believe they're going to go forward with it."

"It was the reason we sent you to Normandy."

"I know that, but we barely were able to investigate Dieppe. The Gestapo and Abwehr killed or captured every Resistance cell we sent in."

"I know. Hambro assumed with Montgomery's help they would be able to kill the raid before it reached

Churchill for approval, but Mountbatten outmaneuvered them."

"Freddy, we don't know anything about Dieppe. Quiberville, Le Havre, Christ even Cherbourg would be better targets at this time."

"It's out of SOE's hands."

"Does the PM know that Combined Operations is planning in a bubble?"

Freddy absently shuffled a sheaf of papers. "One might say that is par for the course in the War Office."

"Christ. Claude will not be happy about this."

Freddy leaned forward in his chair and put his hands together in front of him, much like a doctor would when preparing to deliver some rather terrible news. "I'm sorry, Arch. Hambro did his best to try and dissuade him from the raid, but Mountbatten has already sold this idea to the PM and Churchill is onboard with it."

Cutter's eyes narrowed as the realization dawned on him. "You don't want me to radio Claude, do you?"

"Hambro wants you back on the continent as soon as possible."

Cutter stared absently at the map behind Freddy's desk for a long moment. He opened his mouth to speak, but closed it, taking a moment to control his temper. A flurry of emotions swirled through his head as he struggled with the news. *You damn fool.* Cutter mused. *Did you really think they would keep you out of the field for the rest of the war?* The realization dawned on him slowly but the revelation didn't surprise him. He had beaten the odds, survived the life expectancy curve. The things he knew he couldn't just teach, so why would they pull him from fieldwork? His eyes drifted over the map and locked on Dieppe. "Why the hell did you even bother pulling me out?"

"We weren't expecting to have to send you back."

Cutter nodded but stayed silent.

"We will make contact with Claude and coordinate your insertion. Go ahead and begin planning to stay a while. While you're there, we'll begin setting up more frequent drops with the Lysander squadron so you'll be receiving continuous support to arm the Resistance."

Cutter nodded in resignation. The thought of going back didn't bother him as much as the idea of facing Talia again.

"Arch, for what it's worth, I'm truly sorry."

"Doesn't matter now, old boy." Cutter gave a rueful smile. "You and I both know, an office job wasn't ever going to be a permanent position for me."

Freddy smiled thinly. "Not with all the good you do in the field."

***

"You had no right!" Durand roared, slamming his fists down on the table.

"You were going to let them make off with all of our weapons unchallenged," Talia countered.

"We would have gotten more from the English."

"And wasted three months of work to build up those caches."

"That wasn't your decision to make! I'm in charge of our stockpiles, not you!"

Talia eyed Durand coolly, unfazed by his rage.

"Olivier is no longer here, which means you no longer have a say in our decision-making. You may have had his ear since you had his balls, but that is not the case now."

"Olivier listened to me because of my good ideas, not because of what is between my legs."

Claude had been sitting at the far end of the table, silently watching as the two argued. As annoyed as he was with Talia for circumventing both Durand and him, a small part of him was grateful that she had. "Talia, I think what Durand is trying to say is that you had a special place in the decision-making process because of your relationship with Olivier. With his departure you've been relegated back to your courier duties. Making a unilateral decision to seize the caches, however well-intentioned, was wrong."

The table creaked as Durand leaned halfway across it, his face inches from Talia's. His voice was a low rumble as he towered over her petite frame. "Where are the caches now?"

"Safe."

"Tell us where."

Talia gave a thin smile, undaunted by Durand's attempted intimidation. If she wanted to advance and move past being a courier she had to change how Claude and Durand viewed her. She had leverage, and as soon as she told them where the caches were, she'd be right back where she started. "Let's clear the air, shall we? If it hadn't been for me, those caches that I took would have been seized by the SS. We all know that the SS raided those locations this morning. You aren't mad that I stole them, you're mad that I disobeyed you."

"You little—"

Claude raised a hand and stopped Durand. "What do you want, Talia?"

Talia deliberately took her time and sat down in the chair across from Claude. "I've shown that I'm just as capable as any other Resistance member here. I want to be treated as an equal. I want a voice in making the decisions."

"If we do this, you'll turn over the weapons?"

"I'll give you what you need when you need it."

Durand glowered at her. "And if we refuse?"

"I alone know where the caches are hidden now. If you don't give in to my demands, and keep me as a courier, you'll never get them back."

A hint of a smile creased Claude's face. Her negotiation skills were reminiscent of her uncle. She had learned much from Francois, that much was evident. Perhaps he had misjudged her. He looked over at Durand. His temper had gotten the best of him. Durand would hear none of it. "What's to stop me from taking you into the cellar and forcing the truth out of you?"

"Me," Claude said simply. "Talia has shown her daring and cunning. She risked her own life to save our equipment. What she asks isn't unreasonable."

"Claude, you can't."

"I can and I will." Claude turned to Talia and extended his hand. "You have a deal. Now can we have the machine guns?"

***

"Sir, I'd like to introduce Captain Malcolm Parker of the U.S. Army Rangers," Carver said, as Parker extended his hand to the No. 4 Commanding Officer.

Lord Lovat studied Parker keenly and took his outstretched hand. "It's about time the Americans joined the fight." A toothy smile protruded from underneath his tidy mustache.

"Been here since Saint-Nazaire, sir," Parker shot back, bristling at the challenge.

"A pleasure to meet you and happy to have you with us. How do you like No. 4 Commandos HQ?" Lord Lovat motioned to the entirety of the tavern.

"A real haven for professionals in the art of war."

"Speaking of military professionals, Captain Carver has said nothing but good things about you."

"Captain Carver is being generous, sir," Parker shot back and quickly changed the subject. "I've been told that my company is to be broken up."

"Straight to business. Yes, we will be dividing your forces and integrating them in with the other troops of No. 4 as well as No. 2 Commandos."

"With respect, I'd like to voice my opposition to that."

"I sympathize with your opposition and agree. However, powers much higher up than you and I made that decision and we must obey."

Parker grunted, but remained silent.

Lord Lovat handed Parker a pint of beer. "I'm giving you command of B Troop. As it happens, I am short a commander. You, your first sergeant, and a few more of your rangers will be attached to No. 4 Commandos; the remainder will be sent to the other commando teams."

Parker took a sip from the beer and nodded. He wasn't happy about the decision but he already knew there wasn't anything he could do about it. Although it wasn't ideal, he had complete trust that his two lieutenants could handle things on their own, which was why he had decided to send them both to the other unit. Both he and Adams had agreed that by sending them together they could watch each other's backs and better ensure the safety of the rangers with them. It would be Adams's and his job to do the same with No. 4.

"Sir, I'd like to augment Parker's troop with two of my men. Captain Parker is familiar with them, and they can help him get to know the troop. Sergeant Callum and Corporal Tarbor both served with him during the Saint-Nazaire raid."

"That's awfully generous of you."

Carver shot Parker a wink. "Just trying to set Captain Parker up for success, sir."

"I agree. Have them transferred over tomorrow morning and they can begin training in earnest."

"Will do, sir."

Parker nodded his thanks and looked over at the tavern entrance as another commando walked through the door. He was a tall, lean individual with ghoulish features.

"Tom, nice of you to join us. Pull up a chair." Lord Lovat waved him over and motioned to the bartender for another ale. "Captain Parker, this is Major Rackham, my executive officer."

Major Rackham hobbled over to the bar, favoring his left leg, and sat down hard on a stool. "Nice to meet you." He nodded to Parker, but didn't offer his hand.

"Everything alright, Tom?"

"I was running through Lieutenant Boyce's mountaineering class this morning on the crag of rocks down by the harbor and busted my knee on my way down the rock face."

The bartender handed him an ale and Major Rackham nodded his thanks. "If we're going to have to scale any cliffs, it's going to be damn tricky, especially in the dark."

"I suppose we'll need to start getting the lads used to playing in the dark."

"My thoughts exactly, sir."

Parker looked at them in confusion. "What exactly is the mission?"

"You'll know soon enough," Lord Lovat said with finality, signaling that the topic was not up for discussion. He took a sip from his glass and squared himself with Parker. "Now, I believe all business of the day is finished. On to more serious and stimulating conversation. Captain Parker, can you please explain to me the finer points of American baseball?"

Parker cracked an easy grin, hiding the disappointment that he wasn't going to get any more information about the raid. "Well, sir, it's a little different from cricket . . ."

***

Cutter hated flying; more importantly he hated flying in Lysanders. The cramped cockpit of the small aircraft seemed like it was designed solely to make the passenger vomit as much as possible. Cutter had barely eaten before the flight yet was amazed by how much had come up the past three times, and was grateful he had packed extra airsickness bags.

"We're almost there," Cutter's pilot, Flight Lieutenant Ives called. "Should be landing soon."

"Are you sure?"

"No! Remember when I told you this flight would be a piece of cake? Well, I lied. These are the worst conditions I've ever flown in! For all I know we're over Germany!"

"I didn't need to know that."

"There's a fog over the landing zone, but I think I can land." Ives started to descend and begin the landing cycle. The whole time, Cutter clenched the handles next to his seat until his hands hurt.

"Oh Christ!" Ives cried and pulled back sharply on the stick, pushing Cutter back into his seat. *This is it, I'm going to die in this fucking plane.* The plane hit the ground hard and bounced. The engine started to sputter and Cutter felt the plane push forward as Ives pushed down on the nose and pulled back on the throttle to keep the Lysander from ballooning. They started to slow and Ives started to apply the brakes.

"Another happy landing," Ives called cheerily. "Now get off my plane."

"Sod this." Cutter quickly undid his straps and opened the hatch and climbed out. He tapped the glass and quickly cleared the Lysander as Ives increased power to the engine and started to taxi for takeoff.

Cutter cleared the Lysander and watched as the silhouette of the aircraft faded into the blackness of the night. "I miss my desk job already." Cutter looked around, searching eagerly for a familiar face.

"Olivier, is that you?" a voice called from the darkness.

"*Oui.* Durand?"

Durand appeared out of the black. "I was wondering if they were sending you back."

"Can't get rid of me that easily." Cutter hefted his suitcase and approached Durand.

"Come, we must hurry. The noise of the plane will no doubt draw out Amsel and his thugs." Durand led Cutter through the field to a dirt road where a horse-drawn cart was waiting.

"No car?"

"Much more conspicuous. This is better." Durand motioned for Cutter to get in the back. Cutter paused as he started to climb in when he heard the sound of clucking chickens.

"How is this less bloody conspicuous?"

Durand said nothing but moved past Cutter and fumbled around in the back of the wagon till he found what he was looking for. His fingers caught on an edge of the bottom of the wagon and he pulled. A portion of the bed of the wagon lifted up to reveal a secret compartment underneath where the wagon driver sat. Durand motioned for Cutter to get in.

The compartment was small, and even for Cutter's slight frame he struggled to fit. His suitcase would have to remain out in the open, but he managed to fit his entire body in the compartment before Durand quickly closed it and cracked the reins to get his mare moving.

"This is how I die," Cutter mumbled as he lay motionless in the cramped dark compartment for what seemed like an hour. Every time he heard a commotion or a car drive by, he tensed, half expecting to be stopped and searched, but it never happened.

When the wagon finally came to a stop and the compartment opened, the sun was starting to creep over the horizon.

Cutter struggled out of the compartment and shielded his eyes as they adjusted to the light. He looked around and struggled to get his bearings.

He slowly realized they were on the outskirts of Quiberville at Madame Renault's house. Cutter dusted the dirt from his trousers and stretched his legs before he noticed Talia and Claude standing next to the house along with two other men Cutter didn't recognize.

Cutter stopped stretching and walked over to them.

Claude smiled and extended a hand. "Olivier, I thought we had seen the last of you."

Cutter smirked and took the outstretched hand. "Oh, you'll find that I show up at the most peculiar of times." Cutter's eyes found their way to Talia's and he grimaced at the disinterested look she gave him. She was just as riveting as the first time Cutter had seen her, but the stony look on her face said enough about how she felt about his arrival. "Clearly, I could've been gone longer."

Talia ignored his comment. Crossing her arms and jutting her chin out, she motioned to the briefcase. "What did you bring us?"

"What do you mean?"

"We need munitions and explosives. Did you bring any?" Claude explained, motioning for everyone to go inside.

Cutter shook his head. As they moved into the cottage, he followed Talia inside and noticed the bulge of a pistol under her sweater lodged in the waistband of her trousers. *Didn't see that before.*

The safe house was very basic in accommodations, with an armchair in the corner and a small love seat along the wall. The group of Resistance fighters shuffled into the kitchen where there was a large enough table for them all to sit around.

"So what are you doing here?" Claude sat down at the head of the table, and motioned for Cutter to take a seat next to him.

"I'm back to further develop intelligence and to start sabotaging German operations in the area."

"What makes you so sure we need help?" Talia challenged.

Cutter looked at her but said nothing. He noticed Durand and Claude exchange glances. Clearly, his arrival was less than welcomed. He couldn't blame them for the lukewarm welcome, but he didn't understand the hostility.

"Did something happen while I was gone?" He looked around the table with a hint of annoyance, attempting to put them on the defensive. "Last I was here we established supply drops as well as a set communications line across the channel. What's changed?"

Talia shrugged. "You left us."

"I was only gone half a month."

Durand cleared his throat uneasily and smiled diplomatically at Cutter. "Olivier, we are thankful that you have returned, but your abrupt departure and return is . . . suspicious."

"Suspicious?" Cutter parroted. "What the hell is suspicious about my return?"

"Why are you back? The only reason we can think of is that your military is about to conduct another operation." Claude turned and motioned to the rest of the Resistance members. "Naturally, we will assist, but after your abrupt departure last time we were left to suffer the Nazis wrath after those raids we conducted."

268

Cutter ran a hand through his sandy blond hair in frustration. He didn't have time to rebuild relationships. He forced himself to appear amicable and nodded his head in understanding. "What happened?"

"The Gestapo has been taking a more aggressive interest in Quiberville. People are disappearing." Durand sat down on the other side of Cutter. "People are being sent to Dieppe and haven't come back."

"Who is taking them?"

"The SS."

Mention of the Schutzstaffel sent a chill down Cutter's spine. "The SS are here?" It was one thing to have the Gestapo and Abwehr ambling around with the regular German army; it was another if they called the SS in. They were only called on if the Gestapo wasn't getting the necessary results with soldiers from the army.

Durand nodded silently.

"Why? When?" Questions filled Cutter's head.

"We think they're after our cell."

Cutter turned and looked at Claude. "Why do you think that?"

"They've recruited a handful of officers from the local ranks. Oberleutnant Amsel was recruited by them and promoted to Obersturmführer. He's been aggressively pursuing spies and Resistance members."

Cutter nodded. "I'm sure he jumped at the opportunity for more power and authority." He looked over at Talia. Her blank stare and expressionless features reminded Cutter of the Greek and Roman busts at the Ashmolean. He had expected a rough reception, just not one this chilled.

"We are happy you are here," Claude said earnestly, "but will you be leaving just as suddenly this time?"

Cutter put his hands on the table and opened them palms up, it was time to be honest. "I don't know. I need your help and I need more information on what is going on in Dieppe."

A grunt rumbled in the back of Claude's throat. "You're asking a lot without giving much back." He crossed his arms, "What do we get in return?"

"What do you need?"

"Explosives, firearms, mortars if possible." Claude handed Cutter a handwritten list.

Cutter took it and gave it a cursory look. He saw grenades, Bren machine guns, rifles, and a twenty-millimeter mortar on the list. It wouldn't be too difficult to get, but he'd have to radio back to Atkinson for it. "I can get you this."

"You do realize how dangerous Dieppe is, right?" Durand shot Claude a nasty look as he spoke. "We've sent people there before and every time they were either captured or killed. The last three cells we've set up there were destroyed."

"I know, but I wouldn't be asking if it wasn't vital." A dirty thought entered his mind as he spoke; he was behaving no differently than Hambro had when he persuaded Cutter to come back to Normandy.

Durand nodded slowly, uncertainty dripping from his voice, as he said, "I don't know how, but we'll do what needs to be done."

Cutter looked at the group of Resistance fighters and wondered what had happened in his absence. Something wasn't right. Durand had never been this confrontational with Claude, and Claude looked strung out. Was this all because of the SS?

Claude rubbed the bridge of his nose in resignation. "We'll get started immediately." He gestured to the two other Resistance members in the room. The pair of them nodded and departed the safe house.

Claude turned and looked at Cutter. "What are we going to do with you?" He leaned back in his chair and crossed his arms, deep in thought. "I think it would be best if you continued to stay with Talia." He gave Talia a questioning look. "What do you think?"

Talia eyed Cutter with a sanitized disinterest. "We need to keep his cover intact. It makes sense for him to stay with me."

"Very well, I think we have everything we need to get started. Olivier, why don't you come by the bakery this evening and we can discuss our plans further."

Cutter nodded and stood up as Claude and Durand moved to leave. Claude clapped a hand on his shoulder as he walked by. "It's nice to have you back, Olivier."

Cutter smiled weakly and turned back to Talia. She eyed him coolly.

"I suppose I'm the last person you want to see, let alone live with."

Talia eyed Cutter with a hint of annoyance but kept her facial expression set in a combination of disinterest and aloofness.

"So you're a full-on Resistance fighter now?" Cutter pursued, changing topics.

"What makes you think that?"

Cutter walked over to a cabinet and grabbed the tea tin. "Just that bulge in your lower back. Walther?"

"Sauer 38H."

"Small, easy to hide. Preferred for assassinations."

Talia's face remained expressionless.

"Did you start carrying that after we ambushed that supply convoy or is that more recent?"

"Does it matter?"

"Of course it does. Has Amsel been bothering you more?"

"It's not for Amsel."

"Who is it for then?"

"You," she said matter-of-factly, her voice betraying nothing. "If there's one thing you taught me before you left, it's that when it comes down to your survival, you will do anything. Therefore, you can't be trusted."

Cutter eyed her warily. His stomach tightened and he struggled to keep his face blank. He knew it was unlikely, but in his heart he had hoped their reunion would be a little more amicable. The sanitized disinterest Talia exuded toward him was like a dagger to his heart. All those months trying to keep her at arms length. Cutter had realized it may have been the safe play for Olivier Deschamps, but it was tearing him apart. "Well, I hope to change that quickly."

CHAPTER 12
Bedlam

Parker checked his watch, the luminous tritium on the hands showing it was 11:30 at night. Carver was late for the rendezvous. If he didn't show up soon, Parker would have to move without him. The lads were anxious; Parker could feel it in the air. This was the fifth night exercise in as many days, and every time Lord Lovat had thrown a surprise into the exercise for them to react to. *Was Carver's tardiness the wrinkle?*

Parker scanned the woods they occupied, his eyes darting back and forth, using his periphery vision to watch for movement. He had thirty minutes to seize the objective.

First Sergeant Adams crouched next to him. "Fox Troop is late, sir." he said, his Southern drawl smushing the words together, in a sharp contrast to the British accents of the fellow members of Baker Troop.

"I know. We need to make a move."

"What're you thinking?"

Parker looked around. They sat at the edge of the woods. Right in front of them was a clearing that led up to a farmer's house. He had studied the map of the area extensively prior to the exercise and knew that on the opposite side of the field from where they were was a cottage and a barn. Their objective was an individual inside the house.

"We've been here nearly an hour, and we're almost out of time." Parker bit his lip as his mind raced. "This doesn't feel right."

"What part? The fact that our target is in a large, open area, or the fact that we have seen no indication of activity around it?"

"Both." Parker toyed with the shoulder strap of his Thompson submachine gun, a nervous tic he had developed since Saint-Nazaire. "Screw it. It's a new moon; no one will be able to see us without firing off a flare. Hold here with Carter's and Murray's teams to provide machine gun and sniper cover as required. I'll take Tarbor's, Ferguson's, and Callum's teams. If we take contact, light them up and we'll pull back."

"Will do, sir."

"We'll move in five. Go." Parker duckwalked toward Callum, Ferguson, and Tarbor. "Your teams on me. We're going in to seize the objective. Ferguson, you will be our base. Halfway to the objective, deploy your team to provide cover. Watch the tree line. Tarbor you will be the support team. Deploy your team fifteen meters before the objective, cover the assault team's entry. Callum, your team is with me. We'll seize the objective. Questions?"

As expected, there were none. They had practiced this sort of exercise dozens of times both at night and during the day. They could do this sort of thing in their sleep.

"Step off in three from right here. Go."

The three team leaders dispersed to go brief their teams. Parker checked his watch. They had twenty minutes to seize the objective. Where the hell was Carver? He was late, but it didn't matter. Part of being a ranger was being able to improvise; that's what he was doing.

He scanned the darkness one last time, the hairs on his neck standing on end.

The three teams converged on him and each team leader confirmed they were ready. First Sergeant Adams quickly moved up to Parker. "Ready when you are, sir."

"Alright. We go now, just like we've practiced." Parker clucked his tongue softly and the assault team moved out.

They moved quietly and deliberately. Parker was in no hurry to make a mistake. He reasoned twenty minutes was plenty of time to seize the house. He continued to scan the field as he moved.

Their pace was slower than a tortoise's. The assault team was patient; better to be precise and direct than move fast and make a mistake. When they finally reached the halfway mark between the farm and the wood, Ferguson's team spread out and dropped to the ground and covered Parker and the assault team.

Parker slowly moved, planting his feet deliberately and testing his footing before putting his weight down. They had learned weeks before about the dangers of moving fast at night. Lord Lovat had rigged a number of booby traps during a previous night's exercise, and Parker's troop had paid dearly for their mistakes. The morning after they had been forced to endure the punishment of moving fast by having to bear crawl around the parade deck for an hour. It was a mistake Parker refused to make a second time. He inched closer and closer to the cottage.

As they neared the cottage, Tarbor's team split off and dropped to the ground like Ferguson's team, laying fields of fire to provide support to Parker and Callum if required.

They were in the home stretch, Parker thought. It took every ounce of discipline for him to not speed up their movement toward the cottage.

They moved up along the wall and it took a minute for Parker to find the door. When he finally found it, he took a moment and strained his ear to listen. He couldn't hear anything inside, but that didn't mean it was empty. Callum moved up next to Parker and motioned to one of his team members, Corporal Devon, to open the door. The rest of the team set up near the door and prepared to move in.

Corporal Devon quietly worked the door to the cottage; it resisted and creaked slightly but made little noise.

This is it, Parker thought as he moved through the doorway, taking a moment to let his eyes adjust to the darkness. He paused a moment and strained his ears. The room was empty.

Callum moved silently past him into the room and paused a moment longer as he listened for a noise. "There's no one here."

Parker chewed his lip in silence for a moment as his mind raced. "To hell with it. Fall back to Tarbor's team. We'll push back to the treeline. I—"

BANG!

Before he could say any more he was cut off by an explosion. An audible *pop* emanated from the woods to their right. Parker and Callum exited the house just as a streak of light raced up into the sky from the edge of the woods. It was a flare.

"Contact right!" Devon screamed as the assault team sprawled out in the grass, using whatever uneven terrain they could find for cover.

Parker ducked back behind the door. "We're gonna catch hell for this, sir," Callum grunted as he leaned against the wall in a low crouch.

"End of exercise!" a voice called from the wood.

Parker instantly recognized the voice. It was Major Rackham, Lord Lovat's executive officer.

"Bugger, sir, that's the exec." Callum stood up and shouldered his Sten. "You think the old man is with him?"

"Lord Lovat isn't one to miss an opportunity to observe his commandos at work." Parker slung his Thompson over his shoulder and walked out of the cottage.

The flare was slowly burning out, but Parker could see Rackham along with Lord Lovat and Carver making their way toward the cottage. Parker turned away from them and spotted Tarbor and his team moving toward them.

"Tarbor, get the rest of troop over here, please."

"Right away, sir!" Tarbor turned back toward where the rest of Baker Troop was. "Baker! Rally on the cottage!"

"Good evening, Captain."

"Good evening, sir. I suppose we weren't as nimble moving through that field as we thought."

Lord Lovat shook his head, his face shadowed by the dying light of the flare. "On the contrary, you did well."

Parker looked at him in confusion.

"The flare was to be fired for two different reasons: conclusion of the exercise at midnight or if we thought the objective was being raided. We had no idea you were conducting the raid," Major Rackham explained.

"So we didn't complete the raid in time?" Parker looked over his shoulder and spotted First Sergeant Adams and the rest of Baker Troop standing off at a distance from the four officers, but well within earshot.

"Not necessarily." Lord Lovat walked over to the cottage and lit a lantern hanging near the door. "You failed to rendezvous with Captain Carver."

"Yes, sir, Fox Troop failed to meet us at the designated rendezvous point at the appointed time."

"So you decided to seize the objective on your own?" Lord Lovat demanded, his tone much harsher.

"Yes, sir."

"Why?"

Parker looked at Carver, his face betrayed nothing. "The mission wasn't to rendezvous with Fox Troop, it was to seize the cottage. Not having them with us didn't change the mission."

Lord Lovat nodded in satisfaction and turned to Major Rackham. "I told you they could handle a wrinkle in the plan."

"Indeed, sir."

"I ordered Captain Carver not to rendezvous with you. I wanted to see how your team responded to adversity. And you didn't disappoint. You made the best of the situation and you accomplished the mission."

Parker looked at Carver in confusion.

Carver shrugged but gave a weak smile.

"Gentlemen, I've kept my reasons as to why I did this to myself this whole time. Now I will tell you why." Lord Lovat motioned to First Sergeant Adams and the rest of Baker Troop to come closer.

The troop shuffled up next to Parker and stood silently waiting for Lord Lovat to explain.

Lord Lovat directed his gaze toward the whole troop when he spoke, "The primary mission of commandos as well as rangers is to sabotage, raid, and disrupt enemy operations. This almost always involves us operating alone and deep in enemy territory. Mission success is dependent on a number of things, but the one thing that can determine mission success or mission failure is communication." Lord Lovat spotted Corporal Tarbor and motioned him forward. "Corporal Tarbor."

"Yes, sir?" Corporal Tarbor's eyebrows shot up in surprise that Lord Lovat knew his name.

Parker couldn't help but suspect that Lord Lovat knew every one of his commando's names and at least a few details about them.

"Step forward, lad, I'm not the King," Lord Lovat chuckled in good humor and continued his inquiry. "During your raid on the cottage, what was your team to do if Captain Parker was ambushed?"

Corporal Tarbor stepped forward and hesitated, not keen about being called out and being asked a question by the Lieutenant Colonel. "Sir, if we were ambushed I would lay down cover fire and cover Captain Parker's and Sergeant Callum's teams.

"Would you have immediately started firing or would you have waited for orders from Captain Parker?"

Corporal Tarbor balked, "No, sir. I would have started shooting immediately."

"Why?"

"It's what needed to be done, sir."

"Exactly!" Lord Lovat smacked his hands together for emphasis. "It is what needed to be done. Thank you,

Corporal Tarbor, that is all. You seem keen to get away from me and back to your mates. I'll try not to take it personally."

Tarbor smiled sheepishly and retreated to the safety of his team as a rumble of chuckles swept through the troop.

"Corporal Tarbor is exactly right, he would return fire because that was what needed to be done. He understood that if he didn't return fire, Captain Parker wouldn't be able to finish the raid and therefore the mission would be a failure. Here in No. 4 Commandos I don't need some slack-jawed fool who can follow orders. I need critical thinkers who can both understand verbal orders and the intent of what we're doing." Lord Lovat pointed at Captain Parker. "Fox Troop failed to rendezvous, so Captain Parker, knowing that the mission was the seizure of the cottage, improvised and accomplished the mission anyway. In other words, communication failed but he was able to operate alone." Lord Lovat turned back to the Troop. "Why do you think I'm putting such emphasis on this?"

"Because in combat things never go according to plan, sir," Sergeant Callum announced.

Lord Lovat flashed a grin that glowed yellow in the lantern light. "Sergeant Callum is absolutely right! He took part in the Saint-Nazaire raid; he knows exactly what happens when things don't go according to plan." He pointed at the troop. "Some of you have conducted raids, others haven't. In the end, raids can go horribly wrong. Things get confusing, leaders are killed, the enemy does something we didn't want them to, but one thing is constant . . . ," he paused for effect, "that you are all commandos and the bedlam of a raid is your bread and butter." A cacophony of satisfied chuckles echoed through the commandos as Lord Lovat said this.

"You all know we have a mission coming, we just don't know where. What I can tell you is that it's soon, and I am confident that with the intensity of training you have undergone, we will succeed wherever Command sends us." Lord Lovat turned to Parker. "Well done, Captain. Get the lads home. We will finish the debrief in the morning."

"We doing bear crawls tomorrow, sir?" a commando called from the darkness.

"I think you've earned the morning off."

Parker grinned as the rest of his troop let out a roar of approval. He couldn't help but feel that whatever their mission was it wouldn't be a repeat of Saint-Nazaire. His boys were trained and professional. Whatever Command had in store for them, No. 4 Commandos would excel past expectations.

***

Squadron Leader Faraday killed the power to his engine and started to climb out of the cockpit of his Spitfire. Both Sergeant Roland and Flight Lieutenant Chris Vance, Faraday's executive officer, stood next to his wing waiting for him.

"Oh joy, if it isn't the Angel of Death and Satan himself."

"I'll assume Sergeant Roland is Satan," Vance chuckled. "How was the flight?"

"Didn't see a thing." Faraday looked across the runway at another Spitfire that was shutting down.

"Any issue, sir?" Roland asked. "If so, I could always make them worse. After all, I am Lucifer."

"No, she flew great. And I'll keep that in the back of my mind from now on, thank you." He started to walk toward the other Spitfire.

Vance followed after Faraday. "Sir, I have a few fuel requests and ammunition requests I need you to sign when you get a chance."

"Will do, Vance," Faraday said, not entirely listening. He was hyperfocused on the pilot hopping out of the Spitfire.

Vance noticed where Faraday was focusing his attention. "Who is that? O'Brien?"

"No, he knows better. One of our new blokes. Chapman."

"Oh, I see." Vance smirked. "Well, don't kill him, sir. We are short of pilots, after all."

"I'll see you in the shack."

Vance nodded and walked off.

Chapman hopped down off the wing. He was the latest addition to 71 Squadron and barely looked older than twenty. A youthful grin covered his face, no doubt due to the exhilaration after doing a barrel roll over the runway on his approach.

"You stupid bastard!" Faraday roared as he got closer.

Chapman's grin evaporated.

"How many damn times have I said we don't do victory rolls over the bloody runway?"

Chapman wasn't the only one witnessing Faraday's wrath. The majority of the squadron was lingering on the lawn next to the runway on standby. A few snickers could be heard among them, as well as a few groans as one or two recalled getting their ass chewed by Faraday as well.

"I—" Chapman started to speak but was cut down by Faraday.

"No! You don't talk, you listen! If I ever see you do another feckless act like that again in my aircraft, I'll make sure you never fly again. Understand."

"Yes, sir. It won't happen again, sir."

"It better not. Go debrief, then you will assist Sergeant Roland's mechanics with a full inspection of your aircraft to ensure that nothing was broken from your little maneuver."

"Right away, sir," Chapman barked, the look on his face a combination of embarrassment and fear.

Faraday looked at him for a moment and softened his tone. "I don't have time for fools. I need competent pilots. You have the makings of one, but you aren't there yet." He jerked his head toward the ready room. "Go debrief, then get back out here."

"Right away, sir," Chapman repeated and took off. As he passed the lawn he received a handful of catcalls from the rest of the squadron.

Faraday shook his head and made his way back to his office where Vance was waiting for him.

"Is Chapman still in a flight status?"

"For now, yes." Faraday unzipped his Mae West and hung it on the coat rack in his office. He took off his bomber jacket and hung it as well and sat down. "What am I signing?"

"Ammunition requests for our guns."

"How many rounds?"

"One hundred thousand."

Faraday grunted, "That should hold us over for a month." He signed at the bottom of the request and handed it back to Vance who gave him another request.

"This is for fuel."

Faraday didn't bother to ask, implicitly trusting his executive officer, and quickly signed the document.

"You have a meeting with Group in three hours."

"Yes, I know."

"I believe Air Vice-Marshal Leigh-Mallory will be there."

"Anything in particular I should mention?"

"Big wings don't work." Vance shrugged with sly laugh.

Faraday chuckled, remembering the last time he told Leigh-Mallory that his beloved big-wing tactics didn't work, "My ass hasn't grown back from the last time Leigh-Mallory chewed it."

He finished signing a handful of other documents Vance needed and got up from his desk. Without a word to anyone, he strolled out of the shack and hopped on his old Norton motorcycle, revved the engine, and took off. RAF Martlesham Heath was roughly a two-hour drive from RAF Uxbridge where No. 11 Command was headquartered, and Faraday looked forward to every second of the drive.

As his old Norton roared through the English countryside, Faraday turned his mind off and allowed himself a respite from being a squadron leader and just enjoyed the ride.

The ride felt quicker than two hours, but when Faraday finally arrived at Uxbridge he quickly made his way to the auditorium where the other squadron leaders were waiting impatiently for Leigh-Mallory.

As Faraday inspected the bleachers, looking for a few familiar faces, he noticed that a number of squadron leaders were absent. Faraday understood why. The war stopped for no one, and not everyone was able to pull away from their commands for five hours. The only reason Faraday had come was because he had heard a rumor that there was going to be a significant change in how the RAF was going to fight the war.

He continued to scan the crowd and spotted Michael King and walked over to him.

"Good Morning, Mike, how goes the war?"

"Ian, surprised to see you here."

"I heard we were going to discuss some new tactics today, that's why I came."

"As long as it isn't big wing tactics, I'm all ears."

Faraday chuckled, "God I hope not. How is the one twenty-first?"

"Good. We've been conducting an aggressive amount of Rhubarb missions over Normandy."

"Likewise. It would seem that the Royal Air Force is getting her pound of flesh from the Eagle Squadrons."

"I was hoping to bring up crew rest today. It's becoming a major concern again. We need more pilots or fewer missions."

Faraday rolled his eyes and shrugged. "Good luck with that. That's a War Office problem."

"You'd figure your American brethren would pick up the slack. When do you think you'll be transferred over to the US Army Air Corps?"

"Hopefully never. I have dual citizenship because of my mother, so I'm sure I can parlay that to stay with the RAF."

"I'd keep that close to the chest if I were you. Don't bring it up until you have to."

Faraday nodded in agreement and looked toward the auditorium door. He spotted Leigh-Mallory's aide-de-camp and a few other members of his staff loitering near the door. As if on cue, the door opened and Air Vice-Marshal Leigh-Mallory strode into the auditorium.

Someone called them to attention and King and Faraday quickly shot up out of their chairs. Leigh-Mallory quickly put them at ease and made his way over to a handful of squadron leaders he recognized and shook their hands.

"Ever the politician," King observed quietly.

Leigh-Mallory returned to the center stage and gazed impassively out at all of his squadron leaders. "Good day, gentlemen. I've asked you all here because we will be conducting a fundamental change to our tactics and priorities in how we conduct sweeps over Normandy and other regions." He motioned to a member of his staff, who brought a large chart out and quickly set it down behind Leigh-Mallory. "As you no doubt have heard, these past few months the army has finally started to put some points on the board. In order for them to continue to make progress, we need to begin focusing not only on engaging targets of opportunity but also gathering vital intelligence so our land forces can begin to decisively engage Nazi forces on the ground."

Faraday leaned his head closer to King's and said, "I thought we were already doing that?"

"It wasn't in a verbal order from Leigh-Mallory, so it wasn't official."

Faraday shook his head slowly in annoyance. "We do this already."

Leigh-Mallory continued to speak about the importance of continuing to provide up-to-date intelligence to the Army, and the continued effort to engage enemy logistics trains across the channel. As Leigh-Mallory continued to speak, the aide behind him switched charts and presented a map of Normandy. This garnered Faraday's interest.

The map was detailed and showed a number of routes that Faraday's squadron conducted sweeps around. What made it so interesting to Faraday was that it also showed the sweep routes of other squadrons. They were all focused on Normandy.

Faraday turned and exchanged glances with King; they'd both noticed it.

"You think it's the invasion?"

King shook his head. "Far too early. Must be something else."

Faraday nodded and continued to listen, hoping Leigh-Mallory would explain the map.

After thirty minutes of lecturing, Leigh-Mallory still hadn't expounded on the significance of the sweep tracks on the map.

Faraday groaned softly as Leigh-Mallory continued to drone on about targets of opportunity and occasionally pointed to the map but never discussed it.

"Just get to the point man," King murmured. As he spoke, Leigh-Mallory's aide got his attention and motioned to his watch.

"Forgive me, gentlemen, I hate to cut this short, but I have a pressing meeting I must depart for." Leigh-Mallory smiled gamely. "The Prime Minister is requesting a brief on our successful air campaign." He nodded to them and turned and without another word strode out. Someone called them to attention as he left and Faraday and King shot out of their seats.

"What just happened?"

Faraday shook his head in confusion. "I honestly have no idea. You call every squadron leader in for a briefing and then you leave in the middle of it? What a waste of time." The auditorium started to empty as squadron leaders started to disappear out the door to get back to their squadrons. Faraday and King walked over to the maps that had been left by Mallory's aide and started to study them.

"Look at this one." King pointed at the last map. It was a detailed layout of west Normandy and showed multiple airfields in Southern England.

Faraday shifted his weight from foot to foot as he studied the map. "Maybe it's a raid?"

"Like Saint-Nazaire? It definitely looks bigger."

"And closer. We'd have a longer flight time over the target."

"If that's what it is, you can bet that the Eagle Squadrons will be taking the lead for it."

Faraday studied the map intently. Whatever it was, he was sure it would be an attack *en force* by the RAF. "I suppose we'll find out soon enough." He checked his watch. "I gotta get back to Martlesham Heath. I'll see you soon, Mike."

"Enjoy the drive. Say hello to the chaps for me."

***

Cutter looked up and down the street, eyeing the shops next to Claude's bakery. The entire street was vacant, and there was a palpable tension in the town. As small and quaint as Quiberville was, its main street rarely lacked business. But with the growing presence of the SS in the area and the murmured rumor that the Gestapo were there, too, fewer people were on the roads and those that were avoided socializing in the open.

Cutter looked around in a daze. He couldn't believe how much had changed in less than a month. The shadow of the SS and Gestapo occupation had finally forced the villagers to hide during the day for fear of being stopped and questioned. The derelict town made Cutter feel isolated. He surprised himself by absently reaching for Talia's hand for comfort only to feel her limply return his grip.

"We reaped what you sowed."

"I'm sorry this happened." Cutter watched as a young boy scampered out of Claude's bakery with a loaf of bread and darted through a hedgerow.

Talia eyed Olivier impassively. He seemed earnest, but she had no way of knowing if his sorrow was genuine. The hurt look on his face when she had told him that the pistol was for him had pained her. But she couldn't tell what was and wasn't an act with him. "Not nearly as sorry as we are," she said bitterly.

Cutter gave Talia a anguished look but kept his thoughts to himself. Words would do little to sway her.

"It's changed so much . . . but is still the same."

"Is it not as friendly as London?"

"Maybe friendlier. You should meet my boss," Cutter chuckled, trying to lighten the mood. He looked over at Talia, his smile fading as she shot him a look of annoyance. "Right, I've seen enough." They walked back to the cottage in silence, Cutter making a handful of mental notes as they went, looking for any clues to a change in the German occupation. "Other than the SS and Gestapo being here, is there anything else I should know?" he asked when they walked back inside Talia's house.

"The garrison has been moved closer to Dieppe. They're now in Varengeville-sur-Mer, along with an artillery battery."

"By the church?"

"Down the road from it."

"Sounds like Varengeville-sur-Mer is being used to protect Dieppe's flank." He thought about the geographic placement of all the garrisons. At a glance it looked as though the Germans were surrounding the city with fortifications. It made sense. As the largest municipality in the region, Dieppe gave them a hub to control and defend the region from. That didn't surprise Cutter. What worried him was how big were the defenses? If Mountbatten's raid was going to be as big as Hambro said, you could forget any chance of surprise being a key factor for success. It would be a true test of Hitler's Atlantic Wall, and if that were the case, there was little room for error in appraising the Nazi defenses. "I hate to say it, but I think we need to go to Dieppe."

Talia's eyebrows raised in surprise. She had wanted to go into Dieppe for some time, but Claude had thought it too risky. The last person she had expected to want to go there was Olivier. Her eyes narrowed. *Why now?* She

290

studied Olivier for a moment. He had said he changed but had that been said for her benefit or did he mean it? "It's risky. We could get caught or killed. Are you sure you want to take the chance?"

Cutter's shoulder's drooped as he let out a long breath but nodded. "We must."

"Why?"

"Because I said so."

"That's not a good enough reason anymore, Olivier."

Cutter eyed her for a long moment. She had changed since he had last seen her. He couldn't blame her for doubting him. Cutter ran a hand through his hair and leaned against the kitchen counter. *Time to be up-front with her.* He sucked in a breath and gave a low whistle between his teeth as he exhaled. "We're raiding Dieppe. That's why I'm here."

"You said you were here to help us fight."

"Technically, I am."

"You lied to us again."

"I didn't lie."

"You weren't honest."

"Touché."

Talia fixed him with a stern look. "You've lied to me twice. Give me a reason why I shouldn't kill you."

A small smirk tugged at the corners of Cutter's mouth, but Talia wasn't amused. "I just told you the truth. If you can't see how difficult that was for me, then maybe you should go ahead and shoot me. I could have just as easily fed you some rubbish about how I needed a firm assessment of all cities in the area, but I chose to tell you the truth because I trust you."

Talia crossed her arms and leaned against the kitchen counter. "Why?"

"It's difficult to say."

"Is it more difficult than getting shot?"

Cutter shook his head and looked up at the ceiling, searching the wooden timbers for an answer. "When I went back to England the only thing I thought about the whole time was what you said to me before I left."

"You're telling me the truth because I hurt your feelings?"

Cutter paused, unsure how to respond. When he did, his tone was soft and fragile, his voice a husky whisper. "No, it's because I have feelings for you."

Talia stayed silent, still unconvinced.

"The thought of you thinking of me as a coward or something less drives me crazy. The whole time I was home I couldn't think straight. The memory of us in your bedroom . . ." Cutter trailed off, unsure what else to say.

Talia looked away from Cutter, her long chestnut hair obscuring her face,. "So you came back because of me?"   Cutter watched as the gears turned behind Talia's eyes. She was deliberating on what to do. Cutter could tell that what he said had touched a nerve. He wondered which one and what she would do. After a long pause, Talia opened her mouth, her words measured and her voice firm. "We'll see how true your words are. I still don't trust you, but I am willing to give you a chance."

"That's all I need."

"What now?"

"We need to see Dieppe."

"And if we're arrested?"

"They have no reason to arrest us. Our papers are in order, my cover is intact, and it's not unusual for two lovers to go into the town for a day."

Talia frowned but her eyes had a look of amusement in them. "Don't go and think all is forgiven, Olivier. It's not."

Cutter nodded. "I'll get the car." Without another word he strolled back outside and started the car. A few moments later, Talia followed him out.

"This is a bad idea. Just so you know," Talia murmured as Cutter put the car in drive and rolled out of the alley. "Claude would have a heart attack if he knew."

"Claude can sod off. Do you have a better idea?"

Talia remained silent. They rolled through the main road of Quiberville, passing Claude's bakery. As they passed the church where they had witnessed Amsel execute the priest and Jewish family, Cutter decided to say something. "So about that night, after we went to the church . . ."

"What about it?"

"Was I just a source of comfort that night?" Cutter snuck a quick look and took his eyes off the road.

A smile briefly flickered at the corners of Talia's mouth. "You have a lot to learn about women."

Cutter grunted but said nothing. He continued to drive in silence unsure of what to say. He looked back at Talia anxiously, the words choked in his throat as he said, "I thought about you a lot in England." His face turned red at the admission, but he continued, "When I was told I was coming back, it was a real ballbuster. The only thing that kept me from losing it was knowing I'd see you."

Talia turned and looked at him, her eyes softened and she stared at Cutter for a long moment. He did his best to split his focus between the road and her. He thought she was about to tell him off but spotted a tear forming in the corner of her eye. Just as he saw it, she turned away and pretended to look out the window.

They drove on in silence the rest of the trip, with Talia giving directions occasionally. It wasn't long before they reached Dieppe. As they drove into the outskirts of the town, the hairs on Cutter's neck stood up as he spotted numerous Nazi flags hanging from windows. The last time he had been in a Nazi-occupied city had been Paris, and being in Dieppe brought back a number of memories he had wished to forget, chief among them being Victor. Cutter proceeded to make a series of turns, deliberately taking a prolonged route to the town center to best assess the city and the garrison. German soldiers in their dark gray uniforms walked the streets either in pairs or as a squad. Most were armed, but a few appeared to be enjoying the French city for the day.

"They occasionally get a day or two of furlough." Talia nodded to the unarmed soldiers. "Sometimes they come down to Quiberville and get drunk. They've stopped recently, after the Resistance kidnapped and hung three in a barn."

"I'm sure the Nazis loved that." Cutter turned down another road. As he turned, a checkered guardhouse came into view.

"What do we need for the military checkpoint?" Cutter asked, his heart jumping slightly.

"Just your papers. We should be fine." Talia rummaged through her purse as they approached. Cutter reached into his pocket and pulled out the fabricated documents Freddy had given him and made his usual silent prayer that they were inspection-worthy. He rolled down the window as they got closer to the checkpoint and gave a friendly nod to the German soldier.

The German couldn't have been older than eighteen. He was still a gangly youth and was a bit clumsy in his movements as he reached for Cutter's papers and struggled to keep his rifle on his shoulder. Cutter shivered at the memory of the boy he killed in Paris when he had to escape.

"What is the purpose of your visit?" the soldier asked in broken French.

Cutter wrapped an arm around Talia's shoulder and beamed up at the guard. "Taking in the sights with this beautiful woman."

The soldier bent down and looked through the window at Talia.

Talia deliberately bent over pretending to search for her papers. She was wearing a blouse with the top two buttons undone. At the angle she was at, the German soldier was getting a good view of her chest.

Cutter suppressed a chuckle as the soldier made no secret that he was enchanted with Talia's breasts. He continued to stare until just before Talia looked up to give him her papers. He took the papers staring at them in a perfunctory way, but Cutter doubted his mind was on the task.

"Is everything alright?" Talia asked innocently. "Your face is flushed."

The soldier gave a weak smile and struggled to find the words. He handed them their papers. "Everything is in order. You can go." He turned and quickly motioned for the gate to be lifted.

Cutter thanked him and started to move the car forward. When they were past the checkpoint he looked at Talia. She stared back at him in silence and they both erupted in laughter.

"You're a dangerous woman."

"Indeed I am."

Cutter smiled. It felt as though the tension between them had relaxed. Her laughter excited him and calmed his nerves. They drove down to the harbor and found a place to park.

"Where do you want to go?"

Cutter looked around and spotted a small cafe along the harbor walk. "We're in no rush. Let's go and sit down for a while at that cafe."

They casually strolled over, taking their time and peeking into shop windows as they walked. Cutter made a handful of mental notes, observing how busy the street was and how many soldiers he had spotted. They walked over to one of the cafe's outdoor tables and sat down.

A waiter approached and asked what they wanted. "Two coffees please." The waiter bobbed his head and walked back inside.

Cutter looked around the street casually, a look of general disinterest etched on his face. Talia leaned back in her chair and stretched. A playful smile ran across her face as she enjoyed the sunshine. Cutter couldn't help but notice the buttons on her blouse were straining as she stretched.

"Are you still cross with me?"

Talia's smile curled into a smirk. She wanted to believe Olivier, but she was still hesitant. The pain was still fresh from how he had treated her the morning after they had made love. "I'm warming up to you, but I think I'll hold on to the pistol for a while."

"I believe that's the default position for any romantic relationship."

Talia cocked an eyebrow, but let his remark go unchallenged. "I haven't been to Dieppe in ages." She looked around. "Whenever I came from Paris with my family, we always stayed in the village."

"You never talk about Paris."

"It's hard to talk or think about with so many horrible things happening there."

Cutter nodded and decided now wasn't the time to pry.

"What was it like when you were there?"

Cutter shrugged but didn't say anything. Sitting at the cafe brought back vivid memories of Paris. Of times when he would sit along the Seine with Victor and his wife and daughter just enjoying the evening, taking a respite from their daily duties of building a circuit in Paris and tailing Nazi bureaucrats. The waiter arrived with their coffees and quickly departed to tend to three German officers who had just sat down at one of the tables outside.

Cutter shot a quick look at the three officers and was relieved that he didn't recognize any of them. Two were majors in the army, but the third was a lieutenant colonel in the SS.

"Don't look, but over your right shoulder are three senior officers." Cutter brought the coffee cup to his lips, maintaining a look of disinterest. "One of them is an SS lieutenant colonel."

"Does he have a scar above his lip?"

Cutter waited a moment and casually looked toward the three German officers, as if waiting to get the waiter's attention. It was difficult to see since they were on the opposite side of the cafe, but he could make out a disfigurement. "Yes, he does."

"That is Obersturmbannführer Weber. He is in charge of the SS detachment in the city."

"How come I've never heard about him before?"

"He arrived a few weeks ago. Rumor is that he came from Casablanca."

Cutter nodded and darted a glance back over to the German officers. As he did so, a tall gentleman in a dark suit and black leather trench coat walked up to the Germans' table. "Someone else just walked up to the table. Gestapo, if I had to guess."

"We haven't been able to identify any Gestapo agents."

Cutter watched the four Germans with his peripheral vision, never directly looking at them. He couldn't hear them, and could only guess at what they were discussing. He watched their body language surreptitiously. The three officers treated the man in the trench coat with deference. *If he wasn't Gestapo, what else could he be?* There weren't any administrative positions in Dieppe that were being run by any German bureaucrats. He had to be Gestapo. Cutter chewed his lip, his mind buzzing.

"We should continue to drive around the city." He pulled a few francs out of his pocket and paid their bill. He helped Talia out of her chair and they made their way back to the car, passing the Germans as they did so.

They walked in silence until they got into the car. "Obersturmbannführer Weber has been aggressively ramping up searches for the Resistance. He was the one who recruited Amsel," Talia said as Cutter opened the car door for her.

"Who were the two majors?"

"They are the commanders of the two garrisons that patrol Dieppe and the surrounding area."

"Do they always meet like that? Out in the open, exposed?"

"That is the first time I have ever seen them do that."

Cutter grunted. Perhaps there was a possibility to assassinate the three of them and that Gestapo agent. "Did you recognize the man in the suit?"

Talia shook her head. "If I had to guess, he most likely is from Cherbourg. Claude has been getting occasional word from contacts there that the Gestapo has set up their Normandy headquarters in Cherbourg as well as Caen." She stole a final glance over at the four Germans. Their behavior was so cavalier. *They're overconfident after killing three cells and seizing those caches.* Talia looked over at Olivier. He didn't look panicked about it. It surprised her. She half expected him to be frantically looking for an escape, but the look on his face was similar to a hunter eyeing game. His calm reassured her. *Maybe he has changed.*

"We need to talk to Claude about this." Cutter started the car. "I also need to get on the hook with London." Cutter shot one final glance at the four Germans at the cafe as they turned down a street. An aggressive SS commander and Gestapo agent bent on flushing out Resistance fighters did not bode well for Talia, Claude, Durand, and him; but for some reason, Cutter's instincts told him that there was an opportunity in front of him. He hadn't been eager to kill Amsel because he interacted with Resistance members every day and didn't know it. There was a small logical list of suspects that the Gestapo would rope up from Quiberville if that happened. It was another story to kill the SS commander or senior Gestapo agent. They were big enough targets that the list of suspects would be a mile long.

***

CHAPTER 13
POLITICAL ANIMALS

Hambro chewed his lip as he reviewed the latest report from Cutter. He leaned forward at his desk and set the report down, turned in his swivel chair, and looked at the array of maps that sat behind his desk. As he did so, a knock came on his door.

"Enter."

The door opened and Atkinson walked in. "Good morning, sir. I'm going to be attending a meeting with General Montgomery and the raid commanders this morning. Anything you'd like me to pass?"

"Have you seen this?" Hambro motioned to the report.

Freddy frowned and picked it up. "Must've come in after I left for the night." He scanned the report and his eyes widened. "Gestapo? In Dieppe?"

"Out of the frying pan and into the fire. How long till the raid?"

"A few weeks. Has he been made?"

"I don't know."

"I hate to point this out, but he knows about the raid, sir."

Hambro took his glasses off and rubbed the bridge of his nose. "I know, dammit."

"We need to extract him."

"No, it's too risky. If we pull him, our information network will crumble. There's too much riding on this raid, and it's already on shaky legs with Mountbatten planning it."

"So do nothing?"

"For now, yes. We've suspected the Gestapo were in Dieppe for a time. All this means is that it's been confirmed. Go to your meeting. We'll talk more later." Hambro perched his glasses back on his nose and waved Atkinson away.

"Very good, sir. I'll let you know if the general has anything to pass."

"Good man," Hambro said as Freddy closed the door. He waited a moment to ensure Atkinson was gone before he picked up the phone. "Hello, dispatch? Yes, I have an urgent message that needs to be sent for code name Willow. It shall read as follows: Upon risk of capture, Cartographer is to be executed immediately. Did you get that?" Hambro didn't wait for an answer and hung up, furious with himself.

***

"Are you sure it was the Gestapo?" Durand looked at Talia and Cutter in disbelief.

Cutter's arms shot up in a shrug of feigned ignorance. "I suppose we can't be too sure. He didn't have a swastika on his arm and he lacked a toothbrush mustache."

Durand shot Cutter an annoyed look. "This isn't funny, Olivier."

"No, it's not." Cutter and Talia stood across the table from Claude and Durand in the basement of a cottage between Quiberville and Varengeville-sur-Mer. The owner of the cottage, a cattle farmer, and his two boys were keeping watch as they met.

Claude paced the length of the table impatiently, his hands clasped behind his back and his caterpillar eyebrows furrowed into a unibrow. "I'm sorry, but that is not enough to incriminate a man as a member of the Gestapo."

Cutter stared at the two of them in disbelief. His mind jumped to the memory of the Dieppe cell that had gone quiet prior to his return to London. "The Dieppe cells that we've lost, did we find out what happened?"

Durand and Claude exchanged looks but said nothing.

"What happened?"

"We found two of them," Claude said somberly. "Their bodies were found in a ditch naked and badly beaten. They each had a few fingers missing and a number of burns on their bodies."

"Damn."

They were quiet for a moment. Cutter looked at Claude and Durand. "You have a Resistance cell dead, a new Waffen-SS commander aggressively searching for you, and a meeting between him, the two garrison commanders, and an anonymous civilian. The circumstantial evidence is there. He's Gestapo."

"Olivier is right," Talia spoke up.

Cutter looked at her, surprised that she was agreeing with him.

"Why do you say that?" Claude stopped pacing and leaned forward, resting his hands on the table.

"Obersturmbannführer Weber and the two majors greeted the man as though he were a superior. He may be Gestapo, he may not be, but he is most certainly a German authority, which makes him a target for us."

Claude grunted and exchanged a look with Durand. "I don't know. It's too risky."

Cutter couldn't believe what he was hearing. How could they be this recalcitrant? *They're scared.* Cutter stared at Claude and Durand in surprise. Both were dragging their feet because they were worried about the fallout from killing such an important target.

"This is a bad idea."

Cutter shot Durand a look of annoyance. "And why is that?"

"You're about to tell us that you want us to shadow this man and plan to assassinate him. As soon as we do that we will have kicked the hornet's nest *again*. Every German in Normandy will descend on Dieppe and the surrounding area. That will bring us under a microscope and they will pick us apart."

Cutter chewed his lip in frustration; Durand had a point. The moment they killed a Gestapo agent, let alone the commanders of the garrison, the Resistance cells in the area would be unable to operate due to how aggressively the Germans would be searching for them. But the opportunity to take out not only an SS commander but a senior Gestapo agent was too good to pass up.

Claude pushed off the table and stood upright, his hands open in a diplomatic way. "Perhaps we should hold off on acting on this information until an opportunity presents itself."

Cutter grudgingly nodded his head in agreement. He couldn't force them to do something they didn't want to. He was only there to advise and he didn't want to push them too far in a direction they would resent him for being placed in.

"In the meantime, we were able to get you the information you wanted." Claude handed Cutter a scrap of paper. Durand pulled a map out of his breast pocket and placed it on the table. "We estimate around twelve hundred soldiers inside of Dieppe." Claude pointed to Dieppe on the map. "There are an additional six thousand soldiers in the surrounding area acting as an occupying force."

"What unit?"

"The 302nd Static Infantry Division, a German home guard that was sent to oversee the coastal defense. Most are conscripts. Not the most professional."

"Neither are we." Cutter smirked, not bothering to look up from the map to see Durand's annoyed reaction. "Armor?"

"Tenth Panzer Division. They operate further inland." Claude pointed south of Dieppe.

"I haven't seen any tanks the whole time I've been here." Cutter looked up from the map in surprise.

"They avoid the coast unless ordered. They try to stay near heavily forested areas and locations where they can hide from your aircraft."

Cutter nodded. Getting an accurate number of German tanks in Normandy was a region-wide problem for the SOE and the RAF. "Artillery?"

"We've counted four batteries. One between us and Dieppe near Varengeville, and another three on the east side of the city."

Cutter looked at the map and Claude's notes. "What's the expected time for the division to reinforce the city?"

Durand gave a low whistle and exchanged looks with Claude, who shrugged. "Tough to say. Maybe fifteen hours to be fully reinforced. I'd say two hours before Nazi tanks showed up."

Cutter didn't bother to ask about the Luftwaffe. He knew that a whole wing could be airborne and over Dieppe within an hour of being informed of the attack. He stared down at the map. A little over a thousand men in Dieppe and four artillery batteries established along the coast. That was just what they knew; it wasn't enough, but he couldn't risk having the Resistance dig anymore and being discovered. "It's a good start. We need to keep on the lookout for minefields, troop movements, that sort of thing."

Claude and Durand nodded.

Cutter put Claude's notes in his pocket. As he did so, an idea came to mind. "I think I just figured out how to deal with this Gestapo agent. Can we find out where he works, where he sleeps, what patterns he shows?"

Talia gave him a puzzled look. "What do you have in mind?"

"I'd rather not say just yet. Just get me that information, sooner rather than later, please."

Claude hesitated but gave a slight nod. "We can do that, but nothing more." He looked around the room to see if there was anything else. "If that's everything, I received this message the other night and feel you should know about it." He pulled another piece of paper from his pocket and handed it to Cutter.

Cutter looked at it suspiciously and read it.

Upon risk of capture, Cartographer is to be executed immediately.

Cutter shook his head in annoyance and crumpled the message up. He knew the message was from Hambro. The cold calculations of ensuring operational security wasn't something Freddy was fond of or willing to speak

306

plainly about. Cutter had to give Hambro credit, he got to the point of things.

"Thanks, boss." Cutter lit a match and touched it to the paper, igniting it.

"What did it say?"

Cutter was quiet a moment. "It says kill me if I risk being captured."

The room went quiet, no one entirely sure what to say.

"I'll do it myself, don't worry."

Talia studied Olivier for a long moment, the stalwart look on his face betraying nothing. "How can your leadership order that?"

"It's the way of war. Let's not dwell on it," Cutter said softly. He looked up at Claude. "Thank you for giving me that. I expect to hear from you in two days and I want to know where the Gestapo agent works."

Claude nodded. "I'll have it. I promise."

"Good, let's get out of here. We've spent too much time here as it is."

***

Faraday sat under his Spitfire inspecting the vertical stabilizer. "The pedals felt a bit sticky."

Sergeant Roland moved the stabilizer left and right with his hands. He bit his lip in frustration as he assessed the problem. "It could be rust on the cables. I'll add some lubricant to it as a quick solution. If it gets worse, let me know."

Faraday nodded and rolled out from underneath his aircraft. As he stood up, he spotted Vance making his way toward him.

"Sir, a courier just arrived with orders."

Faraday frowned. "Why weren't they just radioed?"

Vance looked around to ensure no one was around. "They're from SOE, sir."

Faraday shot Vance a quizzical look but said nothing, his mind already predicting what the orders said. He started to walk toward his office and Vance fell in step next to him. "Any idea what they want?"

"No idea, sir, but when SOE comes knocking, it's never good."

Faraday nodded in agreement. The word "SOE" was not something the RAF looked favorably on when orders originated with them. SOE missions were synonymous with low life expectancy for RAF pilots, and Faraday did his best to shield his pilots from those missions.

"Most likely a low-altitude recce."

"Can't say for certain until we see the orders, sir," Vance said in his usual analytical way.

They walked back over to the office and found a courier straddling a motorcycle, waiting patiently with a dispatch bag.

"Sir, are you Squadron Leader Faraday?" the courier asked as Faraday walked up.

"I am."

"Can I see some identification?" The courier wasn't taking any chances. Faraday couldn't help but notice that one of his hands was resting dangerously close to his Webley revolver.

Faraday produced his identification card and the courier nodded. "Thank you, sir." He took the dispatch bag off his shoulder, pulled a folder out, and handed it to Faraday. He then saluted and started his engine before Faraday and Vance had a chance to return the salute.

Faraday looked over the folder. It had the usual confidential markings covering it, along with the letters S.O.E embossed across it. Faraday tucked the folder under his arm and walked into his office and set it on his desk.

He sat down hard in his chair, took a deep breath, and broke the seal on the folder. He read through the usual verbiage and letterhead that came with official military documents and skimmed down to the mission details.

Within 48 hours of reception of this order, Number 71 Squadron will execute a sortie flight with the intent of destroying building number 7 (see attachment 3). Building 7 has been identified by multiple sources to be housing high-ranking German officials vital to German operations in Normandy. Building 7 is to be destroyed at all costs.

Faraday set the orders down and thumbed through the attachments and found attachment 3. It was a large aerial photo of Dieppe with markers indicating where building 7 was.

Vance read the order over Faraday's shoulder. "They're asking us to minimize collateral damage and level a single building."

"That's unrealistic."

"What're we going to do?"

Faraday studied the building. It was smaller than other buildings surrounding it, and fortunately had a large, open road leading up to it, making it easier for a fighter to drop a bomb accurately. "We're gonna slap a large bomb to the belly of one of the Spitfires and hope it gets the job done."

"Spitfires don't have the capacity for any sort of large payload."

"No, but we can hit the building low to the ground and it should compromise the structure."

"I don't think that will be enough." A hint of doubt in Vance's voice.

Faraday chewed his lip as he worked the problem. "Who has the most experience with bombs?"

Vance paused for a moment as he racked his brain. "Faust, I believe. He participated in a training course implementing heavy ordnance on a Spitfire a few months ago. Rumor was that the research team tried to keep him."

"Alright, let's talk to him."

They walked out of Faraday's office and over to the ready line where a number of No. 71's pilots sat and lounged. Faraday quickly spotted Faust.

"Danny!" Faraday got his attention and waved him over.

Faust turned and jogged over to him. "Good afternoon, sir."

"Danny, what can you tell me about bombing from a Spitfire?"

Faust shot him a confused look. "Sir?"

"You heard me."

Faust's lip curled into a wicked grin. "It's damned tricky, sir."

"I heard you were a subject-matter expert?"

"Not to be arrogant, but I can hit any target you give me with a five-hundred-pound bomb."

Faraday and Vance exchanged looks and motioned for Faust to follow them back into Faraday's office. Once they were securely inside and away from prying eyes and eavesdroppers, Vance and Faraday started to ask more detailed questions.

"Could it take out a building?"

Faust put his arms akimbo and screwed up his face in thought. "How big a building are we talking about?"

"Three stories, and you have a clear approach to it."

"Am I trying to disable a factory? Because there are better ways to do this."

Faraday grabbed the SOE folder and tossed it to Faust.

Faust gave the front of the folder a long look, his eyes lingering on the SOE lettering, no doubt thinking the same thing every pilot thought when they saw an SOE mission come across their desk. He quickly recovered from the surprise and opened the folder. He started to read the order and study the photos. After a few minutes, he closed the folder and laid the photos out on the desk.

"This is feasible," Faust said with some finality. "If I come in from the west I can line up the target and come in fast and drop the bomb. I can send it through the front door of the building easily, and be out of the city before anyone is the wiser."

Faraday and Vance exchanged looks, and Vance shrugged. Faraday nodded slowly and turned back to Faust.

"I want this building blown up by 0700 tomorrow morning. Come up with a flight plan. I want a brief in four hours."

***

Flight Lieutenant Daniel Faust checked his map; he was ten miles off the coast of Normandy. After reviewing the maps of Dieppe and the surrounding area, he had quickly realized he would only have one chance to interdict the town before enemy antiaircraft crews would bring all their firepower to bear on him. He wouldn't be able to slow down over the city to locate the building, which meant he had little margin for error.

Fortunately, the building wasn't hard to locate. It was at the end of the main road that ran along the eastern side of the harbor. All Faust had to do was come in from the west, line up on the east side of the harbor, and head inland. He was sure he could identify the building in the seconds he had before releasing the bomb.

Faust checked his readings; his fuel was good and he was flying at one thousand feet MSL. As he got closer to the coast, he gradually descended. He checked his map against the terrain he was flying over and confirmed his position and swung east. He quickly flipped a switch and armed the bomb attached to the belly of his Spitfire and keyed his mic. *"Control, this is Reese 5. Feet dry."*

"Roger, Reese 5. Good hunting," the cool, detached voice of the female dispatcher replied. *"Control out."*

"Alright, Jerry, let's see if you're early risers." Faust opened the throttle. The Spitfire bucked, pushing Faust back into his chair for a moment, and roared low over the hills of Normandy. In a matter of seconds, the city of Dieppe came into view as Faust crested a hill.

As soon as the city came into sight, puffs of bluish-black smoke started to appear around him. Faust swore softly as flak exploded around his aircraft. It wasn't concentrated, which Faust thanked God silently for, but a lucky shot could still knock him out of the sky. He quickly scanned the city, spotted the harbor, and maneuvered his aircraft inland over it. He checked his vector, made sure he was following the eastern harbor road, and started to frantically search for the target building.

"Come on. Where are ya, you bastard?" Faust scanned the port frantically. "There she is!"

At the end of the road, standing out against the other white stone buildings around it with large Nazi flags hanging from the windows, was his target. Faust adjusted his angle of attack and started to take aim. He intently eyed the large Nazi flag hanging over the main entrance. The large swastika acted like a bull's-eye. Flak continued to pepper his aircraft, and he could feel a few bits of shrapnel tearing through the fuselage. He hadn't lost control of the aircraft and hadn't been hit yet, so that was the only input he needed. He pulled back gently on the stick and raised the nose of the Spitfire, his hand hovering over the bomb release lever.

Confident in his vector, he released the lever. He felt the Spitfire jerk slightly as five hundred pounds of drag suddenly vanished from his aircraft. He quickly pushed the throttle forward and banked hard to the left, turning the Spitfire back out to sea.

Faust stole a quick glance back toward the city. Smoke billowed from where the bomb had landed, but there was no way to determine whether or not the bomb had done its job. However, he was confident in his work. He scanned the skies around him, double-checking that there were no enemy aircraft around, and gradually pulled the throttle back to conserve fuel. *"Control, this is Reese 5. Feet wet, bomb dropped on target. Returning to base."*

"Roger, Reese 5. Continue on your present course and climb to Angels 5."

"Roger, Control. Reese 5 is climbing to Angels 5." Feeling jubilant, Faust couldn't help himself, adding, *"And heading to London to buy you a round."*

"See you at the Fox and Hound in Piccadilly," she shot back without skipping a beat. *"Control out."*

***

"It's done." Claude stood at his usual place at the table in the barn.

"And the Gestapo agent?" Eagerness filling Talia's voice.

"Obersturmbannführer Weber as well as the suspected Gestapo agent were killed by the bombing."

"There'll be repercussions." Durand shook his head remorsefully.

"Calm down, we're going to lie low for a week and see what happens. Things should cool down quickly. We've done a good job compartmentalizing everything, so we should be fine." Cutter did his best to sound confident.

Everyone around the table nodded hesitantly, not entirely believing that everything would be alright.

"I hope this was worth it." Claude muttered, "We've never gone after the Gestapo before, they'll react violently."

"It was necessary," Cutter defended. He looked over at Talia, who nodded in agreement.

"Amsel will come after us." Durand shook his head, doubt scribbled over his face. "Even if he knows nothing, he will make life difficult for the nearby villages."

"All will be well," Cutter reassured. "We'll wait a week and see if this blows over."

Claude opened his mouth but quickly closed it, unsure of what to say. As the commander of the circuit he had the ultimate say on the matter, but it didn't matter. They had made their move. Now all they could do was wait. He studied Cutter, his eyes narrowing suspiciously. "I don't know why I didn't think of this before, but the last time we did something like this it was before the raid on Saint-Nazaire."

"Yes, and?"

"You'd tell us if something was about to happen, right?"

Cutter opened his mouth, a quick lie dangling from his tongue, but he stopped himself. "No."

"No?" Durand looked at him in surprise, his visage quickly reddening. "What the hell do you mean *no*!" He took a step toward Cutter, his hands clenched into fists. "You better tell us what you know!"

Claude's eyes didn't leave Cutter's. He placed a hand gently on Durand's shoulder. "Settle down, lad."

Durand opened his mouth to protest, but quickly closed it as Claude's grip tightened on his shoulder. "It's time for us to go." Claude's eyes lingered on Cutter, understanding in them. He realized why Cutter couldn't tell him the truth, and appreciated that Cutter hadn't tried to lie. For some it may not have meant much, but for Claude he was grateful that Cutter hadn't tried to piss on his back and tell him it was rain. He gave the slightest of nods and, without a word, he departed the barn with Durand in tow.

"Olivier, you can't leave them like this."

"I have to." Cutter furrowed his brow and looked up at the ceiling in frustration. "I can't reveal the next step. If one of them is captured . . ."

Talia gave him a conflicted look and watched in sadness as Claude and Durand walked toward Durand's horse-drawn wagon.

"I'm sorry, but there is more to this game than a matter of trust. The less they know, the better off the Resistance will be."

Talia frowned and looked at Cutter in bewilderment. "How can you be so passionate with me one second and so cold and analytical with Durand and Claude the next? Are they just cattle you need to keep calm before the slaughter?"

Cutter remained silent for a moment and motioned for Talia to follow him out of the barn toward the car. "I've been with you every day I've been here. I can't say the same for Claude or Durand."

"But Claude is the leader of this cell."

Cutter gave Talia a quizzical look and opened the car door for her. "It's funny you should say that. Since I've returned, it would seem that Claude and Durand follow your lead sometimes."

"Is that a question?"

Cutter got behind the wheel and started the car. "I guess my question is what happened after I left?"

"You mean after you abandoned us?"

Cutter frowned but didn't take the bait. "Talia, what happened?"

It was Talia's turn to frown. She debated how much to tell Olivier. Blackmailing Claude and Durand into letting her help wasn't something she was proud of, but it had granted her the opportunity of controlling her own life. For that alone, she felt justified in her actions. She wondered if Olivier would have done the same in her situation, and suspected he would have. As much as he annoyed her she couldn't help but notice a number of similarities between them. They both were fighting to control their own destinies. Where he was still fighting to do so, she had succeeded. Talia looked up at Olivier and decided half the truth was enough. "After you left, the Nazis started conducting aggressive searches of all the villages. It put a lot of pressure on Claude and Durand. We lost a lot of men and women during the searches and a lot of equipment."

"This is the first I'm hearing about this. Why didn't the SOE know?"

"We were constantly moving the radios. After you left, there was hardly time to transmit anything."

Cutter drummed his fingers on the wheel in frustration. "Bugger all, no wonder you've resented me this whole time. So what did you do?"

"I started moving our weapons and equipment to caches further away from the villages."

"By yourself? Christ, that took balls."

Talia shrugged. "No one else was doing it. If I hadn't, the Resistance would have lost everything we had built these past few months."

"And that's why Claude and Durand listen to you now?"

"More or less."

Cutter frowned and weighed his next words carefully. "Thousands of lives are on the line. If this raid isn't a surprise, many will die. I have to protect this secret. I'm not ready to trust Durand and Claude with this, but I'm willing to trust you."

Talia wondered how much truth was in his words. She wanted to believe him, but his words the night before he left for England still hung in her ears. "But how can I trust *you*? For all I know, you're just telling me what I want to hear."

Cutter grunted and turned the car down the alleyway to the house. He put the car in park and silently studied the stones in the low wall. After a long pause he finally spoke. "I am a spy. My job is to serve as a provocateur for my country and conscript others into her services. I lie easily, and I change who I am like I change my clothes."

"Yes, I know."

"Let me finish," Cutter said sharply. "When Victor died, it was the first time a contact died as a direct result of my decisions, and it wasn't pretty. He and I were close, but even then I always told him what he needed or wanted to hear to keep his mind on the mission. I always minimized the risk when talking to him."

"And what about me?"

"I'd like to think that you always knew the risk when working with me. I may have been deceitful about myself, but I never lied about the risk or what we were doing."

"No, you just withheld information."

"That doesn't mean I lied."

Talia gave an exasperated sigh and eyed Cutter coolly. "So why tell me all this?"

"I—" Cutter's face turned crimson. "I want to keep you safe. I want to take you back to England with me."

The revelation stunned Talia. For a long moment, they sat in silence. As the seconds ticked by, Cutter started to worry that he had said too much. He had exposed himself in a way he had never done before and it terrified him. He could feel hot blood filling his cheeks and opened his mouth to say something, but stopped as a small smile crept over Talia's face.

"Do you have a plan?"

Cutter grinned in relief. "Of course!"

***

"Sir, what do you think the mission is?" Callum asked Parker.

Parker sipped at his beer and looked around the table at First Sergeant Adams and the other team leaders of Baker Troop. "I'm not sure."

"I think it's a night raid," Ferguson said as deadpan as he could.

"No shit, Fergy, what makes you say that?" Murray laughed. "One thing is for sure. Shimi has been training each troop ragged. Whatever it is, it will involve all of No. 4."

Parker exchanged looks with Adams and nodded in agreement. They had been thinking something similar.

"Don't call Lord Lovat Shimi. You and he ain't friends," Adams growled.

"It's going to be close to here." Callum took a deep draft from his beer and set his mug down. "After Operation

Claymore, they sent us to Sierra Leone to train to invade the Canary Islands. If you ask me, it's going to be France again."

"If that's true, then I'd be willing to bet we're going to Normandy," Adams grumbled as he motioned to the bartender for another round.

"Your old stomping grounds, First Sergeant."

"I was in Champagne not Normandy, you idiot."

"It's the one place we haven't raided," Parker agreed.

"If so, Jerry is going to be right and proper ready for us." Tarbor belched and swiped a meaty paw across his face, removing any stray beer.

Carter nodded in agreement and looked at Parker. "The boys are well trained, as long as Command does their job, we should be able to do ours."

"Clearly, you weren't at Saint-Nazaire," Sergeant Callum chuckled bitterly.

Parker's mind quickly flashed to that panicked scene on the *Campbeltown.* The memory of manning the ten-pound gun and carrying Tarbor to the boat quickly jumped out in his mind. As quickly as it came, Parker turned his mind from it. The fear he felt that day was something he couldn't afford to feel now. As a troop commander, the last thing he could show was fear, especially for the unknown.

"Wherever they send us, No. 4 Commando is all we need. To hell with Command." First Sergeant Adams locked eyes with Parker as he said it, as if he had read Parker's mind.

"Damn right, Sarge." Murray saluted with his pint and drained it. As he did so, the bartender came to their table with a tray of beer.

"Well, lads, how'd it go today?" the bartender, Mr. Rowan, an elderly man with a grizzled beard, asked.

"Those Japs won't know what hit them, Mr. Rowan! You can count on that!" Carter grinned as he reached for a beer.

"Japs? I thought we were fighting Jerry?"

"You heard wrong, old man. They're sending us to Burma," Callum said as Tarbor handed him a mug from the tray. "That's why the Yanks are here." He nodded to Murray and Carter. "These two are fluent in their gobbledygook language."

"Where the bloody hell is Burma?"

"Africa, I think?" Ferguson laughed.

"Christ almighty, you lads don't even know who you're fighting! How the bloody hell are we going to win?"

"That's why we have the Royal Navy, Mr. Rowan." Parker smiled.

"Damn fools." Mr. Rowan put the tray under his arm and fixed First Sergeant Adams with a serious stare. "I better have a closed-out tab from you lot before you all leave."

First Sergeant Adams frowned, but fished into his pocket and pulled out a few quid. "This should cover it, Mr. Rowan, and one or two more rounds."

Mr. Rowan snatched the money from Adams's hand with unusual alacrity, like a snake striking. "Thank you kindly, Mr. Adams."

"Mr. Rowan, make sure you don't tell anyone what we're talking about. Loose lips sink ships, and all that." Callum smirked.

Mr. Rowan waved an annoyed hand at them and started to walk off. "Wouldn't matter if I told anyone; they'd just look at me and call me daft."

"Just wait, our orders are actually going to be for Burma." Tarbor laughed once Mr. Rowan was out of earshot.

"I certainly hope not. My brother is there. He says the bloody Japanese are savages. They behead prisoners," Ferguson said seriously.

"That's some nice tavern banter, Fergy. I appreciate that," Murray said with a hint of annoyance.

"I was just saying," Fergy protested.

"Well, just say that somewhere else," Tarbor agreed. The table went quiet at that. Parker looked over at the door. A handful of His Majesty's sailors had trickled into the bar along with a few girls from the town.

Parker checked his watch. It was getting late. He took a hearty draft from his glass and stood up. "Well, gentlemen, I don't know about you, but I think I'll call it a night. I don't want to hear about any of you getting into any scuffle with our naval service brethren."

First Sergeant Adams stood as well. "I think I'll turn in too, sir."

"First Sergeant, you should stick around! The amount of money you gave Mr. Rowan was enough to buy the entire pub a round five times over!"

"I thought I gave him one pound and twenty-five pence?" First Sergeant Adams frowned and looked back over at Mr. Rowan. The old man was studiously scrubbing a smudge out of the bar.

"You gave him five bob, First Sergeant."

"Goddammit!" First Sergeant Adams roared. He turned and glared at Mr. Rowan, who had coincidentally proceeded to take the sailors orders.

"Nothing you can do about it, First Sergeant. Good night, gentlemen. I'll make sure they stay out of trouble," Callum said quickly, motioning the two of them toward the door.

Parker nodded, not entirely confident in that statement. Adams frowned but nodded slowly, and they departed the tavern. As they stepped out onto the street, a haze filled the air. A fog had rolled into the harbor, giving the interspersed gas lanterns along the road an ethereal glow.

The pair of them walked in silence, stewing in their own thoughts. Parker's mind wandered to Saint-Nazaire, to Normandy, to anywhere that he thought they could be sent. The unknown and lack of information drove him mad. He shot his First Sergeant a glance, his face a wreckage of conflicting thoughts. If Parker had to guess, Adam's mind was on similar topics.

"Penny for your thoughts?"

Adams chuckled, his eyes never leaving the cobblestone road. "Sir, I don't think you want to know."

"No, I really do."

Adams bit his lip. "I was at Cambrai in the Great War. It was the first time American troops saw combat. We lost forty-four thousand men in over two weeks. We won the battle, but it was costly. I like to think part of the reason for that was the introduction of new techniques and equipment. I can't help but wonder if we're about to repeat the same thing on a smaller scale."

"You don't think we're ready?"

"No, I think we are. I'm just concerned, the more complex a mission the more likely it is to fail. I'm worried whatever our mission is, it's going to be very complex."

"Because of Lord Lovat's insistence on being adaptable?"

"I think he understands that our dependence on external units will be a considerable crutch."

"So what's your point?"

Adams shrugged. "I guess I'm worried that whatever the mission is, we'll get left behind. That's what everyone is telling me happened at Saint-Nazaire."

"That was a one-time thing."

"I don't know, sir. I'm hearing a lot of rumblings from fellow senior enlisted men. I'm hearing that Combined Operations Command is very results-oriented. They don't care about the body count." They had kept walking while they talked and had arrived at their quarters. Adams took a deep breath. "All I'm saying is that Lord Lovat better be planning our own egress for wherever this raid is."

"I'm sure *Shimi* has the same concerns, First Sergeant," Parker said with a sly grin.

"Oh, you and he are thick as thieves now, sir?"

Parker laughed. "No, never. The boss is a member of the British aristocracy and I'm the lowly son of a longshoreman."

"Better than the son of a crook."

"And look how far we've come."

"True." Adams nodded. He turned and looked out past the harbor, his eyes searching for nothing in particular. "Eerie isn't it?"

"What's that?"

"Here we are, in a sleepy little English town, perfectly at peace, and less than sixty miles away sits the Nazi war machine."

"Makes you appreciate the Atlantic."

"Ain't that the truth." Adams tuned and saluted Parker. "Good evening, sir."

"Good evening, First Sergeant." Parker returned the salute, and turned and made his way toward his quarters. Adams's observation reverberated in his head. He couldn't help but agree with what he had said. Combined Operations headquarters seemed apathetic to the loss of life their raids cost. Carver had told Parker a few nasty rumors about Lord Mountbatten, including that he had taken time away from planning the upcoming raid to assist in the production of a movie about his escapades in Crete. What made the rumor more disconcerting was the fact that Mountbatten's ship was sunk at the battle of Crete. How was that worth making a movie about? Parker tried not to think about it. He trusted Lord Lovat, and for him, that was enough.

Part III
The Raid

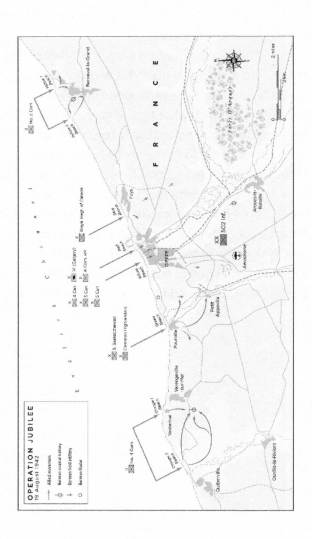

CHAPTER 14
MARCHING ORDERS

"Gentlemen, please take your seats!" Lord Mountbatten called to the room full of commanders of Army, Air, and Naval forces. The War Office conference room was packed with a variety of senior leaders. Hambro did a mental roll call and spotted a number of familiar faces. He spotted Leigh-Mallory and Lord Mountbatten, the brain trust of this operation, at the head of the table, and continued to scan the room. He spotted Field Marshal Montgomery along with General Roberts of the Canadian Army. There were a few other senior commanders whom he didn't recognize immediately. Overall, it was a motley crew of commanders from a melting pot of services and nations.

Freddy Atkinson urgently strode up to Hambro and sat down. "Sir! I went over and looked at the map. There's no marker on it for the tanks Cutter told us about, or a few other inland garrisons he mentioned."

Hambro nodded knowingly.

"I don't understand. I thought we told Combined Operations?"

"We did," Hambro sighed. "But since Leigh-Mallory's aircraft have been unable to spot them on any reconnaissance flights, and since we were unable to provide photographic evidence, Mountbatten is disputing their existence."

"Surely, you can't be serious! If I tell you the stove is hot but the metal isn't flaming red, are you going to touch it anyway?"

"That isn't a bad analogy."

"What about Cutter?"

328

Hambro frowned. Since putting him back in Normandy for the raid, both Hambro and Freddy had yet to figure out a viable extraction plan for Cutter. After the raid, it would be difficult to make any movements around Normandy, and Hambro wasn't keen about the prospect of Cutter staying a second after the raid ended. He studied the map of the area of operation and an idea flickered through his mind. "I think I have a solution." Hambro spotted Lord Lovat across the room. *It's possible; a bit risky, but it's possible.*

The lights in the room dimmed and Lord Mountbatten took his position at the lectern. "Good morning, gentlemen. Today is the day we have all been waiting for. I just came from the Prime Minister's office, and Operation JUBILEE is a go." He turned and looked over at General Roberts and motioned for him to begin.

General Roberts stole a quick glance at General Montgomery, who gave a barely visible nod. With the approval of his commanding general, General Roberts stood up and looked about the room. "Good morning, gentlemen. As you can see on the map, the Canadian 2nd Division will be bearing the brunt of the raid on Dieppe. We will be landing at Green, Red, White, and Blue beaches."

Hambro listened with limited interest, but eyed the map excitedly. To the west of General Roberts's beaches was one additional beach, and it belonged to Lord Lovat and was only a few kilometers from where Cutter was.

***

"Everyone gather around!" Lord Lovat called from the front of the sand table. A giant layout of the beachheads around Dieppe had been constructed out of the dirt and a tent sat over it to shield it from the rain.

Members of No. 4 Commandos and the handful of rangers gathered in close.

Lord Lovat tapped a swagger stick against his thigh as he waited for everyone to get into view of the sand table; Parker, Carver, and First Sergeant Adams moved to the fringes, where the other officers and senior staff noncoms had gathered.

"Right. No doubt all of you have been wondering what the bloody hell we've been training for the last month." Lord Lovat pointed his swagger stick down at the sand table. "Our mission is to raid the French town of Dieppe in northern Normandy. As you can see, we will be assaulting along six beachheads: Yellow, Blue, Red, White, Green, and Orange, going from north to south." Lord Lovat circled his stick around Red, Green, and White beaches. "Canadian forces along with the Essex Scottish regiment and a commando detachment will be the main effort pushing into Dieppe. As soon as the beachhead is established, armor will roll onto the beach and provide support to the infantry as they move into the city. While this is happening, additional attacks will be happening along Blue and Yellow beaches to protect their left flank." Lovat moved his swagger stick down and tapped it on Orange Beach. "As all this is happening, we will be seizing Orange Beach. Latest intelligence reports indicate that a German artillery battery is garrisoned in vicinity of the town of Sainte-Marguerite-sur-Mer. Our mission is to land at Orange Beach and destroy that battery." Lord Lovat paused and looked up at his men, making sure they were understanding what he was saying. "We will be landing in two locations: Orange Beach I and Orange Beach II." He pointed to both locations. "Captain Aldridge will take Charlie Troop and land at Orange Beach I. It is important to note that this beachhead is not your average landing site. A cliff face lies along the entire stretch of Orange Beach I, with the exception of two crevices that we have been told can be scaled."

Captain Aldridge raised his hand. "Sir, where are we getting this information about the crevices?"

"I'm afraid I can't say, but I believe the source to be credible."

Captain Aldridge grunted, not entirely convinced. He turned and looked at Lieutenant Boyce, searching his face for some sort of confirmation about the rock face.

Lieutenant Boyce bit his lip, his face contorted as the mountaineering expert grappled with the news. After a long pause he shrugged. "Shouldn't be an issue. I've made you chaps go up some pretty difficult terrain."

"Once Charlie Troop has scaled the crevice, they will conduct a reconnaissance of the battery and confirm its location and hold tight until the rest of us get into position." Lord Lovat dragged his swagger stick down to Orange Beach II. "As this is happening, A Troop, B Troop, and F Troop will be landing at Orange Beach II. Captains Parker and Carver will take B Troop and F Troop south along the Saâne river and sweep north to hit the Battery from the rear while Major Rackham and I take A Troop west to form up on C Troop's right flank. Once B Troop and F Troop are in position, they will begin the attack as the main effort with A and C Troop remaining in support. Once the battery has been destroyed, we will move in and secure the perimeter and defend against any German forces attempting to reinforce Dieppe." He looked around again to make sure there were no confused looks on his men's faces. "As we are conducting our attack on the ground, we expect the Luftwaffe to attempt to interdict the beaches and disrupt our landings. The RAF will be flying *en force* to engage whatever air support the Germans send our way. There will be a lot of ordnance being dropped during this operation from both the naval bombardments and our fighters. It is imperative that our unit maintain communication as much as possible as we move. Radios will be provided to each troop as our primary means of communication, followed by smoke signals and runners."

Parker eyed the terrain model. He liked the plan. It was simple, and in comparison to the rest of the raid, lacked the complexity that risked failure. The only thing he still worried about was their retreat. He raised his hand and Lord Lovat nodded to him. "When will we withdraw?"

"We will hold our ground as long as possible so that the main effort can safely retreat from Dieppe. However, if our situation becomes untenable, we'll fall back through the tree line and down the cliff to the beach. We will deploy smoke grenades to help cover our retreat and move like hell to create some distance."

Parker nodded, unsure of how strong the raid's chances were for success. He suspected he wasn't the only one. He looked over at First Sergeant Adams and saw the same concern etched on his face.

Captain Carver raised his hand. Lord Lovat nodded to him. "Sir, you mentioned armor. Will any be landing with us?"

"No, all armor will be landing to support the seizure of Dieppe. We will be carrying anti-armor weapons and mortars to help repel any armored attacks."

"What time do we land?"

"Before first light. We'll have darkness as we move in."

Parker saw Callum and Tarbor exchange glances, but said nothing. He had an idea of what they were thinking. They had handled a number of raids and had learned quickly that the smaller the raiding party the greater the chance of success. Saint-Nazaire had displayed the issue with raids by force. The element of surprise would be fickle for such a large assault, and if lost prior to the assault, it could lead to the entire force being thrown back into the sea before they seized any of their objectives.

Parker didn't like it, the looks going around among his team leaders weren't denoting confidence. He looked back at Lord Lovat and wondered how confident *he* was in the plan. He looked back over at Adams and saw him raise his hand.

"Sir, what is our egress plan?"

"The boats we came in on are to remain in place on the beach. The last thing I want is for us to retreat and not have boats waiting for us because a naval officer called them away. I made it very clear to the Combined Operations Command that No. 4 Commando will not land unless the boats we are on belong to us and not some prat aboard a battleship." Lord Lovat locked eyes with Adams, the implicit understanding between them was obvious. "The boats we come in on will have a commando on each one." Lord Lovat read Adam's mind. "They're our lifeline back to England. And although I trust our esteemed colleagues in the naval service, I trust our commandos more to see us home."

Parker smiled in satisfaction. Lord Lovat wasn't taking any chances; the commandos who stayed on the boats would kill the yeomen before letting them leave without the raiding party. No. 4 Commando had learned from past mistakes and wasn't going to be left behind.

"Good. I don't want the Resistance smuggling me out again," Carver muttered to Parker.

"Unless there are any questions, that's all I have. Go brief your troops."

***

Cutter anxiously looked out the window. It had been days since he and Talia had parted ways with Durand and Claude. The Germans had increased their patrols but had done little in the form of searching French houses. At first it had unnerved Cutter that the Germans weren't taking to the streets with the gusto he expected, but as the days dragged on he started to believe that the Germans thought that the bombing was a result of an RAF attack conducted without Resistance support. Obersturmführer Amsel had done his usual rounds, giving Cutter his usual veiled threats as he continued to pine for Talia, but other than that there was little change in the day to day. As the days continued to drag by with little to no interference from the Nazis, Cutter started to believe that the Resistance had gotten away with its assassination unscathed. Could they really have been that lucky? It was hard to believe, but was a huge windfall. To be cautious, Cutter had convinced Talia to wait another day before meeting up with Claude and Durand.

"You are far too cautious," Talia had said in annoyance. After spending four days in the cottage with nothing but each other for entertainment, they were both ready to step out into the sunlight.

Cutter couldn't help but chuckle to himself at the bitter irony of being locked in a house for multiple days with a pretty woman. Any other chap would have a tale of promiscuous sexual escapades; all he had was a tale of loss playing Faro, Belote, Old Maid, and Cribbage.

On the fifth day, they ambled out into the sun like a pair of golems. The smell of rain on the air and the feel of a soft spring breeze on their faces were welcome.

Talia stretched and looked about. "Maybe the Gestapo are hiding behind that flowerpot waiting for us to step away from the cottage," she teased.

Cutter looked over and shook his head. "Doubtful. I'd suspect they're behind that oak over there."

"Five days in that house was a bit much."

"Better safe than sorry."

They made their way through the town, taking their time to stretch their legs. The town was still deserted, but for Cutter it didn't feel as desolate as before. He wondered if it was because of their self-imposed exile in the house. Coming out of the stiflingly cramped quarters made everything enjoyable in comparison.

The two of them meandered down the street, the heels of Talia's shoes clicking against the cobblestones of the main road, their fingers interlocked intimately. As bad as things were, Cutter was happy. In the past five days the friction between him and Talia had slowly eased. The lack of trust Talia had for him had ebbed away and was replaced by the foundation of a strong, workable relationship. It hadn't been easy, but Cutter had earned Talia's trust by being honest. He looked over at her, a happy grin filling his face. "I'm sure Claude will have something for us."

Talia's eyes narrowed and she pursed her lips. She was less exuberant than Cutter, and by the look on her face wasn't as optimistic. "No doubt. Let's just hope it isn't bad news."

Cutter nodded, the grin dissipating from his face. "Let's hope you're wrong."

The pair of them made their way up to Claude's bakery and found him somberly sitting behind the counter.

Cutter nodded to him and his eyes narrowed as he caught a whiff of the pungent smell of bourbon. He looked at Claude and noticed his eyes were red. He was drunk. Cutter exchanged looks with Talia but said nothing. *This can't be* good. Claude's behavior was uncharacteristic of him. Cutter had rarely seen him not in control of his emotions, let alone drunk.

"*Bonjour*, Claude. What's wrong?"

Claude shook his head, his speech slurred as he said, "Durand has gone missing."

"What?" Shock covered Talia's face, she shot Cutter a concerned look.

Cutter motioned for them both to calm down. "Are you sure he didn't just leave for a few days?"

"His brothers don't know where he is."

"How long has he been missing?"

"A day and a half." Claude pulled a half-empty bottle of bourbon from below the counter and poured a heavy glass. "Herr Amsel has snatched him up."

"We don't know that." Cutter drummed his fingers on the counter, fear rising in the back of his mind, but he quickly stifled it. If Durand was captured, they had little to no time before Amsel would be coming for them. Cutter started to go through the contingency checklist in his head of what he needed to do if capture was apparent. For the most part, the majority of the list was completed or inapplicable. He and the Resistance operated off different code books and Cutter would need to destroy it once he sent one final transmission on the radio, before destroying that as well. He looked over at Claude. "Where is the radio."

Claude took a hefty draft from his glass and gave Cutter a dead-eyed look. "I already destroyed it."

"What?"

"I told them we were compromised and I was preparing to destroy the radio." Claude recharged his glass. He pulled a piece of paper from his pocket. "Before I destroyed it, they sent me this message for you." He raised the glass to his lips but Cutter stopped him, grabbing his wrist. "Stop drinking. We don't have time for this." He deftly took the paper from Claude and pocketed it. He would decode it at Talia's house.

Talia looked at Claude in confusion. "What will we do now?"

"We?" Claude shrugged off Cutter's grip and downed the glass of bourbon. "There is no 'we.' *We* are done, finished. I'll head south to Toulon in the morning. I have a cousin there."

"And what about Durand?"

"You and I both know if he isn't already dead, he will be soon."

"I assume this is goodbye?"

"Were you expecting us to sing "Auld Lang Syne"?"

"Well, no need to be a prick about it Claude," Cutter said with a hint of annoyance. "Best of luck. If you get captured, burn Durand, don't burn us."

"How can you say that?" Talia looked at Cutter in horror.

"Durand is burned; no harm in throwing him under the bus at this point."

"You really are an ass, Olivier," Claude said heatedly as he stood up, "but you are right." He tentatively extended a hand. "Good luck."

Cutter took it, his icy demeanor thawing a little. "Claude, I hope to see you after this war so we can laugh and cry about it. Good luck."

Claude gave a weak smile and nodded. He turned to Talia and kissed her on the cheek. "Be safe. Watch over her."

"I will." Cutter gently grabbed Talia by the arm and motioned her to the door.

"This is happening too fast."

"I know, but we need to stay calm," Cutter murmured under his breath. They walked back to the house. Cutter pulled the message from his pocket, grabbed his code book, and started to decode it. It was a short message and didn't take long to translate. When he read the message he slumped back in his chair. "Christ almighty."

Invasion tomorrow. Await retrieval at safe house B.

Talia looked over his shoulder and read the message. "Which safe house are they referring to?"

"Madame Renault's. We'll leave tonight."

"We will?"

Cutter looked up at her. "You're coming with me. I meant what I said."

"Will your supervisors let me?"

"I don't think they can say no when you're standing on English soil," Cutter said glibly as he stood and walked over to the fireplace. He put a log and tinder in and quickly lit them.

"What do we need to do?"

"Just grab some warm clothes you can move in. Everything else should be prepared," Cutter said as the fire caught and started to blaze. He grabbed the code book and the message, threw both in the fire, and watched as they ignited.

***

CHAPTER 15
JUBILEE

The steady churning of the Channel was the only other sound Parker could hear over the din of the gunboats' diesel engines. The fleet had left England hours ago and had been at sea for roughly three hours. Parker absently toyed with the shoulder straps of his Thompson as he went through a mental checklist. It was too late to do anything if he had forgotten something, but he felt confident in his men. He had ensured his team had done sufficient gear checks of each other prior to their departure and was confident they would do their job adequately. Their training had been rigorous; he had made sure of that.

After experiencing Saint-Nazaire, Parker had added a few additional training requirements to his troop. Marksmanship, squad tactics, and advanced explosives training had been emphasized by him, and he had pooled resources from No. 4 Commando to ensure the instructors were professionals in their respective fields. He shivered as the spray of jetsam doused his clothes. The gunboat bucked violently as it hurdled over a swell, the prow rising with the wave and crashing back down into the surf, showering Parker's team in cold Channel water. Parker ignored the cold wet as best he could and looked around his gunboat. The two men nearest to him were rangers, First Sergeant Adams and Corporal Murray. The rest of the boat was comprised of British commandos. Hardly a word was spoken by any of them. They all kept their heads up and out, keeping an eye out for land.

"Any minute now," Murray muttered.

Parker took a deep breath and steadied himself. Adams eyed him calmly. "We'll be alright, sir. The lads are ready."

Parker nodded in agreement and looked back up. He could barely see anything in the dark, but as he strained his eyes he spotted the beaches of Normandy. *Moment of truth*, he thought. As he gazed out at the dark silhouette of land, silent recognition permeated the gunboat like electricity as raiders anxiously shifted their weight and started to do quick checks of their weapons. No one spoke, but there was an implicit communication among them that their work was about to start. Parker instinctively reached for the grenades on his web belt, double checking that the pins were taped and secured. He had heard stories of pins falling out of grenades accidentally at the worst possible moments and was terrified of the thought of it happening to him.

He ran his fingers over the tape strips and made sure that the adhesive stuck to the metal pins. As he did so, a thunderous crack echoed overhead as the guns of the four destroyers supporting the raid started their barrage. Orange explosions lit up the sky in front of them as the ships' rounds exploded around Dieppe. As plumes of light from the explosions filled the sky, Parker quickly scanned the beach, doing his best to get his bearings. He could see that it was low tide; a large stretch of pale sand was exposed. Parker bit his lip. It was a lot of open beach. If there was just one machine gun nest overlooking the beach, his men would be cut to pieces.

"Everyone wake up," Adams shouted, shaking everyone out of their daze. "If they didn't before, they know we're here now. Guns up, heads down!"

Parker looked around; he could make out the other gunboats plugging away toward shore as explosions flashed. He looked back down and double-checked his Thompson submachine gun. He pulled back on the charging handle and chambered a round and made sure the safety was on.

"Three minutes!" the helmsman shouted.

Parker nodded and looked over at Corporal Sykes. The commando manned the Browning machine gun that was secured to the gun rails. Parker had selected him to stay with the boat to cover their retreat. He had taken solace in leaving Sykes with the boats. If all else failed, Parker knew Sykes would scuttle a gunboat before letting it leave without his troop.

Sykes scanned the horizon, his finger hovering over the trigger. He caught Parker looking at him and shot him a grin, an ugly scar curving across his upper lip twisting his smile into a chilling sneer. "Don't worry, sir, I'll be here when you get back. I'm not repeating Saint-Nazaire."

Parker nodded but said nothing. He ran a hand over his vest and absently checked his web gear again and made sure everything was secure. He had three grenades, seven magazines, a compass, a map of the region, two canteens, two K rations, and a flashlight. He adjusted the straps to his helmet and brought his Thompson up and aimed it at the shore.

"Thirty seconds!"

"Alright, boys, clear the beach quickly and get to cover," Parker said as he felt the bottom of the boat begin so slide against sand.

"Go! Go! Go!"

Parker and the rest of his team emptied from the boat into the waist-deep water. Sloshing through the surf, they sprinted up the beach as fast as they could.

The sand gave under Parker's weight with each step and made running across the beach difficult. By the time he dove for cover by the dunes, he was gasping for air. He struggled to steady his breathing and looked around. Silhouettes of rangers and commandos came out of the darkness like phantoms as they sprinted from the surf and dove behind the dunes next to Parker. Their forms rose and fell in the darkness as Parker listened to their ragged breathing.

We need to do more beach training, Parker thought absently, making a mental note, *if there ever is a next time*. He looked up and down the beach, searching for any stragglers, but found none. He waited a moment and listened. He couldn't hear anything other than the roll of the surf and barely, from a hundred feet away, the muted rumble of a handful of diesel engines.

If any Germans had been on the beach, their landing would have been much different. Parker stood up and in a low crouch ran across the beach, searching for his team leaders. The white sands reflected the moonlight well and made it easy for Parker to spot his commandos and rangers. A bulky body came up to him in a crouched run. "Captain Parker?" the commando asked in a loud stage whisper.

Parker recognized Corporal Tarbor before he even started to speak in his thick Scottish accent. His bulky figure was difficult to miss, even in the moonlight. Parker planted a knee in the sand and nodded. "Yeah, where's your team?"

"Both mine and Sergeant Callum's are assembled down that way." Tarbor jerked his thumb back the way he had come. "Captain Carver is formed up further down the beach. Lieutenant Colonel Lovat wants a situation report, but Captain Carver is having trouble with his radio."

"Okay, we need to move fast. I'll talk with Lovat on my radio. I need both your and Callum's teams to push over the dunes and set up security. Once secured, Carver and I will bring up the rear. We need to get moving."

Tarbor grunted and shifted his weight, adjusting the Boys anti-tank gun on his shoulder. "Got it, sir." He turned around and jogged back over to his team and started to issue orders. They quickly shouldered their machine guns with a few strained grunts and started to move over the dunes with Callum's team.

Parker turned and looked around and spotted his radio operator and First Sergeant Adams. He duck-walked over to them and motioned for the headset.

"Looks like we're in the right place," Adams said as the radio operator handed Parker the radio headset.

"Yeah, but we need to get off this beach. We're fish in a barrel if any Germans see us on those cliffs," Parker said, nodding to the steep hill to the west as he put the headset to his ear. "*Whiskey 1, this is Baker 6. Orange II is open for business, moving to secure assembly area.*"

The crisp British accent of Lieutenant Colonel Lovat replied on the radio, "*Roger, Baker 6. Proceed with seizure. Orange I is open for business; Charlie 2 is conducting reconnaissance of Objective 1.*"

Parker nodded; satisfied that everything was going as planned. *Nothing wrong yet.*

"Be advised, Baker 6, we have received word that our armor is floundering in the Channel. As soon as Objective 1 is secured, be prepared for follow-on assignments."

"Roger, Whiskey 1. Baker 6 copies all. Baker 6 out." Parker handed the headset back to his radio operator. He wondered what follow-on assignment Lovat was talking about but quickly dismissed it as he watched both Tarbor's and Callum's teams move over the dunes.

Parker turned and spotted his two other team leaders, Sergeant Carter and Corporal Ferguson. "Carter, Ferguson, as soon as the assembly area is secured, I want your teams over this dune. Make sure to check your mortars and make sure they're clear of sand."

"Will do, sir."

"Sir, Tarbor just radioed. They're over the dune," the radio operator said, pointing in their direction.

"Alright, let's go. Carter, get your guys moving."

Parker clambered over the steep dune with Adams and his radio operator in tow. As he slid down the back side of the dune, he found Corporal Murray waiting for him at the bottom.

"Sir, the rest of us are spread out right here as a base of fire if anything comes our way. F Troop is up a ways," Corporal Murray whispered, the twilight glinting off the scope of his Springfield sniper rifle.

Parker nodded. "Hold here. The rest of Baker will be coming over the dune. Get them sorted and ready to move." He turned and quickly surveyed this side of the dune. The sand quickly gave way to lush green vegetation as rolling hills swept the landscape. Their objective wasn't far away, but as the sun started to rise, Parker became more aware that they needed to move quickly. Soon the cover of darkness would be gone and the element of surprise along with it. Parker made his way up past Tarbor's and Callum's teams and started to see members of F Troop scattered among the brush and foliage doing their best to remain invisible against the encroaching sunlight.

He spotted Carver and duckwalked over to him.

"I think we have everyone," Carver said.

Parker nodded and looked up. The naval bombardment had ceased as they came ashore, but for some reason cannon fire could still be heard.

"That's the Germans. We need to get going," Carver said, and pointed down at his map. He traced his finger along the meandering river that fed into the Channel. "We follow the Saâne river two kilometers, then swing north to hit the battery."

Parker nodded. "I've spoken with Lovat. A Troop has landed along the beach to our north and is proceeding as planned. One of my teams will scout ahead. Yours provide rear security?"

"Sounds good. My radio is limited in range, but I think I can send traffic now."

"We'll conduct radio checks prior to our turn north," Parker said motioning for Murray. Murray scampered over, making a point to keep his rifle and scope out of the sand.

"Murray, we're pushing out for the river. Get us on the west side of it. Roughly a kilometer down we will be swinging north for the battery." Parker circled his finger around the region of Le Mesnil on the map. "We suspect the battery is in vicinity of this village. Realistically, follow the cannon fire; if it gets louder, we're going the right way."

"Keep to the woods; it'll give us better concealment," Carver added.

"Right," Parker agreed. "We need to get moving. If you see anything, let us know."

Murray nodded wordlessly and went back to his team.

Parker turned and waved the radio operator back over and grabbed the headset. *"Whiskey 1, this is Baker 6."*

"Roger, Baker 6. Go ahead."

"Assembly area secured. We have both Fox and Baker Troops ready to proceed to Objective 1."

"Roger, Baker 6. Proceed to Objective 1."

***

Cutter worked the action of his pistol and inspected the barrel, making sure it was clear of dirt. He hadn't been able to sleep, and had already cleaned it three times in the past four hours, but it was all he could do to keep his mind off the raid. Dawn was fast approaching, and with it, the riskiest part of the mission.

Cutter had no idea what was waiting for them at safe house B, but he could only hope it was a commando team with a quick egress plan. His thoughts turned to Talia and he couldn't help but wonder how he would bring her with him to London. He knew Hambro would be pissed as hell, but he figured he could weather the consequences. The Gestapo had backed them into a wall.

With Durand's disappearance, bringing Talia back with him could be justified. *I can worry about it when we get to England*, he thought. Right now, all they had to do was make it to the safe house and the commandos would get them home.

Cutter stopped fiddling with the pistol and set it on the table. He debated trying to eat something, but thought better of it. He doubted he could hold anything down, and simply brewed a pot of tea.

The ceiling of the kitchen creaked and Cutter listened as Talia started to get ready. He sipped at his tea as she made her way downstairs and checked her appearance in the living room mirror. She was dressed smartly in a pair of dark trousers and work boots and a blue wool turtleneck.

"They should be landing in the next thirty minutes."

"How will we get to the safe house? You still haven't told me your plan."

"As soon as the raid commences, the Germans will be too busy to the east to bother with us. We'll take the car to the safe house and await the commandos there."

"I don't see it being that easy."

Cutter gave her a knowing wink. "O ye of little faith." With his foot he slid his trunk out from under the table. Talia hadn't noticed it before, but bent down and opened it. Inside were two Sten machine guns and four magazines. "Call it our back up plan."

"Where did you get these?"

"If there is one thing I always have, it's a contingency plan. There's also a timed explosive rigged to the car, and four grenades in the glove compartment. Well before I started sending weapons to the Resistance cells, I set up a cache on the outskirts of town."

"Why is it that this is the first I'm hearing of this cache?"

Cutter's smirk faded from his lips and he shifted uncomfortably in his seat. "Well, at the time I didn't trust you."

"But you do now?"

"That should be obvious."

"Time will tell," Talia said simply, and walked over to the kitchen window and gazed out into the twilight. "We still haven't heard from Durand." She didn't want to admit it, but she suspected he was dead.

Cutter nodded but didn't say anything, unsure of whether or not he should jump to the most probable conclusion.

"It's been a week since the bombing. A body hasn't been provided by the Germans like they normally do to discourage us, and no one has seen him."

"You think he betrayed us?"

"That or he was captured and will be tortured into answering questions, and we both know everyone talks eventually."

Cutter grunted, "We've been through this. If the Gestapo had captured him, he would be in one of their cells being tortured till he begged for death. If we encounter any issues, we have the Stens and the grenades."

Talia nodded absently. She reached down and grabbed one of the Stens from the trunk and inspected it. As she did so, an explosion shook the house. Plates and cups rattled in the cabinets and the sound of dogs barking could be heard outside.

Cutter jumped at the noise. "The raid has begun." He immediately felt like an idiot for pointing out the obvious. He grabbed his pistol from the table and put it in his shoulder holster and checked to make sure his F-S knife was secured in his waistband. "Talia, you have everything you need?"

She nodded and placed a magazine in her Sten and handed Cutter one. She paused and took one final look around her uncle's house. A whirlwind of emotions swept through her in an instant. The sadness of leaving behind her family home quickly was replaced by a feeling of elation at the knowledge that by the end of the day she could be in England. As she thought about that, a fearful realization washed over her. "For all I know, I may never see this house again."

"Never is a long time," Cutter said as he pushed the magazine into the Sten and cocked it. "I promise we will return."

Talia gave a curt nod and looked at Cutter. "I never said this, but I'm glad you came back."

"Me, too." Cutter smiled and shut off all the lights in the house and opened the back door. Lights were on throughout the village as everyone was awakened by the sound of the artillery. Cutter waited a second to let his eyes adjust to the dark before walking outside. As he waited, a German half-track raced past the car.

Cutter watched impassively but felt the knot in his gut tighten. *If they're rolling through here with a half-track, they no doubt have more vehicles up the road.* Cutter grumbled and walked back into the house.

"German's have a half-track. We can't take the car."

"It's still dark and the safe house is a mile away. Could we walk?"

Cutter's mind turned as he contemplated their chances and shook his head. "Too risky. We could easily be mistaken for raiders and shot. We'll wait thirty minutes and then drive."

***

Squadron Leader Faraday hated flying at night; the thought of crashing into another aircraft always scared him. Fortunately, the sun was beginning to peek over the horizon, making it easier to identify the rest of No. 71 Squadron's aircraft. The whole squadron was in the air for this raid. From what Faraday had gathered when Leigh-Mallory had given the briefing, all three Eagle Squadrons were supporting the mission; an unusual happenstance that Faraday suspected was fueled by politics to show that America had officially entered the war.

Faraday checked his heading and made sure they were on course. Their orders had changed an hour before takeoff. Rather than just drop their bombs and gain altitude, their mission was now to conduct interdiction operations on one of the artillery batteries, code-named Hitler Battery, inland of Dieppe and intercept any German air support before they could attack the raiders.

"*All flights, listen up. This is Saxon Leader. Reese and Victor Flights will conduct interdiction operations while Swift covers the skies. I want tight, efficient work . . . no heroics.*" Faraday stressed his final words. It was meant mainly for the seven new pilots that had joined the squadron two weeks prior.

"*Roger, Saxon Leader,*" Faust, Tombs, and Chambers, the three flight leaders, chorused.

As the sun started to creep into the sky, the coastline started to come into view. Faraday could just barely make out the shapes of the boats transporting the raiders below him. He turned and looked over his shoulder to inspect his pilots. Spread out in a wing formation, nineteen Spitfires churned through the air. As much as Faraday questioned the tactical potency of the big wing, he couldn't help but marvel at the site of his whole squadron moving as one. It was a terrible beauty, one that the Germans would no doubt regret ever laying eyes on.

The sun glared off the windshields of each aircraft, obscuring the heads of his pilots and making the Spitfires appear all the more like an inhuman beast. A chill went down Faraday's spine, a combination of fear and excitement at the thought of this being his first large-scale operation as squadron leader. He said a quick prayer, hoping that he had done everything he could to ensure his pilots had the proper training and preparation for this mission.

"Alright, lads, heads on a swivel. Swift Flight, call out any bandits, and all of you watch that crossfire from the ground."

"Saxon Leader, this is Paddington aboard the HMS *Fernie. We will be vectoring you in. Correct your course to 1-6-4."*

Faraday pushed down on the rudder and brought his aircraft onto the designated course. *"Roger, Paddington. Changing course to 1-6-4. Any bandits identified?"* He looked over his shoulder to make sure the rest of the squadron adjusted course as well. They were all listening in on his conversation with the controller aboard the *Fernie*.

"None at this time. Proceed with your mission. Be advised, coastal barrage from the Navy will conclude in two minutes."

Faraday acknowledged him and switched his mic to speak with the rest of his squadron. *"All flights prepare to conduct initial gun runs on Hitler Battery. Deploy bombs and begin engaging targets at your discretion."*

All flight leaders acknowledged him and started to break off from the squadron formation. Swift Flight started to climb to get a better view of the battle space while Reese and Victor moved into position for their initial gun run.

As soon as the naval barrage ceased, Victor Flight split up and started to dive on the battery.

Faraday watched as the bombs detonated, destroying at least one artillery piece. Reese Flight followed suit and mimicked Victor with their approach and dropped their payload. Faraday watched in annoyance as the blast from the bombs had little to no impact on the three remaining artillery pieces. *"Victor Flight, this is Saxon Leader, replace Swift Flight on overwatch so they can conduct their bombing run."*

Victor Flight quickly climbed and replaced Swift Flight as they started to descend. Faraday positioned himself behind them as they flew in on their bombing run and dropped his bombs with them. He gave a victorious whoop as he pulled back on the stick and watched as their bombs landed on target, knocking out the rest of the battery. Faraday banked and turned sharply. As he turned, a puff of smoke appeared next to his wing and a pressurized *thump* rocked his aircraft. Faraday quickly pulled back on the stick and started to climb. Tracer fire and flak saturated the sky as antiaircraft guns and machine guns started to target his squadron.

Faraday pulled back hard on the stick, moved into a tight turn, and pushed forward on the throttle, going into a corkscrew. He felt his body squish down in his seat as the force of gravity started to exert its weight on him. He tightened his leg muscles and grunted, slowing the blood rushing down away from his brain as he quickly turned. Faraday kept the gun crews on the ground guessing as he darted across the sky, never flying straight for more than a few seconds. His eyes scanned the skies, hunting for their real target.

"*There they are,*" he heard Faust call out, his voice flat and monotone like he was commenting on the weather. "*Messerschmitts to the south. Looks like a whole squadron.*"

"*Tallyho.*"

***

An hour ticked by before Cutter and Talia felt that it was safe for them to leave. The naval barrage had lasted an entire hour before the whirring buzz of aircraft started to drone overhead. With the arrival of the RAF, and the realization that an aerial assault from paratroopers wasn't occurring, the Germans had started to frantically move toward the beaches and antiair batteries.

Cutter checked his watch; it was nearly 4:00 a.m. "It's now or never. The roads should be clear."

"You'd best let me drive. I know these roads better and can get us there quicker."

Cutter nodded and once again checked the road outside the house; it was clear. He shoved the Sten underneath his coat and walked out to the car. Talia quickly followed and climbed into the car and started it. Cutter did one final check of the road and got in. "Drive fast, but don't look like you're in a hurry."

"What the hell does that mean?"

"Never mind. Just drive."

***

Sergeant Callum checked his bandoliers and adjusted the shoulder straps of his pack with a wordless grunt. He searched the faces of the men around him for any doubts, any loss of nerve, any fear. He had done nearly a dozen raids like this one, and had come to accept two things: Nothing ever went according to plan and the enemy never did what you expected or wanted them to.

He watched Captain Parker and First Sergeant Adams as they checked the map. He trusted both of them. Captain Parker had proven a quick study during Saint-Nazaire and wasn't afraid of asking the hard questions. His composure under pressure was a rare trait among his peers, but the one thing that worried Callum was Parker's ability to make the tough decisions that came with command. For that, he trusted Adams to be a solid backstop. As a relic of the Great War, Adams understood that there wasn't always room for compassion or neatness as a commander. Sometimes a decision had to be made that would end peoples' lives, or would have a messy outcome.

"Christ, that's a lot of fighters," Tarbor observed through the breakage in the trees.

Callum looked up. He could see contrail plumes covering the sky in multiple directions as aircraft started to engage in multiple dogfights.

"Think we're winning?" a commando whispered.

"I suppose if we weren't, the Luftwaffe would be attacking us instead."

First Sergeant Adams looked up from the map and shot them a murderous look. "Quiet!"

Callum bobbed his head apologetically and resumed scanning his sector as they waited to see what the holdup was. They were making slow work navigating through the forest. Aerial intelligence hadn't seen this, nor had any brief mentioned the thickness of the foliage. Between the tightness of the trees and the thick underbrush, forward movement had stalled twice in the past thirty minutes. Callum briefly wondered if when their armor reached shore they might encounter similar issues. He looked around; both troops had resorted to walking single file through the woods to move faster. They had followed the meandering river as far as they could and had already crossed to the other bank.

Callum watched eagerly as Corporal Carter bounded through the woods back toward them. "Sir, Murray says they've reached checkpoint one and are sweeping north."

Parker folded the map and shoved it into his jacket. "Good, Tarbor. Once we're clear of the woods, push your team wide to the east and cover the right flank on the advance." Parker turned and looked at Callum. "Do the same with yours to the west, and I'll bring up the middle with the rest of Baker Troop."

Callum nodded and turned to his boys. "Alright, lads, break's over. Devon, you're lead scout. We've got the left flank. You know the drill." He checked his watch one last time as they started to shuffle out of the trees. The pale light of morning had set in, and as far as Callum was concerned, the element of surprise had sidled away with its arrival. They needed to make up for lost time quickly if they wanted to remain undetected much longer. By moving so far inland and looping behind the artillery batteries, it was a sure thing that they would surprise the Germans by attacking from the south rather than from the seaside. But going this deep into enemy territory had its trade-offs. If a single German spotted them, the game would be up.

Callum hopped over a dead tree and looked up in annoyance. The incessant buzz of aircraft overhead started to aggravate him, like a mosquito flying around his ear and refusing to fly away.

"That noise really is annoying," Adams murmured as he fell in step next to Callum.

"Indeed."

"Make sure your boys are quick on their feet if we come into contact. I don't want anyone freezing up, especially in the open."

"You don't have to worry about my lads."

Adams shot Callum a skeptical look. "If I had a buffalo nickel for every time I heard that. Just keep them moving." Without another word he stepped off toward Tarbor's team.

Callum watched him for a brief moment. He liked Adams. He had dealt with few American senior enlisted men, but he liked what he saw of the grizzled old man. In the few weeks he had been attached to Baker, he had become a force of stability and had quickly earned the trust of the British veterans. His experience and demeanor made it so that he was easy to approach with a problem while simultaneously being someone you didn't want to make angry. Although Captain Parker was their commander, there was no question that First Sergeant Adams was the father of Baker Troop.

"Sergeant, Fox is splitting off from us," Reynolds murmured, nodding his head toward the far side of the field. Captain Carver's troop slowly started to disappear into the adjacent woods.

"Eyes up. We aren't far from the battery. Magar, make sure your explosives are secured, we're gonna need them in a hurry."

Callum's Gurkha assistant team leader nodded his head and patted the satchel on his hip. "Don't you worry, Sergeant."

Callum nodded and eyed the nasty-looking kukri knife that swung from a sheath next to the satchel. He pitied the German that would have to face off against that. In close quarters, Magar had proven unmatched in his prowess, both with his fists and with his obtuse angled dagger.

One of Carter's men, an American ranger, shuffled up next to Callum. "Sarge, we just passed the first checkpoint. Moving to objective one."

What the bloody hell is a Sarge? "Thanks. Get back to the center."

The ranger nodded and scampered across the thirty-foot gap Callum's team had created between them and Parker's main force.

"Eyes up, lads. Don't be surprised if an enemy listening post is out and about."

The troop quickly closed the remaining distance of the field and reentered the trees. Callum breathed a sigh of relief once they were under the verdant canopy of the forest. He had felt naked and exposed in the fields. As he looked around, he noticed that the trees were much more spread out than the dense foliage along the river. It would make moving much quicker. Having thoroughly studied the map of the area, Callum knew that they weren't far from the artillery. If they stuck to the woods, they would end up at a crossroads that was right next to the battery.

The troop started to pick up the pace and started to cover ground quicker. As they moved through the woods, Callum noticed that the drone of the aircraft overhead had abated. Now, aside from the muted rumble of the artillery, it was dead quiet. The crunch of pine needles and the rustle of equipment on the raiders' backs was a cacophony. Callum hadn't seen any birds or other wildlife that usually inhabited the woods and it made him uneasy. He exchanged glances with Magar.

"I don't like this, Sergeant."

Callum nodded and motioned for the rest of the team to slow down. Sensing danger, his arm signal was mimicked by commandos up and down the line as the entire troop slowed. They struggled to find cover wherever they stood, and did their best to conceal themselves.

Callum looked around. Sunlight danced among the trees as the shady branches shifted with the wind. "Reynolds, take Devon. I want—"

"Contact front!"

Callum ducked down just as an MG42 machine gun started to bark. Bullets whizzed around them, cracking off the trees and snapping branches. Callum stuck his head up and looked to see where the gunfire was coming from. The muzzle flash of the machine gun was easily visible in the early morning light. A German machine gun team had holed up on the second floor of a cottage at the edge of the forest near the intersection of the second road.

Callum looked over to where Captain Parker was and spotted Tarbor next to him, arranging the machine gun section. The machine gunners in Tarbor's team were already laying down a heavy barrage of fire from their Brens.

Seeing that Tarbor had already started to trade fire, Callum got into a low crouch and sprinted a short distance, ducking behind a heavy oak tree that had fallen over. "Devon! Reynolds! Lay down fire! Magar, you're with me. We're going to take out that gun!"

Magar jumped up, sprinted past Callum, and dropped down below a shallow dip in the earth. He started to return fire with the machine gun nest.

Callum looked over toward the center of the line and spotted Captain Parker moving with Carter's and Ferguson's teams. He heaved himself up and sprinted a short distance past Magar and ducked behind a tree. He repeated the process a few more times, leapfrogging between cover as they got closer and closer to the house. The whole time the German machine gun nest continued to fire, traversing a withering hail of rounds across the entirety of Baker Troop's line of attack. As Callum sprinted from a tree and threw himself behind a small boulder, he watched Carter's and Ferguson's advance stall.

The German machine gunner was smart and knew what he was doing. Focusing his fire on Baker Troop's center he had all but halted their advance. If Callum's team couldn't flank and destroy the nest quickly, there was a good chance the entire troop could be outflanked by German forces in the area.

"Moving!" Magar called as he stood up and sprinted past Callum and dove behind a decrepit fence that sat along the side of the house.

Callum cast one more sidelong glance at the rest of Baker Troop. Barely anyone was returning fire. *Oh Christ.* He pulled a grenade from his web belt and took a deep breath to steady himself. "Moving!" He quickly bounced off the tree he was behind and sprinted the last fifteen feet to the cottage and got tight against the wall. In a single fluid motion, he quickly pulled the pin and tossed the grenade up into the window where the German machine gun team was. The muted explosion of the grenade was followed by the sharp scream of pain as shrapnel, both metal and wood, shredded both Germans.

"Guns down!" Callum shouted, after waiting a minute to see if the machine gun fire would resume. He looked at Magar. "On me!"

Magar sprinted up next to him, his Sten at the ready. He kept the gun up with one hand while he drew his vicious kukri with the other. The pair inched toward the door slowly, straining to hear any signs of life in the house.

"Ready?"

Magar nodded his head.

"Do it."

Magar pushed off the wall and, with a running start, barreled into the door sending it crashing open. Callum quickly moved through the doorway behind him, his Sten at the ready. They quickly swept the first floor and moved upstairs. They found the machine gun nest in the bedroom. The two Germans manning the gun were dead.

Magar stuck both corpses with his kukri for good measure. "Last thing we want is these bloody Bosche waking up."

Callum nodded. "Come on, let's get back to it." As the two made their way back outside the house, Parker ran up next to them.

"All clear?"

Callum nodded.

"We need to get moving. No doubt the battery heard that."

"There wasn't a field phone or radio with that machine gun nest. It won't be long before they send a squad down here to investigate and check in."

Parker nodded and peeked around the corner of the cottage. The intersection was less than fifty feet away. A small berm ran the length of the road acting as a natural barricade surrounding the farm where the battery was located. He could distinctly make out the tops of the battery's guns above the berm as they fired.

Smoke puffed from the barrels of the guns. With each shot, the barrel recoiled downward from the force of the blast and bounced back up to firing position like an angry piston. Parker watched as German soldiers scrambled into firing positions, alert to Baker's location after their engagement with the machine gun in the cottage.

"They know we're here."

Callum peered around the corner of the house. He could see a handful of Germans across the road by the battery diving into foxholes, but none of them were firing. "Why aren't they firing on us?"

"I don't know." Parker looked to his left and right; his entire team had moved up through the forest to the edge of village and was well hidden by either the houses or the foliage.

"I don't think they know where we are," Adams said in disbelief.

"We need to make a move before they get wise."

"*Whiskey 1, this is Baker 6. We are in position,*" Parker said as he made hand gestures, arranging his forces as best he could. He motioned for Carter to move his

362

mortar team between two houses and motioned for Tarbor's team to move up to the intersection. First Sergeant Adams motioned to Ferguson and Murray to move with him around the left flank.

"Roger, Baker 6. When ready, proceed with seizure of objective one."

"Roger, Whiskey 1." Parker darted toward the intersection, with Callum following after him. He looked down the road and spotted First Sergeant Adams with Ferguson and Murray covering their left flank and Carter between the two houses with his mortar team at the ready. They each gave him the thumbs up.

Satisfied, Parker got back on the radio. *"Fox 6, this is Baker 6."*

Carver's voice clicked metallically over the radio. *"Go ahead, Baker 6."*

"Baker is ready to assault. What is the status of Fox?"

"Fox will be ready in one, I repeat, one minute."

"Roger. We will attack at that time." Parker checked his watch. He raised his index finger and shook it, making sure everyone understood. Adams, Callum, and the rest nodded their understanding. Seconds ticked by slowly as they waited.

Callum swore it was the longest minute of his life. He reached for his bandolier and made sure he had a magazine ready for when the one in his Sten ran out. He looked over at Parker. "Having fun yet, sir?"

Parker shot him a dirty look. "Fuck off, Callum."

Magar and the rest of Callum's team snorted in laughter.

"Alright, lads, lock it up. Let's get back to it."

"Twenty seconds." Parker tensed and planted a hand firmly on the berm, preparing himself to launch over it first.

Callum watched him and frowned. "Sir, you don't need to go over the top first. This isn't the Great War."

Parker opened his mouth to respond but the sound of a machine gun erupted to his right. Parker's head snapped in the direction of the sound and he quickly realized that Fox Troop had opened fire. *Goddammit, they're early*. Parker looked over and saw Carver's troop charge across the empty field along the Germans' flank.

Germans screamed as Carver's troop hit them. They had been expecting an attack from Parker's position and had been caught off guard. Parker quickly stuck his head up over the berm and spotted the Germans picking up their guns and trying to direct them toward Carver. Now was their chance.

"Let's go!"

Sergeant Callum gave a whoop and hurdled over the berm, his team following quickly after him. Parker clambered over the berm a second after him and started to run. He sprinted twenty-five feet before a single German noticed him. Parker could see the look of shock on a German's face fifty feet away, still not entirely sure who Parker or his commandos were. Callum, a few steps in front of Parker stopped in his tracks and took a well-aimed shot at the gawking German. The round hit the German's helmet and blood poured down his head like a can of tomato soup. The impact of the round propelled the German's body backward into one of his comrades who was setting up the machine gun.

The tall, lanky German took one look at his fallen friend and gave a quick shout. Parker could see the shocked look on his face and before Parker could shoot him he ducked below a sandbag. Shouts started to sound across the German line as they started to react to Parker's assault. A handful of machine guns started to reposition to their original locations, while half of them continued to try and repel Carver's assault on their flank.

Parker aimed his Thompson submachine gun and gently pulled the trigger, firing off multiple bursts at the machine gun nest. As he emptied his magazine, one of Tarbor's men chucked a grenade at the nest.

"Get down, sir!"

Parker dove behind a divot in the earth and quickly reloaded as the grenade went off. He charged his Thompson and stood back up to find the machine gun nest a smoking mess of carnage.

"Keep moving! Keep laying down suppressing fire!"

Callum moved past Parker and continued toward the battery, encouraging his men as he went. Magar hurdled a barbed wire barricade and rolled behind a dirt mound and started to fire his Sten at the battery. Meanwhile, Devon and Reynolds moved past and jumped into a shallow trench that intersected the battery.

"Sergeant! Magar! Get in the trench!"

Callum and Magar quickly leapfrogged through cover and entered the trench system with Devon and Reynolds. The floor of the trench was waterlogged and muddy.

"Shit!" Magar groaned as his boots sunk below the ankle into the mud.

"Keep moving!"

Callum poked his head up over the trench for a split second to survey their progress. He looked over and saw Carver's troop moving up on his right flank. They were making quick work of any Germans in their path and were gaining ground. Callum spotted Parker with Tarbor's team trading fire with one of the machine gun nests. The nest was only a few meters from where Callum's team was and the Germans hadn't seen them dive into the trench.

"Magar, prime a grenade!" Callum shouted as he pulled a grenade off his own web belt. He pointed in the general direction of the machine gun nest. "Four meters! Ready? One, two, three!" Both Magar and Callum tossed their grenades.

A split second later the grenades detonated and the machine gun fire faded. Callum stuck his head up over the trench and motioned to Parker and Tarbor that the gun was clear.

Parker nodded and started to move out of cover only to be beaten back as machine gun fire raked the ground in front of him kicking up clumps of dirt.

"How many damn machine guns do they bloody well have?"

"Don't ask questions, just keep shooting!"

Callum and his team trudged through the trench and made their way further into the heart of the battery with little opposition. The Germans were so focused on their left flank and front, they had all but forgotten their right flank. The machine gun nest Callum and his team had just taken out must have been the only defense covering this side of the battery. They were now close to the first artillery piece.

"Alright, the first gun is right around this corner. Move fast. Magar, stay back. As soon as this gun is secured, I want it detonated immediately. Ready?"

Callum's team wordlessly nodded.

"Alright, let's go!"

Callum rounded the corner of the trench and found himself face-to-face with a German soldier. The look on the German's face was one of shock and surprise, but being taken off guard didn't slow the German down. Before Callum had a chance to react, the German shoved Callum back into the corner of the trench and fumbled with his MP-40 submachine gun.

Before the German had a chance to bring his gun up, Corporal Magar was on him. Punching, shoving, and gouging, Magar viciously assaulted the German, keeping him from using his gun. After two quick jabs to the face, Magar quickly drew his kukri knife and drove it into the German's side.

The German let out a pained howl as the knife cut through bone and meat and drove deep into his abdomen. In a quick, fluid motion, Magar pulled the knife from the German's side and, with one hand, pointed his Sten at his head and pulled the trigger.

It was all over in an instant. Magar shot Callum a concerned look, but was batted away as Callum struggled to his feet. "Just got the wind knocked out of me. Go!"

Without another word, Magar, Devon, and Reynolds moved on toward the gun, with Callum bringing up the rear.

They found two more Germans manning the gun and quickly dispatched them. In a matter of seconds, Magar had the artillery piece rigged to blow.

"Fire in the hole!"

With a muted thud, the explosives detonated and left the artillery piece a deformed version of what it once was. Callum looked around and surveyed the battlefield. Most of the gunfire had subsided.

"Clear?"

"Clear!"

"Clear here!"

Callum spotted Parker moving freely through the field as he and Tarbor's team moved up toward the gun. As Parker surveyed the carnage he couldn't help but let a grin crack through his lips. They had secured their objective.

"Nice work, Sergeant."

"Thank you, sir. You didn't do half bad yourself."

Parker nodded and looked up and down the line of artillery pieces. Carver's troop had secured most of the guns, and Parker's troop was moving in to seize the other ones. They had successfully seized their objective without issue. "Demo team up! Team leaders, I want a head count and ammo count."

"I need a medic!" Adams called.

The grin faded from Parker's lips; that was the one demand no commander wanted to hear. Parker looked over to where Adams was and then back at the guns.

"Go, sir, I'll supervise this," Callum said, reading his mind.

Parker nodded and ran over to Adams. Corporal Ives, one of their two medics, was already on the scene.

Adams looked at Parker as he walked over. "It's Murray, sir."

Parker looked down. Murray's face was a pale white, an angry red hole gushed blood from his abdomen. Lying next to him was a German soldier writhing in agony from a narrow hole in his side; it wasn't a bullet wound. Parker looked around and saw that Adams's bayonet was red and dripping with blood.

"We need to get Carson over here." Parker turned to call the other medic over.

"Sir, hold fast on that."

Parker stopped and turned back to face Adams and shot him a questioning look.

"That bastard shot Murray, and after he went down, came over and starting kicking him in the face and body. Wasn't enough to bring Murray within an inch of his life. As far as I'm concerned, he's waived his right to receiving medical aid from us."

Parker looked back down at Murray and noticed for the first time that his face was covered in blood. It had been difficult to see earlier since everyone's faces had been painted in black. Parker locked eyes with Murray and saw the anger and fury in his eyes; if able to, he would have already strangled the German.

"As much as I agree with that sentiment, it's our moral duty to give him aid." Parker turned back toward the artillery pieces to call over the other medic.

Crack!

Parker jumped at the sound of the gunshot and spun around. The back of the German's head was gone and blood oozed from a bullet hole in his forehead. Parker looked at Murray who had his arm outstretched with his 1911 Colt .45 pistol gripped firmly in his hand, still aimed at the German.

"He was reaching for his knife," Murray argued before Parker could say a thing. Parker gave him a hard look but stayed silent.

"Sir, Captain Carver is heading this way," First Sergeant Adams said quickly, attempting to alleviate the tension from the situation.

Carver hopped over a piece of barbed wire and walked up next to him. "Nice to see you in one piece, Malcom."

"Corran, appreciate the help. Was wondering when you were going to join the fight." Parker scowled, his eyes still on Murray as Ives treated his chest wound.

"Well, that's why I thought you Yanks joined the war." He looked down at Murray and watched as Ives plunged a shot of morphine into his thigh. "Will he be alright?"

"He can walk it off."

"I daresay, that other chap won't be doing so," Carver said, nodding to the German. "Jerry put up quite a fight. Did you lose anyone?"

Adams nodded. "Three dead and seven wounded."

Carver made a face. "Better than us. I had hoped the confusion from both of us attacking would provide us with some security. But one of their machine guns was aimed directly at our direction of assault from the beginning. They chewed my first team to pieces and nearly wiped out my second. I've got nine dead and six wounded."

Parker nodded, but said nothing, if it hadn't been for Carver's team opening fire first, his team would have had just as many casualties. He looked around and spotted a shallow trench he had nearly fallen into during the

370

assault. "We should colocate our wounded for treatment; right there would do nicely."

"I'll have my men start moving our wounded." Carver agreed. He gestured toward the direction his team had assaulted from. "A and C Troops should be moving in soon from the north. We should begin planning for a counterattack. I'll cover the southeast, you cover the southwest, and we can position our mortar team where the artillery is."

Parker reloaded his Thompson. "Works for me, First Sergeant. Have Tarbor's and Callum's teams start setting up once they detonate the artillery."

"I'll take care of it, sir. I see the old man coming in; you two may wanna see him."

Parker and Carver turned and spotted Lord Lovat with A and C Troops moving on to Objective 1.

Lord Lovat was as indistinguishable as any of his commandos, with the exception of his well-groomed mustache and curly brown hair. He cradled his Lee Enfield bolt action rifle in the crook of his arm the way a hunter would, as he strode toward the battery.

Both A and C Troops fanned out around the battery and started to fill in defensive positions. Lord Lovat strode over to one of the artillery pieces and began to watch as Tarbor and his team started to set charges in the gun's barrel.

"How goes it?" Lord Lovat asked as he bent down, hands on his knees, and watched Tarbor set the charge.

"Wonderfully," Tarbor said politely. "But right now, sir, I need you to move your ass out of the way . . . respectfully, sir."

Lord Lovat chuckled and quickly moved out of the way and spotted Parker and Carver. "Gentlemen, well done. I'm afraid we have no time to rest on our laurels though. We—"

"Excuse me, sir, but we really should get clear of the artillery."

Lord Lovat nodded and hopped down into a nearby trench and was quickly followed by both Carver and Parker.

"Fire in the hole!" Tarbor called, after looking around making sure everyone had sufficient cover. He repeated himself twice more before he pushed down on the plunger of the detonator. The charges in the remaining guns detonated with a muted thud. Parker looked up over the trench after the explosion and surveyed the damage; the whole battery had been neutralized.

"Well done," Lord Lovat said, surveying the destruction. He clambered out of the trench and looked around, studying the hasty defense his commandos had set up. "Major Rackham! I want a CP set up right there." He pointed past the battery near a clump of trees. "Begin communicating with Command about our retrograde from this place."

Rackham nodded, and started issuing orders to his headquarters staff.

Lord Lovat turned back to Parker and Carver. "As I was saying, our primary objective has been seized, but we have an auxiliary mission that needs to be taken care of. He pulled out a map and knelt down and laid it on the ground. It was a map of the area of operation and Lord Lovat pointed at their present location. "We're here." He traced his finger to the west to a nearby town. "Roughly a kilometer away is the town of Sainte-Marguerite-sur-Mer. A British agent is there that we need to extract."

Both Parker and Carver exchanged glances. This was the first they had heard anything about this mission.

"Sir, why wasn't this briefed before our departure?"

The look on Lord Lovat's face was one of annoyance. "I wasn't told the explicit details myself until we were boarding the boats. Apparently, SOE wanted to keep this classified for as long as possible." He stared at Parker. "Malcolm, I need you to take one of your teams and get there. I've been told that there is a house on the east side of the village with a low stone wall and dark red shutters. That is the safe house where the agent will be. I've been told the house is one of a kind and easily identifiable. The agent's name is Cutter. I have information to prove his identity to ensure he isn't an imposter when you bring him here."

Parker grimaced. "What if we can't find the agent?"

"I've been told we aren't leaving without him, but we'll cross that bridge when we get to it. You'll find him. I have faith."

***

Faraday pulled the throttle and stick back, stalling the aircraft. He felt the wings of the aircraft strain as he quickly decelerated. A German ME109 blazed past him and quickly dove, taking evasive action after switching from the hunter to the hunted.

"Saxon Leader, watch out! You have another on your tail."

Faraday swore and pushed forward again on the stick and turned into a tight, corkscrewing dive.

"He's staying with you!"

Faraday rolled out of his dive and moved into a rolling scissors, spinning tightly like one strand of a double helix along the horizon.

"Christ, Jerry is all over the skies." Faraday checked his six, scanning the sky for any sign of his attacker, but couldn't see anything. Thinking he had lost him, he leveled off. As he did so, he felt a jolt and out of the corner of his eye saw a flash of light. He turned to look and only saw four giant holes stitching up his right wing. Faraday moved the stick to take evasive actions but felt another jolt as three more bullets raked his aircraft. He heard a loud crack and part of his canopy shattered inward. A round from the ME109's gun had entered and exited his canopy less than a foot in front of him. Two other bullet holes were visible along the engine compartment and smoke started to billow from it as the engine sputtered.

As the engine continued to cough, Faraday watched it for a split second, seeing if it would come back to life. "Goddammit, not again."

The engine continued to sputter and Faraday realized the situation. He toggled the fuel valves and shut off the fuel to the engine, and then cut the engine's power entirely. The last thing he wanted was a fire.

"This is Saxon Leader. I've lost power. I'm going to try and land and regroup with the raiders."

"This is Victor leader. Copy all. Good luck, sir."

Faraday struggled to keep control of the aircraft; the stick bucked violently and the rudder swerved. "I can't land this." He angled the plane inland toward a field, away from any civilian populated areas and started to unbuckle himself from his seat.

***

Parker walked over to Adams. Murray was on his feet, his shoulder covered in a bandage, and his mouth locked in a grimace.

"What's the good word, sir?"

"We got a new mission. We're extracting a British spy. He's about a half a kilometer up the road from here in a safe house. I can explain the details on the way. Right now I need Tarbor's and Callum's teams ready to go. You'll hang back and supervise things here."

374

"Roger that, sir." Adams motioned to Callum and Tarbor.

The pair of them trotted up next to Adams.

"What's the word, sir?" Tarbor parroted.

"We got an SOE agent that needs extraction. He's half a klick up the road."

Callum grunted, "I bloody hate extractions."

"Me, too," Tarbor agreed.

"Did the boss ask your opinion?"

"No, First Sergeant."

"Then stow the bitching and gear up."

"Yes, First Sergeant."

Callum waved his team over. "I assume my team will take point with Tarbor's team hanging back with the anti-tank gun and Bren?"

Parker nodded. "Keep dispersion. We'll stay off the road and in the treeline. Move out in five."

***

Cutter looked up at the sky. Aircraft swarmed all over. He could tell that the raid was in full swing. He grabbed his Sten and made his way into the safe house.

"You think we were followed?"

Talia shrugged. "Difficult to say. It was dark after all. Someone could have seen the lights of the car, though."

Parker nodded and bit his lip. He couldn't help but wonder how safe the safe house really was. He scanned the fields for anything out of the ordinary, hoping to catch sight of the British Commandos that were coming for them. As he watched, a flicker of movement caught his eye, but it wasn't in the fields; it was in the sky.

Cutter looked up in awe as a Spitfire went gliding over the house. The aircraft was no more than two hundred feet off the ground when a heavy wind hit and changed its course, making its tail skid out from behind it. Cutter watched as the aircraft lost control and went from gliding into falling out of the sky. A loud explosion erupted as the aircraft impacted the ground a hundred meters from the house. Flames spewed from the engine compartment where the hydraulics and fuel ignited.

"Oh good," Cutter said blandly, "I'm sure that won't attract any attention."

***

Faraday gritted his teeth as he impacted the ground with a solid thud.

"Bollocks," he grunted as he started to unstrap himself from the harness. He looked around and tried to get his bearings as he drew his Webley revolver. He needed to get back to the beach.

He struggled to his feet and winced as he put his weight down on his left ankle. It was definitely sprained, maybe broken.

"Shit."

He wouldn't be getting to the beach fast in this condition, not walking at least. He looked around. No doubt a German soldier had seen him bail out of his aircraft. He needed to move.

He continued to look around and spotted a cottage a few hundred yards away. Its red shutters standing out against the green scenery. *Maybe they have a car or a horse.* He stood and gingerly placed his weight on his foot and bit down an oath of curses as pain shot up his leg.

He half hobbled, half stumbled toward the cottage, picking up a stray tree branch and using it as a makeshift crutch as he went. As he got closer, he spotted a low retaining wall and quickly slid over it and continued up toward the house.

He cautiously made his way up to one of the windows and peered through it. *No one appears to be home.*

Faraday leaned against the wall of the house and continued to move around to the front. As he hobbled to the front, a French automobile came into view. Faraday couldn't believe his luck. He stumbled toward it and grabbed the door.

"That's far enough, old man," a voice behind him called in English.

***

"That looks to be our house, sir," Callum whispered as they reached the edge of the treeline.

Parker looked out into the field and spotted the lone cottage. Red shutters and on the edge of town; it met the criteria for where the SOE agent was supposed to be.

"Seems we'll be extracting more than one." Tarbor nodded toward the sky. Parker and Callum looked up and spotted a parachute floating down to the ground, a smoking Spitfire gliding toward a crash-landing.

"Shouldn't be an issue. Should we get ready to move?"

Parker shook his head. "No, let's observe a moment. The pilot will probably move toward the house. He can make contact with the agent first."

"And if we're in the wrong place, sir?"

"Then we move fast and aggressively."

"Will do, sir. We'll get the lads ready."

***

Cutter gazed out of the back window of the cottage and watched as the pilot glided to the ground in his parachute. He couldn't help but wince as the pilot impacted the ground. He clearly had limited experience with parachutes, and looked to have hurt himself on landing.

The pilot struggled to get up and quickly removed the parachute harness and drew his sidearm and started to survey his surroundings.

"You've gone and cocked it up soundly," Cutter whispered softly.

German soldiers would no doubt have seen the parachute and would be there in minutes. He watched a moment longer as the pilot started to stumble toward the cottage, then he walked away from the window into the living room. He drew his pistol and double-checked to make sure a round was chambered.

"Olivier!" Talia called softly.

"I see him.

"Are we going to help him?"

Cutter didn't say anything, he was still deliberating on what to do.

"He's coming up to the back of the house."

"Stay upstairs and out of sight until I say otherwise." Cutter moved to the far side of the living room. He watched as the pilot walked up next to the house and ducked behind a bookcase as the pilot stuck his head up next to the window to look inside.

A moment later, a soft thud emanated from the side of the house. Cutter assumed the pilot was leaning against it for support.

Cutter slowly moved toward the front door and watched as the pilot limped toward the car. He was hyper-focused on the car, Cutter could tell, fixated solely on his escape plan and oblivious to all else.

Cutter softly opened the front door and raised his pistol and aimed it squarely between the pilot's shoulders.

"That's far enough, old man."

Faraday slowly turned around and looked at Cutter. He eyed Cutter for a long moment and slouched back against the car, taking his weight off his ankle.

"Your English is very good."

"Well, Normandy once was part of Great Britain. Who are you?"

"Squadron Leader Ian Faraday of His Majesty's Royal Air Force. Who are you?"

Cutter didn't respond.

Faraday eyed him a long moment and looked behind him, half expecting a German patrol. He looked back at Cutter, unsure what would happen next. "Are you going to shoot me or take me to the coast?"

Cutter ignored his question. "Drop the gun." He wasn't entirely sure what to do.

Faraday slowly set the pistol on the top of the car and continued to slouch against it.

Cutter eyed Faraday a moment longer and lowered his pistol. "Christ, get in the damn house."

Faraday grabbed his pistol and stood up. "You look like you really had trouble making up your mind there."

"Who said my mind has been made up?"

Faraday hobbled past Cutter into the house. "I assume you have a plan?" Faraday asked as he collapsed into a chair in the living room. "I'd rather not become a permanent resident here." He propped his foot up and started to massage it.

"If you sit still and be quiet we may get out of here alive." Cutter walked over to the stairs. "Talia! Get down here!"

"Germans are driving up the road toward us!"

"Bollocks." Cutter walked to one of the windows and looked outside. A German half-track and Kubelwagon were driving toward the cottage.

Faraday groaned as he stood up and checked his revolver. "Right. I'm not one to go quietly into the night, and I'm not particularly fond of being a POW."

Cutter looked at Faraday, his mind racing. "Go upstairs with Talia. Keep quiet and I may be able to get us out of this."

Faraday grunted as he moved as fast as he could up the stairs. He checked the nearest room and found Talia sitting under the windowsill.

"You must be Talia, nice to meet you." Faraday slid down next to her.

"Be quiet." Talia racked the bolt of the Sten and chambered a round, her heart pounding in her chest. *This is it*. She had no idea how Olivier would extricate them from this without a gunfight. The sound of the half-track could be heard as it rumbled up the dirt road to the cottage. Their best hope was Olivier getting as many of them out of the half-track as possible before she started shooting from the second floor.

Cutter peered through the window and watched as the half-track rumbled up the path. Obersturmführer Amsel could be seen standing in the bed of the track, goggles covering his eyes and an SS cap sitting atop his head at a jaunty angle. Cutter continued to watch as the track came to a stop in front of the cottage. As Amsel's troops began to disembark the track, he noticed they all had the markings of the SS on their shoulders.

Cutter quickly checked his pistol and made sure it was secure in his waistband in the small of his back. He took a deep breath and walked out. "Obersturmführer, what is going on? Are we under attack? Are the British invading?"

"All is well. Just a failed British raid on Dieppe. I just received word that we are retaking the beach now. No need to fret."

Cutter's heart sank at the news. If the raiders were being thrown back into the sea, he had no chance of being rescued. He smiled gamely and did his best to look unperturbed. "I'm relieved then."

"Perhaps you shouldn't be, Mr. Deschamps. I understand that you make maps in your spare time."

A voice screamed in the back of Cutter's head. He was compromised. He eyed Amsel for a long moment,

380

trying to see if he was fishing. *Maybe he's bluffing*. Cutter looked at Amsel in confusion. "You're mistaken. I deal in antiquity."

Amsel gave a thin smile and switched to English. "So the name Cartographer means nothing to you?"

"*Je ne comprends pas.*" Cutter responded, his face straining to denote what he thought was innocent confusion.

Amsel eyed Cutter with a hint of disappointment and switched back to French. "What about the downed pilot?"

"Who?"

"My men saw a Spitfire go down near here and saw the pilot bail out. Did you see him?"

"I'm afraid not, Obersturmführer."

"*Dommage,* Olivier." Amsel leered at Cutter, his blue eyes alight with amusement.

The bastard knows; he's just toying with me. Cutter threw his arms up in confusion. "What is it that you want, Obersturmführer?"

Amsel shrugged and motioned to his men. "There is nothing you have that I want, but I hope you don't mind if we search the cottage."

"Of course." Cutter struggled to stay calm. They were so close to the finish. It couldn't end like this. His mind flashed to the dark, moldy alleys of Paris. Running through the labyrinth that was Paris' underworld; struggling, raging to escape and survive. Now here he was in some empty farmer's field at the end of a game of cat and mouse with Amsel. Was this his end?

"Olivier, you disappoint me," Amsel mocked. "Durand put up much more of a fight when he was captured."

Cutter's face turned pale.

***

"Who the bloody hell is that?" Faraday asked as Amsel walked up to Cutter.

"Obersturmführer Amsel of the SS."

"Well, this really is a lovely day. You got another Sten?"

Talia shook her head.

"Bollocks." Faraday checked his Webley. "Can your man drive them off or are we about to have a fight?"

"I don't know." Talia peeked through the window. Her pulse quickened; she was terrified for Olivier.

Faraday slowly moved so he could see out the window. Cutter was still talking to Amsel, but by the looks of it, it wasn't going well.

"This isn't going to work. That SS prat knows."

"What would you have us do?"

"Start shooting."

"Not yet."

"They will check the house. At that point we will be out of options."

Talia bit her lip, her finger hovering over the trigger of the Sten, eyes transfixed on Amsel.

"Oh shit, they're coming," Faraday said as Amsel motioned to two of his men. He got into a low crouch and took aim with his pistol.

***

The *snap* of a pistol round whizzing past Cutter made him jump. One of Amsel's men collapsed to the ground, a crimson, bloody hole in his chest. Cutter quickly drew his pistol and took aim at the German nearest to him and fired two shots in quick succession. He was close enough that both found their mark.

The German collapsed and Cutter scrambled back toward the house. As he did so, the Sten opened up, raking the half-track with withering fire. As Cutter got a hand on the door, he felt a concussive force hit him in the shoulder. The initial impact of it spun him slightly, and within milliseconds he started to feel blinding pain and realized he had been shot. He staggered through the doorway, ducked behind the entranceway, and took cover. He took a moment to control his breathing. He peeked around the corner, took aim at the nearest German, and fired. Then gunfire erupted from the right side of the cottage.

***

Parker ducked at the sound of Faraday's pistol. They had seen the Germans arrive in the half-track and had started to creep closer to the cottage. The high grass in the field was giving them good cover, and they were only a few hundred yards away.

Parker looked around and spotted both Tarbor and Callum looking at him for instructions. "Tarbor, have your team lay down a base of fire! Callum, your team will assault on my mark! Covering fire!"

"My team, let's move! Reynolds, Devon, move in pairs!" Callum shouted and stood up.

"Teach, get the Bren up! Allen, help me with the Boys gun!" Tarbor shouted as he worked the anti-tank gun, getting it ready to take out the half-track.

Parker's and Callum's teams moved slowly up toward the cottage and took aim at the Germans as they moved. Parker spotted their officer and took a well-aimed shot and fired. The bullet grazed Amsel's arm as he moved at the last second. He grimaced in pain and ducked behind the half-track.

Parker ducked behind the low wall of the house and started to reload.

"Teach is hit!" Allen shouted, as the Bren was silenced.

"Get the Bren up!" Tarbor screamed, shoving him away. He finished preparing the Boys and took aim and pulled the trigger. The round penetrated the half-track through the engine block with an audible *ping*. Tarbor worked the bolt and took aim again, this time aiming at the driver's seat, and fired. Satisfied that the half-track was down, he quickly went to check on Teach.

Parker scrambled behind the corner of the cottage and took cover. Callum ducked behind him. "Reynolds, Devon, enter the back of the house. Make sure you announce yourself and watch your fire."

"Will do, Sergeant!" Devon doubled back behind the cottage.

Magar peeked around the corner of the house and unloaded his Sten. "Sergeant, those Bosche are SS."

"I bloody hate the SS."

"I'm sure the feeling is mutual," Parker said as he stuck his Thompson around the corner and fired blindly while Magar reloaded.

***

Cutter strained his ears, confused by the new sounds of gunfire. He heard the back door open and quickly trained his pistol on the hallway leading to the kitchen.

"Friendlies! British! Don't shoot!" Reynolds called as he slowly moved through the hallway toward Cutter.

Once Cutter saw who they were, he dropped his pistol. Reynolds duckwalked over to him and inspected his shoulder while Devon took up a firing position at the window.

"Where the bloody hell have you been?" Cutter asked in annoyance as Reynolds probed his shoulder and applied a bandage.

"Took the scenic route."

Cutter groaned in pain as Reynolds applied pressure to his shoulder, his tone changing. "Happy to see you."

"Much better." Reynolds picked his rifle up and started to return fire through the window.

"Talia, Faraday, commandos in the house!" Cutter turned to Devon. "Go upstairs; you'll have a better angle."

Devon nodded and scurried up the stairs.

Cutter picked his pistol back up and peeked around the edge of the door and resumed firing.

A few minutes later the firefight ended.

"Friendlies coming across!" Callum shouted, and he and Parker came around the corner of the house, guns trained on the half-track.

"We got a live one!"

Talia and Faraday made their way down the stairs and surveyed the first floor. The windows were shattered and the walls were full of bullet holes.

Talia looked down at Cutter and dashed to his side.

"I'm alright." Cutter struggled and stood up. His shoulder felt like it was on fire, and was slick with blood. He felt a little light-headed as he negotiated the stairs outside and grabbed Talia's arm to steady himself. He ambled up to Parker. "Who the bloody hell are you?"

"Captain Parker, here to extract you. Identify yourself first."

"Arthur Cutter." As he said his name, Cutter saw the look of shock on Talia's face and couldn't help but feel guilty about having never told her his real name.

"Arthur Cutter?" Talia said the name slowly, as though she were trying on a new pair of shoes.

"I'm sorry. I should have told you sooner."

Talia hesitated for a moment but gave a small smile. "You look like an Arthur."

Parker looked at the pair of them in confusion. "Never mind, we'll prove who you are later. You ready to go?"

"You're extracting me, an RAF pilot, and a French agent."

Parker hesitated but nodded as Faraday walked out of the house.

"Who are you?"

"Captain Parker, US Rangers."

"Christ, 'bout time you entered the war. I'm Squadron Leader Faraday. Get us out of here."

"Will do, sir. We've got a bit of walking to do and need to leave before we get cut off. So if you'll follow us, we can get out of here."

Cutter nodded but paused a moment. He walked over to the other side of the half-track where Tarbor was standing over the wounded Obersturmführer Amsel. Blood and mud stained the Obersturmführer's gray tunic. His hand covered a jagged hole in his shoulder where he had been shot, and his SS service cap sat unattended in the dust. Cutter looked down at the leering skull perched atop the cap's visor. The taunting smile looking more like a twisted grimace. A heavy gust of wind picked up the cap and sent it flying into the field. Cutter watched with mild disinterest as it cartwheeled off. He knew he didn't have much time, but part of him wanted to savor the moment, the one time he would ever be able to put a face and name to his enemy, a defeated enemy. There was something romantic about it, good overcoming evil. A part of Cutter, a piece he had locked away during the war, the boyish scholar, yearned to witness this conclusion. He crossed his arms and looked down at Amsel. For all his bluster the prancing peacock was beaten.

"Well, how the tables have turned," Cutter said softly in French as he stood over Amsel.

Amsel looked up at Cutter in wide-eyed surprise. A combination of terror and fury filled his eyes. "You coward," he spat, "Scurrying around here as a spy, too cowardly to fight man to man."

Cutter winced as he struggled down into a low crouch, his arm burning with every movement. He looked Amsel in the eye. A devil was getting his due, but the moment was bitter-sweet. Amsel had hurt a lot of people, and Durand's fate was still unknown. "Being called a coward by you means as little to me as your life." He looked up at

Tarbor and gave him a nod. Tarbor moved back toward Parker and Callum.

"Where's Durand?"

"What makes you think I'll tell you?"

Cutter didn't hesitate; he aimed his pistol at Amsel's knee and pulled the trigger. Amsel let out a howl of pain and swore up and down at Cutter in German.

"I won't ask again."

He looked up as Parker, Faraday, and Talia walked back around the half-track. Parker moved to stop Cutter from continuing the interrogation, but Faraday and Talia stopped him.

"Ease up, lad, this needs to be done," Faraday said, his voice calm but making it clear that it was an order. Parker grimaced in disgust and walked back to his team.

Cutter nodded his thanks and turned his attention back to Amsel. "What happened to Durand?"

"We spotted him loitering around our headquarters a number of days prior to when the RAF bombed it. We assumed he knew something and collected him."

"What did he tell you?"

"Enough." Amsel grinned, blood coming down his chin. "My men killed your man Claude this morning. Your Resistance is broken, and your raid has failed."

Cutter looked up at Talia and saw tears forming in her eyes. "You're lying." She spat.

"Why would I?"

Talia frowned but did her best to stifle the hot tears she felt filling her eyes. She wouldn't give Amsel the satisfaction in his last moments. *Her parents, her brother, Francois, Durand, now Claude. . .* she let out an anguished breath and looked over at Cutter. He was one of the last people she had, and she hardly knew him. *That's not true,* she realized, as he looked at her in concern. She could tell his worry was genuine. For all his distancing and bottling up of his feelings, Talia could tell by the anxious look on his face that he cared for her. That feeling of loneliness and isolation she had first felt when Francois had been killed dulled as that realization dawned on her.

She walked up next to Cutter and put a hand on his shoulder. There was little they could do for the remainder of the cell, and as for the raid, that was well out of his hands. Cutter raised his pistol and without any hesitation pulled the trigger. Amsel's head snapped back as the bullet bore through his forehead and exploded out the back into the ground. Cutter stood up in silence.

He looked at Talia. Her face was like stone as she wiped her eyes and nodded to him.

Faraday eyed Cutter for a long moment, conflict covering his face. "Cutter, that man was unarmed."

"Our rules don't apply to the SS," Cutter shot back and walked over to the group of commandos. "Come on, it's time to go."

Parker glared at Cutter, but Cutter could care less. He thought back to when Amsel had killed that Jewish family and the priest at the church, and felt justified. He thought about the SS soldier who had killed Victor. He knew it wasn't Amsel who had pulled the trigger, but a sense of closure washed over Cutter, as though he had avenged his friend. He knew what he had just done would do little to bring his friend back, but Cutter took solace in the knowledge that Amsel wouldn't be able to hurt anyone else.

"Lead on, Captain, we have a lot more to do before this war ends."

Parker said nothing but turned and motioned for them to move out.

They made it back to the artillery battery just as Lord Lovat was ordering his commandos to retreat. The staccato of machine gun fire could be heard a hundred yards down the road.

"Back just in time." Lord Lovat walked over and shook Parker's hand. "Where's Cutter?"

"Sir, I'm Arthur Cutter, call sign Cartographer."

"What's your sister's last name?"

"Bailey."

Faraday's ears perked up at the mention of Bailey. "You related to Sharon Bailey?"

"Aye, what of it?"

"You know Peter?"

"Aye, he's my brother-in-law. He was shot down a few weeks ago."

"Small fucking world," Faraday chuckled.

Lord Lovat studied Cutter for a long moment. "Tripoli."

Cutter quickly recognized the code word. It was one he hadn't used in years, but he quickly responded, "Trafalgar."

Lord Lovat nodded and turned his attention to Faraday and Talia. "And who are you two?"

Faraday stepped forward. "Squadron Leader Ian Faraday, No. 71 Eagle Squadron, sir."

Lord Lovat nodded and looked at Talia, expecting an explanation.

"She's with me, sir, that's all you need to know," Cutter interrupted. He would explain himself to Hambro but had no intention of explaining himself to anyone else.

Lord Lovat shrugged and seemed to take Cutter's word. He turned and surveyed the destroyed artillery battery. "Captain Parker, get these three to the boats. Captain Carver and the rest of your troop are pulling back as we speak. This position will be swarming with Germans in minutes."

"Yes, sir." Parker motioned for Cutter, Faraday, and Talia to follow him.

Cutter paused and looked at Lord Lovat. "Sir, was the raid successful?"

Lord Lovat looked at Cutter and pulled his watch cap off his head and ran a hand through his curly brown hair. "We won't know the full effect of this raid for a few days, but by my estimates we just pissed away a large contingent of Canadians and commandos."

"A damn shame."

Lord Lovat shrugged, "No shame in it." He paused and a smirk tugged at his mouth. "No planning either."

"We can agree on that." Cutter extended his hand. "Thank you for getting us out."

Lord Lovat took his hand and shook it. "Go on, lad, we got a whole lot of war left to fight."

Cutter smiled and nodded. *On that we can agree.* He followed Parker through the woods back to where the boats were. As they boarded, Lord Lovat and the rest of Parker's troop as well as Captain Carver's came sprinting through the woods and jumped onto the boats.

First Sergeant Adams clambered into their boat and quickly made sure everyone was there. Satisfied, he started shouting orders. "Get us underway! Go! Go! Go!"

As the boats pulled away and started to sail back to England, First Sergeant Adams walked over to Parker.

"We lost four."

Parker frowned. "Who?"

"Davenport, Neely, Best, and Hawkins. Twenty wounded."

"Dammit."

The raid was a failure and Parker had no way to justify the deaths of his men. He looked over at Cutter.

"Let it go, sir," Adams said quickly, reading his mind.

Parker ignored him and walked over to Cutter. "Why did we do this raid? You must know something!"

Cutter looked at him and couldn't help but feel sorry for him. Parker had obediently followed orders and had taken part in a raid that Cutter had known from the start had little chance of success. Before Cutter could respond, Sergeant Callum interceded. "Sir, it doesn't matter, you know this."

"Yes it does, *you know that*."

Sergeant Callum shook his head. "Sir, our job is to keep the Germans on their toes. Sometimes we catch them flat-footed, sometimes we don't."

"So we're expendable?"

"Sir, you were at Saint-Nazaire. You know better."

Parker looked at him in surprise and looked at First Sergeant Adams.

First Sergeant Adams shrugged. "It's part of the job, sir. How many times do you think I went over the top in the Great War with the expectation I was going to be killed in a failed attempt at gaining ground?"

"I don't understand. This was a waste."

Callum nodded. "It was, but we can't look at it that way. We engaged the enemy, and with these surprise attacks we're keeping Jerry unsure of where the big invasion will happen."

Parker grunted and looked at Faraday. "How many pilots did you lose today?"

Faraday frowned; since they had clambered into the boat it was the only thing he could think about. "Definitely a few."

"And you're okay with that?"

Faraday walked over to the railing of the boat and shook his head. "I'm not. I understand what you're feeling. I felt the same way after the Battle of Britain. I lost a lot of friends to sorties and Rhubarb missions over France, for no reason other than the off chance Command thought they would get lucky and destroy a supply train or something. It kept me up at night and I nearly lost my nerve."

"What stopped you?"

Faraday shrugged. "My mates, I suppose."

Cutter looked at Parker and put a hand on his shoulder. "Mate, this is the hard part, sometimes you need to be emotionally vacant." He looked up at Talia as he said it and changed his mind. "No, actually that doesn't work. That makes you no better than the Nazis. For blokes like us, if we can ask ourselves if it's worth it and the answer is yes, then there you have it."

"And you think this was worth it?"

Cutter paused and locked eyes with Talia. Her eyes were unwavering but the look in them was different. There was a warmth and familiarity Cutter hadn't seen since the night they had slept together. Cutter patted Parker's shoulder. "When we get back to England, the lot of us can down a bottle and we can sort it out." He moved past Parker and back to Talia and reached for her hand.

"Durand, Claude, the others—"

Cutter raised a hand and stopped her. "There is nothing we can do for them now." He gently put his arms around her and held her. She stifled a cry and her body shuddered. Cutter slowly lowered her to the deck and they sat with their back to the bulkhead. Cutter continued to let her sob quietly as he held her close. He looked up at the faces of the men who had rescued them.

He spotted Teach and Tarbor in the aft compartment. A cigarette dangled loosely from Tarbor's lips as he wrapped a new bandage around Teach's chest. Another commando had his arms around a ranger as he shuddered and hyperventilated, struggling to get control of himself. Cutter turned and saw Faraday and Parker leaning against the railing sharing a cigarette, talking about home and continuing to discuss compartmentalization of what had just happened. Sergeant Callum and First Sergeant Adams moved among the commandos, checking the emotional and physical status of each man. They both floated among the soldiers, exchanging a good word and comforting those that were distraught.

Cutter watched in fascination as the commandos took care of their own. This brotherhood was something absent in SOE. He respected them for their daring, but respected them more for the love and affection they showed each other.

Cutter continued to watch them until the rocking of the boat and fatigue dragged him into a heavy sleep. When he finally awoke it was to Sergeant Callum kicking his foot.

"Oi, spooky, we're home."

Cutter looked around in confusion. Talia was already awake and standing. Cutter struggled to his feet, careful not to further injure his shoulder.

"Welcome to England." He walked up to Talia.

"Are you sure they won't send me back?"

"I'm sure," Cutter lied. He honestly had no idea how he was going to convince Hambro to let her stay.

As they clambered onto the docks of Newhaven, Cutter spotted Hambro and Atkinson waiting for them on the road.

"Oh shit."

A huge, toothy grin spread underneath Atkinson's mustache as he spotted Cutter. "Home is the soldier, home from the war." He walked up and shook Cutter's hand. "Good to see you Arch. The boss is pissed, so tread lightly." He said the last part softly so Hambro wouldn't hear and turned to let Hambro greet Cutter.

"Arthur, it seems you brought a stowaway."

"Well, I figured leaving her would only compromise us. Her entire cell was killed this morning."

"SS?"

Cutter nodded.

Hambro nodded and locked his bespectacled eyes on Talia. "What is your name?"

"Talia Crevier."

"Tell me what happened, Ms. Crevier."

Talia looked at Cutter for guidance. Cutter nodded to her and she started to explain in English the past few days of how Amsel had captured and tortured Durand and had started to systematically execute every member of her cell. When she finally finished, Hambro took his glasses off and started to clean them. He did so silently, and when he finished he turned and looked at Cutter. "So Amsel is dead?"

"Killed him myself."

"You did the right thing. Ms. Crevier will be thoroughly reviewed, but if everything is as she says, she will be granted asylum."

Cutter couldn't believe his ears but didn't betray his emotions. "So what now?"

"You'll come back to London for a thorough debrief and we will go from there." Hambro motioned to the car that was waiting for them.

Cutter nodded and couldn't help but grin. He looked at Talia. The look on her face was a combination of relief and joy.

"Monsieur Hambro, what is to happen to me after a debrief?"

Hambro's features softened for an instant, but quickly returned to a blank facade. "Mademoiselle Crevier, what is it that *you* want?"

Talia didn't say anything for a long moment. She understood his question and looked over at Cutter, as if appraising his life. Cutter's work had brought him to the gnawed and frayed edge of his wits; had brought him to the breaking point. Was it something she wanted for herself? She had an opportunity to seek asylum in England and wait out the war, or she could contribute in a way few women could. She pivoted her gaze back to Hambro and locked eyes with him, making him blink. "I want to fight."

***

CHAPTER 16
THE MARTIAL CIRCUS

Hambro strode into the War Office and made his way down to Mountbatten's office. As he walked, he couldn't help but notice the buzz of activity inside Combined Operations. News of Jubilee's failure had done little to stifle the mood, as staff ran to and fro with sheaves of documents under their arms, and service-members went about business as usual. As Hambro waded through the office space of the senior leadership he couldn't help but notice that most of the people running about were new. *Christ, looks like Jacobs wasn't the only one who jumped ship,* Hambro thought as he looked around.

Almost immediately after Jubilee, Commander Jacobs had quietly reached out to Hambro asking about a possible reassignment to SOE. Hambro had eagerly granted the talented commander his wish. It was rumored that Montgomery had also poached two operations planners as well.

Mountbatten's unwillingness to collaborate with adjacent organizations, but instead ramrod his plans through political subterfuge, had done little but alienate Combined Operations from other parts of the War Office. As a result, any member of Mountbatten's staff who wasn't a sycophant was looking for any excuse to escape Combined Operations.

Hambro shook his head at the thought of Combined Operations, a novel organization with potential to be an effective force against the Nazis, being run by stuffy, incompetent bureaucrats. It truly was a travesty of the British military. He didn't let his contempt for the organization show as he smiled at Mountbatten's secretary, handed her his coat, and waited for her to let Mountbatten know that he was there.

"Mr. Hambro! My dear fellow, how are you?" Mountbatten cried as he was let into his office.

"I'm well, Dickie, thank you, and you?"

"Very well. I've been in meetings all morning coordinating planning for future operations. How goes it with SOE?"

Hambro shrugged. "We're staying busy. Montgomery asked me to help develop some of his war plans."

"Wonderful. Is there a role for Combined Operations?" Mountbatten asked in a conspiratorial tone. "With the success of Jubilee, we are a hot commodity."

"The success of Jubilee?"

Mountbatten looked at him in confusion. "Yes, the success. Jubilee did exactly what it was meant to do. It flushed out the Luftwaffe and gave Leigh-Mallory the ability to cripple their air force."

Hambro looked at Mountbatten in shocked anger. "How the bloody hell can you consider Jubilee a success? We suffered around two thousand casualties, nineteen hundred forty-six captured, one destroyer destroyed, and one hundred aircraft. In return, the Germans only lost a submarine, forty-eight aircraft, and around five hundred casualties. The only objective that was successfully seized and destroyed was Lord Lovat's!"

"I believe those numbers to be incorrect." Mountbatten's facial muscles tightened, but his confident facade remained intact.

Hambro eyed him coolly but chuckled, "I'm sure that's what you told the PM."

"The PM agrees that this raid had valuable lessons learned in preparation for the invasion."

"Theoretical reasoning always is a safe harbor for those unwilling to accept their mistakes."

"Mr. Hambro, is there a reason you are here or did you just come to speak ill of the dead?"

Hambro glared at Mountbatten, but didn't take the bait. He had learned much from watching Mountbatten over the past six months, and had learned when he was about to step into a political bear trap. "Yes, I came to tell you that Operation Torch is on schedule and at this time we will not be requiring Combined Operations' support."

"Nonsense, I have two commando units participating." Mountbatten waved his hand dismissively.

"Yes, but they will be falling directly under General Anderson."

"What game are you playing at?" Mountbatten's face turned crimson as he struggled to control his emotions. "On whose authority?"

"On the PM's," Hambro said simply. "After Jubilee, I recommended that commando units be more heavily incorporated into regular army units. The PM agreed. Tactical control of commando units until further notice will be with the commanders on the battlefield, not someone behind a desk in the War Office."

Mountbatten's mouth opened and closed multiple times in stupefied shock before he spoke. "You had no right, you—"

Hambro moved to stand up, a glimmer of a grin peeking out the corner of his mouth as his own bear trap snapped closed. "Dickie, my recommendation: Sit this one out. Let the commanders win the war." He didn't wait for a retort, but turned on his heel and left the room.

As Hambro left Mountbatten's office he couldn't help but smile. For once a little political maneuvering may have done some good. Hambro wasn't proud of it, but he knew it had to be done. He strode out of the War Office, his eyes following various personnel as they scrambled through the hallways to meetings as operational planning was conducted.

Staff jobs were a necessity Hambro understood all too well. He hated to admit it, but the War Office served a vital purpose even though it often took two steps forward and one step back. He doubted many of the lessons learned from Jubilee would make it out of the locked cabinets inside Combined Operations. For all the lessons Mountbatten cited as making the raid worthwhile, the most valuable ones pertained to the gross blunders in preparation and planning by Combined Operations. To acknowledge such mistakes would be an admission of incompetence by Mountbatten, and for that reason alone the most valuable lessons worth learning from the raid would never be revealed.

Hambro trudged out of the War Office into the motor pool and found his driver waiting for him. "Where to, sir?" Sergeant Monmoth asked as he climbed into the car.

"Back to HQ."

Sergeant Monmoth gave a wordless grunt and sped away.

Hambro watched as they passed a city block of burned-out buildings. The shattered windows and crumbling brick walls served as a reminder of what the SOE was fighting for. He watched as a young woman helped a group of men sift through the rubble for survivors. The hard, determined look on her face reminded Hambro of Talia Crevier. She had left a lasting impression on Hambro when he had first met her at the docks. Her willingness to contribute after barely escaping Normandy with her life was inspiring. It was the people like her that gave him encouragement. People like her and Cutter were the reason Hambro believed they would defeat the Nazis.

THE END

Acknowledgments

Writing *Jubilee* was a passion project for me that started while on a deployment to Sicily in 2017. What started as a writing exercise, slowly expanded into a novel and developed into something that I eventually wanted to publish. That said, if it weren't for a handful of people who had the patience and diligence to work with me, *Jubilee* would have never come to fruition.

Special thanks to my wife, Jacquelyn, whose love and patience was invaluable. I cannot count the number of times she was asked to reread the countless drafts that were written, safe to say it was more than a few dozen. Without her, this book would be wasting away in a folder on my computer.

My editor, Michele Rubin, and the people at Cornerstones US. Thank you for providing vital insight regarding character arcs, development, and motivations. Your guidance in navigating the editing process as well as helping me develop a publishing strategy was invaluable.

To my parents, thank you for instilling in me an aggressive appetite for reading. If it weren't for you I would never consider writing as a hobby.

ABOUT THE AUTHOR

Conor Bender, born in Atlanta in 1990, went to the College of Charleston and graduated in 2013 with a degree in Classics. Upon graduation, he commissioned as a 2nd Lieutenant in the Marine Corps where he served as a logistician and foreign military advisor for six years. In 2019 the Marine Corps Gazette published an article from him, and it encouraged him to begin work on *Jubilee*. Mr. Bender currently resides in Dallas, Texas. To review more of his work, visit his website at www.conorbender.com.

Made in the USA
Las Vegas, NV
10 March 2023

68850106R00236